In Defence of

Her Honour

Sara Powter

Bible Quotes from King James Version

ISBN: 9780645441567
Paperback edition

ABN 99 768 734 831
Pacific Wanderland Publications
Kincumber Australia NSW 2251

saragpowter@gmail.com
www.sarapowter.com.au

1st edition 2024 printed by Kindle
an Amazon Company; available on Kindle Unlimited & KDP
2nd edition, 2024 Pacific Wanderland Publications

Cover Painting
The background
https://dictionaryofsydney.org/media/1354
Parramatta River,
George Penkivil Slade

Girl Inset
"My Name Day"
By Edoardo Tofano
Girl with yellow flowers

Chapter Graphics all in Public Domain

Cover by
Beckon Creative
beck@beckoncreative.biz

Acknowledgement of Country:
In the spirit of reconciliation, I acknowledge the Traditional Custodians of
country throughout Australia and their continuous connections to land, sea
and community. We pay our respects to their elders, past and present, and
extend that respect to all Aboriginal and Torres Strait Islander peoples today.

Australian Historical Novels
(All stand-alone books)

A First Fleet Story (1788)
Gentle Annie Soames *(2024)*

The Hunter to Macquarie Collection (1795-1822)
When Upon Life's Billows *(2025)*
Saddler's Song *(2025)*
Tuppence to Pass *(2025)*
His Majesty's Pageboy (2025
Far From the Whispering Sheoaks (2026)

Unlikely Convict Ladies Trilogy (1792-1840s)
Dancing to her Own Tune
(co-authored by Sheila Hunter & Sara Powter)
Amelia's Tears
A Lady in Irons

The Lockleys of Parramatta (1800-1900)
Hands Upon the Anvil
Out Where the Brolgas Dance
Diamonds in the Dirt
The Earl's Shadow
Once a Jolly Swagman
Jonty's Journey

The Convict Birthstain Collection (1830s-1840s)
No More, My Love
The Vine Weaver
Scotch at The Rocks {*Sequel to The Vine Weaver*}
Waiting at the Sliprails
Convict Shadows of the Past
In Defence of Her Honour
I Can't Stop Tomorrow *(2024)*
Madeline's Boy *(2024)*
Jam or Marmalade for Tea *(2025)*

Shelia Hunter's
Australian Colonial Trilogy (1840s-1850s)
Mattie
Ricky {*Jonty's Journey is a sequel*}
The Heather to the Hawkesbury

Note:

The Rear Admiral Duncan Inn

stood in Church Street Parramatta
and was named after Admiral Adam Duncan.
(He became Rear Admiral in 1787)
He was the first naval officer to sail his ship into the middle of the defeated the
Dutch fleet in the Battle of Camperdown in 1797,
where he fired his cannons from both sides of his ship.
This manoeuvre was a game-changer in future battles,
and his friend, Admiral Lord Nelson,
followed his example numerous times.
The two men knew each other well.
Governor Lachlan Macquarie admired both.

THANKS:-
I say thanks to all those who came before us,
including the Naval doctors who oversaw the wellbeing
of our convict ancestors.
They were heroes in themselves.
To those who served their time in chains.
To those convicts in our families who did survive
the atrocities dealt to them so unkindly by
those who were in charge of issuing the punishments.

Thanks to my husband,
Steve, for all his support in my writing.

To Roby Aiken
for your patience in correcting my punctuation
and
to my Beta readers
Noreen Robertson, Linda Upcroft, & Lee Boehm
for doing the final read-throughs
and to
Rebekah Robinson for my cover.
Cover by Beckon Creative
beck@beckoncreative.biz

Table of Contents

The grammar and language in this book are
Australian English spelling

~ Time Passing

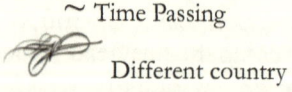

Different country

Chapter 1 Friends

*T*hree boys sat in the well-appointed classroom. Their tutor, Algernon Makepeace, was a born teacher. He loved sharing his knowledge. One would have expected the three desks to have been in a row; however, one of the students was not of equal standing. William Miller, known as Bill, was the butler's son. He was permitted to sit in on the lessons due to the pleading of the youngest son of the household. Cuthbert Edison-Browne refused to attend classes unless his best friend was also permitted to come. Sir Percival Edison-Browne, a baronet, preferred peace to an argument in his household; hence, Bill had been included in the classes but sat at the back.

The teacher approached his desk. "William, I wish to congratulate you on that fine Latin assignment."

Bill was the youngest boy by some six months, so the tutor was surprised that he outshone the two older boys, especially considering he was only a servant's lad. He had taken him into his class with some trepidation; however, Bill was a bright boy and soon outshone the other two students. Now, Algernon wondered if there was some way this lad could gain entry into Eton or Harrow.

Time would tell.

Having just turned twelve, Errol would sit his entrance exam next week, and he wondered if he would even pass. He knew Bill would have passed if he sat the exam, and he was only ten. Hopefully, with a word or two to his employer, he could persuade Sir Percival to sponsor the lad to go to school with his son. He knew he was supposed to mark the other two papers; however, his mind kept wandering. All three were currently copying a page of Latin grammar. Algernon found out earlier that Bill already knew this off by heart. He heard him reciting it to his father in the staff dining room.

Jerome Miller was now the butler. He, too, sat in classes with his friend Percy when he was a lad. He also did well with his lessons; he had been sent to Eton with his friend at his employer's expense. He served as under butler for decades. At the grand age of fifty, he had finally been permitted to step into his father's shoes. That was eleven years ago, and Sir Percival also allowed him to marry. William was a massive surprise to Jerome and his thirty-five-year-old wife, Letitia, who had been the housekeeper. Jerome was now sixty-one and had ten-year-old William to bring up by himself. Jerome was a doting parent, as were all the staff of the big house. They all adored the very well-behaved young lad.

Ellen Ross spoiled him rotten from the moment she entered the household. She came and filled Letitia's empty shoes. The new housekeeper was a very young widow with a little girl whom she called Molly. Being the only two staff children in the house, the little ones were brought up as all but siblings.

Jerome's father, Herbert Timothy Miller, was the Edison-Browne's butler before anyone else on the staff could remember. They expected that Herbert would hold on tenaciously for many years. He was still alive but could no longer stand upright. His back was so bowed that seeing his toes was not a problem; unfortunately, lifting his head to see where he was walking was a different matter.

Bill adored his grandfather. He lived in one of the tiny back rooms of the big house in London. He was offered a pensioner's cottage, but being unable to look after himself, he requested he stay with the only family he had. That was Jerome and Bill. Herbert's wife, Grace, died soon after Jerome's birth. Letitia had died having Jerome's second child when Bill was three. Neither man would have coped if it had not been for the supportive house staff. Sir Percival was Jerome's friend since childhood and understood their difficult situation. He, too, had lost his wife early during childbirth, along with their third child, a little girl.

Algernon shook his head, trying to get his thoughts back on his work. He returned to mark the other two papers. He read the answers of the two older lads and cringed and had to re-read them to realise that both had failed dismally. He looked at his charges with a frown buried deep into his forehead. His eyes fixed on Bill, and he stayed gazing at him.

Bill was astonished when he met the master's intense gaze. Mr Makepeace was looking at him as though he had done something wrong. Bill coloured, then asked in fear, "Sir, have I made an error?"

Algernon saw the other two were still hard at work. He walked to Bill's desk and crouched beside him, whispering, "No, William, your work was perfect." He placed the marked paper on his desk in front of the boy.

Bill gasped when he saw "100%" written on the top in red ink. "Sir, really?" His face was glowing with excitement.

Glancing at the other two students, the tutor nodded, then put his finger to his lips and whispered, "I need to see you after the class, lad."

Bill returned his smile with a big grin and a nod. "Yes, sir."

Algernon returned to his desk. The other two papers nearly burned a hole in the timber, 32% and 40%, respectively. How was Errol going to get into a decent class at Eton? He stood holding the papers. He noticed his hands were shaking. He was here to teach the two sons of the household and prepare them for Eton. Neither had excelled at Geography; Bill had. Both of the baronets' sons had barely passed mathematics; again, Bill excelled. As Bill typically completed his homework in class while the other two were plodding on with their set work, Algernon had started Bill on learning the basics of Classical Greek. Again, his ability to drink in the knowledge laid before him was astounding. This was not a subject that was even discussed in class. All study on this was done in the butler's room before his father was off duty. Algernon knew that Jerome and Bill spoke French between each other when off duty, so Bill's French was perfect. Even his accent was flawless.

With Bill's excellent results across all subjects, a seed was sown in the tutor's mind. He would submit his name for a scholarship at Eton. If the next twelve months continued in the same vein, he would probably be offered a full scholarship. Only one or two of those were available each year, and he felt Bill might get one.

Algernon asked permission from Jerome to submit the boy's name a year early. There was always the possibility that he could get a partial scholarship. However, the exam practice would be a good experience for the following year. At least with the new system, Bill had a good chance of an education. The National Society for Promoting the Education of the Poor was now allowing underprivileged children to learn.

~

Seven years flew by since Bill received the offer of a full scholarship on his first try at the exam. He had completed Eton and duxed it. He did not need to apply to Oxford as they offered him a full scholarship upon completing his years at Eton.

Jerome was mourning his aged father when he had to farewell his son as he left for Oxford. The butler was still shaking his head in wonderment. "A scholarship at Oxford University, I can't believe it. I hope you know just how proud your grandfather was, and I am, of you and your successes in your studies. He told me the morning he passed away that for you to top all your subjects at Eton surpassed any expectations from either of us." He had just folded his son's new uniform and placed it carefully in the shiny leather suitcase. "Son, for you to be a King's Scholar, though, astounds me." Jerome looked at his son. They now stood eye to eye, and the handsome young man before him took his breath away.

Bill had just been enfolded in a big hug, and Jerome noticed that Bill had something stiff in his shirt.

When Jerome released him, he asked, "Bill, what's this?" He tapped his jacket and felt something there.

Bill's mouth twisted with embarrassment. "Today's mail, Papa. I meant to tell you, but we sort of got side-tracked." Bill dug into his shirt and produced the letter. The crest on the front of the envelope was becoming familiar to both men. They had received many official envelopes over the five years since Bill won the full scholarship. Each missive acknowledged a new award or honour of the bright young student. Bill was becoming seriously embarrassed at all the accolades he was winning. He had tried to keep them quiet as both boys in the house barely passed their exams. Initially, Bill had assisted them until they both rebelled. He still beat them both.

As they had little money, Bill was not tempted to spend his time frivolously. Sure, he joined the boys as often as possible, but rather than being bored when he had no money to party, he studied. Sir Percival had even given him free access to the library at home. Although Algernon Makepeace was long gone. Basil Gomes, the archivist and librarian, was an Oxford Scholar in the Classics. Bill adored the elderly gentleman and was often quizzing him for information, or they conversed in either Latin or Ancient Greek. Basil was delighted as his language skills had been getting rusty since Bill had gone to school. Sadly for both men, Sir Percival's library did not extend to many tomes on the classics or ancient literature.

Jerome carefully lifted the already broken seal on the letter and read the information. If he was proud before, now he was floored. "You are the Oppidan Scholar from Eton? Seriously? Bill, this means that as both Kings Scholar and Oppidan Scholar, you have letters after your name and haven't even left school. KS and OS, you astound me, son." Jerome glowed with pride in his boy.

Bill just grinned and gave a shy nod. "I wanted to tell you alone. Papa, we have to keep this quiet for as long as possible. Errol failed a subject in his final exam and must repeat or take a lesser course."

"Damn!" The exclamation was almost forced from Jerome. "That boy is trouble with a capital T. He will never pass anything unless he spends some time at his books." He knew Errol had just scraped through most of his final exams but now must re-sit the Latin to enter Oxford. He had overheard Sir Percival shredding his son. Bert wasn't doing much better, although, older than Bill, Bert was a year behind him. He was at least passing his exams but excelling at nothing.

Bill was a little jealous of his boyhood friend. If it weren't for lack of funds, he would be eager to join him on his many outings and the evening fun. He stayed silent for a while before adding, "Well, Papa, I'm not sure what good this will do me. Here, I'm still just a butler's son. It's not as if I can do anything with my new credentials. I could stand for parliament, but who would listen to a seventeen-year-old? I may as well go to college and see if I can change my lot in life. At least by the time I graduate, I will be an adult." Bill sat on his bed, somewhat dejected. "I hate the system here, Papa. Obviously, I have brains. However, I remember Mr Makepeace initially objecting to me being in his class as I was 'only a servant's child.' But I discovered he submitted my name for early entry into Eton." Bill saw his father smile knowingly, and then he gave a nod. "You knew?"

Jerome nodded. "He asked me if I would mind. Why would I? Neither of us expected you would get in the same year as Errol. I'm glad that Bert never held it against you. Percy and I went there together and were study partners."

Bill didn't even tell his father about the animosity between his previous best friend. He shrugged in reply. Since the news that Bill had passed all his exams leaked out, Bert would not even talk to him. Errol snubbed him as he was so much younger than his peers.

The farewells the following morning were difficult. Thankfully, Jerome still had his work, which kept him busy. A hackney carriage called at the servant's entrance and collected Bill and his cases. The trip to Oxford would be completed on the mail coach. No private carriages for him. He may have won a full scholarship to Oxford, but money was still tight. He and his father only had the butler's salary to live on; if Bill wanted money to spend, he had to work for it.

Before Bill left, he ensured he was in the library when Molly Ross, the housekeeper's daughter, was cleaning the fireplace. Molly was being trained to take over her mother's role one day. She was now fifteen, but oh, so pretty, and she had a smile that would melt the hardest heart. Bill's heart was far from hard; it had melted long ago. The staff may have treated them as brother and sister, but his feelings for her were anything but brotherly. Whenever he was home, he would try to spend whatever time he could with her. It was usually only snatched moments here and there, but he liked her. No, he more than just liked her, and she never rebuffed his gentle attentions, so he thought she possibly also liked him. Basil Gomes had discreetly been expanding her reading skills in the years since Bill was away. Bill had started her lessons when they were children. She was only five, and he was eight. Being the only two staff children, they often found themselves alone. Basil kept on her back to keep reading, or she would lose the skills she had. Molly didn't wish to learn languages but delighted in literature and discussing Divinity with her mentors.

The rocking coach took him further from her every moment that passed. Bill touched his cheek as he sat wedged between two other travellers. Molly had kissed him on his cheek as a goodbye. Her warm lips felt as though they had seared a burn on his face. With her loving action, he realised he really liked Molly, far more than he should. She was like a young sister to him for most of his life. But that long kiss on his cheek was no sisterly peck, though. He looked out the window past the smelly farmer's wife, who sat beside him. On the other side of him was the woman's husband. He figured they must have had a fight as they had not said a word to each other since entering the swaying vehicle. When the oversized woman had stepped into the ancient carriage, Bill wondered if the wheels would fall off. She plonked herself next to the window and refused to move.

With his hand dropping back into his lap, Bill's mind returned to the years of study ahead of him, and he wondered what it would bring. Would a degree make any difference in his life? If he finished his course, what job could he get? Politics, teaching, diplomat? He was sure he would be offered the butler's role when his father died, but his father was fit and healthy, so that would not be for years anyway. Bill leaned forward and dug out the prospectus from Oxford from his bag under the seat. He silently blew out his cheeks with excitement as he again read the subjects he would be doing in his first year: Greek and Latin, rhetorical reading, mathematics and something called natural philosophy and declamation. He wondered if that was more than just learning the skills associated with Public Speaking. He had learnt to love debating. He kept reading; the following year, he added algebra and geometry. Physics was an optional course, and finally, chemistry. He would also try to keep up his Latin and Ancient Greek as he loved them. Hebrew was a language he also wished to learn. He would ask about that. They had rhetoric, logic, philosophy, and some political theory for his final year. Then, there were the subjects for the Divinity course. He looked forward to studying Old Testament Theology, Canonical Law, and the numerous other courses offered. He intended to keep up his European languages from year one. He lay back on the worn squab seats and thought about the years ahead of him. However, his thoughts were not on the subjects, the university, or even his rooms there. They had returned to Molly's kiss. She would be eighteen by the time he had finished university. Who knew what would happen then? He would certainly make sure that he returned home every chance he could. Even though his ancient grandfather had now gone, Sir Percival's magnificent house was the only home he knew.

Bill again lay back on the squab seats of the mail coach. He hoped the couple on either side of him would only stay for part of the trip. With the frequent stops to change horses and collect and drop off passengers, the journey should only take about three hours. He wished the road was not so bumpy so he could read his Sophocles. He adored the ancient Greek stories and often took one of the many books in the library to bed with him. Basil and he were the only two who ever used that section of the extensive library. The leather-bound tomes were lovingly cared for by his elderly friend.

By noon, the carriage was pulling into the university town.

~

Errol didn't make it to Oxford. He decided to re-sit the exam and actually knuckled down to study. He passed it well but still did not beat Bert. Errol enrolled at Cambridge rather than be in the same year as his younger brother. Bert, however, followed Bill to Oxford.

In the second year at college, even though they were heading to the same destination, an offer for a lift was not forthcoming due to an incident two weeks before. In Bert's final weeks at Eton, he made the grim discovery that Bill had won the coveted Oppidan Scholarship the year before. On his arrival home, he had cornered Bill one evening after imbibing a few too many drinks.

Bert accosted him with a finger poked into his shoulder, digging at him repeatedly. "Why did you keep this tidbit of news hidden, Bill? Ashamed that we would find out you are a brilliant student?" Bert was partially drunk, as he often seemed to be now. "Well, mister butler's son, let me tell you, this is no secret. You've beaten both of us at every exam and every test we've ever sat since Makepeace's days upstairs. Why stay silent now?"

Bill knew that arguing with Bert was a useless task. As he had already consumed more alcohol than he should have, he stayed mum.

Bert didn't give up. "Eh, Bill, why so quiet?" He was not speaking softly, and out of the corner of his eye, Bill saw Molly and her mother appear on the staircase. Bert's voice grew louder as the alcohol took effect. He, too, saw the staff watching, "Dux of Eton, everyone, did he tell you all that? Our little butler's boy beat us all."

Molly gasped. She caught Bill's apologetic glance towards her. Molly saw that there were now various other faces hanging over the staircase railing.

Sir Percival even appeared at his office door. "What's this, lad? Did I hear Cuthbert say you duxed Eton?"

Bill watched as his boss moved from his office door to stand beside his son.

Sir Percival placed a passive restraining arm on his son's shoulder. However, his fingers pressed so hard into his shoulder that Bert was sure there would be bruises tomorrow. While still smiling at Bill, Sir Percival said so only the three of them could hear, "Bert, behave yourself. Lower your voice and act like the gentleman you are supposed to be." He then turned to Bill and, in his normal voice, added, "Why keep this good news quiet, lad? Was it because of this sort of behaviour?"

Bill gave a single nod.

Bert's eyes still glared at his old friend. For once, he shut up.

Sir Percival understood both sides of the incident. The claw-like pressure on his son's shoulder still bit into his collarbone. For a servant's son to beat his boys was a bitter pill to swallow. Algernon Makepeace had tried to tell him early on how brilliant this lad was. Sir Percival disregarded him. The boy was a motherless butler's son. However, he managed to bestow his congratulations on him before ushering his half-drunk son into his office.

The holidays that had just finished were a series of similar incidents where Bill narrowly avoided his old school friend's ire. As he had no exams to study for, he had stayed in the servant's quarters and the below-stairs areas, far from the reach of the two angry young men. At least Molly was often there when she wasn't cleaning upstairs. He noticed she sought him out, and they would discuss life, the universe, and the various unfair status discrepancies. She ironed while he polished the silver.

~

Bill returned to university for his third year. After two years, the buildings and streets were now familiar. Although he was set down not far from his destination, he realised he would need to get a hackney to his digs with his luggage. He hated travelling in his university garb, so it was safely stowed on the top of his carry-all bag. His father had shown him how to pack it so it would not crush. His academic hat sat carefully protected in the gown and the rest of his college paraphernalia. Even his academic gown caused a problem with Errol. Cambridge University students did not seem to value the status that the academic outfit meant to the Oxford scholars. Bert's gown was of much better quality but was typically crushed, and the board of his hat had at some time been creased. Bill's outfit was immaculate. He also had colours on it from his successes at Eton. Bert's was unadorned, as was Errol's.

Soon, his years of study would be behind him. Then what? A post-graduate degree? He was sure he would get a scholarship again as he'd topped nearly everything, but for what purpose? Who would employ a butler's son with a degree?

Chapter 2   One Door Closes

$\mathcal{A}$t the end of July 1816, his university years were finished. Bill, now aged twenty-one, had returned home.

A month later, Bill and Jerome stayed up late one night discussing his graduation, his excellent results, and what he wished to do. Many ideas were raised in the discussion; however, direction had yet to be reached by the time they retired. Teaching was the only possibility.

Bill was floating through life, assisting his father with his butlers' duties and generally being helpful. He could turn his hand to many things but was master of none. He knew he must seek employment soon, but Jerome enjoyed having his son around.

More than once, Bill had been required to collect one or other of his master's sons from overindulgence at a club after having a good time. He was well known at White's club by the doorman, as Errol was frequently tossed out due to his behaviour. Bill was always on hand to escort him home. Occasionally, one of Errol's friends needed to assist in all but carrying the insensible young man home.

Bill had been home just over a month when his father did not appear at breakfast one day. It was three days after their long conversation. Bill ate a leisurely meal and returned to their apartment in a relaxed manner. He expected to find that his father had slept in for some reason. Maybe he had a day off he had forgotten to tell him about.

It was not to be so.

Jerome Miller was lying on his side in bed, cold and stiff. Unbelievably, his father was dead.

Bill stood beside the bed and gazed at his father's face for what would be all but the last time. Numb and in deep shock, Bill froze. What now? Where would he go? What would he do?

Bert's animosity had only grown with each one of his successes. Bill had won accolades and awards for everything he did. Yet now university was finished, and he had a double degree in Classics and Divinity. However, he had no qualifications or experience in anything at all and now no home. The only practical thing he knew how to do was to be a butler. He was still frozen to the spot, wondering what to do next, when he heard a noise behind him. He turned slowly as though in a daze and saw Molly and her mother standing at the door.

Ellen spoke. "Bill, it's not like Jerome to be late. Is everything all right?" Ellen and Molly Ross both stood watching him.

Bill shook his head. Not trusting himself to speak much, he simply said, "He's gone, Aunt Ellen."

Ellen checked on Jerome; he had died peacefully in his sleep. His cheek was cold to the touch and stiff.

Molly went to Bill's side and slipped her hand into his.

This simple act was Bill's undoing. At twenty-one, he was too old to cry, wasn't he? Apparently not! Molly's comforting action had sent his emotions spiralling uncontrollably, and soon, he was sobbing on her shoulder. She was crushed in his arms.

Ellen stood beside them both with a hand on his back. She knew that Sir Percival must be told, but he would not yet be up. They had a few minutes where the lad could grieve with only friends near him. She would stay with Bill while Molly was there. They would have little enough time together soon, and she was unsure what Bill's life would now entail. He may even have to leave the house. However, in the meantime, she would clean out his grandfather's old room on the ground floor.

Bill regained control and gently withdrew from Molly's caring arms. He stroked a hooked finger down her cheek. "Thanks, Mol, I needed that, and you." He dug in his pocket and found a freshly laundered kerchief.

The following hours were torturous for Bill. Once he controlled his overwrought emotions, Ellen sent Molly to their rooms while she went to inform Sir Percival.

Bill stayed with the empty husk that had been his father.

Jerome Miller had been a healthy sixty-nine. He had mentioned to Ellen that he had been getting breathless but had felt no pain.

Ellen had no need to tell Bill, but she and Jerome had become close. They had worked together for two decades and shared many an evening sitting in the butler's room while she knitted and he cleaned the silver. Being the only two staff members with children, they shared many of their joys and sorrows. They even talked about a possible union between their children one day. She would miss him greatly. She was doing what needed to be done at the moment without thinking too deeply. She would weep later when alone.

Jerome had been her backstop, sounding board, and generally, he just listened to her vent over the little things that disturbed her during the day. On the other hand, he would listen with a saint's patience. The more than twenty-year difference in their ages had meant he treated her like a daughter. But she loved him so much as he was the only one who knew her background.

Ellen had to wait until Sir Percival's valet was called and had finished dressing his master. Only then was she given entry to see her boss.

"Had he been ill, Mrs Ross?" The news was delivered with Ellen barely holding back her own tears. The shocked look on Sir Percival's face showed that the information was as unexpected to him as to everyone else.

Ellen shook her head. "Not that he mentioned, sir, a little breathless sometimes, but not precisely ill."

Sir Percival nodded. "I'll be along shortly to pay my respects. You had better call the doctor and then arrange things. Is his son home?"

Ellen nodded this time. "He is, sir, and in deep distress."

Sir Percival, having had many recent discussions with his sons, knew the once close bond that had once been between the three had long since evaporated. For the two older boys, the jealousy of being shown up at university by a servant's son was humiliating for them. He was also aware that Bill kept well out of their way. He would still use the library but would vanish as soon as the various carriages were heard on the crushed gravel driveway. He lived in the house like a ghost. With Jerome now gone, his son soon would be, too.

Sir Percival sighed. "I suppose he will have to find somewhere to live now. There's no hurry for that, but he must move from the butler's apartment as soon as possible. I will need a replacement as soon as I can find one."

Ellen expected this. Bill had even broached the subject with her already. She suspected that he had already thought about where he would go. She wondered if the university would have him back as a paid tutor. However, at twenty-one, that was unlikely.

~

Even though Jerome Miller was Percy's friend, he was only the butler. So, there was no swathing of the knocker, no official period of household mourning, or any of the usual rituals after a death. But the staff felt his loss severely; their work was done automatically. All were deep in grief for the loss of their beloved confidante. Many, if not all, had taken their woes to him at one time or another. Jerome's cheery outlook and firm faith gave them a valuable perspective on life that was unique to him. From the youngest kitchen or laundry maid to the oversized cook, all had taken their grievances to the butler at one time or another. Now, all were in shock.

Bill missed his father greatly, more so because no one knew what to say to him, so they would vanish as he approached. Molly and Ellen didn't. Although Bill was not permitted into their rooms, he and Molly were frequently found sitting at the staff dining table and talking. Ellen had released her from chores to be with her grieving friend as he needed her.

Bill was still unsure of a direction for his life. He was permitted a week's grace before he needed to make a decision. However, he moved into his grandfather's old room the day after his father died. Their old quarters brought back too many memories.

~

Mid-morning, a week after his father's funeral, he received a summons from Sir Percival. Not knowing what he had done wrong this time and expecting an eviction notice, he approached Sir Percival's office with some trepidation. This multiplied as he drew closer. Even with the door shut, he could hear the heated conversation from inside.

Errol's voice was shrill. "I do not want that person to remain in the house. He has shamed us so often that I would rather he be gone."

Sir Percival's softer reply to his spoilt son's comment was somewhat surprising. "Shamed you? Ha! If you had studied harder and partied less, the difference may not have been so pronounced. I need a butler, and he knows the job. His father was my friend, and I miss him. Although I owe Bill nothing, I can't just throw the lad out. Bert, it will be your decision. We have one vote for his staying and one for him to go."

Bill was rooted to the spot; his life would be in Bert's hands. Stay or go, he wondered if he really wished to be the most educated butler in the country. His hand was raised, ready to knock, when Bert's words were heard through the closed door. "Take him on as butler, Father, but make sure he knows his place and keep him there. After all, he is only a servant." Bill heard a small scuffle, then silence. He knew Errol would have punched his younger brother. Bill heard their father's single word, "Behave!" There was then silence.

Anger seethed through Bill. All he had ever done was work hard and help them whenever possible. He helped them both study, assisted them with assignments but refused to write them completely, and even helped them cram for exams when he should have been studying. He checked behind him; his father would generally have been in the foyer waiting in case he was needed. Today, as it had been for the last week, the atrium was devoid of his beloved presence. He almost felt his father's hand on his shoulder as his words came to him. "Son, breathe deeply three times before saying anything." Bill stood erect and took three deep breaths, knowing he had little choice but to take the job. Once again calmed, he knocked. Waiting for the order to enter, he thought he would look around for a teaching placement on his days off.

"Enter." Sir Percival's edgy voice was audible from the hallway. He was obviously somewhat tense.

Bill was pleased to see the two boys gazing out the window onto the beautifully manicured lawns. "Good morning, sir; I believe you wished to see me?" Bill stood in the same stance he had seen his father perfect over the years. His feet were slightly apart, and his hands were clenched behind his back. He had not bowed on entry as he was not indentured to them or paid by them... yet. At the moment, he was free and knew he ran rings around them all academically.

Sir Percival took a sly glance at his sons. They almost had come to blows with Bert's comment. He had needed to separate them before violence ensued. Pleased to see the boys were still out of earshot, he turned to the young man before him. The butler's boy was a well-presented, handsome young man. He drew a deep breath and said, "William, with the sad demise of your papa, I am lacking a butler, and you also need a position, or you will have to vacate the house. We have agreed that we shall offer you the role first. I know you have ably assisted in this position since you were in short trousers and even earlier. It would mean you could move back into your original quarters and have no need to leave us at all."

The smooth, even fulsome tone in which he spoke belied the earlier conversation Bill had overheard. He bit back the words and comments that sprang to his lips and found himself bowing and accepting the job. At twenty-one, he would be one of the youngest but also the best-educated, fully-trained butlers in London.

~

Knowing the role and doing the job were vastly different things.

Bill discovered how sore his feet became when he had to stand still for some hours while a dinner party or special function was on. He knew all the tricks of cleaning the silver and selecting the wines. He knew what all the keys were for and precisely what the job entailed, but he hated every moment of the work. He hated being subservient to the rude and cocky young men he had grown up with. He had footmen under him that were a decade older than he was. They were also overheard spouting their snide remarks. He later discovered that both Ellen and Molly became a buffer far more than he knew. Even with their assistance, the position rankled with him. He had no intention of being a butler all his life. However, Sir Percival and the boys kept him far too busy to seek another position, even if he knew what he wished to do; to put it simply, he was miserable.

Molly knew and did what she could to alleviate his frustrations. Her mother had caught them hugging more than once. Although it was only a hug, Ellen knew he could not and would not overstep the line he had drawn for himself. She knew he cared for her daughter but would not make any approach to her until he was settled enough to support her.

She was correct. Bill knew that until he had some form of security in his life, he would not approach Ellen for Molly's hand. She was eighteen, so they had time. He had purchased a large bunch of white roses with a few yellow ones to mark the special occasion of her eighteenth birthday.

~

Six months after his father's passing, Bill reluctantly settled into his new job. The only job-hunting Bill had done was peruse the newspapers for teaching positions.

Bert, however, was itching to find fault with Bill; however, he couldn't. The butler was, like in all other aspects of his life, just too good at what he did. Bert did, however, manage to put him down at every chance he could.

Bill stood mute, accepting each and every insult. Occasionally, Sir Percival would step in, but usually, Bill stood and took the insults and abuse without flinching. Yesterday, Bill fled to the butler's room and punched the wall angrily. As the walls were of stone, all he succeeded in doing was hurting his fist. His knuckles still hurt, and the tight white gloves didn't help with the pain.

~

The Easter after Jerome's death, tragedy struck below the stairs again. Basil Gomes, Bill's mentor and friend, tripped and fell down the servant's stairs while coming from his room to the library.

Bill had seen the entire thing and felt like it all happened in slow motion. Basil had first fallen to his knees, and as Bill ran towards him, he toppled forward and almost rolled down the narrow staircase.

Bill had no chance to stop his fall. He broke his neck on the first roll. He had often asked that a lamp be left alight on the steps so his elderly friend could see his way. Being right had not helped.

Basil's death occurred on April 7, 1817.

Bill was surprised to find that his friend had been eighty-seven.

Chapter 3   Defending Her Honour

$\mathcal{B}$asil's funeral was arranged for two days later.

It was Bill's day off. Basil had no family, as he was the only child of his parents, and he had never married.

Sir Percival was overseas on an extended business trip, and the boys lived it up while he was absent. Sir Percival had instructed his overworked staff to have some respite while he was away on his journey. However, that did not happen. The boys had partied hard. Bill had to be on call to bring the drunken men home. Occasionally, one or other of their friends assisted him. Errol's friend, Marquess David Lockley, was often nearby and came to assist. Sometimes recently, his younger brother Edward took his place. As Bill was a servant, they didn't even notice him.

Ellen sought Bill out. "Would you mind if we accompanied you to the funeral, Bill? I didn't know him well as he kept to himself. However, I feel we should be there for you. Molly, of course, was his student, so she asked if she could come with me."

Bill was delighted. "Aunt Ellen, the last thing I wish to do is to attend a funeral alone. However, it's uncommon for ladies to appear at such a service."

Ellen knew that, but they both wished to support Bill. "Lad, you've been through enough alone and having to deal with what you do above stairs. We would both like to support you today."

Bill would be appreciative of their company. They chatted about the unsettled state of the household. "Aunt Ellen, I'm not sure I will last long in this position if they continue their antics. As you know, James is the under-butler and makes so many errors they are permitted to slide. He is never corrected on a single thing. On my last day off, he served a white wine with beef and forgot to bring in the port. There are fingerprints on everything he cleans, as he hates wearing gloves. Oh, Aunt Ellen, give me a classroom of rowdy children any day. I could cope with them much better. I think even pulling ales in a pub might be preferable."

Molly sat silently but looked aghast at Bill. After a few moments, she said, "You would leave?"

Bill saw her apprehension. "I may have to, Mol. If the boys continue on like they… well, it's becoming intolerable."

Some of the other older male staff accompanied them to the funeral. They could only stay briefly as they all needed to return to work. As it was the day off for those in the first carriage, they sat in the park enjoying the spring sunshine before returning to the house. They dismissed the hackney and walked for a while, watching the pond's swans and cygnets hunt for food.

~

Two hours after the funeral, the three again called for a hackney carriage and headed home. A friend's tattered old cab dropped them in the mews at the back of the house, and they wandered inside.

From the back door, they could hear a commotion in the foyer. They decided to investigate the noises rather than go upstairs to their rooms.

Ellen followed the two young people into the entranceway. As they entered, she saw a group of strange men.

Bill immediately saw James in a state of confusion. The situation was beyond his ability to cope. Bill was in his best clothes and immediately assumed the role of senior butler. His spotless white trousers and dark coat were obviously not livery, but he spoke with an air of authority. "Gentlemen, how may I be of assistance?"

James took a step backwards and relinquished his position to Bill.

The rabble silenced for a moment. Bill stood tall and asserted his authority. "Sirs, please cease this noise. Would one of you please step forward and explain this commotion."

A rotund gentleman stepped up and threatened Bill with a clenched fist. "If I find who hit my little girl, I'll have his guts for garters."

Molly was still at Bill's side and clung to his arm for protection. She thought the angry, round man would hit one or both men.

The angry man approached the couple, and Molly shrank to Bill's side, cowering against him in fear. His words were clipped. "Who are you?"

Bill bowed and replied, "I am the butler, sir."

The angry man raised his voice. "You the butler? You're mighty young to be one. However, I was told that it's you I need to see."

As no one knew when Bill and the ladies would return, in his absence, James had sent for assistance to Sir Robert Peel and requested that one or some of his policemen attend the house.

Before Bill acknowledged anything further, he wished to know the root cause of the disturbance. "Sir, please, may I ask, to whom am I addressing?"

The rotund man stood as straight as possible. His belly protruded from the unbuttoned white-trimmed coat. "I, young man, am the child's father run down outside this establishment. She has been taken to the hospital with her mother. On enquiry, I was informed that you were the culprit."

Again, Molly stepped closer to Bill, only this time protectively. She said, "Sir, we have just returned…"

Bill cut her off. "Molly, say nothing. I have a feeling I know exactly what has occurred." He motioned with a lift of his head toward the library door. It was open just an inch or two, and Errol and Bert were peeking out.

Again, the rest of the people in the foyer started talking at once.

By the time Bill could figure out who was who, the police had arrived, with Sir Robert Peel accompanying them.

James answered the knock on the front door. As the police entered, Errol and Bert finally emerged from the library. The newcomers joined the rowdy throng of angry people filling the foyer.

Bert was dressed in clothing similar to Bill's. He was wearing his best white trousers with a dark cutaway jacket, and they could easily have been mistaken for each other.

Sir Robert stepped up and soon had the affray sorted. It should have been dealt with by an apology and an offer to pay the hospital bills, but at that moment, Bert approached and spoke to Sir Robert. He tried to banish the various onlookers. The angry man was found to be a Mr Fulcher, and his daughter had run out onto the road as a carriage approached. Thankfully, she had only been mildly injured.

Bert glanced at Bill and met his gaze with a sneer. "Sir, my brother and I were in the library studying for our return to university when we noticed the speeding carriage pass, turn into our house, and then proceeded into the mews. We heard the disturbance out here from the peace in the library. We believe that, in reality, the butler was in the carriage that had just arrived, sir, and that maid was with him."

Sir Robert smelled spiritous liquid on Bert's breath, and he was finding that even standing still was difficult. Errol was not in a much better state. Knowing that these two young men had caused much trouble in the town before, he doubted their story. However, he turned to the young butler and awaited his comment. "Sir, what say you? Have you just returned in a vehicle?"

Bill gently shook Molly's hand from his arm, distancing himself. "I have, sir."

Sir Robert continued his questioning. "Did the said carriage you were in draw into the mews?"

Bill looked at Bert as he replied, "It did, Sir Robert."

Molly refused to be shaken off. She slipped her hand in his and whispered, "Bill, tell him the truth."

Sir Robert heard her whispered comment. His eyebrows flicked up, "Before you answer, lad, come with me." He looked around at the remaining people in the vestibule. "If you are not personally involved, be gone." He stood and waited while some of the twenty sticky-beak people left. Soon, only the rotund man, Sir Robert, and the household members were in the room.

Sir Robert turned to Bill. "Come, lad." Their conversation was to be private. He turned to walk into the room Errol and Bert had recently vacated. He held the door for Bill and snapped it shut behind him.

Bert was not impressed having the door closed in his face.

Rather than stand near the door, Sir Robert moved across the room to the fireplace. "I believe your name is William Miller."

Bill dipped his head in a bow of acknowledgement.

Sir Robert knew that Bert's accusation could see that the young lad before him could be arrested and transported for his crime. "Lad, I wished to question you alone as somehow I don't believe that the allegation made by the somewhat inebriated man outside is correct."

Bill was not afraid of the repercussions. He replied, "Sir, what I said was perfectly true, only I had just returned in a hackney carriage; however, I was with the housekeeper and her daughter, having just returned from a staff member's funeral. As it is our day off, we sat in a park for an hour or so before returning here. There will be witnesses to us being there. We hit no one, and the ruckus was already in progress when we returned. You may ask Mrs Ross, sir. She is a woman of good repute and known to be truthful." Bill's gaze held his own without flinching.

Bill neither looked to the left nor right, but Sir Robert could tell the lad was undoubtedly telling the truth. "If this accusation is false, then how do you explain that?"

Bill wondered precisely about that question. He was about to answer when he noticed the bookshelves move aside, and the ordinarily unused archivist's entrance opened quietly.

Molly silently came to Bill's side. "Sir Robert," she gave a small curtsy, "I don't know what Bill has said, but we were not even here when whatever it was occurred. Mother, Bill, and I have just returned from a funeral."

Sir Robert smiled at the attractive young girl defending her friend. "I believe him, miss. However, I cannot just dismiss Mr Cuthbert's words. I need a reason to dispel them." He looked from one to the other.

Bill had taken Molly's hand and given it a squeeze of thanks.

Sir Robert saw a frown and slight shake of Bill's head to Molly.

Molly's expression did not remain passive. "No, Bill. I'm sorry, but you're not taking the fall for him this time. You've done that for them both far too often."

Bill flicked his eyes from Molly's to Sir Robert, then back again, but stayed silent.

Molly harrumphed. "Sir, it started when Bill was educated with the boys. He beat them on all the tests and exams and won school and university scholarships. He completed his degree last year, and although younger than both, they are still trying to catch him up. He duxed both colleges, and they can't forgive him. Sir, it is pure jealousy."

Bill flushed scarlet. "Molly, enough, please. I'm just the butler."

She turned on him. "And I'm just a maid, Bill, but I won't tell untruths for those drunken sots so they can get off scot-free again. It's about time they owned up to their debauched activities." She turned back to Sir Robert. "Ask the child's father if the vehicle that hit his daughter was an old hackney or a private carriage. Trust me, you can't mistake them. I know our hackney driver, and he will confirm our trip."

Sir Robert nodded. "Wait here." This one question may sort out the issue. He exited the room, leaving the young couple alone.

As the door closed, Molly rounded on Bill. "Bill, you are not to accept this. As I told Sir Robert, they must pay, not you." She held his arm with both hands. "Please, Bill, I need you here." She lowered her voice. "I want you here with me."

Bill saw her eyes go glassy, and his heart was racing. "I have nothing to offer you, Mol. I don't want to leave, but I have no future here. I'm not even twenty-two yet, and I'm at the top of my career as a servant." He drew her to him, cradling her lovingly, her luscious curves pressing against him.

She lifted her face to him. "I don't care, Bill. I don't care at all about that; I care only about you."

Bill couldn't resist and bent to give her a peck on her inviting lips. She wrapped an arm around his neck and deepened the caress as he did. Bill responded in kind, and soon, the fracas outside was forgotten. Moments of sheer ecstasy turned into an eon of time; both were blissfully unaware of the passing minutes. They were in the moment and enjoying every second of it. However, hearing the approaching footsteps, Bill gently broke apart and pushed her away slightly. "You have no idea how long I've wished to do that, Mol," he said softly before Sir Robert entered the room.

As the door opened, Molly had a chance to whisper, "Me too," before Sir Robert, followed by the three men, came to their side.

Bert opened his mouth to say something, but Sir Robert shut him down with a lifted hand before he uttered the first word. "Silence! I shall ask the questions. Sir, any information you have will be recorded if required later." Sir Robert now spoke to the child's father. "Sir, did you notice if the carriage was a hackney cab or a private carriage?"

The rotund man looked at the three equally well-dressed gentlemen before him. It was hard to believe that one of these men was a butler, but none looked old enough for that position. "The carriage was definitely a private one. It was a shiny mahogany one with puce and black livered footmen."

Sir Robert asked Bill, "Sir, do you own or have access to a private carriage?"

Bill shook his head. "No, sir, I use hackneys or walk." Bill saw Sir Robert give a micro wink. "Gervais Harrow was our driver today."

Sir Robert said sternly, "Ahh, well, therein lies a problem. The accused could not have been the culprit. I suggest we now adjourn to the mews and investigate the vehicles."

Bert, who had sobered up a little in the intervening minutes, sulkily said, "Oh, don't bother. You'll find the carriage you require in the coach house. I have already sacked the driver, but I had hoped to blame the butler to finally get rid of him." He then very childishly poked out his tongue at Bill. He was swaying as he stood. Then he said to his brother, "So much for me getting into the wench's skirt. You suggested this, Errol. You said you had it planned so I could have at her. I bet he's in her bed behind our backs anyway."

Errol shook his brother. "Shut up, you stupid fool; they had nothing on us until you opened your mouth. Now you've blown it! We'll both be in the nick soon enough."

Bert may have spoken so because of alcohol, but it was too much for Bill. He heard Bert's snide comment and the slur on Molly's character. He was trying to pull himself from Molly's grasp.

Bill said, "Bert, you know I would never touch her in such a disrespectful manner. I would not..." He was seething. He was unable to finish due to his anger. He said, "Sir, I demand satisfaction here and now!"

"Not blooming likely, Bill." Bert didn't let up. He jibed at her morals again, slandering her reputation. "I do not doubt that you have had that pleasure of such satisfaction with her already. She is just a maid and a saucy bit of fluff at that. I doubt she would have said no to you."

"Satisfaction, be damned!" Bill was now livid. He would not let that slide unnoticed. He muttered and swung.

Bert had no chance to say more as he soon lay unresponsive on the library floor. His nose was at an odd angle and oozed red gore on the luxurious rug. The claret pooling around his head did not come from a bottle this time.

Bill had hardly moved from his original position. His response was lightning fast; if Sir Robert had not been already watching, he would have missed it altogether.

Errol was momentarily stunned that Bill had laid his brother out flat. "You've killed him, you fiend!" He turned to Sir Robert. "I demand you arrest him. I want him charged with assault." He, too, had hardly moved. He had not even bent to attend to his drunken brother.

Bill did and turned his old friend on his side.

When Bill stood, Sir Robert grabbed Bill's arm more to halt further action. "Lad, I have no choice now. I must arrest you for assault."

Bill nodded. "Sir, I would not let that slug insult my girl. Arrest if you must, but please do not leave her here alone with them. Please call her mother." His eyes bored into Molly's. "Sir, I love her. I always have. Please keep her safe for me."

Sir Robert had seen the connection between them and knew his following actions would tear them apart irrevocably. "Say goodbye to her, lad, while I deal with the first matter, I must, however, arrest you for this."

He saw Bill tug twice on the bell pull and then go to Molly's side.

She was gently weeping as he took her in his arms for a quick hug.

Bill did not kiss her but released her and gently rubbed his hands up and down her arms. "The die is cast, my sweet Mol. I will go where they send me, but I couldn't let the scoundrel cast aspersions upon your character. You are good and true. If we are meant to be together, the good Lord will work that out. Trust Him, my sweet." Bill pointed heavenward.

Molly nodded. "I will, and I do."

Only then did Bill kiss her. He had just lifted his lips from hers when her mother entered.

Ellen went directly to her daughter's side. "Sir, you called." She looked at the prostrated Bert and the fuming Errol. She instantly summarised the situation. She looked at Errol and awaited an answer.

"No, woman!" Errol jerked his thumb towards Bill, "He did."

Bill nodded at Ellen. "I did, Aunt Ellen."

The three had enjoyed a delightful time in the park, and now he would see Molly no more. He already knew assault on the gentry carried a hefty sentence. He may even be transported. He wouldn't mind that so much, except he would miss out on a life with Molly beside him. He would let no man insult her. He would stand in defence of her honour at any time. He loved her too well for that.

Ellen knew she would get the full story from Molly later. For now, she knew she needed to support Bill.

Sir Robert silenced Errol and took control. He had things well in hand.

For a second time, Bill checked that Bert was breathing. Bert had retched soon after falling, and the disgusting vomitus oozed over the floor. The simple act of turning him on his side had saved him from choking on his spew. After checking Bert was still breathing, he knew that most of the reason he was unresponsive was due to the excess of alcohol. His punch had not been that hard.

Sir Robert turned to Errol. "Send someone to fetch the doctor. I think most of the damage will need to be slept off, but it's better to be safe than sorry." He was intrigued that his attacker was the only person to attend to the injured man. Sir Robert waited for Errol to leave, then turned to the housekeeper. "Ma'am, sadly, there was an altercation, and I must now arrest William Miller for assault. I shall also be charging the other two men with various crimes, including that the accusation was both defamation and slander. It was not perjury as they were not under oath, but they both attempted to incriminate William with the crime they had committed." He turned to look at the prostrated figure. "Mr Cuthbert there admitted the incident, and Mr Errol substantiated his comments. I will charge them with bearing false witness."

Sir Robert suggested that Bill apply for a writ of *habeas corpus* once arrested instead of trusting a magistrate for a just judgment. "Lad, if you are taken before a judge, I will stand witness for you. You will not get off without punishment; however, my testimony will assist in the sentencing."

He turned to Ellen. "Mrs Ross, a private word, please."

Bill and Molly had no idea what he wished to say to Ellen, but Sir Robert quietly told them to say the last farewell while he distracted her mother. He waited until Ellen had her back to them, and Bill again drew Molly into his arms for their third, but most likely, final kiss. His heart was nearly breaking, but he would protect her with his dying breath. It was now unlikely that he would see or hold her again. He poured his heart into that kiss.

Molly clung to him.

When Bill released her, she sobbed as though her heart would break.

Chapter 4   Old Bailey

$\mathcal{B}$ill was charged with assault and sent to Newgate Prison, where he was placed in the shared wardroom near the refectory cells where the worst criminals were held. He knew this building was situated next to the Old Bailey, where he would be taken before the court judges.

Sir Robert's petition to stand witness for him was granted, and he had also prepared a submission in writing, which he would file before the case was heard.

Thankfully, before arresting him, Sir Robert had suggested that Bill changes out of his best attire. He then returned to the room, where he and Errol were finally escorted from the house. Two of Sir Robert's finest 'bobbies' or 'peelers' took them to Newgate, where Bert would later join them when he was well enough.

Errol, however, had refused to change his attire, and his entry into the unsavoury prison was an eye-opening experience for him. He was incarcerated in what was known as the debtors' wards. Bert joined him there three days later. This wing had a slightly better class of prisoners but was still vile. Although assured of a bunk on the better side of the prison, the place stank, and there was no privacy. They remained in the squalid cells until their father's lawyer bailed them out. They had to return to face the judge but had already agreed to pay all the hospital costs for the injured child and cough up some compensation. They would get off with a slap on the wrists again.

Their father was still away on his overseas trip. He was circumnavigating the globe on a diplomatic mission. Bill worked out that he should now be on his way back from New South Wales.

Bill was content to sit back and wait his turn for trial. He had learned to be patient years before. However, having nothing to read was frustrating. Sir Robert had twice come for a visit, and both times, Bill had forgotten to request a book to read.

As Sir Robert left after his second visit, he was still within earshot and, through the locked cell doors, heard Bill groan and say, "Damn, I forgot again!"

Sir Robert turned from the end of the corridor and asked, "Something eating at you, son?"

Bill didn't think he had even spoken aloud. He was somewhat in awe of the special attention he was getting from Sir Robert. "No, sir, I was going to ask you if, by any chance, I could have something to read."

Sir Robert chuckled as he returned to Bill's cell door. "I'll see what I can find. Any preferences?"

Bill was thrilled, and his face lit up with joy. "Anything ancient, in Greek, Latin or similar, would be wonderful, sir. Euripides, Plato, Pliny, Seneca, Aristotle, for example, and it doesn't matter if it's in the original language, although a Latin translation would be fine too." Knowing that most of the others he shared a cell with could not even read their mother tongue, he wasn't too worried about the book being pilfered.

"You read Latin and Greek?" Sir Robert asked, somewhat stunned at the education of a mere butler. Molly had mentioned something, but he presumed she had exaggerated. Robert returned to the grill, which separated them so that others could not overhear their conversation.

Bill met his enquiry with an honest gaze. "Yes, sir, ancient and modern Greek, Hebrew, German, Spanish, and French, of course, and I have a smattering of Cyrillic languages, like Russian. I lose the skill if I don't keep up with my reading."

Sir Robert questioned him further. "Where did you study? Private tutor? Miss Ross said you attended college."

Bill again gave an honest and very innocent answer. "Sir, as Molly said, I did a double degree in Classics and Divinity at Oxford. I believe that you did something similar, sir. If I remember Father's words, you also achieved a double first in Classics and Mathematics from Oxford. It's why I had hoped you may have some of the books I would like."

The man outside the cells looked at the prisoner. "But you are a butler; who paid your fees?"

Bill again answered honestly but with great modesty: "No one, sir; I won full scholarships to both Eton and then to Oxford. At Eton, I won the Oppidan Scholar award, and I was the King's Scholar in my final year. I was placed at university before I applied. I got a double first there, too." The young man stated the details so simply that his achievements sounded underwhelming.

Sir Robert gazed at his charge with his mouth agape. Finally, swallowing, he said, "You're an O.S.? Seriously?"

Bill nodded in the affirmative. "K.S., O.S., sir. Not much help, though, is it?"

Astounded, all Sir Robert could say was, "Then why are you a blasted butler for those two young upstarts?"

Bill shrugged. "I wasn't intending to stay there. It was only because Molly was there that I stayed to protect her from them. Papa was the previous butler, and my grandfather was before him, so I knew the job. I stayed while I looked around, but nothing came up. I'm considered too young to be a tutor of any calibre or a lecturer at a university, even though my degrees are higher than those lecturing there. However, I've already delivered a few language lectures at Oxford. Oxford offered me some crumbs of tutoring or guest lecturing, but I would rather teach children than spoilt rich boys like those two." He gave a half smile as though embarrassed.

Sir Robert looked at the boy behind bars anew. "Having known other spoilt rascals like those in the other cells, I can understand your comment." He paused, then said, "You didn't hear me say that, by the way, lad." He grimaced.

Bill grinned. "No, sir! Of course not, sir." Bill was biting his top lip, trying hard not to laugh.

Sir Robert turned to leave, then returned. "You really have guest lectured at Oxford already?" The illustrious gentleman shook his head, astounded at the young man before him. "Hold tight, William; when those two are released, as I'm sure they will be very soon, I'll try to move you to the debtors' cells. You would not wish to be near them while they are still there. At least in the individual cells, you will have fewer bodies sharing in the wards and better lighting to read. I will bring you a few interesting books to while away your time."

"Thank you, sir." Bill was pleased that he had asked for the reading material now. He knew that Sir Robert would check his credentials before coming again, but he was happy about that, as everything he had told him was accurate and well-understated. He had not just passed his Oxford exams but topped every one of them except physics. He had only gained a second in that subject, but it was only done as an extra course, so it didn't affect his degree. Bill settled down to wait for the next meal to arrive. Keeping his mind active, he decided to recite the words of the Ancient Hebrew *Shema*; this was something his father had taught him when he was very young. He had seen him praying every night and heard him say this prayer aloud often. He bowed his head in reverence to the mighty words. "Hear, O Israel: The Lord is our God, the Lord alone. You shall love the Lord your God with all your heart, and with all your soul, and with all your might. Keep these words that I am commanding you today in your heart." Once said, it was followed by *The Lord's Prayer*. He was reminded of God's power and was content to hand his life over to him. Then, he also decided to revise all the ancient language alphabets. He went through each alphabet in each of the languages he knew.

He had often done this exercise when unable to sleep at university. This exercise typically took about half an hour. Tonight, by the time he had finished, the bell had clanged for the gruel's arrival. Considering the delicious food served at Sir Percival's house, Bill was pleased to be given anything to eat. He laid back on the wooden pallet bed and waited.

~

A parcel arrived for Bill the following week. Thankfully, he had been moved into the debtors' wards and placed in a solitary confinement cell, which was often left unlocked. Sir Robert had waited until this had occurred to keep his books safe. The parcel contained a note with information about his trial and the books. One of which he had only ever seen in a London Museum behind glass, plus an edition was a copy of the Nuremberg Chronicle. He didn't even know that this book had more modern copies. *Liber cronicarum cum figuris et ymaginibus* by Hartmann Schedel was the second book ever printed in 1493, after the Gutenberg Bible. He had never even seen a replica of the illustrated encyclopaedia. To actually hold a reproduction of it in his hands amazed him. It would undoubtedly occupy him for some time. The other three textbooks were standard classic texts that would be good to while away the hours. They were modern editions of Oedipus Rex, Pliny, and Sophocles.

With these books, the days before the trial passed in a flash. Bill hardly lifted his head from the magnificent library he had been loaned. Deep in the study, Bill lost track of time. He spent his days with his head once more in his beloved books. He knew it had been early April when he was arrested. He had spent three weeks in the squalid wards before being moved into the debtor's prison section just days before his books arrived. Here, he found sanctuary and peace.

For him, being locked in a cell twenty-four hours a day and having food and drink delivered was an academic scholar's delight. As he never noticed what he ate, the food quality went unnoticed. It filled his stomach, and that's all that mattered.

~

After more weeks in the debtors' cells, Sir Robert came again to inform him of a date change for his trial and asked how he liked the books.

Bill grinned. "I don't like them, sir; I love them. I while away the hours, thinking it must be nearly midday when I find the entire day has gone. Oh, and thank you for moving me here. You tell me that it's mid-June already, and I find that the time has gone so fast."

Sir Robert's smile was reassuring. "I wondered if you had seen a copy of Schedel. I was given it after one of the first cases I helped solve. It was a murder, and the gentleman involved was a rare bookseller. I have no idea how many copies of this exist, but with your background, I thought you might appreciate it. I admit I've not had more than a cursory glance at it, as work keeps me far too busy."

Sir Robert had come to tell him that his trial date was now August 28th. "William, I will be away, but I have delivered a character reference to the judge. I have also given him a letter of recommendation. I'm sorry, lad, but if the date had been July as was originally planned, I could have come as promised. I shall see you when I return and collect the books. Hopefully, we will know what the future will hold, but I was thinking about recommending transportation for you. You would have a fresh start in the colony, and once your term is served, you could teach or do whatever you liked."

With the last comment, Bill's eyes pricked attentively. "I could teach after being a convict. Truly, sir?"

Sir Robert nodded; he knew that what happened in the Antipodes differed vastly from London. "Lad, the world will be your oyster over there. I believe Governor Macquarie is stirring things up out there and is permitting emancipists to return to their previous status and rank they held before their convictions. The land is cheap, and opportunities abound. Should this be the outcome, I will write to him and give my recommendations to you. William, I mean precisely that when I say you could do anything you wish. There are many free settlers there with children who will need tutors, or you could even teach at your own school. However, I'm sure the Lord will open a door for where He wants you, and mayhap Miss Molly could join you?"

~

Bill's case went before the judge, and he was summoned to attend the overcrowded court.

The prisoners being tried sat in a central square section of the courtroom. In front of them was a semicircular-shaped desk; around this sat twelve wig- and robe-clad men, whom Bill presumed were the jury. Above them, in an elevated dais-like structure, sat more men whom, from their position, Bill assumed to be the judges.

Bill could watch the proceedings for some time as he was not the first case to be heard. He sat quietly, observing the way the system of justice worked. He saw the prosecutor addressing the judges from his seat in the prisoner's box. He watched the animated stance of the man while explaining the charges against the poor girl now called to stand trial. As with each one before her, she would be found guilty. None escaped the punishment metered out by the elderly men seated so high above them.

Bill sat intrigued, watching the wheels of justice turn, forgetting that he would soon be at their mercy. The cacophony of voices from the public sections of the court needed to be admonished frequently.

As the day progressed, the numbers decreased. The officials retired for a meal, and then half an hour later, on their return, the court once again had to stand for their entrance. Bill's case was heard at three o'clock. His name was called, and he was escorted to the stairs leading to the elevated platform to stand trial. Sir Robert had Ellen sent in his best clothing, and he had donned these for the court case.

Bill stood and waited.

Generally, by now, the judge would have asked some questions. A frown settled on his brow; he wondered what the hold-up was. He turned to the prosecutor with a cocked eyebrow.

The man shrugged in response to his silent question.

Errol and Bert had been called to the front, and they sat in the witness boxes, wondering what the hold-up was.

Bill had not seen them since the debacle at the house and noticed that Bert's handsome face was now somewhat altered. His nose sat at a peculiar angle on his face. A smile slid over Bill's lips; Bert would not forget him now.

It seemed to take an age, but finally, the senior judge spoke. "William Miller, please stand." The elderly, bespectacled judge did not see Bill already was in place as he was watching Sir Percival slip into the courtroom and take a seat at the back.

Bill said, "I'm here, sir," as he lifted his hand from the dock.

"Ahh," the judge said. "I have a letter here, boy, that explains the entire case from the main eyewitness who will remain nameless. He has given a detailed description of the extenuating circumstances. He has also corroborated your educational history. You have an interesting background, lad, and I congratulate you on bettering yourself. I also congratulate you for standing up to drunken bullies. Nevertheless, what you did is breaking the law, and your crime of assault will be upheld. You shall have to pay for your action; however, I will agree on a term of a maximum of three years from today and for that time to be served in the Antipodes. Transportation to the colony will be forthcoming, and once there, the remainder of your term will be served as the letter suggests." The judge's gavel banged onto the base, and Bill heard him say, "Dismissed! Next case."

Bert stood to protest. He shouted at the unfair term of Bill's minimum sentence. Bert's snivelling whine was heard in a lull in the proceedings. "I say, sir, that's not fair! I was given no chance to state my case."

Errol had earlier seen his father enter somewhat late. He glanced at his father's face; he could see a storm brewing on their return home.

The judge glared at Bert. "Did I ask you to talk, sir? No, I did not. If what I read in this letter is accurate, and knowing the author personally, I know him to be fully truthful, you may, of course, try to present a case; however, I know for a fact that as you were both before me last month, for failing to render assistance to a child you had hit with your carriage. I may well change my mind and send you both to prison for perjury. This letter fully outlines this incident as a precursor to today's case."

The old man's bushy grey eyebrows furrowed. He dropped his head again to read Sir Robert's screed. The courtroom silence was such that you could easily have heard a pin drop. With a gasp of satisfaction, the wig-clad head nodded. "Ah yes, here it is. You, sir, apparently inferred that you wanted to have the butler accused, as you wished to, and I quote, '*have at,*' a certain young lady who is soon to be betrothed to this young man. Is this so?"

Before Bill could reply, he heard a voice from the public gallery: "This is true, sir, for I am the lady." Molly stood in her place, and with her head held high, she stood her ground.

Ellen sat beside her, trying to stop her from speaking.

The courtroom erupted in booing, and someone threw something at Bert, who, unfortunately, ducked.

Bill stood with his back to the judge, gazing at his lady love. He didn't realise she was there. Everyone else in the room had all but vanished for him. He drank in her presence and wished he could be at her side.

The courtroom marshals eventually got the rabble to be silent once more.

The presiding judge watched the entire fiasco with interest. The judge beckoned Molly to the dock, "Come here, girl; I wish to speak to you."

There was a murmur of disquiet rippling through the room. This was against the proceedings. She was an unacknowledged witness, but the judge had the right to call whom he wished.

Bill saw Errol grab at Bert's jacket as his brother went to say more. "Shut up, you blithering idiot," Errol said in anger. "Bill was to be sent away until you opened your stupid trap. Shut it, you twit. With him gone, you could have had the floozy to yourself."

The room fell silent as Errol's final words were spoken. Every person in the room heard his comment.

The judge, jury, and court all caught the incriminating words. Now glaring at Errol, the presiding judge waited for Molly to move from her seat to stand at Bill's side. The judge saw an attractive young woman climb the stairs to the dock and take her place beside her beloved. He saw the simple action of her slipping her hand into his and the look of adoration on the young man's face.

Bill had not taken his eyes off his beloved since he heard she was in the courtroom. In the four months since he had seen her, she had blossomed into a beautiful and confident young woman. She stood beside him in a white sprigged muslin gown and a small straw bonnet. As the courtroom was hot, she had removed her shawl. She said, "I am sorry for the interjection, Your Honour, but I still have trouble with that young man in question."

The judge nodded. "The letter states your name, but for court records, please confirm it so everyone can hear."

Molly nodded. "My name is Mary Ellen Ross, and I am known as Molly."

The judge checked his records. "Yes, they concur. Continue, tell me, how long have you known the accused?"

In a confident voice, Molly answered, "For all but two years of my life, Your Honour. My mother was required to seek a position as a housekeeper when my Papa died. I was two years old. Mr Jerome Miller, William's father, interviewed the candidates and chose my mother, as she had a child. You see, sir, he had a small child too. He is just three years older than me." She glanced at Bill, and the smile she gave him silenced the remaining comments from the public gallery. "Sir, Bill and I have been constant companions ever since. We were brought up as almost brother and sister and drew closer as we aged. He has been away at university until recently. On his return, his Papa died, and through our joint grief, we realised we felt more for each other than as honorary siblings. As we are unrelated, our relationship had no barriers in that way. However, it was only on the day in question that we declared our feelings towards each other were more than just friends." As she finished, she stepped closer to Bill. She had not released his hand.

Bill had not taken his eyes from her as she spoke.

The judge had a strange look on his face. The harsh, wrinkled visage had softened into a smile.

Molly realised the stern old man was a romantic.

He waved for her to continue.

Molly's voice was clear and concise. "And then, sir, those two men accused Bill of knocking over a child. As we three, mother was with us," she motioned to her mother in the gallery, "...had been at the funeral for a beloved staff member, we had only just returned in a hackney carriage when everything went haywire. We entered from the mews to a commotion in the foyer. The constabulary was called, and Bill was accused of the accident. Even with those accusations, William Miller, known to me as Bill, refused even to belittle the drunken actions of those two standing over there." She pointed at the accusers. "Bill held his temper, and I think he may have even accepted the responsibility for their actions once again. He had done this often since they were all children, protecting them from their own folly."

The judge and jury sat spellbound.

The judge said, "Oh, has he now? Well, that's interesting; go on."

Molly said, "Well, sir, a senior policeman took Bill aside and questioned him privately. Unbeknownst to him, I knew a private way into the room and joined them shortly afterwards. I corroborated Bill's story, and those two were called in to explain. It was after Mr Cuthbert finally admitted that it had indeed been their carriage that had caused the incident and the reason for his vile comments about me that Bill demanded satisfaction." She gazed lovingly at her beloved. "Bill, I'm sorry." She swallowed, then continued, "Mr Cuthbert did not cease with his attentions, sir. His comments were brutish and derogatory, not to mention seriously inflammatory. When he described his wishes for his actions towards me, Bill defended my honour, sir. Moments later, Mr Cuthbert found himself prostrated and insensible." She paused and smiled, "His nose still bears witness to the incident." She chuckled, and the public gallery joined her in a hearty belly laugh at Bert's expense.

The judge thoroughly enjoyed the break from protocol and hearing this charming lady's tale. "So, William, you defended the honour of your lady love and best friend, and I gather, sir, you would do so again?"

Bill tore his eyes from Molly and looked at the judge as he spoke. "I would, Your Honour and would do so to any person who spoke such vile statements against her." Bill again dropped his eyes to Molly. He said in a low and ardent tone, "She is all that is good and pure, sir. I do so love her dearly."

The judge and jury heard the searing heat of passion in his voice.

One juror wiped a tear from his eye. He muttered loud enough for his peers to hear, "Ahh, such true love."

The judge nodded and dismissed Molly. "You may return to your seat, miss. Your story matches with the details in the said letter."

Molly gave Bill's hand a big squeeze, more she could not do in such a public setting. She turned and elegantly stepped from the dock.

As she walked past the witness box, Bert said in a coarse tone, "Whore! I bet you are not so pure and innocent."

Molly was close enough to spin around and slap him with her open palm on his cheek. She gasped moments after she did so. She had just hit a gentleman in full view of the court. Her mother's position would be terminated in an instant. However, she spun around and faced the judge. "Did you hear what he called me, Your Honour?"

"I did, Miss Ross." The judge was beginning to find this case was not to his liking after all. The more he heard about these two spoilt miscreants, the less he liked them. He addressed Bert, "Sir, you will stand and apologise to her so everyone can hear."

Bert said petulantly like a small child, "I won't. She is… she withholds her favours only for him." He pointed to Bill.

The judge's face grew red. He stood, and with hands on the bench before him, he roared, "You will apologise, and you will also pay her financial damages for such wilful derogatory comments."

Errol gasped. "You are a blooming idiot. Apologise before I knock you insensible myself."

In a very sullen voice, Bert muttered a few inaudible words. His half-hearted effort was only discernible to a few, and he sat down almost instantly.

The judge thought to teach the sullen, rude, rich brat a lesson. "Louder man, I did not hear you. You will have to speak up."

Bert again stood. "I'm sorry for my ungentlemanly behaviour and rude comments." He turned to Errol. "There, are you happy now?"

The judge was beginning to see red. He stood and said, "He may be, but he is not the injured party. What is your yearly allowance, sir?"

Bert answered without standing, his arms folded in annoyance. "I get a measly £5000, and Errol gets £8000."

The judge nodded. He turned to Molly with a sly grin. "What is your yearly salary, Miss Ross?"

Molly had not moved. "Eight pounds, Your Worship."

The judge nodded. With a sly smile, he took his seat as he considered the situation. "As I thought." He bit his lip momentarily. "That shall be rectified." He nodded to Molly, then said, "People of the court, I presume you have all heard the commotion going on before me?" He watched many nodding. "My judgement is, and I use this term lightly, gentlemen, you shall not dismiss Mrs Ross as your housekeeper, nor Miss Molly Ross as a maid in your father's employ. Mr Edison-Browne and Mr Cuthbert Edison-Browne, for your joint rudeness and disparaging remarks, you will both immediately pay her compensation of your entire yearly allowance. After receiving it, Miss Ross shall pay you the princely sum of her yearly salary to you as compensation for her slap, but only after you have paid her."

The judge beside him heard his following comment and muttered not so softly. "Pity he didn't have many more of them while growing up."

The junior judge beside him choked back laughter.

The senior judge caught a glimpse of Sir Percival's posture. He was surprised to see him glare at his sons and then give the judge a nod of thanks.

The presiding judge motioned for Molly to return to her mother. He watched as she did so, then said to Bill, "I shall change my conviction, Mr Miller. You are still to be transported to the Antipodes. However, your sentence will finish on arrival, whenever that may be. From there, make yourself a new life away from these two." He watched Bert and Errol's faces as he spoke, knowing it would make them livid; he just smiled and banged his gavel. "Next case!"

Chapter 5   At an Impasse

*A*fter the case concluded and Bill was taken to his cell, Molly and

Ellen returned to the house, knowing that Bert and Errol would do everything they could to make their lives uncomfortable.

Sir Percival summoned all four to the library as soon as they returned. He had already read the riot act to his sons. He was disgusted at their behaviour and dealt with them by not replacing their allowance. They would return to university, their extracurricular activities would be banned, and all future expenditures must be pre-approved by him. No new clothes, outings, parties, women, horses, or any other frivolous pursuit; they would study and pass or repeat every year until they did.

Both young men were horrified.

When Ellen and Molly joined them some minutes after their roasting, they were met by two somewhat chastised young men. Their angry and absolutely apologetic father stood with his back to his sons.

Molly clung to her mother's hand as they entered, fearful of the reprisals they would encounter. The ladies had not even realised that Sir Percival had returned from overseas in time to attend the trial.

Sir Percival gave her a nod of acknowledgement on their entry, something he never usually did. "Mrs Ross, Miss Molly, as you know, I heard everything that was revealed in the courtroom. I am sincerely sorry that you have both had to experience the rudeness of my sons. This is not how they were brought up, and they will apologise to you both." He turned and glared at his sons. "Sadly, I cannot undo the damage they have done to William, but they shall pay. I do not just mean financially, although they will feel that, but in other ways."

Molly was still clinging to Ellen. She did not wish to stay in the house with either of them but had nowhere else to go.

Sir Percival called his sons, and reluctantly, they came at his bidding. One by one, they politely bowed and offered a profound apology.

Only time would tell precisely how sincere they were, but it was a start.

~

Some months after the trial, Sir Robert called to see Sir Percival.

Ellen had taken in the tea tray and been summarily dismissed.

They sat sequestered in his den for over an hour before Sir Percival again summoned her. Sir Robert and Sir Percival stood at her entry. "Mrs Ross, as you may guess, I have come on William's behalf. It is beginning to get cold in the cells. Although women are normally not permitted to visit the men's section, I have arranged a meeting in the superintendent's office for you to bring William some warm clothing and bedding."

A week later, Bill was impatiently waiting for them. He had been dragged from his cell in a show of false protest for the benefit of the other prisoners. He only played along because he was told he would get to see Molly. He heard footsteps approaching, and Ellen opened the door; he greeted the housekeeper with a peck on the cheek as usual. She had been a surrogate mother to him for most of his life. Then, as he had done when young, he greeted her with "Hello, Aunt Ellen, thank you so much for coming." His eyes had already left hers and rested on Molly. He had not even noticed Sir Robert's presence. Ignoring the two adults, Bill took Molly's hands. "Hello, my sweet girl." He dared not kiss her in front of these two people, but how he wished to.

His greeting made Molly's heart sing. She stood gazing lovingly at him, unsure of what to say in her mother's presence. She flicked her eyes over at her mother. "Hello, Bill. I missed you." She cringed; it sounded so corny, but what else could she say with the other two so close at hand? "We brought you some warm clothes. Sir Robert arranged everything and... and... I have so much to tell you." Again, her eyes flicked to the two adults.

Sir Robert interrupted. "Go sit in the alcove, lad; I have to chat with Mrs Ross." He shooed off the two young people while he occupied her mother with some banal chatter. He wondered what the now star-crossed lovers would do. William was marked to be transferred to a prison hulk when he was allocated a berth on a convict transport. It was not time to reveal this to the three of them. Soon, they would have to part forever, and they should know. Some twenty minutes passed before Sir Robert called them back to his side.

He revealed the next part of Bill's conviction. "Lad, I do not have a date for your transportation yet, but it will probably be mid-next year. A few months before you leave, you will be taken to Portsmouth and held on a prison hulk. The transport will collect you from there, and you will leave England's shores forever. With your education, you should be able to obtain a good position doing whatever you want."

Bill was gutted; just knowing he was in the same country as Molly had sufficed. However, he knew that she had to get on with her life. He could not hold on to her and must say farewell. Both knew it, but both refused to acknowledge this melancholy fact. He had kissed her once since she arrived, which was brief. As much as he wished almost to devour her with his kisses, nevertheless, he knew it was unfair to her. He would leave, and she must get on with her life. While still holding her hand, he sat listening to Sir Robert's instructions.

Ellen told both men that the money had been paid. £5,000 was from Bert's allowance, and as the judge said in Sir Percival's hearing, Errol's £8,000 allowance was added to Bert's. Sir Percival was as good as his word, and some £13,000 less the £8 fee now sat in a new bank account for Molly's use.

Both young men were sent back to their universities in disgrace. Letters preceded them that neither were to leave the university grounds other than for study-related excursions. Both would be forced to knuckle down and study. Neither had access to funds, so they had no choice but to obey. They were both grounded.

Bert seethed with anger. He was determined to have Molly one day. She was far too pretty for him to leave well alone, and the more he thought about Bill, the more his rage boiled.

With them both at college, life at home had settled down. Molly and Ellen were treated with respect by all the males in the household. From the new butler to the youngest houseboy, all males had been instructed to treat all the female staff with great respect. Even Sir Percival stood when Ellen entered a room.

However, Molly was rarely seen above stairs anymore. Rather than tempt fate with the two boys upstairs, she had chosen to assist in the laundry or kitchen. She discovered that she loved the kitchen work and asked the cook to teach her the skill of making some of the delectable dishes she presented. Soon, she made the most delicately light scones and delicious afternoon teas they had eaten. Even Sir Percival noticed the changes.

~

As the autumn progressed and winter hit, Ellen and Molly were permitted to take Bill more clothing and some food.

Sir Percival accompanied them on one visit, wanting to see the cell where the boy was incarcerated. What he saw in Newgate took his breath away. He realised that his sons had brought the boy to this place.

Ellen and Molly stayed in the office while Bill showed his previous employer through his section of the prison. Bill escorted him to the various wards and described how many shared each room. The facilities were stark and necessities few, but Bill seemed happy enough. He was clean and reasonably well-fed. They arrived at a small cell on the far side of the men's prison courtyard. The door was closed but not locked. Bill could come and go at will, but he usually kept it locked from the inside. His room was spartan; two grey woollen blankets lay neatly on the pallet bed, and a small pile of clothing sat neatly folded with a spare pair of shoes on one end of the single shelf.

Sir Percival saw the shelf laden with aged leather-bound volumes as he turned. "What are those, William?" he asked while pointing to the old tomes.

Bill gazed lovingly at his borrowed books. "Ancient texts, sir. They are mostly owned by Sir Robert, who frequently changes them for me. We both studied Classics at university, but his collection is vastly better than I had access to." He looked at Sir Percival with some embarrassment, knowing he spoke of his own library. "It keeps me occupied, sir, and my mind sharp." Bill gave a slight shrug. "My situation here is somewhat ambiguous. I am neither a debtor nor a criminal. My time will expire as soon as I arrive in Sydney; however, I have little wish to leave as I get to see Molly and her mama once a month."

Sir Percival frowned, then nodded.

No one had told Bill what punishment the boys had received, and he was somewhat taken aback when Sir Percival informed him that they were on financial bread and water rations. He knew what that was like as he also had no money to spend at university. His scholarships paid all fees and extracurricular subjects, but his father had little money for an allowance. What money he did have went towards his clothing. He had tutored to earn that spending money.

Sir Percival motioned for them both to sit on the bed. "Son, I'm so sorry that things have reached this state of affairs. I should have noticed their behaviour much earlier. By the time I did, you had won the scholarship to Eton and were gone. It was almost too late to do much more than keep you separated by then. I failed Jerome over this treatment of you. We were best friends and were in the same situation as you and my boys; I had no animosity towards him. We married late and drifted apart after our wives died. I threw myself into my work, and while I do not need to explain things to you, lad, I have failed in my duty to you."

Bill felt awkward sitting on the pallet bed next to his ex-employer. "Sir, it's not your fault. I shouldn't have hit Bert. I acknowledge I was wrong. I let my temper take control."

Sir Percival looked up quickly, shocked. "Bill, you did it in defence of a lady, and Miss Ross is certainly a lady. I had no idea your feelings toward her were more than friends, though."

Bill gave a slow nod. "The feelings have been longstanding, but it was only a recent understanding between us, sir. My tendre for her has been growing for some time, but I was not financially able to do anything about it. I knew that as a butler, I could not marry without your permission. However, I would have asked you for that on your return." Bill looked a little embarrassed, as he had not even thought about permission from his boss. It had all happened too fast. Now, it was too late.

Sir Percival realised that the two ladies were still waiting for them. "Come, lad. She awaits you. I have taken enough of your precious time together."

Bill's face brightened.

They returned to the office, and Molly once more slid her hand into Bill's. Their time together raced away far too soon. During this visit, they had no opportunity to have a farewell embrace. He was not permitted to leave the office unattended, and she had to go. Their hands slid apart as Ellen drew her daughter away. She turned again at the door.

Bill saw a single tear slide down her downy cheek. He wished to comfort her and draw her into his arms; instead, the office door was slammed shut behind them. It echoed deep into his soul.

~

Christmas approached. This year, there would be no stuffed goose or pheasant, no baked salmon or glazed ham for Bill. The Christmas fare in prison was an extra serving of gruel with spotted dick pudding and custard for dessert. He adored the current steamed pudding the cook had made at home; the prison fare was hardly recognisable as the same dish.

He wondered what Molly had been given for Christmas from her mother. He thought of all the lovely things he wished to buy her. She had always wanted a golden cross necklace. One day, he would buy it for her, and it would have a strong chain she could wear daily. One day... For the first time, his melancholy emotions almost overwhelmed him. He wept.

Christmas at the Edison-Browne's was underway.

Each lady on the staff had received the usual gift of five yards of flannel to make themselves some petticoats. As expected, even after decades, the present never changed other than it was no longer red. At least now, there was an array of colours.

Molly refused to come upstairs as the boys had put a mistletoe branch over the top of the staff staircase.

James, the new butler, had been courting one of the maids and had managed to steal a quick kiss from his girl under it.

Molly refused to leave the kitchen. She would rather forfeit her gift than be caught in Bert or Errol's arms, as she doubted it would stop with just a kiss.

However, her well-intentioned ideas were futile. Bert snuck down to the kitchen while the family changed for Christmas lunch.

Cook had gone to change her apron as she had splashed some gravy on it, and Katy, the undercook, was in the pantry.

Molly was pouring the cranberry sauce she had just made into a dish when she sensed someone standing behind her.

Bert had silently shooed away the two scullery maids, and before Molly realised, she was alone with him, and his hands grabbed her waist and slid up to her breasts. He twisted her around and bent to kiss her.

She still had the now-empty cast iron skillet in her hands from the sauce. Without thinking, she swung it and caught him on the side of his head.

Bert crumpled to the flagstone floor. He lay insensible, with Molly standing over him. The wooden spoon and dirty skillet were still in her hands. She was dazed at what had just occurred.

Cook returned and heard the sound of his collapse. She noticed Molly frozen to the spot and staring at the ground at her feet.

Bert was not visible from the doorway.

Cook asked, "Molly, what's wrong?"

Molly was unaware that snow was falling outside. Unaware of noises or of where the staff were. Unaware of anything except that she may have killed Bert. "He came at me, Mrs Pearce; I had the skillet in my hand, and… and… I just swung it." Her mouth hung open in stunned shock. She stood still, holding the spoon and pan aloft, both still covered in cranberry sauce. She had let go of neither. "Oh, Mrs Pearce, whatever will I do?"

As she approached the cook took in the situation, she also noticed the typically frantically busy kitchen was empty. "Where are the other girls?"

Molly had not even noticed she was alone. She shrugged and shook her head. "I was busy with the sauce. I have no idea, Mrs Pearce."

As she spoke, the two young kitchen maids returned. Both volunteered the information that Mr Bert had sent them out.

Mrs Pearce turned to the older one and said, "Go find Mrs Ross and bring her here. Make it snappy, miss."

The maid vanished in an instant.

Ellen arrived from her room down the hall and saw her daughter still frozen to the spot. Bert was insensible at her feet, and although there was no blood, he was obviously injured as his face was severely deformed. "Oh, honey child, what have you done?"

Molly melted as she heard her mother's pet name for her. "Mama, he attacked me from behind. I had the pan in my hand and swung without thinking." Her hands shook, and she finally dropped the heavy skillet on the floor. It fell with a tremendous crash, bringing other staff running from their dining room.

Until then, the kitchen had been strangely silent. Considering they should have been preparing for a Christmas feast, that alone was unusual.

Ellen demanded an explanation.

One of the footmen said, "Mr Bert had poked his head in the room and told us to stay there for a while. We had not dared to move as we knew his temper."

Ellen sent one of the footmen to bring Sir Percival. "Toby, you are to say that he is needed outside. Do not explain why until he has left the room. Phillip, go for the doctor, Cedric; go find Sir Robert Peel if you can; if not him, then the most senior policeman on duty."

The three young men didn't move.

Ellen clapped her hands and said, "Move, now, all of you. Just go!"

The three fled.

Two went to grab their hats and coats; Toby took the stairs two at a time. He arrived at the upstairs sitting room puffing.

James was instructed to summon Sir Percival as quietly as possible. He knocked, entered when beckoned, walked to his boss, and whispered, "Sir, you are urgently needed outside."

Sir Percival looked up in surprise but followed his butler.

Toby was waiting and quietly shut the door as he exited, bowing to him. "Sir, Mrs Ross has requested that you join her in the kitchen. An urgent issue has arisen." Toby bowed again as his nerves were now showing, and he needed to relieve himself; such was his state of anxiety.

The gentleman looked aghast. "Can she not come to me? Must I attend to her below stairs?"

Toby gave him a third bow. "I do apologise, sir; however, the matter is urgent and cannot wait. Please be good enough to follow me." Toby walked to the staff staircase with his employer on his heel.

The scene that met Sir Percival's eyes was one of utter confusion. His glance took in his prostrated son lying insensible on the floor.

Molly was weeping in her mother's arms, and she was comforting her as much as possible.

His cook was fanning his son, and the maids and other house staff stood in various groups weeping and muttering to themselves.

He said, "What the devil has happened this time?"

Ellen extracted herself from her daughter's arms and said, "Sir, there has been an unfortunate incident."

Sir Percival frowned. "I can see that, but what the hell is my son doing in the kitchen in the first place? I banned him from below stairs." His eyes swept the room, taking in who was there. Seeing only Molly in tears, he knew immediately what had occurred but asked, "Who rendered him insensible this time?"

"I did, sir," came a plaintive voice from Molly. "I was dishing up the cranberry sauce, and he came upon me from behind. I had the pan in my hands, and… and… I swung around, not knowing who it was." She choked a cry. "Sir, I'm so sorry. I had no intention of hurting him, but I got a shock and was frightened. I had no idea it was him, sir; it could have been anyone. I didn't mean any harm."

"Damn, damn, damn," came the cry from the prostrated man's father. "I told him to keep his hands off you and all the other maids; having said that, your reaction was vastly overdone, miss." Sir Percival finally knelt to check his son was breathing. He was, but he could see that his jaw was misaligned.

Molly pleaded about her reaction. "Yes, sir, I know, sir, but it was an accident. As I said, I had the pan in my hands when he entered; I had no idea who it was. He spun me around, and I raised the pan. It could as well have been James, or Toby or... or... even Bill if he were here." She sniffed before saying again, "I just spun around, and he was so close...." Molly was rocking back and forth on the stone step into the pantry. "I didn't know who it was. I didn't, sir, truly I didn't."

Bert was beginning to come around.

His father went to his side and leaned over him.

Cook heard the boy's father murmur, "You blooming stupid fool. I told you to leave all the maids well alone, and Molly especially. She is not your property to abuse."

Bert groaned and held his jaw. It looked disturbingly crooked. He opened his eyes to see his father's seethingly angry face leaning over him. "She hit me with a pan, Father," he muttered through his clenched teeth.

His father gave him no sympathy. Knowing the trouble his son had already caused Bill and that Molly had been the innocent cause, he said, "Shut up, you fool. It sounds like you deserved it. If you had left her alone, she wouldn't have needed to hit you. Why were you even down here?"

Bert could only speak with his teeth clenched together while holding his chin. He was sure his jaw was broken. It hurt like hell. "I want her charged father. I want her charged with assault." His words were almost unintelligible.

His father's livid words were enough to chastise a saint. "She could well charge you with the same thing. You're a damned fool and an idiot, and I wash my hands of you. When you are healed, you will be sent to my business in Canada for a few years and see if you can mend your ways. You disgust me!" Sir Percival stood and turned his back on his youngest son.

Bert attempted to sit up; the effort made him surprisingly woozy. Cook was still by his side and supported him.

At that moment, the doctor and a policeman entered, escorted by the footmen who had summoned them.

The doctor attended to his patient, and the policeman went to Sir Percival's side.

Moments later, Molly was beckoned.

Ellen helped her as she was still shaking.

The policeman asked for a quiet area and was shown to the staff dining room.

Molly and Ellen were hard on his heels.

Sir Percival followed, but before he vacated the room, he turned and banished most of the staff. With a dismissive wave, he said, "Christmas luncheon is cancelled."

The doctor and Toby lifted Bert, and the three footmen carried the injured man to his room. His face was already showing a mass of discolouration. His jaw was quite obviously distorted. The movement had seen him pass out before reaching the bottom of the staircase; this made transporting him much easier, and he was soon being carried into his bedroom.

His valet had preceded him and was preparing his bed as they entered. While still insensible, the doctor and valet stripped him and had him in his nightshirt before he roused again.

Errol had heard the kerfuffle and had followed in their wake. He realised something was afoot when his father had not returned. When he saw the footmen carrying his unconscious brother up the staircase, he followed. Christmas luncheon should have already been called, and it was late. Errol was hungry, so he had gone searching for the cause of the mysterious summons.

Bert was groaning in pain but still insensible.

The doctor was leaning over him and prodding his displaced jaw. Errol heard him hum and har before nodding his head. "Definitely broken, possibly in two or three places." A poke along the hinge and Bert fainted again.

The doctor turned to his brother. "I'll set it while he is out cold."

Errol had moved from the doorway to his brother's bedside. He rudely pushed the valet out of the way and watched as the doctor ministered to his patient.

That action was the final straw for the valet. Brant Coleman had taken on the valet role for both sons when they returned for the holidays. He had been in the household for some years as a footman, and when Sir Percival offered him the role, he jumped at it; now, only a few months later, he was already considering looking for a new position. The behaviour of the spoiled men made his work extremely difficult. He was not expecting the disgusting rudeness of his charges or their slovenly and disrespectful ways. They often spoke as though he did not exist, and he learnt many of the ungentlemanly pursuits they got up to at their universities. Brant thought that, for once, Bert had got his comeuppance.

All the older staff had protected Molly. Both she and Bill had been adored by them all. When Bill was arrested for defending her honour, many wished to resign. They only stayed to help protect Molly, who was unable to leave. For some time, he stood watching the tableau occurring before him. Without waiting to be dismissed, Brant left the room. That alone was a sackable offence. He walked up to his quarters and started packing. He wanted to have nothing to do with such a person as Bert. He had enough funds to tide him over until he could find another position. He would not work for men without respect for such a lovely young woman. However, that meant he would need to leave without a reference.

Meanwhile, downstairs in the staff dining room, Sir Percival did all he could to protect Molly rather than stay at his son's side.

Unfortunately, the policeman had seen that she had inflicted grievous bodily harm on a member of the gentry. "Miss, you will be charged with malicious wounding the said gentleman. Regardless of the fact that you were attacked and that you were defending yourself. I'm sorry, Miss, but your weapon of choice could well have been lethal."

Molly gulped. "But sir, I was cooking a sauce. The pan was already in my hand when Mr Bert grabbed me from behind and spun me around. I didn't mean it, sir." She turned to her employer. "Please, Sir Percival, I didn't mean it, honest. I didn't, you know that. You know what he's like."

At that, Molly fainted.

Ellen and Sir Percival grabbed for her before she hit the ground.

The policeman hovered, waiting for her to come around. He was somewhat surprised that the prostrated gentleman's father championed her rather than his son. However, he had a job to do, and she had broken the law. As soon as she came around, she would spend the remainder of Christmas Day in Newgate Prison.

Chapter 6   Hell Hath No Fury

$\mathcal{B}$ill's Christmas passed quietly. He had hoped that Molly and Ellen might be able to get away and visit him; sadly, no one had come for him that day. Sir Robert had brought him some new books last week, and he lay on his hard bed reading Euripides. The tome he held contained all nineteen of his works, including one he had never read. He had always loved the ancient Greek plays and rarely had time to relax and enjoy them.

The following morning, soon after dawn, Bill was awoken by the cell doors opening. A familiar voice was heard, and he jumped out of bed and pulled on his trousers.

Sir Robert stood at his door as he tugged on his shirt. "Up, lad, and follow me as fast as possible." He turned on his heel and walked through the courtyard.

Bill grabbed his shoes and jacket and was hard on his heels. He caught up to him as they reached the office door. He didn't ask what had occurred, knowing he would be told soon enough. Whatever it was, it was urgent enough to get Sir Robert out of bed at dawn on Boxing Day.

Sir Robert knocked on the prison office door once. It swung open, and Bill saw a distraught Molly waiting for him.

As Bill entered, she flung herself into his arms. "I didn't mean to, Bill, it was an accident, but he attacked me."

Bill's arms enfolded her. His heart was beating twenty to the dozen. He turned his eyes to the policeman. "Sir, what happened?" He knew he would get no sense from Molly as she sobbed uncontrollably.

Sir Robert explained the situation. "I knew that young whippersnapper would not leave her alone. His father tried hard to halt the arrest, but my constable did his duty as he saw it, and she has been charged with unlawful wounding, malicious wounding, or inflicting grievous bodily harm; take your pick. All are imprisonable offences. Young Bert is pressing charges, and his father has no say as his son is of age." He released a long sigh. "I'm sorry, William, but Miss Molly has been placed in the women's part of this prison and will be tried as soon as I can arrange it." He turned to Molly. "Miss, there is a silver lining to this, though."

Two pairs of eyes immediately turned to him. He had their full attention. Sir Robert continued. "She will be found guilty and then transported too. I will ensure you are sent to the same place if I can. From there, it's up to you, William. You will be freed on arrival, and I will write and ask that she be assigned to your care."

Bill still had Molly in his arms. He had not kissed her and now pushed her away slightly. With a hooked finger, he knuckled away the tears from her cheeks and gazed lovingly at her. His care and compassion for this wonderful girl almost overwhelmed him. "Mol, did he hurt you?"

She shook her head. "He didn't have time to, Bill, but you know what he is like. He cornered me in the kitchen and banished the rest of the staff. He caught me as I was dishing up the sauce, and I swung at him with what I had in my hands." Her tears once again flowed. "I didn't mean to break his jaw or knock him out, but he came at me unawares, Bill."

Once again, she was drawn close and cradled to his chest. Her hacking sobs tore through him. His hands were stroking her back in long, comforting, massage-like actions. "Mol, something good will come from this. As for Bert, he deserves everything he got. He was warned more than once and didn't listen." He laid his head on top of hers.

She heard him whisper, "Oh, Mol, I am so sorry you had to have this happen." Her curvaceous body was pressed hard against his, and he forgot they were not alone.

Sir Robert stood watching the young couple before him. He had not been at the house and did not know if her words were true. However, he did know the accuser was an out-and-out bounder. He did not doubt her story happened exactly as she claimed. "Lad, I will do what I can for her. When she is convicted, which she will be, I will get her transported as quickly as possible. More than that, I cannot promise. I enforce the law with my men; I can neither divert nor pervert the course of justice." He took a moment to let that sink in. "I brought her here myself as she must soon appear in court. I read through the charges each morning, and when I saw the names, I guessed what had occurred." His attention was now focused on Molly. "Miss Ross, again, I shall write to the judge and hope and pray that it is the same one who tried your case, William. If it is, then he will know the history of the accuser.

If not, then my letter will explain much. I doubt you will see each other again this side of Sydney, so say your adieus." He turned his back to the young lovers.

Molly lifted her tear-stained face to Bill.

Silence reigned, and they took the moment of privacy for a much-needed kiss. At least now, they had the possibility of a future together.

~

The scene unfolding at the Edison-Browne's establishment was one of anger and extreme frustration.

Later, Errol went to his room to find his valet, Brant, had resigned. None of the footmen would assist in undressing or shaving him.

Sir Percival had sent his valet to the boys.

Brant had left a note and explained that he could no longer serve such men who would dishonour such an innocent lass.

Sir Percival agreed and wrote an excellent reference for him, and included two months' advance salary; these he left with Ellen. He did not blame him for leaving. He was aware other staff would follow him. But this young man would not be punished for abandoning his post because of his son's appalling actions.

The following day, Errol had attempted to shave and had nicked himself three times. Finally, he had to call his father and ask for assistance. He found that his water was only lukewarm when it was delivered. Then, at breakfast, his toast was burnt, his eggs were overcooked, and his bacon was soft and greasy.

His father just smiled. He found that servants had a way of punishing his sons far better than he ever could have achieved.

Bert had finally roused to discover that his face was to remain bandaged for at least eight weeks, and he was to consume no solid foods until the bandages came off. If he moved his jaw or attempted to speak, it could easily be twice that long. Once it was healed, he would be sent to Canada until his father called him home. He would need to work for his living at the family shipping firm in Halifax. If he did not mend his ways, he would stay over there until he did. He would be given no allowance, so he would need to work for his money.

Errol was put on notice. After just one morning, he realised that his life would be vastly different if he did not conform to the rules.

~

After a week, there was a noticeable negligence of any work associated with either of his sons; Sir Percival summoned Ellen to his office. "Madam, please come in and shut the door behind you."

He had seen James and Toby loitering in the foyer. He discovered that all his staff would jump to the defence of the Ross's. He had two choices: sack them all or negotiate a truce. He decided to try the latter.

Sir Percival Edison-Browne had never felt intimidated by anyone until meeting his housekeeper that day. He had his arms folded, waiting for her to be seated, more because she stood a shade taller than him than anything else. He acknowledged that his sons had been in the wrong; however, he needed a functioning household. "Mrs Ross, please take a seat."

After a few minutes of standing in a similar stance, Ellen harrumphed and did as he requested. However, she sat erect in the chair across the desk from her employer. She would not be intimidated by this man whose family had caused such harm to two people beloved to her. She again folded her arms and sat silently. She had yet to decide what to do with her life. If Molly were transported, there would be nothing left for her here. She thought she might go as well.

He sat looking at the angry woman from his comfortable office chair. He knew she was unhappy, and quite honestly, he didn't blame her. His housekeeper did not need to say a word to work that out. Her body language spoke volumes. Even after she sat, her arms were re-folded. He wondered where to start in attempting to appease the distress his family had caused her. Where to start? He began with a grovel. "Madam, Mrs Ross, I find I am at your mercy. My household has almost come to a standstill, and I am at a loss to know where… no, how, to go on from here."

Ellen was still seething that he had allowed Bert to become so undisciplined to attempt to seduce her daughter.

Each day since Christmas, she had grown more and more angry. Nine of the staff threatened to leave, and they weren't all maids. Only by persuading them to rotate the room service did they stay. Bert's demands as a patient were also wearing thin on everyone, and to make matters worse, his father was never around to hear his whining.

Her plan had worked until Bert left his room. Only his jaw was injured, and sadly, he refused to remain confined to his suite for long. He had even made a play at James's girl, and that was the final straw. All the maids refused to be anywhere near him. Toby, Phillip, and Cedric found they had new roles in delivering things to the two young men.

The footmen, too, were furious at the callus treatment of their friends. Ellen had not asked the staff to work on a go-slow, but they had obviously had such a discussion without her knowledge. She had noticed that rooms customarily used exclusively by the boys were no longer cleaned, nor were the fires set. Yet the rooms used by the master were pristine.

Ellen had smiled at the staff's actions. It seems, however, that their efforts had been noticed. "Sir, let me say, I have had nothing to do with the behaviour of the staff. I, too, noticed that rooms your sons used are now only serviced by the footmen, as the maids will no longer enter them when they are there. Sir, your youngest son may well have his jaw bandaged shut, but they told me that is not the part of him they are wary of." Ellen looked at him with a cocked eyebrow. She was being crass, but she needed her employer to understand both his sons' horrific behaviour.

Sir Percival was stunned at her comment; he jumped up from his seat and paced the room as he spoke. "Do you mean to tell me that this has not been nipped in the bud? The inconsiderate and undisciplined whippersnapper is still at it?" His hands raked through his hair with anger.

Ellen nodded. "He manhandles any maid he can get near. Mr Errol is not quite as bad, but they have not stopped their inappropriate actions."

The infuriated father said, "I cannot believe that he will no longer take instruction from me." He turned and met her gaze. "Do you have any solution?" He watched as a smile slowly appeared on her lips. He continued pacing the room.

Ellen had been waiting for this question: "I do, sir. I believe the grouse hunting season is over, and your hunting box in Scotland is all but empty. I think a long holiday in the far north of Scotland, staffed by only males, would do them wonders." Her eyes twinkled with mischief as she realised their father was as angry with them as she was.

He swung around to face her again. "Mrs Ross, I think you are correct. Bert can heal in the cold climate at Inverness-shire as well as here." He rubbed his hands together. With a smile, he said, "Oh, ma'am, I do think that is a wonderful idea. Errol has finished his university. He excelled at nothing but did manage to pass his final exams. Much good the qualifications will do him. Bert did slightly better, but his behaviour is appalling. If only they had taken a leaf out of young William Miller's book, but that, too, is now water under the bridge. I do think your idea has merit." He now paced with his hands behind his back. Again, he turned to her. "Mrs Ross, can you mobilise the staff to get them packed without them knowing?"

She smiled and nodded to him. "Yes, sir, I think that could be arranged. However, unless you explain to them why they are being banished, the trip will be pointless." She wondered if she sounded impertinent.

He stood before the fire, tapping his hands behind his back. His brow was deeply furrowed, and he was deep in thought. He swung around and faced her. "I have an idea, Mrs Ross; however, I will need your assistance." He coughed and cleared his throat. "Rather than send them to the hunting box, which they may actually enjoy, I have a long-standing offer to visit my friend in Scotland. Hamish McKenzie owns a place in Stornoway on the Island of Lewis. I believe it is extremely remote and can only be accessed by their private boat. Hamish is a direct descendant of the Viking invaders of old and is the most fearsome chap you could meet. He refuses to come south of the border again due to the unruly conduct of today's young men. My two sons fit that mould well. I think some behavioural modification under Hamish's hands will do the trick." He grinned at her. "Bert will still be sent to Canada after that, but some time of deep contemplation will do them no harm. I shall set to write to him today."

Ellen was thrilled; they would have strict oversight under a stern Scottish Laird. She had heard of this strict authoritarian and his blow-up in parliament when he came south of the border for his once-in-a-lifetime trip to the city. "Sir, how will you get them there, though? Kidnap them?" She was now smiling, and her arms had unfurled.

He threw back his head and laughed. "I like the way you think, Mrs Ross. I think that will suffice nicely, don't you? I think a day out sailing should suffice. I have a ship in the harbour waiting to set sail. I will ensure we have had a long conversation beforehand, though. I shall also write a letter to them to read on their journey. Ensure the staff pack all the appropriate clothing for sailing and frigid conditions. I may not like their behaviour, but I don't wish any harm to come to them, but a bit of roughing up won't hurt them." He smiled to himself. "Why ever did I not consult you before?"

That was a question she refused to answer. She smiled and gave a half-tilt of her head, then a nod, but remained silent. She released a quiet sigh of relief. The maids would be safe from unwanted attention for at least the next few months. She still had to sort out her own situation. "Sir, with the possibility of Molly being transported, I need to discuss my future while I have your attention. I am in two minds about staying on here. I think I may even follow her to Sydney if that's where she is sent."

Sir Percival seated himself with a plonk. He had not even thought about the possibility of her going. "You would leave? Truly? Oh, I am so sorry to hear that."

Once again, she folded her arms, more as a defence against his wrath than anything else. "All those I hold dear are either dead or in the process of banishment from these shores. If I stay, I shall be utterly alone. Molly and Bill have been my life, sir. With them both gone, I have no reason to remain."

He gasped, not realising the state of her thoughts. "You have no one else but the two young ones, ma'am?"

Ellen shook her head. "No, sir, my only close relative other than them was my younger sister, who passed away last year." She swallowed, as a lump had formed in her throat. It wasn't entirely true, but she was estranged from her father, stepmother, and much younger half-sister, Mary. The death of her beloved sister, Narelle, had been gruesome. Her husband had always had a temper; one evening, he had taken to her after a drinking session. Battered and bruised, he dragged her to bed, used her vilely, and then abandoned her. Narelle was found unconscious the following morning by her neighbour. Her state of undress and the black and blue bruises were cause enough to call in the local magistrate. However, Narelle had named her husband, Michael, as her abuser. He was entitled to use her as he wished. He was found passed out in a ditch, arrested, fined, and returned home to drink again. Narelle had died at his hand the following day. Thankfully they had no children. Ellen knew they had a half-sister and numerous illegitimate half-siblings, but she had never met any of them.

She took a deep breath and replied, "No, sir, I only have the young ones. I shall probably follow them to Sydney and see if I can ease their life path. It all depends on Molly's sentence." Her words sounded final, but they were far from that. Was she brave enough to leave all she knew to cross the world? Could she do it?

Sir Percival knew his family had been the cause of her distress. "If that is your wish, then so be it. I shall give you a glowing reference and pave the way for you as best I can, and that is for you all. I have various shipping contacts there and will supply you with letters of introduction. I have great hopes Miss Ross will not receive that punishment, though. If she pleads that it was an accident, I shall ensure Bert is not around to cause further injury to anyone, and if possible, depending on the trial date, I shall take the stand in his place and acknowledge he was at fault. If I am away, I shall leave a letter."

~

It was not to be.

The court case finally occurred three months after Molly's arrest.

Again, Sir Percival was called away on business.

Errol and Bert had just returned from Scotland when the case was heard in late March. Rather than the young men returning from Scotland chastised and reformed, they had returned angry and even more bitter than when they had departed. And having abstained from their pursuits for three months, they were now chasing after anything in a skirt.

Bert's jaw had healed enough to eat soft foods. Despite that, he kept it strapped most of the time and rarely went out. His face was now distorted because he had not kept it still. The bones had knitted out of alignment, which complicated things. His face would never return to the handsome visage it had once been, but his lusts were more pronounced.

Each morning, when he looked in the mirror, his anger grew. Being selfish and narcissistic, he did not blame himself for starting the incident or even acknowledge that bedding a maiden out of wedlock was wrong. He refused to acknowledge any responsibility at all. Bert heaped all the blame on both Bill and Molly. In his eyes, he did no wrong. Molly was just a servant and should have welcomed his attention. He felt all the maids he chased should want him. His family paid them for whatever service he required, and that should include bedding him. He harrumphed again with frustration.

Only days after their return, a scream sounded from a maid, and Ellen realised that their reform plan had failed dismally. The first change she made in the household was to move all the maids into one dormitory room, and they were to lock themselves in each night. New footmen were now required to clean the rooms if the brothers were around. They were, in fact, male maids. If the brothers were out for any length of time, she personally oversaw a thorough cleaning of the two apartments and whatever other rooms they used.

The maids were always supported when the brothers were in the house. A footman would accompany her and always remain with her if one must attend to something upstairs.

~

Molly was taken before the same magistrate who had overseen Bill's case. Sir Percival and Sir Robert had both written letters, and the judge read both while the court sat waiting in silence.

Bert tried to play the part of the wounded victim; however, he did not take his father into consideration.

Molly was called to take the stand. She knew her mother was in the gallery. She stood proud and erect as Sir Robert had instructed her to do. She remained silent until given leave to speak. She wore the same pretty muslin gown as she had worn last time. Her mother had sent it to her for her appearance today, though this time, she wore no bonnet.

The judge was reading the two long letters associated with this case.

Ellen knew that both Sir Robert and Sir Percival had written covering letters. Sir Robert's letter was a character reference, and Sir Percival's screed was far more detailed. Although she knew he had written it, she didn't know what it contained.

The bespectacled elderly judge gazed at her. "Miss Ross, are you not the young lady who was previously insulted by this same young man last year?"

Molly nodded in the affirmative; her voice had deserted her.

"Do you plead guilty or not guilty?" She saw the judge's head shake slightly.

Ellen gasped; even the judge wished Molly to plead not guilty.

Molly saw his sign, frowned, and then ignored his instruction. "Well, I did hit him, sir, but it was not intentional. You see, he attacked me unawares, and I happened to have a pan in my hands as he spun me around." Molly blushed. "I lashed out at whoever it was. I do not allow my private personal bits to be groped by anyone, sir."

"Mr Cuthbert Edison-Browne, what say you?" The judge leaned back in his chair and folded his arms. He raised one bushy eyebrow in anticipation of a snivelling answer.

Bert stood to speak. The bandages on his face did little to bestow confidence; they hindered him. "Your Honour, it was Christmas, and I just wished for a kiss under the mistletoe. Nothing more, I assure you, sir."

The judge half-laughed and said, "Then, in that case, sir, why did you pursue her to the kitchens? I presume there was no mistletoe above her or elsewhere in that room. Why, then, did you banish the staff and approach her by stealth from behind? If your motives were as innocent as you say, why was she hiding in the kitchen in the first place? Huh?"

Bert shrugged rudely but made no sound.

The judge was furious at his rudeness. "I asked, what say you, sir?" The judge enquired again in a louder voice. "Speak up."

Bert had not learnt his lesson. "I say, sir, that this woman, this wonton trollop, enticed me below stairs with her saucy ways, then proceeded to attack me with a lethal weapon."

The judge chuckled. "Oh, sir, I do believe you are correct for her saucy ways. If I read correctly, it was cranberry sauce. I believe she thwacked you with the cast iron skillet she already held, and it contained more of the sweet and sticky substance. Had you been her employer and attacked her, she probably would have clouted him, too."

Bert objected. "My father would not have treated a maid so, sir. How dare you!"

This outburst was exactly the situation the judge wished for. "True, Mr Edison-Browne. Your father, Sir Percival, whom I know quite well, is a true gentleman, unlike his sons. I can see the injury she caused you is disfiguring and likely to be permanent. I would like to say that is punishment enough; however, I have little doubt that I will see you back here again on some other trumped-up charge. You seem not to listen to your father's instruction, and you certainly have not listened to mine."

The judge turned to Molly. "Miss Ross, having admitted to hitting him, I must find you guilty, especially as his injuries are permanent. However, I feel that should you be returned to the household, his attentions would not abate. Therefore, I sentence you to three years imprisonment from the date of your arrest and transportation to Sydney Town as soon as it can be arranged. One of the letters here also contains a character reference for you and absolves you from any intent in this matter. Had that not been so, you would have received the death penalty, which may or may not have been commuted to life. I shall give instruction that you should be assigned to Mr Miller on your arrival if you so wish."

She had nodded, but on those final words, Molly fainted.

A court attendant went to her side.

Ellen stood in the gallery as the judge mentioned Molly's sentence. She watched as her daughter crumpled. Unable to do more than observe, she released a groan of agony. Her only baby was going to be transported. Ellen was stunned, but her hands were tied.

The judge looked up and noticed her focus on her daughter. He saw that behind her and sitting in the public gallery were half the staff from the house.

James had permitted them to go and support their friends. The skeleton staff on duty had all served there for less than two years. James's girlfriend, the maid who was friendly with Molly, called in her cockney accent.

"And what of Mr grubby-hands gentry-man then, eh Mr Judge? Is he gonna get orf scot free as usual? There's more than one of us he's 'had at', sir, and we can't stop him, either!"

The judge saw an angry, uniformed maid standing with her hands on her hips. He glanced at Bert, then back to the maid. He lifted his hand to silence the jeering in the gallery. When it was quiet, he said, "Miss, whoever you are, the young man in question, who I will not call gentry, will, upon conclusion of this case, be banished to Halifax in Canada for a minimum of two years with no allowance. His father has arranged passage already, and you need not fear him any more. He may or may not be permitted to return."

The entire courtroom erupted in a cheer.

Ellen watched the judges confer. All were smiling at his pronouncement.

The gavel sounded, and the order was given for the next case.

Molly had by now roused and sought her mother's face for reassurance. Ellen sadly had to leave her daughter to the ministrations of the courtroom marshals. She waved a farewell and blew a kiss. She put her hands together to remind her to pray. She saw Molly nod and give a wave in reply. At least Bill would be in Sydney, and she would be assigned to him. Hopefully, somehow, they would be able to find each other. Sir Robert assured her that he would arrange a meeting in the superintendent's office once the sentence was handed down. His letter had achieved that.

Molly was dragged out with her eyes still fixed on her mother's.

The presiding judge watched her as she exited. She had not bellowed or screamed. Until she fainted, she had stood tall and accepted the sentence. The judge turned to Bert and saw him and his brother slapping hands and cheering. His ire was raised. "Get those two spoiled jackanapeses out of my courtroom, and if they return, they had better be in irons in the dock." He watched four burly marshals take an arm of each man. They manhandled the brothers from their seats and dragged them unceremoniously from the chamber.

Bert heard the raucous laughter of the public gallery at the indignant sight of the so-called victor being jostled roughly from the room. He let out a growl of anger and spewed forth a verbal spiel of filth directed at Molly.

The judge heard every word, but Molly was now well out of earshot. Oh, he wished he could make them pay, but his hands were tied. He wished there was more he could do to protect the innocent girls from filth like these two so-called gentlemen. Just before Bert exited, the judge saw a raw egg hit Bert on the back of his head, followed by someone calling from the gallery, "Filthy dogs!" The judge dropped his head and smirked.

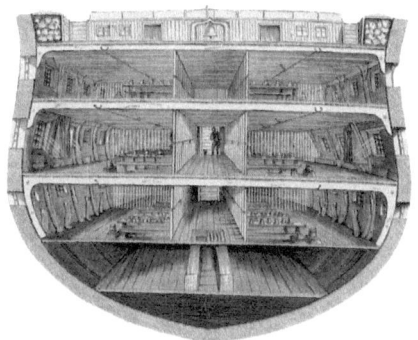

Chapter 7   Hulks and Transports

$\mathcal{B}$ill was impatient; he knew that Molly's case was on now, and he could not be with her to support her. So, he prayed. It was all he could do.

A visit from Sir Robert a few days earlier had brought word that he was to be transferred to the prison hulk *Leviathan* at Portsmouth harbour at the end of the week. He would not see Molly for nearly half a year, if not longer. He found that his cell now felt claustrophobic. He was a prisoner, yet not one. He was given freedoms way beyond his cellmates, and Sir Robert's patronage had permitted privileges not granted to others. Yet the only thing he wished was refused. He wanted to protect Molly. She was so close, yet so far. They worked out that they could see each other at the weekly chapel service. The men sat on one side and the women on the other. They each managed to sit on the aisle at the back and could whisper to each other. They had been permitted two visits after she had been convicted. Then, last Sunday, she didn't appear. He knew he had to go to Portsmouth soon and was awaiting word of the day. He had wished for a final farewell.

Sir Robert called in later that week to say they had fast-tracked her transportation, and she was already *en route* to Sydney on board the *Maria*.

Bill was shattered; Molly had gone and would arrive before him. In vain, he asked Sir Robert if he could arrange to get him on the next ship.

Sir Robert's hands were tied, but he did get a date for the transfer. Bill would leave for Portsmouth on May 25th, ten days after Molly had gone. For the first time, Bill lost heart; he was worried.

~

The day before his Portsmouth departure, he had an unexpected visitor. Sir Robert had collected his books on his last visit, and time hung heavily on Bill's hands. His cell was all but empty. His few belongings were to be folded into his blankets and carried on his back. What the hulks would be like, he could not imagine. He had been lying on his bunk, staring at the ceiling. He had been incarcerated for over a year, and visitors had been few and far between; however, this one was very unexpected. Sir Percival called in to say farewell.

Bill was not sure if he was happy or sad about that. This man represented his old life, which the lack of parental discipline had ruined. Neither Molly nor he had deserved any punishment, but that was the way of the gentry and servants. The gentry did the crime; the servant did the time. His father used to say to him, "Grin and bear it, son." Well, he didn't want to. He felt like lashing out. As the door in the office closed, when he saw who awaited him, he wished to turn about and leave.

The tone of the voice speaking stopped him. Sir Percival half expected this reaction. Bill had no reason to either like or forgive him and his family. The man said, "William, no, Bill, I have come to give you some news. Did Sir Robert mention that Ellen Ross has left my employment?"

Bill angrily spat, "No sir, did you sack her?"

His ex-employer understood his ire. "No lad, she left of her own free will and took an excellent reference, severance pay, and the ability to start a new life as well as the funds in the form of a bank draft. She has preceded you both to Sydney and will apply for Molly to be assigned to her when she arrives. I have ensured she has enough funds to set the three of you up in whatever life you wish. On top of the money my irresponsible sons have given Miss Ross, her mother carries an endowment for you. You deserve no less. I should have done this earlier, but, well, in here, it would not have lasted long."

Bill frowned and asked bluntly, "Why?"

The man looked to have aged ten years since Bill saw him only months ago. "Why? Because I'm ashamed that my son caused all this angst. Neither of you deserves anything that has occurred. This money will give you both a fresh start." The man stood and walked around the small office. "Bill, I heard that Bert arrived in Canada and immediately got into trouble in a similar way. He is currently in prison in Halifax, and I refuse to bail him out, so he is sitting in gaol over there. I have tried everything but tough love. Mayhap this will get through to him. Errol seems to have settled somewhat and has joined me in the business." He ran his fingers over his brow as though to wipe the memories away. "I miss Jerome and the happy and peaceful house when you four were children. I got busy and left the boys alone without parental guidance. It's easy to see now, but that's hindsight for you. I knew nothing about children. I was too old to be a single parent; at least you had Mrs Ross as a surrogate mother. My boys had neither; I suppose I should have married again, but that, again, is hindsight. I supplied food, shelter, and education and stupidly thought that was enough. I did not know what more to give them. Bill, I'm sorry! I have failed you all dismally. I'm just pleased your father is not around to witness my incompetence."

Bill was not a father; he didn't understand those feelings. Hopefully, one day, he would. "Sir, if I get a chance to be with Molly, then it will all be worth it. For even here, I could not have married her."

The penitent man said, "I would have let you marry lad, but I never saw the attachment. I was blind to too much, and I'm now paying the price." This time, he wiped his hand across his eyes.

Bill had no answer, so he stayed silent. Much water had flowed under the bridge; he would embark on a new life. He wanted this interview to end, and soon. Every day now could not go fast enough. Molly was now ahead of him; however, the good news was that her mother would arrive before her, and she would be safe.

Sir Percival was about to leave when he turned to Bill and said, "Sir Robert tells me that you will be permitted a little more freedom on the hulks, and so I have forwarded some books for you. Amongst them are *Tacitus*, the *Gallic Wars*, and something he said may really interest you, so I have added *De vita et moribus philosophorum* by Burlaeus Gualterus. I believe you mentioned to him that you had not seen this. Bill, these books are to accompany you on your voyage to Sydney. There are others, and they are now yours and my way of apologising to you. They are worth little compared to what has been taken from you; however, I believe you may have a better chance at life in the colony than here. Unfortunately, the convict stain will follow you forever. Sir Robert added one or two more books he found for you. I'm not sure what they are. He said he doubted that you had read them." He walked to the office door, paused and turned back. "William Miller, you are one of the most brilliant men I have had the honour to meet. Don't let anger eat you up. Make something of yourself as your father would have wished. Be happy, lad. Marry Molly and have a quiver of beautiful children. Be a better father to them than I have been to mine." With that, he opened the door and left without waiting for an answer.

Bill's eyes watered. He stood rooted to the spot; a frown settled on his own brow. For the first time, Sir Percival seemed almost human. He had previously seemed impervious to the behaviour of his wilful sons. Bill's eyes still bore into the closed door. The man was back to the person he remembered as a child. Bill shook his head; his life would move to the next stage tomorrow. He heard footsteps approaching; it would be the warder coming to return him to his cell. He shrugged off his melancholy; Molly would be awaiting him alongside her mother. She would be safe.

~

Bill's transfer to Portsmouth was accompanied by seven others who had been tried in Shrewsbury eight weeks ago. Considering he had been held since April the previous year, he was somewhat angry when he found they had been fast-tracked. The prison wagons took them to the dockland, where they saw a row of prison hulks along the river edge. Some were more derelict than others, and he wondered which one they were to be incarcerated in; he knew its name was the *Leviathan*, but none seemed to have names painted on them. All looked like they were about to sink. The wagon pulled up with a jolt. It had been a hot day, and the eighty-mile trip had been made at speed, not taking into consideration the prisoners in the unsprung wagon. The roads had been so rutted that resting had not been an option. All eight men had held on for grim death lest the vehicle overturn and kill them all.

With Molly now arriving before him, Bill was keen for the time to pass. Even the descent into the abyss of the hulks no longer daunted him. Sir Robert had been on board some of these and advised Bill to cover one eye as soon as he arrived on the ship. He also suggested which areas were a little better than the rest. As soon as they were sent below deck, he uncovered his eye. He discovered that he could see immediately. Once again, Sir Robert had been correct. Bill chuckled as he saw the other seven men stumbling in the darkness. He walked straight to the suggested bunks that his mentor had mentioned. He was surprised to see although there were other men already ensconced below decks, none had taken the aft bunks. Once all seven were down the stairs, which apparently on board were called ladders, the hatch above slammed shut with a thud.

Bill had never liked being in the dark. In Newgate, his cell had been close to the warder's office, and he had a lamp constantly burning outside his room. In the hulk, the darkness threatened to overwhelm him. Before the hatch shut, Bill saw a bump in the bunk in the row next to him. The bump uttered a groan as the slam rippled through the ship's timbers.

Bill asked quietly, "Who's there?"

A muffled voice from under the blankets replied, "Tom."

Bill wondered what the voice's owner looked like. He didn't sound young. "Tom, what? I'm Bill Miller. Are you all right?" Bill heard a rustle but no words.

Bill thought that as he would share a bunk for a few weeks, he'd better get to know the man. "Don't you like the dark either, Tom?"

"No! Hate it," came the reply.

Bill tried to sound friendly. It was the last thing he wished to do. He said, "So do I, but if you sit up carefully, you can actually see some light through the rear gunport. I had a friend tell me that these are the best summer beds. We should get a bit of air through them, too. Look, you can see it's still daylight outside." Bill's eyes had now fully adjusted to the darkness. He could see that they were on a gun deck, and the hatches were letting in shafts of light. The big hatches had been sealed up, but the smaller ones could be opened easily, as the scuppers along the floor could, too. He wondered why no one else had done so. Maybe they didn't realise. Or perhaps that was why Sir Robert had suggested the rear bunks. Maybe only these opened. Bill felt his way to the back and poked around near the shaft of light. He found a board had been slipped across two holders. He lifted it off, and the sunlight streamed through the tiny opening. He found more of these and, one by one, unlocked them. "Tom, look, you can see now." A wrinkled head poked out of the blanket. Bill gauged him to be middle-aged, if not a bit older. What sparse hair remained was beginning to go grey, but he still had colour in his straggly beard. Bill encouraged him to get up. "Come on, Tom, look outside. See, the darkness is gone."

Tom pulled himself upright. His thin blanket was pushed back, and he slowly came toward Bill.

By nightfall, Bill found out why the hatches were kept shut. Rats! They were drawn by the stench of the unwashed bodies and buckets of excrement thrown overboard. They seemed to stay away during daylight, but as soon as night fell, they climbed out of the river and through any aperture they could. Once on deck, they were as pleased to chew on a living body as easily as the foul-smelling by-product the convicts produced. When the first rat was seen climbing the ship's timbers, Bill shouted to Tom to help shut the hatches.

One huge beast made it on board before Tom clobbered it. "I hate rats too, Bill. Watch out, there it is…."

Bill heard a scuffle.

"Got it!" Tom crowed gleefully. "Did you know they eat these in some countries?" He had the enormous, thankfully dead, water rat by the tail.

In the dim light, Bill could still see Tom. "Ewww, that's disgusting!" Bill dry retched at the thought. "You'd have to be pretty hungry to resort to that."

Tom gave a toothy grin, not that Bill could see more than an outline of him now. "Skinned and roasted, they aren't too bad." He paused, then added, "I've been that hungry, Bill; it's why I'm here. I got done for swiping food. Seven blooming years, mate, but from what I've heard, it's pretty good out there in the new colony. A bloke's got a chance to make something of his self if he wants to. I might have a go once I done my time."

Bill's future would be different, but he didn't reply.

Molly was weeping as she had no time to say farewell to her mother or Bill. She doubted she would ever see her mother again and was distraught. The women were hustled from their cells and rounded up in the courtyard with little notice. Molly knew from previous experience over the last weeks why this was done. A riot ensued when the two earlier shipments of convicts were notified they were leaving. The angry women destroyed what little furniture there was, and Molly and some of the younger girls had taken refuge away from the crowd. This morning, on arrival in the courtyard, over one hundred names were called and amongst them was hers. All the others were sent back to their cells.

Two by two, they were shackled and chained together, then escorted through the prison gates. Once outside the walls, they were loaded onto over twenty hackney carriages that waited for them. The last group Molly knew was rabble-rousers. She noticed their departure was in a very degrading manner. Each was not only shackled in pairs by the wrist but also by leg irons. Previously, they were forced to watch as these poor souls were herded into the older wagons. Today, cries of pain were heard as the wrist or ankle irons bit into their skin.

Molly had winced when the irons were clamped onto her wrists; however, being young, they did not bite into her skin like the more endowed, older women. She had lost the rounded blossom of health that she had when first arrested. Her irons were both heavy and uncomfortable, yet some of these poor wretches were triple-ironed as they were also in a neck collar. As she climbed aboard the vehicle, one poor, large Welsh lady had blood dripping from her wrists. She noticed a well-dressed lady overseeing the loading of the convicts. She stood beside the prison warden and directed the loading of the women. Molly had seen her before but had yet to find out her name. She was loaded into the first vehicle to set off. The trail of carriages was long and cumbersome, with over one hundred and twenty convicts to be shipped out.

A turnkey was to accompany each of the last six carriages. Molly had previously heard of processions of convicts over the six-mile journey to Newgate's wharf; however, they had been by open wagons. She knew them to be one of the most humiliating experiences. On those journeys, the women had been pelted with rotten eggs, off-food, and even excrement. Such open wagons had taken the women for the last two musters. However, on this trip, by travelling in closed carriages, they were only greeted with jeers and shouting. They were protected from the things thrown by the rabble along the route. The journey seemed to take forever. It had been after dawn when they were first called, and Molly's hackney departed mid-morning. By the time they reached Deptford, an angry mob trailed alongside the slow-moving prison transports.

Molly noticed the pristine white of the lovely lady's high-backed mob cap soon after she arrived. She now stood with a man who was obviously the captain, and the lady was directing the boarding of the convicts. Molly overheard the captain refer to the lady as Mrs Fry. She had heard about this woman before from one of the other prisoners. Mrs Fry had visited the gaol and distributed clothing and fabric packs, which Molly had missed receiving. Few other visitors were permitted or wished to enter the filthy prison cells, and Mrs Fry's presence on the ship delighted Molly. Her mother had visited as often as allowed, but that was only once a week. She lifted her eyes heavenward and thanked the good Lord for sending her. She prayed that she would be kept safe.

Mrs Elizabeth Fry had noticed the small action, and soon Molly and a group of younger girls were singled out; others soon joined them. They were loaded onto the waiting ship and told to stand on the deck to await instructions. Mrs Fry had accompanied Molly's group, and they stood together on the quarterdeck, and their irons were removed. She sorted the two groups into smaller batches of twelve, then six. From the slightly elevated position, Molly watched the pairs of women be divided into more groups. One was the mothers and their children; another was younger women; they were sent up to join her, and the others were rowdy women and troublemakers. The latter group had their leg irons removed, but their hands remained shackled until they were sent below.

Once below deck, Molly and her five companions, who were slightly better dressed and young, were sent to the ship's stern; the mothers with young children followed them. Molly was relieved to find the rebellious women were all sent to the forward cells and would be separated from the children. She had already had various run-ins with some of these obnoxious females. Once they had secured their bunks, the women wondered how they would occupy their time. Night had by now closed in, and once a meal had been served, they settled down as best they could in their new pitch-black quarters.

Dawn was met with the sounds of movement above decks. The ropes were being cast off, and the ship moved away from the wharf. Molly had often watched the ships going with the ebb and flow of the tide as they came and went up and down the river. She knew the process and watched it often. The outgoing tide would carry the vessels downstream until the tide changed; the ships would anchor to the side of the channel, and the incoming tide would take the next lot of ships upstream. She was, therefore, not surprised that the vessel anchored shortly before noon. She explained the activity to her bunkmates.

Shortly after they anchored, the hatches were opened, and fresh air poured in through the vents. Molly was surprised to find Mrs Fry had returned with others. A small group of ladies accompanied her with a massive pile of bags beside them. Group by group, they were called above deck, and each stood before the gracious lady. One by one, they were called to stand before her. Each was given a small pile of clothing and a calico bag of sewing fabric, notions, knitting wool, and needles. The absolute delight on their faces was a joy for Mrs Fry to behold.

Molly was the first to bob a curtsy as she received her bounteous gift. Others following her repeated the respectful bob. As Molly stood waiting for her group to receive their gift, Mrs Fry enquired if anyone could read or write. Molly's hand slid up. Two other girls soon joined her and were asked to stand aside for a later discussion with the grand lady.

By the time the midday meal of slops was ready to consume, the entire complement of prisoners had received new clothing and a gift of fabrics or knitting material. From this, they could make some things to sell for extra rations or a fresh start in life. A few earlier parcels contained some embroidery threads and silks and some lovely fabric offcuts in fancy patterns; Molly was lucky enough to receive one of these bounteous bundles. Once most of the parcels had been distributed, Molly heard that the remainder of the pile was to be taken to a room at the stern for use later. All had been asked if they wished to listen to what Mrs Fry had to say; the few who accepted the offer came from Molly's group.

Mrs Fry now stood in the centre of the attentive women. She called the readers close to her and gave them instructions. Near them were the mothers with children aged four and above, and behind them, others who wished to hear what their benefactor had to say. With the captain by her side, the attending surgeon, and a blue-coated major on the other, Mrs Fry addressed the remaining groups. "My dears, before you is a difficult, many months-long journey. If these young ladies who claim to be able to read are willing, then the captain…" she motioned to the man beside her, "…is willing to allow you to teach those wishing to learn and also the children. You will find that there is a supply of slates and some books, as well as some copies of the Holy Scriptures. From this good book, you can learn to read and write and learn about Christ's love and forgiveness. His love and compassion are why you have received the gifts today from people concerned for your welfare. Take this opportunity to better yourselves while in confined quarters. Even if you only learn to write your name, it will assist you in your new life in the Antipodes."

One or two of the women groaned and were quickly shushed by the others. Molly felt two of the girls she now bunked with grab her hands. Rebecca and Sophie were fifteen and sixteen. They had been friends since they were young, and their fathers had been soldiers killed at Waterloo. The girls were arrested for stealing food for their families.

Mrs Fry continued, "Now, I believe the ship will remain anchored here for some weeks while provisioning and getting you settled. I shall return when I can. I shall take the items you have made and sell them so you will have some money to purchase necessities. Use these weeks wisely, settle in and ladies, be industrious." Mrs Fry left the ladies to the captain and doctor. They had been introduced as Captain Henry Williams and Surgeon Superintendent Thomas Prosser.

Doctor Prosser had come aboard in early March when he received his commission. The first convict passengers arrived fit and well, although others from county gaols were not so lucky. They had been transported in open wagons and had arrived cold, chilled and ill from exposure. Many were affected with coughs and treated while awaiting the full complement of convicts to be boarded. Now, all had recovered, and he was satisfied that they had no infectious diseases of any consequence. Once the convicts were cleared of disease, paying passengers were permitted to board.

Chapter 8   Anchors Aweigh

The lady was as good as her word. Mrs Fry returned almost daily over the five weeks the ship remained anchored in the Thames River. To their delight, the Naval Agent, Captain Young, requested that the better-behaved prisoners be allowed on deck when the weather warranted. This being granted, the women who conducted themselves well were permitted access to this privilege for the entire trip. Once up on deck again, Molly discovered the ship was now anchored between Deptford and Woolwich. She recognised some of the riverside buildings.

Unshackled prisoners were permitted to sit on deck sewing, knitting, or learning to read. Molly set about knitting as she taught the young children to learn their letters. She mentally thanked Basil Gomes and Bill for making her learn to read; she set about her work. She decided to knit sailors' caps as she could sell them to the crew whilst onboard rather than wait for arrival in Sydney. She had made them for the grooms and stable boys as they had to work in the frigid cold weather. Others knitted sweaters or even shawls. Many sat sewing on the warm spring days. Molly and the other girls who could read divided the children into age groups. One took the young ones and taught them their A, B, and C's; another instructed the older children. Molly found that many mothers and other women also wished to learn, and she took on their education. There were twenty-five children on board, and fourteen were of an age to learn to read and write, and many women wished to learn while they had the chance.

Mrs Fry had asked the teachers if they required anything else, and Molly requested more slates and chalk as many were keen to use their time wisely. Wooden crates of educational materials arrived, along with a box of small Bibles and many bags of damaged fabric and remnants. These included water-damaged bolts of print cotton, needles, thread, and notions for completing garments.

Early on, Mrs Fry also discovered that many women did not know how to sew. On the subsequent visit, the amazing lady was accompanied by friends who set about remedying this situation. They brought scissors and taught the women to draft and cut out a pattern. The scissors needed to be returned after each session as they could be used as weapons.

There were few paying passengers, and most of those were men. Only one travelled with his wife and family; they were kept well apart from the convicts. One elderly woman was isolated by her cellmates. She had the unpleasant habit of fouling her bunk each night, whether by intent or accident. The stench of this predisposition was extremely vexing to her bunkmates. Eventually, the doctor was able to have her isolated in an unused corner cell. Thankfully, she vanished the night before sailing as the doctor said her condition would cause problems on board. She was marked as unfit to sail and offloaded. The only major issue the doctor needed to deal with was the itch many complained about. He had no way of knowing if it was lice or uncleanliness. He treated all of them with sulphur, both internally and externally.

By the time they set sail in mid-May, the unwilling passengers were well on the way to mastering new skills. Mrs Fry elevated Molly to the senior teacher as she was astounded at her educational skills. Few prisoners could read and write; for Molly to know Latin and various other exceptional subjects was a delight, and she knew this girl could continue the lessons on the journey. After five weeks anchored in the river, Mrs Fry arrived to make her *adieus* for her final visit on May 14th. She asked that all the women be gathered together on the quarterdeck, and then, facing them from the deck above, she addressed the crowd. The sailors, wishing to know what was occurring, shinnied up the rigging and viewed the scene from above. The silence by all was profound. In the weeks since this woman had been ministering to all the convicts, she had won them over with her care and compassion.

Elizabeth motioned for the women to sit. Once they were comfortable, she pulled out her small Bible and read a passage aloud. The morning air was still, and her voice travelled over the water. Nearby, two other vessels could hear her speak. Crews from other ships were up in their rigging and hanging on her every word.

Surrounded by the silence of so many, Elizabeth quietly closed her Bible. After a short pause, she knelt on the deck and implored a blessing on the work of Christian charity. Her loving words, accompanied by her actions, had broken through into the lives of so many women who had been shown little love, care, or compassion. One by one, they wept.

Her departure from the ship was supposed to be without fanfare, as in her previous trips. This time, however, all stood in silence, honouring the lone woman who had stood up to the authority and archaic rules to give the women back some self-respect. Her simple act of restoring their dignity and caring for the least of them had broken through into their shuttered and shattered lives.

Molly and all the other convict women stood at the quarterdeck railing, waving farewell to the departing long boat; they farewelled her with applause. The crews along either side also stood and joined them. Many were loaded with male convicts, and one ship, the *Glory*, was due to sail with them.

At dawn the following day, their ship weighed anchor and caught the receding tide. It was still a few days to travel down the Thames River. The sea was finally reached, and they began their journey to the Antipodes. Having already had five weeks to settle in, the trip ahead started with a semblance of order. The ship's surgeon, Thomas Prosser, had already loaded on board enough wine and lime juice for daily distribution to ward off scurvy. He insisted that meals were regularly served. The first meal was at 8 a.m., the luncheon was at noon, and the evening meal was at 4 p.m.

He attended any on the sick list at 9 a.m. as soon as breakfast was over. He insisted that the prison deck be kept as clean as possible and that it was to be sprinkled with vinegar daily and be cleaned and fumigated frequently. The hatches were kept open wherever possible, and ventilation below decks ensured the health of all on board.

As generally happened on such a trip, in the months on board, most women found their monthly flow stopped; the complaint of extreme constipation also accompanied this. He knew that both these conditions were often due to an inadequate diet. Molly found that rather than the delicious foods she had grown used to under her mother's care, the scant rations on board often gave her an upset stomach. More often than not, she brought up what she consumed. Her glowing health soon departed, as did her excess weight. The doctor ensured she had the hardtack ration, but they were unpleasant at best.

~

The months on board were passed in tedious boredom for many. However, Molly was kept occupied teaching and sewing to anyone interested. They experienced many storms, and unfortunately, some of the supplies were not stowed correctly; various barrels of produce had come loose and, in the process, destroyed many others. Due to the bilges not being pumped, the water had risen and seeped into the casks of dried food. So even those barrels not smashed were tainted. The flour had become saturated with salt water. Rice had also been stored in an inundated area with seawater and was now unfit to eat. The salted meats turned Molly's stomach at the best of times, but over the months on board, the now slimy salt beef and pickled pork stank, and many women refused to eat their rations. The weight fell off Molly so much that the doctor often brought her some of his own food; this was of a higher quality and far more palatable. At least the plain rice was edible. She thanked him but found that even his meagre offering was nearly unpalatable. Hunger won; she ate the hardtack biscuits and could keep this down.

Doctor Prosser would stand and watch over the education classes to ensure the three girls' safety. Knowing the voracious appetites of the sailors, and he didn't mean for food, he insisted that Molly and the other girls were kept under guard from carnal attack. He knew of their innocence of all things sexual, and he wished to keep them that way. He was fully mindful that the ship's captain and the guard's captain were aware of the nocturnal visits of various crewmen and soldiers. Sometimes, the guard, supposedly protecting them, participated. As a doctor, he was also aware of the previous occupation of many women locked up below. He knew many would do almost anything for extra rations, and warming the bed of a willing sailor was an easy way to get more food.

Molly, however, was a worry. She ate her meagre ration but never put on weight. She was not ill, *per se*, but as the cruise progressed, she seemed to have little energy. Knowing that they had no access to fresh fruit or vegetables, he could do little about it. Thankfully she willingly ate the sauerkraut, which helped ward off scurvy. She even drank the now-soured wine he brought her, but her health was beginning to suffer. Lethargy set in. Some days, she could hardly pull herself out of her bunk in the morning. Her curves were gone, and her round face was now hollowed and thin. After many months at sea, the spoiled food, such as it was, was served to both passengers and crew alike. All were hungry.

~

The *Isabella*, the *Glory*, and the *Maria* sailed into Port Jackson at Sydney within three days of each other. The first two ships arrived on September 14th, even though they had left five weeks earlier. The *Isabella* had departed London in early April and stopped at Rio de Janeiro, where she met the *Tottenham*. The *Isabella* stayed for a week and then departed for Sydney. The *Tottenham* was dealing with an outbreak of scurvy and remained for some time, although leaving some weeks later, the *Glory* and *Maria* sailed directly to the colony.

Ellen Ross had been the final passenger to book a berth on the departing ship. She was at least pleased she had beaten the *Maria* out of port. She had not even seen her daughter to let her know she would join her in Sydney. Her decision to leave had been made at the last minute after Molly had gone. She had been in two minds about whether she should go. Sir Percival's offer of a fresh start for them all was the clinching argument. His gift of £3000 meant she could hire a proper cabin on board rather than travel in a hammock on the steerage deck. She purchased a first-class ticket and travelled in comfort. Master Edward Pounder and Surgeon William Stewart welcomed her on board and saw her settled into her cabin.

On arrival in Sydney, Ellen had been able to disembark and stay at a relatively new hotel called the King's Arms on Pitt Street. She noticed there were many building projects in the town. A waiting hackney carriage transported her and the mountains of luggage accompanying her to her accommodation. She had all Bill's and Molly's possessions with her and hoped to be settled for some weeks before their arrival. She booked a suite, and the night she arrived, she luxuriated in a long, hot bath. The following day, she relaxed, overwhelmingly glad that the bed didn't rock.

Three days after her arrival, she heard that Molly's ship had just dropped anchor. She panicked and asked the young hotel manager if he could assist her. Ellen approached him with her problem. "Sir, can you direct me to the person in charge of convict placement? I wish to have one assigned to me." She did not let on that it was her daughter.

Mr Stewart took in the elegance of the upright woman before him. She was dressed in the height of fashion, and although her gown was not of the first stare, it was far from cheap. He knew she was registered as Mrs Ellen Ross. She had arrived with far more luggage than the regular traveller. She was not the first family member who had travelled to be with their children or husband, and he guessed that would be her reason to be here. He smiled at her and said, "Madam, if you head along to the new Hyde Park Barracks, ask for Major Downes; I believe he will be able to assist you. He had only recently arrived, so he is settling into the role himself. Major Turner is showing him the ropes, so to speak. Shall I call a carriage for you? You won't need a maid to go there."

Ellen smiled graciously. Unwilling to seem so keen, she said, "Thank you, sir, that would be appreciated. Also, would it be possible for a maid or footman to accompany me? As I said, I hope to employ someone as soon as possible." During the time she was at the hotel, she noticed various advertisements for staff in the newspaper. Many were girls wanting work. She knew a woman alone in such a place would draw malicious comments. Even in London, she had rarely ventured out alone. Normally, she had been with Molly, but should her daughter not be available, one of the maids, Elyse or Jayne, often accompanied her should she need to go anywhere. She did not need a personal maid as a housekeeper, but she had always had one before she wed. When she married Sam, they were comfortable, but money had been tight after his death. Now they had funds aplenty; Ellen decided to seek a needy girl as a maid. She would educate her and set her on a better path in life with good references. Mr Stewart hailed a hackney carriage for her. Ellen travelled up the hill of the small town, and when she alighted at the newly built edifice, she asked the cab to wait for her.

The cabbie wondered who she was, but she was a good-looking woman, and he knew that if she could afford to stay at the King's Arms Hotel, she would tip well. After dropping her off, he moved the horses into the shade of a nearby tree. It may be September, but that was no reason to make the poor beasts stand in the sun. Ellen clutched her full reticule nervously as she entered the solid, barred gates.

A sentry challenged her. "Ma'am, this is a barracks not open for public viewing."

Ellen nervously swallowed. She pulled herself up to her full height. "I am not here to view it, but I would like to see the officer in charge, please."

"I presume he's not expecting you, ma'am?" the sentry frowned; women weren't usually admitted to the young major's office. He didn't wish to offend her, but he couldn't just send her in unannounced.

Ellen shook her head. No one was expecting her, and she'd had no time to arrange anything. "No, sir, but it is quite urgent that I have some time with Major Downes."

The sentry turned and clicked his fingers at a soldier standing outside a sandstone building off to the left. The red-coated soldier came at the double. The two had their heads together for a moment, and then the sentry turned back to Ellen. "Follow this man, ma'am."

Ellen followed the second soldier to the side building. He asked her to wait outside while he knocked and entered. Less than a minute later, a very young major flung open the door and apologised for the inconvenience. He ushered her to a seat and offered her a cup of tea.

She noticed the door remained open, even though she was twice his age; it was protocol, and the sentry guard stood within sight. Ellen was so nervous she swallowed again. "Sir, I have a letter from a London gentleman explaining my request." She dug into her reticule and soon had her hand on Sir Percival's letter. She also had the one from Sir Robert about both Molly and Bill. "Sir, I have come to request that my daughter, when she arrives, is assigned to me. The letters I have will explain everything." She slowly slid the two valuable letters from her bag and placed them in his hand. The fair-haired major only looked about Molly's age.

Major Downes took the two documents, laid them on the table, and went to make her some tea. "Ma'am, here we drink it hot, black, and sweet; I have just arrived myself and am not quite used to that yet. How would you like it? I'm sorry we have no milk or lemon."

Ellen didn't care. Tea at home was often cold before she drank it as she kept forgetting she'd made some. "Hot and sweet is fine, thank you, major." He handed her a big mug of sweet black tea and took his seat with his hot brew. Once seated, he took Sir Percival's letter and flicked open the seal. He spread the letter on his desk and read… and read… and read. She knew the missive was lengthy but did not realise he had written four tightly packed double-sided pages.

The major occasionally lifted his eyes to her and commiserated with an, "Oh, ma'am" or "I'm so sorry," but he kept reading. He turned to the final page and lay back in his chair with a long sigh. "Oh, ma'am, I've never heard the like. I think I'll be able to work with you easily. I'm also pleased you informed me about William Miller. I've never heard the like of his situation."

Ellen realised that Sir Percival's letter explained everything, but he had yet to read the second letter. "Sir, there's the other letter. It's from Sir Robert Peel."

The major sat up to attention at that name. His eyes flew open in surprise at her knowing this man. He refolded the first letter and turned his attention to the second one. As he dropped his head to peruse it, he exclaimed, "Oh, this is terrible," or "The poor lad," which Ellen heard as he read this screed. She had not had the pleasure of reading either letter. She wished she had broken the seals and read them herself, though she knew the stories. Major Humphrey Downes finally finished reading the second letter. His hands fell to the desk with a plonk. "Well, I have never heard the like of this case… no, these cases, madam." He was astounded by the twisted tale of two innocents paying for the crime of such a spoiled upstart. But then again, he had encountered many such spoilt whippersnappers over his short career. Many had been soldiers under his command. They were often second or third sons of the gentry. He was himself, and his father had purchased his commission. The major gazed at the woman sitting opposite him. "You've come all this way, and I understand you left early to be set up before your daughter arrived, only to find she was a mere three days behind you?"

Ellen released a sigh of relief. Sir Robert's letter obviously explained that side of the journey. He had handed it to her just before she departed with the words. "Mention my name should you need to, but this will assist in smoothing your path." It had certainly done the trick.

Major Downes again lay back in his chair and said, "Madam, I have heard of many injustices in my job, but these two take the cake. I shall certainly do everything in my power to assist your plight. The first will be to get Miss Molly off the *Maria* immediately. These convict vessels normally sit in the harbour for up to a week before the surgeon or medical person gives them the all-clear to land. Any passengers will alight first, and then I can extract Miss Ross." He reached out for a giant ledger and flipped it open. "I can't believe people get away with such rubbish and inflict injustice on the young and innocent."

Ellen was nearly beside herself with delight. "You mean, sir, that you will assist me? That you will assign Molly to me?"

Major Downes smiled. "Why, ma'am, of course I will. With references like this, I will do everything I can to aid you. For once, it's something different. Many come protesting their innocence but never arrive with such letters." He tapped his finger on the letters before him. "Ma'am, I will keep these and show them to Governor Macquarie this afternoon, but I will return them when Miss Molly is brought to you."

Ellen was delighted. That was stage one of their plans that worked out. Hopefully, Molly had not been abused on the voyage here. Ellen had heard horror stories of some of the below-deck activities on some ships. Even if she had been violated, she was sure Bill would still want Molly, as she knew he adored her. Ellen had prayed daily for her daughter's safety. She had no idea when Bill would arrive. She was aware that he had still not left London when she departed. Sir Robert had said that Bill had been due to be sent to the hulks in Portsmouth that week, though. Hopefully, he would be here soon. "Thank you, major; I am staying at the King's Arms Hotel until I can find a place to rent."

Major Downes nodded acknowledgment of her comment. "Ma'am, I believe a new cottage is coming up for rent at Cockle Bay. I'm unsure what you plan to do in the town; however, it may suffice until young Miller arrives. I presume that he and Miss Molly will make a match of it? As she is a convict, even being assigned to either you or him, she will need permission to wed from the Colonial Secretary. Miller will also require the same until his paperwork has been finalised." He saw Ellen's face and the fear now on it. "Ma'am, as I said, once I explain to the Governor the situation…" He looked down at the letters before him and tapped them, "…and these do that adequately, then all will be easy. The Colonial Secretary is the cousin of the governor's wife and is very approachable, considering he and the governor are both Scottish gentlemen." He gurgled a chuckle.

Having lived all her adult life in, or near, London, her experience with Scotsmen was minimal. Her only connection with one was through Sir Percival, who had made friends with a duke whose wife was Scottish. Lady Susannah and she had been presented together. Their oldest son, Lord David, was Errol's friend. She said, "Thank you, good sir; I have taken enough of your time. I shall ask the cabbie to drive via Cockle Bay and view the locale. I have seen nothing of the town yet as I've been getting my land legs. I fear that the sea will not see me on it again in the near future." Her eyes twinkled with joy at how the interview had turned out. Molly would be brought to her. She stood to leave and turned to ask if she could have a gown delivered for her daughter to wear.

The major knew that she would wish Molly to start with her convict background well hidden. "Ma'am, sadly, I shouldn't allow it until she attains her Certificate of Freedom at the end of her term. She should remain in her convict garb; however, I believe Mrs Fry has had the women sewing while on board. I have already heard that one of the women has been teaching others to read and assisting with sewing skills. Therefore, I have a feeling that on this arrival, the women will be much better clad than previous cargoes of prisoners. If you bundle up some clothing, I will ensure Miss Molly gets it. Leave it here when you are ready."

Chapter 9   Hyde Park View

$\mathcal{A}$s Ellen left the compound, the hackney cab was waiting for her.

The driver assisted her into the seat and asked for directions.

Ellen thought she would like to look around, "Could we drive around town, please? I would like to see around Cockle Bay as I believe a new cottage is coming up for rent next week."

The cabbie bowed, pleased that this cab fare would pay well. "Certainly, ma'am." He gee'd up the old nag that pulled his dilapidated vehicle. He took off around Hyde Park at a gentle trot from the barracks entrance. He also embarked on a full tour of the settlement.

Ellen noticed some nice houses in this area and wondered if any were available for her purpose. Money was no object, and she planned to buy them something nice.

The cabbie then turned down George Street and headed out to Cockle Bay via the foreshore at Millers Point. In each new area, he spoke to her through the communication hatch. He told her where they were and what the place was like. They travelled through Dawes Point, then passed the dockland where the newly arrived ships were anchored. The cabbie paused for a while; they parked, watching the activity on the foreshore, and then he asked if she was ready to return or if she wished to see more as there was also a nice drive out over on the next headland.

Ellen replied, "Keep driving, please, cabbie. I have nothing to return to the hotel for yet. Thank you so much." Ellen leaned back on the worn squab seats and watched with interest as the strange sights passed. It was so very different to London. As they turned into the next road, she saw that it led to a pretty grassy point near where the *Maria* was anchored.

As they reached the furthest point, she tapped on the roof. "Can we pause here for a moment, please, sir?" Ellen opened the carriage door but did not step down. She drank in the sight of the ship that carried her daughter.

A thought occurred to her. She did not even know yet if Molly had survived the voyage. A tear trickled down Ellen's cheek. She swiped it away angrily, thinking, "I'm not going to be melancholy. Sam would wish me to be with Molly; that is all there is about it. I've burnt my bridges, and I'm not going back." She sniffed back her tears and closed the door. She said through the hatch, "Drive on; thank you, sir."

She thought about the cottage that was for rent and was currently being cleaned of the building debris. They had stopped in front of it and had a long look. The place had been newly built and had a sign, 'Comfrey and Corbett Constructions.' There were similar cottages in the area, and many seemed new. Ellen thought that this would at least be suitable to rent until Bill arrived, and they would work out where they would settle down. But she would rather have something further away from the docks.

The cabbie deposited her at the front door of the hotel. On entering, Ellen asked if there was a newspaper she could browse through. With the click of his fingers, a young lad brought her the current week's news sheet.

Ellen took it to her room and browsed through the advertisements. She saw the notice for the cottage and wondered if she would send for particulars. The hotel manager could send the young boy for the information, but the advertisement was quite informative.

To be LET, at a moderate Rent, a STONE BUILT HOUSE in Cockle-bay, containing two Rooms and a large Loft, with an extensive outlet bounded by water on two sides. The premises are in every way adapted for any purpose that can require Water or Land Carriage, and considerable improvements may be made at a minimal expense to render these extensive premises equal to any in Sydney for maritime or Commercial Purposes.

For further Particulars, apply at 68 George Street, Sydney.

The paper made the small cottage sound pleasant, but the two bedrooms were not big enough. Ellen wondered what living in the growing docklands would be like or even safe. She wasn't sure if she wished for just 'pleasant'. Nor did she want two single females living near many sailors on the waterfront. As they passed, she had counted four public drinking bars and inns and probably missed some. The area was obviously growing, and she didn't particularly wish to live there alone with Molly.

Ellen kept reading. Moments later, she sat bolt upright when her eyes fell on this advertisement. This house sounded much better, and it was in town. It was close to the barracks, so she and Molly could cry out for assistance if required.

TO BE LET. That elegant DWELLING HOUSE, situate at Hyde Park Corner, is now in the occupation of Mr. Edward Riley. Comprising six rooms, a kitchen, a cellar, a coach-house, a three-stall stable, a good well of water, and every convenience for a genteel Family.

Apply on the premises or at Mr Marr's, Castlereagh Street.

Ellen noticed a well-appointed house on the corner near the barracks. It stood out from many of the other dwelling places in the area. Yes, this was the one she would enquire about. She looked around for the bell pull and saw a beautifully embroidered tug in the corner of the room. Giving it two jerks, she then waited. A maid appeared at her door in a matter of minutes.

Less than half an hour later, she was headed back to Hyde Park. She had packed Molly's clothes and planned to drop them off to the major at the barracks. Then, with her new chaperone in tow, she approached the premises and tentatively knocked on the door. From the outside, the house looked perfect. Would the inside hold up to expectation?

It did. By the time they arrived at the hotel two hours later, Ellen took a six-month lease on the house with an option to extend. It came fully furnished and even had some staff should they be required. She had willingly agreed that they all be kept on, but it was up to them. All she needed now was both Molly and a maid. Then, they would sit and wait for Bill's arrival. The six rooms turned out to be an understatement. The six suites were as large as at Sir Percival's home, and there were numerous small bedrooms that the advertisement had not even acknowledged. There was even a small sitting room for staff. She wondered if she could let them out and start an upper-class boarding house. This idea would give her something to do.

~

It took a week for the majority of the convicts on the *Maria* to be processed and released. Molly, however, was the first to be taken ashore once the paperwork was done. She was called to the sick bay five days after arrival and had been told to have her things ready before dawn when she would be called and would disembark. The doctor told her she had to creep out before the others awoke. She still had no idea her mother awaited her, but she knew that Bill probably had not even left England. She presumed that she had already been assigned to some wealthy family due to her reading abilities.

In the pre-dawn light, Doctor Prosser had woken her with a touch on her shoulder and a hand on her mouth. Knowing this was coming, she had gone to bed fully clothed; she wrapped her things in a blanket and followed him silently past her sleeping cellmates. She had hugged Rebecca and Sophie before she went to bed last night. She would be gone when they awoke.

All were used to the doctor's silent ways as he had closely watched his charges. He had often crept below decks and listened to make sure they were not being molested. He had ensured all were well and had adequate food, but rations were still woefully inadequate. Few women had had the normal mensural cycle since London, as their diet sadly still lacked fresh food. Thankfully, since their arrival, he had sourced boxes of fresh fruit and vegetables and hoped the constipation that had plagued many would sort itself out before disembarking. From the stench now below deck, his treatment seemed to have worked.

Only three of the convict women had been wilfully consorting with the soldiers guarding them, but that was their choice, so he was not too concerned. Consequently, there had been little to no abuse of the remainder of the women and girls.

Molly was thrilled that her friends had been kept safe and that most could read and write quite well. She followed the doctor through the corridor and up the narrow ladder to the deck. The chill September morning bit into her uncovered arms. She shivered and wished she had wrapped her blanket around her rather than folded her things.

The doctor arrived at the cabin door. He opened it but did not enter. He softly said, "Come on, hasten up, Miss Molly. You have been assigned, and you have been sent new clothing. I think you may well like the choice." The medic ushered her into the sick bay and pointed to a parcel waiting on the examination table. "I'll wait outside while you change, miss; then, you will be taken ashore. I don't think you will need the rest of your things, but take them if you wish." He closed the door as quietly as he had done everything else.

Molly placed her possessions on the end of the table and picked up the wrapped bundle. She untied the string, and the tightly compressed wrapping burst open. Her own royal blue velvet hooded cloak and best-sprigged muslin gown lay on the top of the pile. The presence of these items meant only one thing: her mother was here. She clasped the glorious apparel into her arms, and a few tears dripped onto the fabric. She quickly stripped off all her filthy clothing, donned the new drawers, stays, camisole, and petticoats that her mother had included, and drew the muslin gown over the top. She knew she stank, but she could do little about that. She wrapped the cloak around her shoulders and snuggled into the warmth of the luxurious thick fabric. The doctor was correct; she folded her old clothing and left it on the table. Some other poor girls could have it; the thin, almost threadbare blanket had a similar fate. She wrapped her few other possessions in the parcel wrapping. Molly didn't need a hat as the cloak covered her head. For the first time in a long, long time, she felt like herself again.

The bedraggled convict who entered the cabin had vanished, and a well-clad, neatly dressed young lady exited the room. As she left the sick bay, she met the doctor's eyes and saw his look of astonishment. Her beaming smile met his gaze.

He said softly, "Well, Miss Molly, you certainly pay for dressing. Let's get going."

They had to make it off the vessel unseen by most of the crew. They crept out of the ship's lower decks and into the dawn sunshine into what would hopefully be a bright future.

~

Breakfast at the hotel was brought to Ellen's room. She had never had the luxury of breakfast in bed since Sam died. He had spoilt her rotten when she fell with child soon after they had wed. She and her sister had fled their home on the same day, and neither had wished to leave the other alone with their father. He had never come looking for either of them. But for him to miss out on Molly's life had been gut-wrenching. Now she was pleased he didn't know what had happened to her. When Ellen found out the cost of the rent for the house, she was surprised that the six-month rate was only £30 plus the staff's wages. Hopefully, Molly would have received her bundle of clothing and she would arrive soon.

The maid had drawn back the curtains, and Ellen had taken her breakfast tray and set it on the small table in her room. From here, she could see the activities in the harbour, and in the early morning light, she saw a long boat leaving the *Maria*. Knowing that Molly would be taken off before the convicts were called for their morning meal, she realised she had to hurry the luxury of her breakfast. She sat and quickly ate the bacon and perfectly cooked eggs, then spread her toast with the tangy Scotch marmalade, cut it into four and left it on her plate. She ate this while dressing and was ready to face her daughter when a knock was heard.

It wasn't Molly at the door but a maid, who had come to say that Mrs Ross had a visitor and she was awaiting her below.

Ellen asked them if it was Molly. The maid nodded. Ellen requested that her visitor be brought upstairs immediately and another breakfast tray brought up for her guest. Ellen refused to greet her daughter in public and be watched by the stares of the other patrons. She stood waiting at the window. Her nervousness detracted from her normal tall, willowy elegance. She stood clasping and unclasping her hands and then folded and unfolded her arms. Where was she? Why was she taking so long?

Another tap on the door and Ellen turned and called, "Enter."

The door slowly opened, and the sight before Ellen made her gasp. Molly was alive and well. Her daughter stood looking as though she was heading out shopping in London.

Molly entered silently and gazed at her mother.

They remained quiet until the door was closed behind her. Then, the space between them was crossed instantly, and they were enfolded in each other's arms and softly weeping. So much had occurred in the months they had been apart. It was six long months since they had seen each other and nine since Molly had been arrested. Ellen felt that Molly was almost skin and bone. Her face looked gaunt and almost haunted. She held her daughter at arm's length and said, "First and foremost, just know that I love you no matter what happened on board."

Molly replied with a smile, "Mother, never fear; I was not abused on board or at any other time. Our doctor was amazing and protected us well.

Certainly, I'm not as innocent as I was, as I both saw things and heard things no lady should see, including helping deliver a baby or two. I learnt many things, mother, but I taught much too. You told me to use my time wisely, so I have, and I prayed. I have done both. I have been teaching the little ones with some other girls on board who can read."

Molly told her beloved mother of Elizabeth Fry's visits and bounteous gifts, how she was tasked with teaching those on board how to read and write, and the privileges this brought. She mentioned her friends' names once or twice but did not elaborate.

Ellen knew that her daughter's time of service was not yet settled. They had to go along and see the young major to make Molly's assignment official; however, that could wait until Molly had eaten a proper meal. Her dear girl had lost much weight but otherwise looked well.

Another knock brought Molly's breakfast, and they fell apart until the door closed again.

When the maid departed, Molly fell to her knees, weeping. She had not seen this much proper food since she was cooking a Christmas luncheon on the day she was arrested.

Ellen knelt beside her and let her cry. She understood there would be much of this. She had to get to know her daughter all over again.

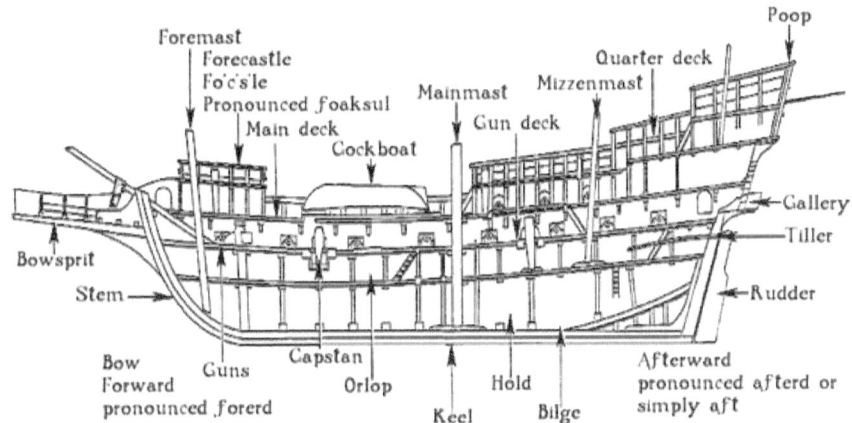

Chapter 10 Hard on Her Heels

$\mathcal{A}$s Ellen left Rio de Janeiro on the *Isabella*, Bill was being transferred from the *Leviathan* onto the *General Stewart* at Portsmouth. He had spent months getting to know old Tom; however, he was surprised that the bent and wizen man was only in his forties. He was not much older than Ellen, but he was nearly bald, and many of his teeth had rotted in their gums, which added to his aged look. Because of his lack of hair, his head was not shaved like all the other convicts. Bill was not used to having a shaven head. His hair had always been immaculately groomed, and his cue naturally curled into a ringlet. Thankfully, he rarely needed to powder his hair unless Sir Percival had a function when he was home from university. Those days were now a thing of the past. The powder was now out of fashion, and the cues had long since been cut off. However, his hair had always been lusciously thick. Now, as his hair grew back, it was filthy, felt like glue, and was horrible. On the hulk, they had their hair roughly removed every month or so. At least it stopped the head lice, but it wasn't so good in the chilly winter on the frigid river. He had never realised how warm his hair kept his head. It had been some months since his last head shave, and he ran his fingers through it to force it into some semblance of order. He itched and presumed that he had nits. He knew from the bites on his body that lice infested his clothing and bedding. There was little he could do about any of it.

Tom impressed Bill as he could turn his hand to anything. He made do with what he had, which was very little, from catching river rats to supplement the meagre rations on the rotting hulks to sewing torn clothing with unravelled thread and a homemade needle. Tom also had the uncanny knack of knowing what would happen before it did, from when it would rain to when the sun shone brightly.

For months, Bill and Tom made the best of their life on the hulks. Some other convicts had been drawn by the light and heard Bill reading to Tom. Sitting out of sight in the darkness, they, too, sat and listened to the strange stories of foreign lands. Bill read from *Apollodorus, Diodorus, Siculus, Hyginus,* and *Euripides*. He found the sagas of the Iliad and the Odyssey were a delight to many stories-starved ears. Soon, a regular time each day was dedicated to Bill's classical education of the captors. Tom was always by his side, ordinarily happy and chatty, as he was no longer alone. He had never had a friend before and became Bill's protector and shadow.

One day in the middle of summer, Bill noticed Tom was sitting in a melancholy heap. He became uncommunicative and sullen. Bill could not get out of him why he was sad. It was not until a thud occurred that the reason became clear. Bill and Tom were sitting in a shaft of sunlight after Bill had been reading one of his books aloud. Tom sat staring at him. The rest of the listeners had returned to their bunks, and Bill sat in silence, thinking over his story of Hercules.

Both were rocked when a massive crash occurred.

Bill gasped.

Tom swore, then added, "You'se wanna know why I'm sad? Well, it's 'cause you'se bloody goin', that's why I'm sad. You'se been a ray of sunshine to me, Bill, and now you'se goin' to be shipped out. Them's upstairs won't take me; they reckon I'll die on board. I bin here three years, and I ain't carked it yet. I only got four more to serve."

The convict roll was read some hours later, and over two hundred and fifty names were called out. As the names were read, the men had to pack their things and move on to the other ship.

Bill wondered if they had missed him until the last two names were read aloud, "William Miller and Thomas Yeats."

Tom was up and dancing a jig. "I'm goin' with ya, Bill old fellow, ol' mate. I'm not being left out this time. You bloody beauty, me little old mate is sticking wiv me, and I wiv him." Within moments, Tom had scrambled down to his bunk and scrunched his things into a bundle.

Bill chuckled at his friend's excitement to finally be transported. He had a lot more to pack.

Tom, too, had delighted in Bill reading him some of the old stories, translating from Greek or Latin as he read. These valuable books had to be packed carefully and transferred along with his clothes and blankets. They owned nothing beyond that.

By the end of the day, they were on the new ship and settled in their berths. The *General Stewart* had a nearly full complement of convicts on board. They were from all over Britain, and roughly half were to serve life sentences. The rest were minimal terms. Bill never let on any information about his crime or punishment. Tom had warned him to say very little.

Although, if it were a crime against the gentry, he would almost be a hero, and he didn't want that. There was a detachment of the 84th regiment to accompany them on their journey. Bill knew this was standard procedure; they would be the prisoner guards.

They soon discovered that the new ship did not have cells but open timber berths that gave no privacy. The guards paced the corridor at the foot of the bunks. The berths on the *General Stewart* were undoubtedly an improvement to the rat-infested rotting hulks. At least here, they had light.

By the time they set sail on the next tide, Bill had calculated that he had already served fifteen months. With another five months or so on this journey, he may as well have been sentenced to serve the full three years. He pulled himself up short. Due to Molly's conviction, she now awaited him in Sydney with Ellen by her side. With that thought, he smiled.

Captain Robert Grainger, a giant of a man, was in charge of the vessel. He had already singled out Bill because he was carrying an obviously heavy crate of old books. "Are you Miller?"

Bill nodded in the affirmative.

"Thought you must be. That box gave it away." The captain turned to the doctor and said, "That's him, Doc."

Surgeon Superintendent Andrew Smith nodded in response to Bill acknowledging his identity. "Drop your things below or get your friend to look after them. Things will go missing quite easily." He paused, thinking, then said, "No, as a matter of fact, bring your stuff and your shadow." He walked off and expected the two convicts to follow him.

They did.

Tom was going to stick as closely as he could to Bill. Following the doctor, he led them below deck and through the dining mess. They were taken into the galley and told to leave their possessions on the bench seat. He led them down a passageway and stopped before a cabin door. Only then did he realise Tom was still with them. The doctor shooed Tom back to the mess room. "This is just for the lad, go and mind his valuables."

Tom vanished; he didn't mind at all. He hoped to scrounge something to eat from the galley, so he went to chat up the cook.

Bill was taken in to meet the leader of the military guard. He discovered that all soldiers on board were under the orders of Captain Arthur Bernard. For some reason, the regiment captain wished to set eyes on Bill. No questions or enquiries were made. After the introduction, Bill was dismissed; only moments had elapsed.

As the cabin door closed, Bill frowned at the unusually brief interview; Bill bravely said, "Sir, was that not somewhat odd?"

The doctor shrugged. "He told me he wanted to meet the man who beat his brilliant little brother at Oxford. I figured you had some learning behind you. Did I glimpse a Pliny in that box of yours?"

Bill replied with a grin, "Amongst others. They were a gift from my accuser's father. It's a long story, and I'm sure it's all on record."

The middle-aged doctor smiled. The lad didn't drop any names, and he could have. He said, "It is, and I have read it all. It is an interesting case, as you are yourself. As you will be free as soon as we land, you will have a little more freedom than other convicts. There is a small unused servant's room that I thought you would like to use as safe storage for your box and for your studies. You can at least place your books in there to keep them dry. It's little more than a closet but still better than below decks." By now, they had arrived in the crew mess area again.

Tom had heard the comment and saw that Bill was about to refuse the offer. "Of course, he'll use it, sir. He has been reading me some of them old Greekee stories, and they be real interesting, if a bit weird."

Bill objected, "...but Tom, you'll be all but alone."

Tom chuckled. "Bin alone all me life, and I reckon I can cope with a bit more. What's more, doc, he's had a pile of us, real criminals, listening to his learnin' too. We sit around him, drinking in the stories. Good for the souls they is. Even when he does a ring in and adds some Bible ones, we doesn't mind. Doc, he said some of them Bible ones is even older than the Greekee ones. I doesn't really care as they is great to listen to."

The doctor was intrigued. "I do the church services whilst on board. Do you believe?" The question was short, but the answer was vital.

Bill knew he was asking about his personal faith. He shouldn't have been surprised, but he was. "Yes, sir, but live it rather than preach it."

The doctor nodded. "I thought as much. If you're willing, I might ask you to do some of the readings." Then, with a quick frown, he asked Bill if he played chess, to which Bill again nodded. "Yes to both, sir."

The doctor chuckled, "Championship level, I bet?"

Bill felt his face flush. Chess trophies adorned his old bedroom, "Yes sir, and backgammon at Eton as well. At Oxford, only chess, sir, as I didn't have much time to play at university, but it was my one form of relaxation."

"Anything you didn't excel at?" the medic asked, expecting a negative answer.

Bill was relieved to reply honestly: "Yes, physics, sir. The rest of the subjects were easy in comparison. I only received a credit for that."

Doctor Smith said as they strolled along the corridors, "Rest easy, boy. That's a subject that throws many. I failed it my first year and had to swat for an extra holiday exam. I scraped through by the skin of my teeth, then dropped it like a hot rock."

Bill nodded. Then he asked, "Oxford, sir?"

Doctor Smith said, "No, Edinburgh, they have the best medical school there."

Tom followed them passively, listening to the conversation of the two in front of him. Bill realised he was not including his friend in the chat and apologised. Tom hastened to reassure him: "Oh, Bill, ignore me. I'm a nothing, laddie. I' se content to be listenin' to you learnéd gentlemen. It does my 'eart good to hear you chatting nice like with an equal, my friend."

Bill objected; he knew about many of Tom's talents and said, "You are not a nothing, Tom. You are amazing at how you have scraped and scrimped to survive. I am in awe of you. We can't all be surgeons or scholars. Every one of us must have different skills to make the world the place it is. The world would not function if they were. We need the workers and those willing to learn to make the place we live in better for all."

By the time the ship was ready to sail on the next day's tide, Bill and Tom had settled into their bunks with the other convicts.

Many of the men from the hulk now clamoured to be near Bill, as they had hoped he would continue his story times. So they had saved the two men a berth in the central area. The doctor had overseen the storage of Bill's precious tomes in the small servant's cabin, and Bill decided that he would only keep one at a time below decks.

They had felt the jump of the ship when the breeze picked up. It was not long before the bay's calm waters turned into the churning seas and rolling waves of the Atlantic Ocean. The sails were fully unfurled, and the winds filled to heel the ship uncomfortably on a tilt. At this angle, the vessel crashed through each wave and shuddered. Surviving that crash, it hit the trough of the next one… and so it continued, day in, day out for the next five months. Bill groaned and vomited.

Tom chuckled. "But Bill, it's not even rough. Wait until the water and waves crash over the deck; then, you have permission to be scared. You'll know about fear if we get rocked to the scuppers."

Bill had never been at sea before, and along with many other prisoners, the *mal de mer* overtook him. The stench of vomit and excrement made being below deck even worse.

Tom hauled his friend up to the deck and laid him near the railing so he could heave his heart out without using a bucket. Tom ministered to Bill and insisted that he drink frequently. This was the last thing Bill wanted to do. He wished to curl up and die. His guts were turned inside out, and he felt rotten.

The doctor visited the convicts each morning and checked on all the seasick patients. He passed out cold boiled water and told each one to drink up. The water had lemon essence in it and went down well. The bitterness of the fluid hit the sourness of Bill's stomach, and amazingly, it helped settle it.

From Portsmouth, the ship headed directly south. Three days after leaving port, Bill awoke to the realisation that his innards were still intact and had seemingly adjusted to the movement of the torturous liquid beneath them, as had his head. Finally, the ship seemed to be moving in unison with his body, and his sickness eased.

The soldiers had been down and checked on their charges. Over the course of each day, the majority of convicts were permitted on deck for some air. They were allowed to walk around and get some sunshine on their bodies. Initially, thirty at a time, but that grew to sixty as the trip progressed.

However, ten of the convicts were shackled to one another. All were sentenced to life terms and were marked never to be released. These men had been locked in special cells on the lower deck each night and were kept in isolation. They were known troublemakers, and Captain Bernard and his Lieutenant, a man named Beamish, were always on deck with muskets at the ready when these ten men were brought up from the bowels of the ship.

Thanks to the doctor's friendliness, Bill and Tom discovered that the only paying passengers were a family, Mr and Mrs George Panton and their five small children. Their cabin was next to the captain's, so access to the top deck was the easiest for them. They were rarely seen when the convicts were exercising; if they were, they would be up on the poop deck.

After a month at sea, the lack of winds impeded the passage south. They had no sickness on board; however, one of the Pantons' small children suddenly became very ill and died quickly. Little George Kerr Panton needed to be buried at sea.

The entire ship was in mourning as the child's body was lowered into the deep waters of the Atlantic Ocean. The doctor, Andrew Smith, conducted the short service, and many attended. Doctor Smith had no idea what ailed the child, but it was not infectious.

Bill read the passage from John chapter 14, verses 1 to 6. "*Let not your heart be troubled: ye believe in God, believe also in me. In my father's house are many mansions: if it were not so, I would have told you. I go to prepare a place for you. And if I go and prepare a place for you, I will come again, and receive you unto myself; that where I Am, there ye may be also. And whither I go ye know, and the way ye know. Thomas saith unto him, Lord, we know not whither thou goest; and how can we know the way? Jesus saith unto him, I Am the way, the truth, and the life: no man cometh unto the Father but by Me.*" Bill wasn't sure that this was the reading he would have chosen for a child's burial at sea, but it took all his determination to make it through the words without choking up.

Soon after the service, the winds died.

With the ship becalmed, the remaining four children had time to run and play outdoors. The convicts were kept occupied below decks with various occupations. The gun deck convicts were now permitted to be unrestrained at all times. The lower deck ones were still confined in their secured cells but were now unshackled.

Squabbles ensued often, and the officers had to break up fights. The group of ten was now split into two blocks. They still shouted and jeered at each other, particularly the soldiers guarding them. The rest of the two hundred forty convicts were exceptionally well-behaved.

~

Six weeks after leaving Portsmouth, the sailor in the crows' nest shouted, "Land ho."

With only one island *en route* to Rio de Janeiro, St Helena's was a welcome stop for the family and crew. However, it meant that the convicts had to be confined below deck. As a gentle breeze blew, it was quite nice.

Bill refused to go up into his tiny cabin. He preferred not to be singled out.

The first days were pleasant enough; however, on the fourth day, the weather changed. The wind dropped entirely, and the humidity picked up. It was stiflingly hot. All hatches were kept open on both convict decks, and although air flooded through the lower decks, it did not relieve the comfort level. The gun deck also had the large cannon hatches opened to release the hot and fetid air. The deck below only had grated porthole hatches and the gunports at deck level, and at least these could be sealed in stormy weather. The temperature below was intolerable. With the Panton family in their cooler cabin, all the convicts stripped off completely and lay on the floor rather than the elevated bunk beds.

Bill and Tom lay on the bunks, wondering why they felt wet. Both had perspiration dribbling from their brows.

The doctor had done his morning rounds and told Bill that the barometer was rising. He warned them that the day would be hot and humid. The temperature shot up; until then, it had been a comfortable 68° Fahrenheit, but it skyrocketed to over 80° Fahrenheit. The humidity was nearly ninety-five per cent. All the convicts were too hot to move.

It was hotter now than when they had crossed the equator some two weeks earlier. At least previously, a stiff breeze blew, and air could circulate through the open gun hatches and port hole covers. As they were anchored, there was not a breath of breeze to ease the oppressive heat and stench from below decks.

Extra fluid rations were distributed, but many were too hot to walk to the drum and drink.

Doctor Smith came back on board and checked on the prisoners. He mobilised the coatless soldiers and brought the lime juice-flavoured water to each man below. He was almost forcing them to drink.

The soldiers usually wore their red woollen coats at all times; however, today, they were in their white linen shirts. This lack of uniform was something generally frowned upon, but today, they had been permitted to remove their jackets. Some had doused themselves in seawater to keep cool. All were glad they were now on duty on deck rather than in the sweltering hell hole.

Amazingly, no one had died.

The paying passengers had decided to stay for two nights onshore so the children could run around.

Doctor Smith made a snap decision. Contrary to the rules, the convicts were permitted up on deck while anchored. Extra hatches were thrown open, and all those unshackled crawled up on the deck and collapsed wherever there was room. The deck was strewn with prostrated, naked men; no one was even thinking about jumping overboard to escape.

Buckets of seawater were drawn up and sloshed over the heatstroke-affected convicts to relieve the discomfort. This action continued for nearly an hour until they revived a little. The lower deck convicts were by far the worst affected. They had been brought up still chained and bolted again to the rings on deck. Soon, the sun began to set, and the temperature dropped slightly. With the cooling evening and the consumption of the delicious lime water, they all slowly recovered. Once the patients, as the doctor now referred to them, tasted the drink, they consumed the entire barrel full of it with gusto.

With the emergency now averted, the men were returned to their bunks. All the hatches had been left open, and the below-deck area had cooled somewhat. Food was cooked and served. Most decided to leave the salty, fishy stew alone until it had cooled. Tonight, it was served with a sort of raw sauerkraut. None hesitated in devouring this. It was the first reasonably fresh food they had been served for months. The doctor had also sourced cases of fresh fruit, which he distributed. He knew that with the trip he had to do tomorrow, he had heard of a place further inland where he could buy bunches of bananas. With nearly three hundred people on board, vast quantities of produce vanished in a single meal. Five huge bunches of bananas would barely be one banana each. He decided to see the farm for himself and order a wagon load of green fruit to be delivered to the ship.

When Andrew Smith sent the convicts below decks, he told Bill to wait in the small cabin, as he wanted to speak to him. When the last convict had once again been locked up, the doctor went to meet Bill.

He knocked, then quietly opened the door and entered without waiting for an invitation. The small room was stuffy, and Bill was already perspiring. "William, today is your lucky day. I have arranged a treat for you. Captain Bernard has given me permission to take you on shore tomorrow. Knowing you are a history buff, I figured you may wish to see where Napoleon Bonaparte is living. He moved into his new dwelling, *Longford House*, some three years ago. I hope he will stay put this time. You should catch a glimpse of him as he often is seen standing on the headland looking seaward." Doctor Smith saw a transformation in Bill's face.

"Really, sir, I'd be permitted to land?" Bill's expression was one of astonishment. He realised he was probably the only convict ever to be granted this permission. However, he was no regular convict.

Doctor Smith smiled with delight, thinking that this lad could well have pushed the privileges he had been granted, but he didn't. The doctor had vouched for the lad's safety and knew he would not break that trust.

In the weeks they had been on board, they had many discussions on various topics. Bill regularly read the Bible during the services the Doctor ran each Sunday. Again, he never usurped his authority. Yes, he could trust him. "Yes, lad, but you must stay with me all the time. Your shadow cannot come, so it's just to be you and I."

Bill doubted if Tom would be interested in the trip anyway, but he asked permission to let him know and explain his absence. Bill trusted Tom to do that. Tom was duly told and promised to cover for him to the other convicts.

~

The following morning dawned, and thankfully, it was much cooler.

Once again, a gentle breeze had sprung up. Boats delivered produce and crew to and from the shore all day. Bill was hidden under a pile of hessian bags and stayed out of sight from the other convicts who watched the activity from the small hatches. When the boat was nearing the shore, the doctor uncovered him.

Bill's first sight of Jamestown was not what he expected, nor was St Helena Island itself.

The town was almost denuded of substantial growth. The valleys were vegetated with low shrubs and a few trees, but the hills were bare. The urban area itself was long and skinny and nestled at the bottom of two steep barren hills. The buildings themselves were colourful, but the whole place was somewhat depressing.

Bill knew the colony's history and that the Portuguese had planted fruit trees somewhere at some stage. He had no idea if they were still producing, but if the fruit bought onto the ship yesterday was a sign of productivity, then he presumed there were more fertile valleys elsewhere. He had read extensively about this small isle in his learning, as it was chosen to house England's greatest enemy. The likelihood of Napoleon Bonaparte escaping from this isolated dot in the ocean was minimal. Now, he was possibly to see the fabled soldier. Bill found it hard to concentrate on the surroundings. The boat pulled up to the small harbour, and they clambered out, and Bill stood looking around him.

The doctor tapped his shoulder and beckoned him.

As they landed, a carriage waited, and a soldier guarded them; just in case, the three set off for the hinterland of the tiny island.

The road through the town rose as it headed along the valley floor. Bill was sitting facing forward, and he, too, was able to drink in all he saw.

The doctor gave Bill a running commentary on the area as they travelled. He had obviously been here before and had taken a tour or two of the island.

They were taken through another town with the strange name of Alarm Forest and, while wending their way through valleys and over hills, eventually came to a single-story house set on a headland overlooking the sea from a distance.

As they drew closer, Bill gasped as he saw a man with a bicorn hat worn sideways. "Is that him? Why are we this close?" Bill craned his neck to savour every glimpse of the famed general.

The doctor shushed him. "Yes, and I have to check he is well and adequately cared for. He may require something, and I have brought you as an interpreter. I speak French quite well, but you are fluent. I believe his French is like his army; he fires it off in a volley. I didn't tell you before; I thought you might be nervous. I believe from others that you will speak a more pure version of French than he does, as he's from Corsica, not Paris. It is also why Sergeant Rex Block is with us. It's not that I don't trust you; it's that I don't trust the damned Corsican."

Bill's jaw dropped. "You want me to meet him? Really, sir?" He was stunned. "Gosh, sir, what an honour. Of course, I will assist." He was so excited at what lay before him. He, a convict, was to interpret for Napoleon Bonaparte, a prisoner. This one afternoon would be worth everything that had happened if nothing else ever came from his studies.

Andrew chuckled. "Bill, just remember, he's the enemy."

Bill nodded with a grin.

Chapter 11   Storm Warning

*T*he interview with the infamous Bonaparte did not quite go to plan.

The deposed warrior banished his staff as soon as the carriage arrived, and the doctor and Bill were invited into his spacious abode and offered sustenance while the sergeant stood guard.

For a while, Bonaparte complained about most things while speaking broken English, except his new house, which he liked. Eventually, he admitted that he was in want or need of nothing. His discontent stemmed from the knowledge that he was attempting to learn English as a third language, and he was exasperated. In utter frustration, he said to the doctor, "Ah bah! This English of yours is *c'est horrible*. No rules and too many exceptions, c'*est impossible!*" He threw his hands in the air in resignation and added. "*Parlera Français!*"

Bonaparte turned to Bill and asked, "*Parli Francese o Talianu? Perchè sia saria bè?*"

Bill nodded and replied in Parisian French, "*Oui, monsieur, je parle Français et Italien.*" Then he turned to the doctor and translated: "He asked if I spoke French or Italian; I told him I spoke both. But I think he asked in Corsican."

Unlike Boneparte, who grew up in Corsica, Bill's French was perfect.

The doctor nodded, and in a similar gesture to Bonaparte's earlier one, he said, "Go for it; I can't keep up with him."

Bonaparte cheered up. He replied in Corsican again, "*Va bè allora parlemu Francese,*" and then, seeing Bill frown, repeated it in French. "B*on alors on parlera Français.*"

Bill translated, "He said, ' Good, then we will speak French. You're right about his Corsican. It threw me for a bit.'

The great man babbled away far too fast for the doctor to keep up.

Andrew picked up a word or two here and there and asked Bill to elaborate on specific topics.

The doctor and the sergeant were lost most of the time. Neither could understand the speed at which the man shot his words at Bill.

Bill's replies were as fast. With the doctor asking questions in English, Bill would nod and translate them into perfect French.

Bonaparte's answers were often long-winded and accompanied by gestures and effusive hand movements that explained his ire at being incarcerated.

Bill translated each verbal torrent *sans* hand gestures, and the doctor took copious notes as Bill interpreted.

The interview lasted for over an hour, and eventually, the doctor thought he had enough material to file his report.

There was nothing they could do to change Bonaparte's incarceration or comfort, so they took their leave and departed with a final *adieu*.

Bonaparte thanked Bill for speaking in his own tongue, something he rarely got a chance to do on an English-speaking island. Although he had an entourage of over twenty staff, all of whom were French-speaking, he was sick of their banal conversation. Having a new face and voice had been a delight. Bonaparte looked almost happy when they departed. He had even seen them to the carriage and stood until they were out of sight.

Bill was still in awe that he had spent an entire hour talking to Napoleon Bonaparte. He could hardly wipe the smile from his face. He sat in silence all the way back to town, barely noticing the surroundings change or that as they neared Jamestown, they had stopped at a roadside farm and purchased five bunches of nearly ripe bananas. Bill's feet sat on one colossal bunch, and others were tucked under the seats.

As they entered the town, Bill looked down. From the corner of his eye, he had caught a movement that startled him. He moved like lightning and curled his feet up to his chest, exclaiming, "Cor, look at that!"

Just about to crawl up his booted foot had been an enormous red-headed, skinny brown centipede. It was at least five inches long, and he knew they could bite.

The sergeant knocked it onto the carriage floor and stomped on it. He said, "Nasty blooming things! I'm told they bite both ends, but I'm not letting it live to find out."

Bill sat staring at the remains of the creepy critter. "I'm not helping lift those bunches if they have those evil things in them. I've heard spiders, frogs, and even snakes can live in bunches of bananas."

That comment kept the three talking, ignoring the passing scenery and fixing their eyes on the fruit on the floor.

Once again Bill was hidden until the longboat reached the ship. His absence had not been noticed.

~

The ship stayed in port for nearly a week before it weighed anchor and headed off on its journey. While there, they stocked up on fruit. The trip southward from St Helena was peaceful for some time. The weather remained fine, and the stiff breeze carried them southward.

The fresh fruit that had been brought on board was eked out for as long as possible.

The farm had supplied over one hundred bunches of bananas, which now hung suspended from the rafters on the convict decks. Three bunches at a time were taken up into the warm sun to ripen. Each convict was rationed with half a banana every third day.

They also purchased other fruits plus vegetables and fresh meat on the hoof.

As the convicts were encouraged to eat the fruit as it yellowed, the bananas had all gone by the time they had reached the southern tip of Africa.

Cape Town came in sight, and the convicts were locked up again.

Gone also was the good weather as the chill set in.

~

A week into their journey's next stage, the doctor told the convicts that the barometer was dropping quickly. He neglected to mention what this would mean for them all.

Tom explained, "It's gonna be a bad one, Bill."

They hit the storm a week after leaving Cape Town and struck the worst weather they could imagine.

The wind was bitterly cold, and the occasional splash of the sea was freezing. The convicts were kept below decks, but all the hatch doors were unlocked, just in case.

Bill had wondered, 'in case' of what?

Then, one giant wave hit, and the ship was tipped almost horizontally.

Tom lay on his bunk and hid under his blanket. He cried out in fear, groaning. "Bill, we're gonna die! It's bin nice knowin' ya, mate."

The gun ports along the entire ship's side were forced open on all decks, and the sea water gushed in.

The convicts raced to batten down the ports and hatches again so the ship would not sink.

The slop buckets were overturned, and the bunks were awash with water, vomit, and effluent.

Screams of fear echoed through the darkness below. It was then that Bill realised that the 'in case' was 'in case they sank.'

Wave after wave crashed over the bow and decks. The ship was rocked to the scuppers, and Bill discovered the warning that Tom had given him way back in London was genuine. He now knew fear. They could hear the water pouring off the deck and emptying from the side scuppers above them as the ship righted after each pounding.

More rolling waves followed, and the toughest of the criminals below prayed hard. Many wept in fear and begged for Bill to pray for their survival. As the now airborne ship free-fell off the side of a wave, screams of terror echoed through their deck.

No one below decks knew how the captain stayed at the helm and kept his ship upright.

For two days, he would not relinquish his post. The frigid sea spray froze on his moustache, and icebergs were seen in the distance. As they sailed onward, he was lashed to the wheel's pedestal and kept his gloved grip on the spokes rather than the slippery wheel handles.

The paying passengers and the soldiers in their hammocks were ordered to stay in their cabins or berths. Like the convicts, they had to eat the dry rations provided for such a storm.

The water barrels were secured, and lids were added to prevent spillage. In such weather, fresh food or hot meals would not be served, and lighting a fire in the galley would be far too risky.

Knowing that ferocious weather was brewing, the captain had supplied emergency food and water to all. Everyone on board was given two days of dry rations of ship's biscuits and access to sufficient water. He hoped that would be sufficient but felt this storm may last longer.

Before the worst of the gale hit, they were all allocated oranges from the Cape Town supply, and other raw vegetables were doled out equally. Rations were also left below decks for the convict's consumption. However, the food remained virtually untouched for the next two days.

During the storm, everyone willingly stayed confined to their beds. The seas churned, and the winds howled, each gust more substantial than the last.

Bill thought of Molly and wondered what would happen if he died at sea. At least Aunt Ellen would be with her. He prayed for them both as he buried his head into the padding on his pallet bunk. He groaned and prayed again.

Tom turned to Bill and said, "Laddie, I don't talk much to the big boss in the sky, but I know you do. Can you start talking to that Jesus fellow and ask that He quieten the storm as He did in the Bible story you read?"

Bill had been praying since he heard the first word of an approaching tempest. "Tom, I've been praying nonstop since the blinking storm started." He was so darned afraid that, like any of the convicts, none had moved to use the slop bucket to relieve themselves, as it was just too dangerous.

The stale urine smell emanating from every bunk went unnoticed.

All the sails but one small one were tightly furled. All lamps and flames throughout the ship had also been doused. Every hatch was battened down, and the crew and soldiers took turns manning the bilge pumps, but the water still seeped in. Often, it came through the leaking hatches or gun doors as they burst open.

The darkened decks stank of vomit, excrement, and the reek of the overturned slop buckets. Those on the top bunks moved onto the lower ones or the floor.

One convict had broken his arm as he had been pitched from his berth.

As the storm blew, the stench below deck increased. Even if the storm was not overhead, the ammonia from below decks was enough to turn one's stomach.

The timber ship crashing down each wave caused Bill and most others on board to wonder if it would survive the next gigantic liquid mountain. Everything not bolted down became a missile, and many would need stitches and wound bandaging when the storm abated. For now, none moved.

The sea was angry, and so was the captain, who bellowed at the young cabin boy to get below decks before he was washed overboard.

The lad was agile and normally at the centre of any activity, but today, he was just too small to fight against the storm's ferocity. He scarpered off as he saw a monumental wall of water approaching.

The captain and the first mate were now both at the helm and tied on with thick ropes. Both were fearful the vessel would not survive this gargantuan waterfall of seawater that now overhung them.

The first mate yelled, "God help us!"

The captain's reply, "He's the only one who can," was nearly drowned out.

The enormous wave broke halfway up the main mast.

A wall of seawater washed the pair off their feet. If they had not been tied on, they would have been washed overboard.

Thankfully, that behemoth of a wave was not followed by another similar.

The water filled the decks faster than the crew could pump out the bilges. The six chain pumps were each double-handled, and all had been manned from the start of the storm.

Although relieved of the upper deck duties, the crew was ordered not to leave their post at the pumps, or the ship would be lost. They took turns pumping the hold, which was in great danger of flooding.

Hour after hour, the crew did what they could to weather the storm. All those on duty were tied to their workstations with ropes around their waists, and only those absolutely necessary were on deck.

At tide change, the winds dropped. Although the seas were still building, the captain was exhausted already. He needed sleep as he realised worse was yet to come at the following tide change in six hours, and the crew would need him. The barometer was still dropping.

The captain took a few hours to rest as the storm lulled, knowing his experienced crew could handle the current conditions. He checked and saw that the barometer was dropping quickly, so he knew the storm was becoming more intense. He peeled off his frozen outer clothing, replacing it with dry attire, took to his high-sided berth, and was asleep within moments.

While the captain had slept, dry rations were again doled out, and water replenished.

~

As expected, the storm grew worse than the barometer had predicted. The strong winds turned into a howling gale, and the rolling blue waves became a raging tempest.

The captain rotated the strongest crewmen hourly; they stayed at the wheel in pairs, but he would not relinquish his post. A hurricane-like storm raged around them, and the ship felt like a small bobbing cork thrown around by the tempest-tossed seas.

For most of the first two days of the storm, the captain had remained at the wheel for all but the four hours of sleep he snatched. After he had napped, Captain Grainger stayed at the helm for another twenty hours straight. During the worst of the storm, it had taken two men to hold the ship upright, knowing that if they lost their rudder or the masts, the vessel would probably be lost at sea, as would all on board.

The first mate began to notice the captain's strength sag. He saw his hand slip from the spoke of the wheel.

The captain refused to relinquish his command at the helm; however, others worked hourly shifts to assist him.

At one stage, the storm was so bad that the captain yelled to his first mate, who was currently tied to him, "If we make it through this storm, I'm buying a farm, and it will be well inland." Although Robert Grainger was a mountain of a man, after four days with little sleep, his energy had been sapped. He was utterly drained and exhausted.

In a slight lull in the wind and seas, the second mate finally relieved him of duty and sent him below deck to get what sleep he could. He could barely stand; he handed the wheel over to two others. He pulled off his sealskin gloves, knowing that as his hands warmed, they would hurt badly. He was surprised to find they were not frostbitten and black.

As he walked, he looked down at his severely blistered palms. He had clasped the timber wheel so tightly that he had not even noticed the blisters forming, let alone burst. Now, the seawater stung the raw flesh of his popped wounds. He doused them with some brandy and tapped his barometer. He sighed in relief as the barometer was now rising.

The worst was behind them. He could now sleep.

As he peeled off his cold, sodden clothing and donned dry storm gear, his mind turned to food for himself. As he all but crawled towards the bed, he thought this storm would delay them further. He couldn't remember when he had last eaten proper food, a biscuit here and there, but little else. He had drunk only water, as he was not prepared to risk drinking rum on a day like this. He needed his full faculties with him.

He saw a plate beside his bed, a slice of buttered bread and jam. It was gone in the time it took to pull on dry socks. He read the note beside it, and it was a report that much of the food below had been destroyed or ruined.

Before he slept, he realised that the rations might have to be cut to have enough food to complete the journey. They could have problems if they became becalmed for the remainder of the voyage. He was too tired to think about that now. He had spoken about stocking sufficient supplies to Doctor Smith when in Cape Town, but the required provisions were unavailable. They purchased what they could, and he realised they would have to make do and cut rations.

Four days without cooking for three hundred or more souls would undoubtedly assist in extending the supplies.

With this still running through his mind, as soon as his head hit his pillow, he knew no more. Exhaustion overwhelmed him.

Overhead, the winds howled, but the seas had eased.

He didn't feel the ship crashing down the waves or see the foam cover the deck.

He didn't hear the creaking of the timbers or the tearing of the furled sails from the mast.

He didn't even hear his own snoring as he slept like the living dead. But now, every wave was smaller than the last.

~

The captain slept eight hours straight.

His first mate checked on him several times. On his first visit, he took the empty plate. On his return visits, he saw his captain had hardly moved. The physical exertion had drained him completely.

At the height of the storm, the crew could only withstand a one-hour shift; this man did over ninety hours straight, with only a four-hour break in the middle.

When Captain Grainger finally awoke, he ate another slice of buttered bread and jam that sat on the bench beside his berth and pocketed more ships' biscuits. His pile of wet clothing had gone, and a folded bundle of fresh clothes awaited him.

He noted the seas were much calmer. The vessel's movement had eased dramatically since he had retired to his cabin. After checking his watch, he returned to duty somewhat angry that he had been left to sleep while his crew laboured on.

They had not woken him as they knew they could cope, and he had guided their ship through the worst of the seas.

They all realised that, but for his incredible strength, they would now be swimming in the briny ocean, if not a watery grave.

As he came on deck, he was given a welcome of applause. He silenced his crew with a filthy look.

~

On the fifth day of the storm, the waves were far less angry. They were still immense, but the regular rolling swell was easier to deal with.

The ship managed them better than the crested monsters of the past two days. They no longer were fringed with white foam, and the ship's movement was less tortured. The crashing of the hull had stopped, and though the movement was still uncomfortable, it was nowhere near as dangerous.

Hour by hour, the sea calmed, and the winds eased further. However, everyone remained confined to their bunks or cabins.

The lower decks sloshed with everything from seawater to unmentionable filth. Some of the convicts, now starving, rose to their feet to eat and drink. Many didn't care if they lived or died.

They had survived one of the worst storms recorded, thanks to Captain Grainger's incredible skill and strength.

~

On the sixth day, the crew finally emerged from their quarters to repair the damage. Only then did they realise that the little cabin boy, Peter Prior, and one of the crew, James Allen, were nowhere to be found.

It was three days since either had been seen.

All were horrified at the discovery that the lad and the crewman had been swept overboard, and no one had even noticed.

Mortified, Robert Grainger fell silent. James had always been an able crewman, and he would be missed. The boy, he loved like a son. On his return to England, he would have to tell the boy's mother he was gone, lost overboard in the Indian Ocean during a violent storm. Thankfully, in seas like that, the pair would have drowned quickly. They were now in the Lord's hands.

When Andrew Smith checked below deck, he found one convict had died, and another had a broken arm. Many needed his services, such as cleaning and stitching wounds. Other than that, the convicts seemed to have no significant injuries. The paying passengers were all unscathed, having stayed in their cabins.

Cleaning the prisoners' decks would take time, but that was minor.

The *General Stewart* had survived one of the most horrible storms Robert Grainger had sailed through in his entire career. The Indian Ocean was known to be rough, but never had he met ferocious seas such as these. He had feared for the ship and now realised when he had seen the barometer dropping so quickly that he should have sailed further north rather than the shorter southern route. This southern path was the route the First Fleet had taken, and he now regretted he had decided to follow them. Having read the reports of their torturous journey, he had thought the journals he read were exaggerated. He now knew the doctor's journal on the *Lady Penrhyn* was correct. They were not exaggerated at all; if anything, they underestimated the ferocity of the icy hurricane. The seas in this area should be avoided at all costs.

He looked up at the tattered sail above him and realised that the spars were lined with long icicles; should these snap off, they would easily spear someone. He knew that he would have to order one of his men to shinny up the rigging and remove the bulk of them.

Onward, they sailed toward their destiny, dodging floating sea ice.

A week after the storm hit, the captain, Andrew, and Bill did a service for the dead convict. They also committed James Allen and Peter Prior's bodies to the deep. However, only one sail-draped body lay on the plank. While shrouded in a white sheet, it was sent to 'Neptune's grave,' as the sailors called it, for James and Peter's bodies were already there.

The child had been a happy lad whom everyone had liked.

All the crew felt a great melancholy at the loss of two friends.

The storm had now fully abated, and the seas calmed.

The ship sailed on in mournful silence.

Captain Grainger figured that by his reckoning, they must only be days from sighting the western coast of the great southland. He had brought out his sextant and adjusted his settings so that he could see both the sun and the stars, day and night. He heard that Governor Macquarie was now calling the land Australia, as Matthew Flinders suggested. Whatever it was known as, he would be pleased to land and replenish the water supplies. Drums of the precious liquid had either spilt or ruptured during the storm. Everything in the hold had moved. The rations would have to be cut. He knew they must stop and replace their water supplies.

He had stopped and refilled his water drums on previous journeys by sending his longboats up the Swan River. He had been hoping to avoid doing this, but the storm made it necessary.

Sacrifices now would have to be made by all but the family of paying passengers and crew.

Captain Bernard had already complained to both the doctor and the captain that his soldiers needed full rations. "How are my men supposed to exist on such scant morsels, sir? They need to keep body and soul together."

The doctor and captain decided to show him the food store situation rather than explain their predicament on descending to where the food was held. Many of the barrels of grain, flour, and other foodstuffs were still scattered in the mire that had once been a neatly stored system of barrels.

The kegs of food had lost lids; the paste on the ground was a mixture of salt pork, flour, raw rice, and goodness knows what else. A few dead rats floated in the gooey mess.

Captain Grainger explained, "Sir, due to the storm's violence, I have little choice but to cut rations for all. I will include myself in that. The crew will not have their food reduced, as I need all of them able-bodied and not lightheaded when they need to climb the rigging. Your soldiers sit guarding locked-up prisoners. What do the convicts eat if I give your men full rations?"

Captain Bernard realised there was insufficient food available for them and the crew. He acknowledged that they needed sustenance more than the inactive soldiers. The soldier was not happy with the explanations of scant stores and water-damaged food but had little recourse, as he had seen for himself the mess below. The dead rats were enough to turn his stomach.

For most of the crossing, the soldiers of the 84th detachment were given the same rations as the convicts. It had been, on the whole, good quality and decent-sized servings. Captain Bernard acknowledged that most of his soldiers were sitting lolling as they guarded their charges, but he was not happy.

As agreed, the crew were kept on full rations to man the ship. Rather than make more complaints, he set the soldiers not on duty to clean up the storerooms, with instructions to save as much food as possible. Some of the chunks of salted meat could have the flour rinsed off and eaten rather than thrown overboard. Flour was also washed from pieces of butter; as they were still edible, much of it could be resealed in empty drums. Rice, too, was rinsed and dried. Even a day or two stretching of the food would make a big difference, but the rescued food needed to be swiftly consumed as they did not have enough fresh water and salt to make new brine. Much of the saved stores was cooked and served as a feast for all on board.

After a week with hardly anything to eat, all relished the filling meal.

The sails filled with a quickening breeze, and the ship sailed onwards.

Chapter 12 Miss Molly

$\mathcal{M}$olly sat at the small table in her mother's room. The tray placed before her would have been an entire day's rations on board, and even then, it would have been cooked as gruel, stew, or slop.

This morning, the eggs were perfect. They were set in the middle but not hard all the way through. The bacon was crisp and crunchy, just as she liked it. The toast was thin and had a tiny dish of curled butter and another full of tangy lemon marmalade to eat with it. There was no hot chocolate, but the pot of black bohea tea was nectar to a girl who had lived for nine months on the stale water of the ship's stores and dry biscuits.

Ellen expected her daughter to be much changed, but for Molly, the time on board and her arrival in the convict town was like she was emerging from a protected cocoon.

Molly had a new poise and confidence that she wore well. No longer was she the meek and timid girl from London but a convict who had to survive a horrific trip in the company of hardened criminals. She had delivered babies and seen death; she had braved storms, starvation, and trauma. She had witnessed men's abuse of other women and learned how to empathise with the victims.

Ellen knew she would have to get to know the new girl sitting before her.

Molly ate what she could but knew better than to overeat after an extended time of scant rations. Food would not be in short supply from now on, so there was no need to hoard it. Hoarding was something she had learnt others did. Molly had lived on the hardtack biscuits and nearly always had one in her pocket. The stories from her cell mates had hardened and educated her about a different side of life. She may have taught them to read and write, but they taught her of poverty, injustice, and hunger, such as she could not imagine. She realised now that her mother and Bill had protected her from the seamier side of life. Molly had never seen the starving masses in London. She knew poverty existed, but her mother had never permitted her to see such horrors for herself. Her new friends included some of those underprivileged hoards. With the means and compensation now available, she was determined to help as many as possible. Her own experience had shown her how quickly the attention of an unscrupulous male could get her arrested and imprisoned. She wondered what Bert was doing now. Molly knew he was to be sent to Canada, but nothing more than that. She now put the man out of her mind. She was here, and she would start a new life with Bill. With the money they now had access to, they would not remain servants, and this fact alone was almost overwhelming. Her mother had told her about their heritage soon after the passing of Jerome Miller. She had yet to discuss it in depth with Bill, as she had only briefly mentioned the topic when she visited him in gaol. He said he didn't care what her background was. He loved her anyway. She smiled, wondering what he would say when they finally spoke.

Ellen had yet to tell Molly much about the house she had rented. The current tenants were moving out that week, and they would move in as soon as she found a maid. "Molly dearest, do you, by any chance, know of any girls on board who we could employ as personal maids?"

Molly's eyes lit up. "I do, Mother. Rebecca and Sophie would be perfect. They became my particular friends, and we could train them as we've done with so many others in London."

Ellen would have said more, but the hotel maid arrived to clear up. She waited until the breakfast had been removed and requested hot water for a bath to be brought.

Molly looked forward to a bath and stripped off as soon as the water arrived.

As Ellen washed her hair, both ladies cringed when they saw the colour of the water.

Molly said, "Oh, Mother, do you realise it's nine months since I had a proper bath and washed my hair with soap? On board, they set up half barrels and a screen; we had saltwater washes, but we felt dirtier than before we bathed."

She slid under the warm, soapy water and relished the pandering like a child. The dirty, bedraggled girl who had arrived hidden under an all-encompassing cloak was once again clean.

Ellen had reserved a pitcher of warm water to rinse Molly's hair. She made Molly stand in the hip bath, poured it over her head, and rinsed off the soap. Ellen noticed that Molly's previous curves were gone. She was skin and bone.

Molly had told her mother they had no privacy on board and soon learnt that her body was the same as most others.

With the pitcher empty, Molly took the towel her mother handed her and all but squealed with delight. "Oh, Mother, I'm clean. Squeaky clean from top to bottom." Her bony frame had no fat left on it. She was as gaunt as a skeleton.

Ellen wiped a tear away lest her daughter see she was upset.

Molly was allocated an adjoining room with interconnecting doors, so they did not need to go out into the public corridor. They set about preparing for an excursion. By mid-morning, two well-dressed ladies descended the broad staircase at the hotel.

Mr Stewart immediately came to their assistance. "How may I help, ladies?" He knew Molly's status as Ellen requested his assistance, ushering her inside.

Ellen smiled at the kindly gentleman. "Would you be so kind as to call us a hackney, sir? I would like to show my daughter around town."

Knowing they had yet to see Major Downes, the manager already had the same cabbie waiting for her. "Ceddie Dickerson will be at your disposal all day, madam. He knows your first destination and is prepared to wait for your orders for the remainder of the day. I have also ordered a picnic hamper, and it is waiting in the carriage, ma'am."

Mr Stewart gave a slight bow as he finished speaking. He had no idea about this woman's status, but she had money, which meant she was equal to quality here. He knew that some gentry had come as convicts. There were rumours of one even living in the colony under an assumed name, and he discovered that the man had a title. He only discovered this as two lawyers had stayed at the hotel recently, and although close-lipped, he had worked out why they had come and to whom they had spoken. Ceddie was a mine of information for that sort of news. Most people did not realise that the drivers easily overheard conversations in a cab. People became relatively free with their talk once the door closed, and Ceddie was paid well to pass on such vital details to Frederick Stewart. It was how he discovered they had a viscount in the community, which could one day prove useful.

Ellen and Molly were handed into the awaiting coach and noticed a large picnic hamper under the other seat. Ellen had not requested the food, but she thought after completing the official paperwork, they might use the day to sightsee around the entire area.

Ceddie again pulled up before the enormous gates, and a soldier was ready for them.

The red-coated man handed them down and escorted them to the major's office.

Major Humphrey Downes had the kettle on the hob stove, and the bakery had made treacle and oat biscuits for morning tea. Everything was ready for the guests' arrival. None of the other convicts from the *Maria* would be unloaded until the following day, so he was relatively free.

The major greeted Ellen and nodded to Molly. "Welcome, Mrs Ross, Miss Ross, please enter. I have asked another officer to sit in on our meeting. I hope you do not mind. He's been overseeing my tuition." The young major grinned, introduced Major Thomas Turner to them, and then closed the office door to keep the room warm.

Ellen had explained to Molly what they were required to do regarding her assignment. The paperwork needed to be recorded, and the two accompanying letters had to be collected. Molly was directed to fill out various documents and was handed her assignment paperwork. "Miss, by rights, you should serve another nine months before receiving a 'Ticket of Leave,' however, I have had a long chat with my learnéd colleague here, and as you will be allocated to your mother, we know that this is much the same as a wife being assigned to her husband. You are not to leave her employment and must live with her until your time has expired unless you receive permission or direction from my office or the governor. You must front up to convict musters, and you are required to attend church regularly. Other than that, madam, she is now fully in your care." He turned to Ellen. "She will not be required to wear government-issue clothing. But consequently, being off stores, she will no longer be eligible for assistance from the government supplies, including forfeiting her food ration."

Ellen smiled knowingly at the major behind the desk.

The other soldier stood rather awkwardly off to the side. She wondered if he had told this man about the letters, so she was unsure of what to say.

Major Downes saw her apprehension and was aware of her glances towards Tom. "Madam, Major Tom has been apprised of the situation and read the letters. I will soon go on leave and have brought him up to date with your situation. Should William Miller arrive during my absence, do not hesitate to seek assistance from Major Tom."

Molly sat silently through this interview but tapped her mother's foot. "The girls, Mama," she whispered.

Ellen gave a nod to acknowledge her reminder. "Sir, there is one more thing, well, two actually, that you may be able to assist. We require maids, and I believe you need to place convict girls. My daughter informs me of two suitable lasses on the *Maria;* we could train them as maids. The names are Rebecca and Sophie."

Molly filled in their details, giving the soldier the names and descriptions of the two girls.

Knowing they were prepared to train young girls, Major Downes wondered if they would take on more. "Madam, I try to place the younger ones charged with petty crimes like food theft and similar offences in private houses rather than send them to the Female Factory at Parramatta. I require such situations, and I was wondering if you would be interested in offering placement to more than just two?" He sat watching her reaction. He was hopeful, knowing that Molly had been teaching with a group of better-behaved women.

Ellen saw Molly reply with a nod to her enquiring look.

Molly replied on behalf of her mother, "Yes sir, I know two more girls, but I did not dare hope to rescue all four. They are Esther and Ruth. Both are Jewish girls and are severely oppressed by the other women. They are also young and poverty-stricken. They turned to theft after their family died. They both refused to go on the streets to sell their bodies. Sir, I would dearly love to have them with us." Molly turned to her mother. "Mama, would you mind?"

Ellen said, "No, dear, if they are good enough to be your friends, they are good enough for me. Which is all the recommendation I need." She was delighted that four girls would now be kept safe from the confines of the female gaol that Major Downes had told her was so horrible.

Before the assignment was finalised, the four new girls needed clothing, and Major Tom offered to take them to Government Stores in town to be fitted out before being brought to the new house on Friday.

With their paperwork already completed, Humphrey Downes was happy that five fewer girls would need to be processed tomorrow. Having been on board the *Maria* the day before, he knew not all would be disembarked; some sick ones would be kept another week before release. Another sixty of the younger healthy ones were to be forwarded to Hobart when a suitable ship was found. He knew he had no choice but to send all the mothers with children to the Parramatta female gaol. He knew this was already overcrowded but needed somewhere to send them. He wished the new prison was finished, but even so, it would only house three hundred. He sighed, knowing that more and more of these vessels would be arriving unannounced. The men were not as problematic as they could be sent to chain gangs or sent out as workers, not so the women. The more he could assign privately, the happier he was. "Should you change your mind and feel you could take more of the young ones, do not hesitate to let me know." He said little as he wrote. The ladies on the other side of the desk waited patiently for the documentation to be completed.

The most important one would be Molly's Ticket of Leave. The major already had this signed by the governor the day before. He had filled it in when he had met with the governor on board the *Maria*.

Within fifteen minutes, the major had processed the paperwork for all four new girls, and they only had to sign their names where required.

The Ross's were now free to view the town; however, the new girls would stay on board until the house was ready for occupation.

~

By Wednesday the following week, Ellen had taken possession of the keys and moved into the Hyde Park house.

As good as his word, some two hours after their arrival, Major Downes sent Ceddie to deliver the four girls. He knocked at the door of the house, "Mrs Ross, Major Downes has sent me with a delightful delivery for you." He stood aside, and the four girls were ushered indoors to their new home.

Molly had intentionally stayed out of sight as she knew the girls would squeal with delight.

The four arrivals were silent, wondering why they had been singled out by name. Molly waited until Ceddie had driven off before showing herself to her friends. She opened the door a smidgeon and saw the backs of all four. She quietly entered and stood behind them.

Ellen introduced herself and told them that they had been chosen by name. "Girls, your benefactress is standing behind you."

With that, the four spun around and saw a very differently garbed Molly beaming at them. "I hope you all wish to learn to be maids, as you have been assigned to us to learn a new job." The five quickly gathered into a group hug. Molly was the first to pull back. She screwed up her nose at their body odour. "The first thing that will happen is you will all be given a long bath and wash your hair. New clothing awaits you all in the washroom, and more things are in your bedrooms. You will share two to a room, so we hope you don't mind."

All four girls now frowned, flicking their gaze from Ellen to Molly.

Ellen chuckled at their apparent confusion. "Darling Molly, you forgot to mention that I am your mother." She turned to the girls. "Molly's story is complicated. Suffice it to say her accuser's father wrote a letter of recommendation for her, and she has been assigned to my care. We need personal maids, and she chose you four. We will fill you in on the details later, but let's get you washed for now. Your lessons will start by learning how to dress each other's hair properly when washed and dried."

The girls didn't know whether they should laugh or cry. In the end, they all chose the former.

Over the next hour, much laughter emanated from the luxurious bathing room near the back of the house. No water was required to be carted up the stairs as there was a big bath in a lockable room just off the kitchen. Ellen had converted one of the small servant's rooms into a bathroom. She knew how hard it was keeping water hot and carting it upstairs. She had purchased two hip baths and a dividing screen so two could bathe simultaneously.

Chapter 13 Bill

*A*s Molly settled into the new house with her mother and four friends, Bill and the *General Stewart* were becalmed off Australia's West coast.

It had been less than a month since the violent storm nearly sunk them, and they were now getting very low on many stores. They were close to a desperate need for water.

For five days, the ship sat almost still in the glassy sea.

Dolphins frolicked in the ship's shadow, but there was little movement other than them. Someone jokingly asked if they could harness a few and get them pulling the vessel along.

The captain was now checking the sextant daily; it showed they were drifting slightly northwest.

They were going backwards!

The captain ordered that every sail be hoisted to catch every breath of wind, and everyone joined Andrew Smith and Bill in the Sunday service to pray for wind.

The reading for the day was from Isaiah chapter 1, verses 17 to 20. *"Learn to do right; seek justice. Defend the oppressed. Take up the cause of the fatherless; plead the case of the widow. Come now, let us settle the matter, says the Lord. Though your sins are like scarlet, they shall be as white as snow; though they are red as crimson, they shall be like wool. If you are willing and obedient, you will eat the good things of the land, but if you resist and rebel, you will be devoured by the sword. For the mouth of the Lord has spoken."*

For some reason, the words from this reading hit Bill like a cricket ball had bowled him over. Two verses had hit him in particular. The first was, *'Learn to do right; seek justice. Defend the oppressed. Take up the cause of the fatherless; plead the case of the widow.'* And the second followed on but meant so much to him. '*Though your sins are like scarlet, they shall be as white as snow; though they are red as crimson, they shall be like wool. If you are willing and obedient, you will eat the good things of the land;*' Bill lifted his eyes and met Tom's as he finished the reading. Tom was twice his age, and he had not a soul to care for him in the entire world. Not one living person cared if he lived or died. Bill was also an orphan, but at least he had Ellen and Molly. He was surrounded by convicts with sins redder than scarlet.

In the stillness of the seas, he tried listening to Andrew's words drone on about goodness knows what. He knew he should be listening to the doctor's sermon, but God's words, not Andrew's, were what had hit him. He knew now what he had to do when he reached the colony. It was not to teach but to provide food and shelter to the poor and hungry. To reach out to the Tom's of the new place and give them love and sustenance. He realised Andrew had finished speaking, and he had to stand to read the Psalm.

The reading was from Psalm 37. Verse 7 struck him as appropriate for what they were experiencing: "*Be still before the Lord and wait patiently for him; fret not yourself over the one who prospers in his way, over the man who carries out evil devices!*"

Considering a shipload of convicts was becalmed off the coast of Australia, and they were running low on supplies, being still was not a problem, but that is not what the words meant. Bill realised he had been somewhat stressed over his life's direction once he reached Sydney. Now he knew God already had it organised. He had to hand his life to God anew. He finished reading the words from the Bible and sat down. He was thinking deeply about what was before them. He felt God had planned a new path for him to take. He had said to Andrew when he left St. Helena that if that day was the only time he used his language skills, his study had been worth it. He was not wedded to learning or teaching; it was that it came so easily for him that he breezed through all his classes. If God were calling him from that path, he would follow that new direction. His studies were now in the past. He had never felt called to teach, and all doors in that avenue had slammed shut. He had been stuck being a butler, inheriting the role far too early, and may have stayed there stagnating, but for Bert.

He thought back to the many nights he had had to go to White's Club or some other place of ill repute in London and bring Bert and Errol home, both so drunk they were almost insensible. It was not a life that attracted him. No, he wanted to help needy people, not the spoilt, rich brats he had been brought up with. Bill felt at peace for the first time in a very long time, and it had nothing to do with being becalmed.

~

Few had made a journey such as this, so they did not realise that a spell of being totally becalmed in this area was unusual.

Andrew Smith watched the joy on the children's faces as they were permitted to play outdoors. The Pantons' four children enjoyed the deck's stillness and ran gleefully around chasing each other. They were the only ones who were seemingly oblivious to the situation. When chatting with her mother, the little Panton girl said, "Mama, why is everyone so sad?"

Mrs Panton replied, "Darling, we're running out of water."

The little girl gazed at her mother's face trustingly. "Then we'd better pray for rain, Mummy. We should put the drums out and prepare the sails to catch the rainwater. If we have water, then it will stop everyone worrying."

Overhearing her words, Andrew was brought up short. The faith of the small child had shown up the so-called learnéd beliefs of all the adults. Admittedly, many of the convicts and soldiers attended the services he ran daily, but they came out of necessity and boredom. He wondered how many actually had any depth to their faith. He knew Bill did, and he could see Tom's growing. He looked over to the crew and could hand-pick which ones showed their Christian beliefs. Thankfully, none displayed the false religious fervour that he detested.

Leaving the child under her mother's watchful eye, he sought out Robert Grainger. He said, "That little girl has more faith in the tips of her fingers than we all do, Robert. She hit the nail on the head; we have food. We only need water. She suggested we prepare the water drums, set up rain sails, and fill the barrels that way."

Robert looked at Andrew as though he was crazy. Then he realised the wisdom of his suggestion. His own faith had been severely tested in the storm. He said, "Damn it, if nothing else, it will keep the crew busy. They have already given all the convicts haircuts and are bored stiff. Well, this will give them something to do. If we have water, then we can cope. Rations will be stretched, but we will manage. Pray for some fish while you're at it, Andrew."

Robert ordered that the crew rig up some torn sails to catch the rain in the water barrels. As the crew was so bored, having scrubbed and repaired everything, they decided to get to the job on the double. At least it was an activity that was different. However, there was not a cloud in the sky, not even a tiny wisp of white fluff.

Night watch took over. The stars shone overhead, and the crisp evening showed the stars of the southern sky. Occasionally, there was a shooting star seen flitting across the heavens. However, the night watch noticed that the moon had vanished by midnight.

An oppressive eeriness had settled upon the becalmed ship. The vessel still needed hands-on duty even on a still night, not that they were going anywhere, but to be ready if required for anything, even if a set line caught a fish.

At two in the morning, the first raindrops started softly falling on the prepared water-gathering sails. None yet flowed into the drums, but soon, the occasional drops turned to a regular pattern. Then, the drumming of the heavy scud overhead was almost deafening. Even in the lamplight, no one could see further than a foot in front of them. It was like a cloud had opened directly above them. The rain continued to fall.

The welcome sounds awoke Robert Grainger, and he went to make sure the drums were positioned correctly. They were, and he was joined by Andrew, who stood at the door to watch the downpour. Soon, the noise was so loud that even Captain Bernard was roused from his dreams of rain to find it belting down. He donned his oilskin coat over his night attire and joined Andrew at the hatch door to watch the heaven-sent blessing fall from above.

Andrew almost laughed at the stiff-upper-lipped captain of the guard's sleeping attire. He wore an over-frilled nightshirt with a long-tasselled sleeping cap. His attire would not have been out of place in a fancy London home, but it looked odd in the middle of the Indian Ocean on a convict ship.

The torn sails were now funnelling the life-giving water into the many empty barrels on deck. The crew brought every empty drum, keg or bath on deck; all receptacles filled quickly. Every single crewman was now dancing a jig, and their deep belly laughs made Andrew chuckle.

Robert took over the watch; he couldn't sleep anyway, as the noise was now almost deafening. A noisy storm would have been expected to accompany that quantity of rain, but there was no lightning, thunder, or wind. Just rain; lovely, heavy, heavenly, drenching rain. It seemingly had come from nowhere.

By dawn, the sun shone brightly again, and there was not a cloud in the sky. The water barrels were all full, and the emergency was over. The mood shifted from melancholy resignation to chuckling jovially. Laughter was once again heard, and even some of the crew whistled as they cheerfully worked at their chores.

One fish was caught on the set line, and someone suggested they throw more fishing lines overboard. Soon, giant tuna were being hauled on deck. Hooking them was the easy bit. Getting the oversized fish aboard was almost beyond them. Robert ended up launching two long boats and bringing the big fish into them. They landed eight enormous southern bluefin tuna before they went off the bite. The smallest was thirty-nine inches; the largest was just shy of the two-yard mark. They estimated it weighed nearly four hundred pounds. Every person on board ate two huge fish meals from that one beast. The skeleton of it made a delicious fish soup. Some of the crew salted strips of the flesh and more meat was put in brine and would be consumed as quickly as possible.

The cook even made salted pickles with brined vegetables and dried tomatoes. None was wasted.

By the time the fish had been preserved, a light breeze was moving them eastward, raising morale once again. They would not need to stop at the Swan River, as all the water barrels were now replenished. The ship continued under full sail and headed southeast along the now towering cliffs of the Great Australian Bight.

~

A week or so later, on Sunday, Andrew and Bill stood on deck waiting for the masses to gather for the regular service. Andrew asked Bill, "Have you ever heard of a story written by Jonathan Swift called 'Gulliver's Travels'?"

Bill's eyes lit up. "Absolutely, sir, it was one of my favourite stories as a lad." He wondered why he would ask about that particular story. Admittedly, tiny figures were visible on the tops of the towering cliffs. He turned to his companion, puzzled.

Andrew saw he was intrigued by his question. "Swift was an Englishman, but he had friends who were Dutch sailors, and their ships sailed these seas. On their return, his friends told him of the land of giants and tiny people, and he penned the story. It, of course, also has political overtones, but that is neither here nor there, as it's a great story. It was one of my favourites, too. As they say, the rest is history. To my knowledge, he never came here, but the story describes the land well, doesn't it?"

Tom and many other convicts joined Bill. They took their seat on the deck, and the service began.

Bill could not tear his eyes from the towering cliffs they were passing. He knew that it was about one hundred years ago that Swift had written his story. His father had read it to him as a little boy. Now, he was seeing for himself the inspiration of the tiny people. He wondered what the indigenous people thought about the invaders. He imagined that they didn't want the white people to come. Andrew had told him they were usually near naked, and their clothing was animal skin, if they wore any at all. He had referred to them as savages, but Bill wondered; or were they just different? They had lived in this dry land for hundreds, if not thousands of years, and had left it untouched if what he read about the place was to be believed. Sir Robert had given him many books about his country of destination. He read every report and book he could get his hands on. Some of the books Sir Percival had given him were what others would have termed boring. To Bill, they were like windows into his new world. Included were some copies of some of the First Fleet journals. He had Governor Hunter's adventurous journeys in a copy of his diary, plus the two publications he had printed after serving as the second governor. He also had Sir Joseph Banks' tomes as he had published a few books.

As the service was underway, the call of 'tacking' was heard, and soon Bill had the cliffs blocked from his view. He sat enjoying the warmth of the sunshine. Here, the wind was cold and almost cut through him, but out of the wind, the sun was warm. It was late November, and the frosts would have started at home in London. Andrew had said they should be in Sydney in about six weeks.

That comment got him thinking, as in six short weeks, his new life would start. Hopefully, Molly and Aunt Ellen would be waiting for him. Hopefully, the letters he carried would be unnecessary as the word that his conviction would end as soon as he landed would have been recorded. Hopefully, he would quickly find a new niche in life, and hopefully, he would be able to help people like Tom. The Bible passage said the widows and orphans. Well, children of all ages could be orphans; he was one himself, and so was Tom.

It had never struck him until that moment that he was now an orphan. Molly's mother and Molly had been part of his life, and they were like family. Aunt Ellen had been a surrogate mother for him most of his life. Soon, she would be just that as his mother-in-law unless Molly had changed her mind. They were adopted family just like God had adopted him, grafted into God's eternal family. Again, his father and Aunt Ellen were the ones who taught him about God. It's what made him different from the other two boys. Sir Percival always put business first, rarely utilising his yearly subscription for his pew in church. He joked once he called church C and E, Christmas and Easter, not Church of England. Bill hated his time in prison as the services there were not very church-like. He missed having Holy Communion and hearing God's word explained each week. He missed the friends he had made there and the outings they would go on after church. On one of those jaunts, his feelings for Molly surfaced. She had been skipping along with all the other young girls. Molly was only fifteen, and one of her friends was engaged. Bill had his nose in a study book, and they had not known he could hear them, but they talked about boys they liked. All the girls giggled and said who their crush was. Molly had remained silent but lifted her eyes to Bill. He met her gaze, and they shared a shy smile. Bill found his heart racing twenty to the dozen. He looked down at the book on his lap. Did she like him that way? Was he her crush? It was as though he had been hit with a battering ram. She liked him, he knew that, but as more than a sister figure. If she returned his affection... his eyes no longer absorbed the words from the book in his lap. His mind was now thinking of a long life with Molly. Soon after, she had given him that first memorable kiss on his cheek. It had been a mere peck, but he felt like they burned a lasting impression from her lips. He remembered the feeling now and touched where she had kissed him. Now, when he should have been listening to God's word, he was distracted by thoughts of her; he shook his head to make the memories move away.

Andrew saw the softening smile on Bill's lips and the gentle touch of his fingers on his cheek. Something or some memory of someone had made him happy. In the months on board, Andrew grew to like Bill more than he had thought possible. Typically, convicts were similar; few were not vagabonds and useless ruffians who took everything they could. Bill was not like that; his difference stood out, and even Robert also admired how the lad did what was asked without fuss. If the moods on the ship were getting irritated, it was often Bill who calmed things down. He would bring out one of his tomes and read the crowd a story about one of the heroes of old. Hercules was a favourite, but the story of David and Goliath was often called upon. However, the passion for these Greek and Roman stories seemed to have left him. Andrew often found him with his nose in the Bible's Book of Isaiah. It was as though he was searching for something lost. He was determined to pull him aside and have a chat. Finally, the service ended.

~

The ship sailed on, tacking and wearing through the frigid waters of the southern seas. Soon, it would turn northward towards Sydney. It would make a stop in Hobart, but all the convicts on this voyage were destined for Sydney. Bill was now getting nervous about arriving. Questions cascaded through his mind. Sleep was difficult, as the question of life ahead of him was so uncertain. Such uncertainty of his future bombarded his mind. Did Molly still want him? Was she still even alive? Did she have a good trip? What would he do? Where would he live? How would he access the money Sir Percival had given him?

Andrew had coaxed some information about Molly out of him. "I've read your file, boy; I know a young lady was involved. I gather it is her you are thinking about?"

Bill nodded but didn't elaborate. She still had to serve her term; the fewer people who knew about her, the better.

Andrew pumped him. "Did the other man hurt her?" He paused and then gasped. "He didn't molest her, did he?"

Bill frowned at him, then shook his head, looking around to ensure no other ears were nearby. Sighing, he said, "Sir, as a doctor, you are under a patient confidentiality promise?"

Andrew nodded this time. "Yes, it's in the Hippocratic Oath."

Bill dropped his voice and replied, "Then, as my case and hers are interlinked, it's the one story. In answer to your question, no, thankfully, she whacked him with a skillet and smashed his face before he could violate her. His father wrote a letter exonerating her. He blamed his own son for the situation. But, sir, she admitted she hit him; it is why she was transported." Bill rubbed his hands over his face at the memory of what she went through. He continued, "Bert had already managed to get me out of the way by provoking her in my hearing. I decked him one with my fists; hence, I'm here. Only I did it bare-handed, not with a cast iron pan."

Bill explained his upbringing and his previous friendship with the two sons of the household. "I was a butler, doctor. His butler! I knocked out my master's son. He was gentry, but the four of us were brought up together. Both sons in the household are older than us, but I was educated with them, though my learning ability seemed much greater. I insisted that Molly learn to read, too. She did, and we would sit for hours in the library with the archivist and pump him for any knowledge we could. Therefore, Molly can also read Latin." He paused and smiled to himself. "I went to Oxford; you know about that. Anyway, Molly kissed me on the cheek just before I left. She was fifteen, and I was eighteen; knowing I had years of study ahead, we kept our relationship platonic. We each acknowledged our feelings were deeper than just the foster siblings we were brought up to be. When my father died, I took his place. This situation suited the boys as I was now supposed to be subservient to them, whereas before, I was academically superior, yet it was an ambiguous position. I was neither servant nor free until I accepted their job offer. Then Bert started on at Molly. It came to a head one day, and I punched him for his disrespect of her." Bill glanced at the doctor and said, "There endeth the saga, sir."

Andrew smiled. "Not quite. You said she thwacked him with a skillet?"

Bill nodded and related the story of the Christmas Day incident as he had been told it. "Sir, the judge was on our side, hence the light sentences. Bert put on a hell of a performance, which the judge saw straight through. He threatened him with prison if he was caught light-skirting the maids. Bert had been a good friend when I was young. Anyway, his father visited me in prison the day before I was transferred to Portsmouth; he supplied me with my books. He informed me that Bert was arrested in Canada for doing the same thing." Bill released a sigh of resignation and sadness.

Andrew watched Bill over the next week. A few days out of Sydney, the lad had big dark patches under his eyes. The doctor was worried about him. "Bill, you can't get sick now; it's only days until you see her again."

Bill had finally admitted he wasn't feeling too well. "I can't sleep, sir; I haven't for days." The doctor checked him for temperature, rash, or itch but found nothing.

Andrew asked, "Have you prayed about it, Bill? It must have been the worry eating at you."

Aghast at his lack of faith, Bill shook his head mournfully. "I don't know what to ask God for, sir. I'm scared. I've only ever been a student or a butler. God is calling me away from both, and I am unsure what or how to step forward into the future."

Andrew placed a caring hand on his shoulder. "Trust Him, lad, and you won't go wrong. Just bide in His time. You can do little else while on board this convict ship anyway. Worry will change nothing and only make you ill."

Bill nodded.

Chapter 14 What a Welcome

Sydney Heads was an amazing sight. Most better-behaved convicts
were permitted on deck until they turned into the harbour. The majestic
vision of the parting of the triple headlands was breathtaking. The towering
cliffs parted into three separate headlands as the ship drew close. Once the
bay to the south was seen, the bulk of the prisoners were sent below decks.

Andrew knew that it would still be a week before they landed, as they
still needed health checks; but Bill was now free, or would be as soon as he
landed. Bill had spoken to Captain Bernard and requested that Tom be
assigned to him.

The once terse soldier said, "Out of my hands, laddie; I just had to get
you here. You'll have to see the chappie in charge here. Major Downes has
just been sent here to take over that job. He's new and only arrived a few
ships before us, but he will probably come on board with the governor." The
captain of the guard had come to admire the brilliant young man. His
younger brother had admired Bill at college, but he'd never admitted that to
the convict boy. He, too, had read the documentation that accompanied his
conviction. His paperwork said that his term ended on arrival. Well, they were
here. So he was now free. With his sentence unofficially ended, Bill was
permitted to remain on deck as they glided almost silently towards their
designated anchorage.

With a single square sail now hoisted, the way forward was slowed.
The crew were up in the rigging, furling the sails securely as they would not
be needed for some time. The crew did everything to put the vessel in ship
shape for a few months at anchor. Bill had not seen them do this in previous
stops, as he had been locked below deck. He held an ambiguous position of
being free, but not yet. The paperwork was the one technicality that had yet
to be completed.

Andrew pointed out the four coves as they passed: Watsons Bay, Rose

Bay, Double Bay, and Elizabeth Bay.

Andrew explained the upcoming procedure. "Bill, if the chief surgeon gives the all-clear, the passengers will be permitted to disembark. Normally, the major or senior officer in charge will come on board and retrieve the convict's paperwork; sometimes, the governor accompanies him. If they are women, convicts, they are more problematic, as there are few places to send them, but if they are male, like the rebellious group in the lower deck, they will be taken and placed immediately in a chain gang and set to building roads, smashing rocks and the like." Andrew saw Bill's face screw up. "That lot has been nothing but trouble this trip. I feel sorry for them as they have had to be shackled for most of the journey."

Bill asked, "Sir, what about Tom? He's too old for such work, and some others aren't in a good way either." Bill hoped and prayed he could help Tom.

The doctor knew the two were close. "I'll put in a good word for you both. I'll have a word with the Colonial Secretary when he comes aboard and see what I can work out. Hopefully, Tom can be assigned to you as you are now free."

Reporting four deaths on board is never easy; having two of the crew wash overboard was gut-wrenching. That one of those was a cabin boy, and it had taken three days to notice his demise was a cruel blow to them all. The loss of the passenger's son was also sad. Andrew knew he must submit his report and surgeon's journal soon. He knew his paperwork was ready, so he stayed and watched the bays pass by. He loved watching the arrival into this incredible harbour. He turned to the young man and said, "Bill, that next headland is where we're to anchor. See that cut-away rock like a giant seat?"

Bill nodded.

"The governor, Lachlan Macquarie, made it for his wife about eight years ago. I came when they first started it, and it had been nearly finished when I left a few months later. Mrs Macquarie is often seen sitting there watching the passing water traffic. It's a lovely cool spot on a hot day like this." As they watched, a carriage paused on the road around the headland. Andrew said, "Look, there she is now."

A lady was handed down from the carriage. Her staff unloaded a rug and hamper. It looked like she had settled in for a while. They watched her settle herself.

They were to anchor off Mrs Macquarie's chair, where the surgeon from Sydney Cove would first check the health of the passengers, crew, and prisoners. They needed to move as the anchor chain was laid out. The large anchor tied up to the bow was readied to be lowered. The crew called, "Anchors aweigh!" The midshipman cut the restraining rope, and the splash was heard as it dropped.

When the anchor was down, two more ladies arrived on the foreshore.

Andrew heard Bill gasp.

As the anchor dug in, the ship swung around, and they had to move to the other side of the vessel. Bill almost ran across the deck. The ladies were there together. He was sure it was them. He stood on the bottom rung of a rope ladder leading up to the rigging, his heart beating twenty to the dozen again. His fears had been unfounded. They were there.

Andrew grabbed him. "Don't jump in; just wave, Bill. They will wait."

Bill's eyes misted. "Andrew, they are here together, and Molly is safe." Bill had not even realised he had called the doctor by his Christian name. Molly was now out of harm's way and was with Aunt Ellen. He sighed with relief.

Andrew saw him swipe his hand across his glassy eyes. He released the back of his jacket. "Just don't leap in; there are sharks and some reports of crocodiles here too."

Bill nodded absentmindedly as he waved gleefully. Laughingly, he said, "I won't, sir; I'm just so relieved to see her here and with her mama." He jumped from the ladder and now stood waving with both arms. Now I'm happy, sir; I have been most concerned, not knowing if she had arrived safely." His comment didn't stop him from waving. He watched the two ladies standing on the foreshore until a small craft came alongside.

Andrew pointed out that the longboat had reached them. "You have to go below, lad. I'll get things sorted as fast as I can."

Bill blew kisses to the ladies as he knew he had to leave. Until he receives his paperwork, he must conform to the rules. As Bill heard the new voices approaching, he slipped through the open hatch and went below deck for what could be the final time. He carefully and quietly closed the cover after him. He could already feel the heat building; it was only nine in the morning. Once the sun was overhead, he knew the convict decks would be swelteringly hot with the hatches closed. He hoped that the surgeon's visit would be quick.

Molly was jiggling with joy at Bill's arrival. She saw Bill wave back. He was obviously pleased to see them. For him to even still be on deck was wonderful. When he blew his kisses to Molly, he saw that she had caught them and planted them on her lips. It was a fun thing they had done as children, but now it meant so much more. The ladies saw him leave as the long boat came alongside. Ellen knew even though Major Downes said that he would see to his paperwork as a priority, it could take days before Bill was permitted to leave the ship. They returned to the house in Hyde Park after unexpectedly seeing him and knowing he was safe.

Once Molly arrived home, she was almost unable to sit still. She was up and down checking and rechecking the windows, just in case he came early. She had already checked and rechecked his room. It was aired and ready. There were new muslin curtains on the windows. His room, with a substantial double-width, feather mattress, looked directly over the lovely parkland at the back of the residence. She had swapped around the furnishings as it had previously been used as a lady's room. Now, with the blue velvet side curtains and less feminine furniture, she was sure he would like it. Hopefully, soon, it would be their bedroom. She was still slightly nervous that he no longer wished to marry her. She knew why he had refused to propose in England, as he had wanted her to have a life without him. Hence, she bit her lip anxiously.

Ellen watched Molly's antics for a couple of hours, and by noon, she suggested they go back to the foreshore to view the ship. Bill may have been permitted back up on deck.

As they were about to leave, there was a knock at the door. Bill, Major Humphrey Downes, Doctor Andrew Smith and Tom Yates stood at the door. Ellen was already downstairs and invited the men in.

Molly was on the landing; she froze when she saw who it was.

Bill needed no invitation; he gave Ellen a cursory kiss on her cheek and walked straight past her. A whirlwind of ruffles and flounces flew down the remaining stairs, and Molly was gathered into Bill's arms. He didn't kiss her but held her close and whispered against her neck, "I wondered if you were safe; I wondered if you still wanted me." He pulled back in her grasp to gaze at her adorable face. It was so thin, and her cheeks were almost hollow, but she was smiling and happy.

Molly grinned. "I do, so very much." She slid her arms around his neck and drew his head down for a long-awaited kiss.

The four adults and the stunned maids stood watching the passionate display.

Tom smirked. "I think she likes him, Missus."

The two men had not yet been introduced to Ellen, but she chuckled at the comment. "I think you may be right, sir," Ellen said with a big smile.

Molly pulled away slightly but was still held lovingly. "So very much, Bill! I've been worried sick about your arrival."

Major Downes cleared his throat. He said, "Young man, we do realise that this is a reunion of the hearts, but mayhap you should introduce everyone first."

Suddenly aware that others were watching them, and they were not even engaged yet, Bill dropped his arms from around Molly. He had intended to ask her to marry him before kissing her, but she had thought differently. She hooked her hands onto his elbow as he said, "Sorry, sir, of course, sir."

Bill made the appropriate introductions. Andrew bowed over the ladies' hands. With Bill's assistance, Tom had scrubbed up as much as possible. Not to be outdone, Tom mimicked the doctor's behaviour but overdid the bow and held Ellen's hand a shade too long. He also actually kissed her hand rather than just making the action to do so. Bill laughed good-heartedly. "Oh, lay off Tom. Aunt Ellen, the good major has permitted Tom to be assigned to me as I'm now free. Do you mind?"

Ellen laughed. "No, of course not, Bill; wait until you see who Molly has brought. It will be a wonderful New Year for us all. Together again after so long apart. Gentlemen, please come into the parlour. We have stood in the hallway long enough." Ellen led the way into the sitting room, and two maids, Esther and Ruth, brought in the tea tray.

As they placed down the tray, Ellen introduced them. "Bill, these are two of Molly's friends from the *Maria,* and there are two more around somewhere. We are training the girls to be good staff. Molly taught them to read and write, so their lives will vastly differ from what they had at home."

The sisters curtsied and waited until they were dismissed before leaving. They were learning their new roles and loving their new life.

Having been a housekeeper in a London establishment, Ellen was used to training staff and was an excellent teacher. When she arrived, the staff members who had come with the house found she knew how to run a household efficiently. They realised they had to either shape up or shift out. Two of the older maids resigned, not wishing to work alongside convict staff, and the sisters asked if they could take their places rather than learn to be personal maids. Soon, the household was running smoothly.

Ellen discovered that the lifestyle in the colony was of just two classes. They were the convicts and the free settlers. Even the ex-convicts, known as emancipists, were not accepted by the free settlers. Ellen's first foray into the church had seen the separation of the new classes. She was ushered into the front pews as a free settler, but Molly and the girls were supposed to sit at the back. Ellen didn't like that and sat with Molly in the rear pews. This seating, in itself, caused an uproar; however, she refused to move.

Over the weeks, the congregation became accustomed to the tall, elegant, efficient lady. She had come to this colony to be with her daughter; one look or a raised eyebrow from her and mean comments would cease. She brooked no misbehaviour from her staff and expected regular attendance each Sunday by them all.

Ellen was at St. Phillips on the second Sunday, and the minister introduced her to the Vice-regal couple. She had seen the surprise on the governor's brow and knew he had read the two letters. Rather than ostracise her, they warmly welcomed her into their eclectic circle of friends. After a lengthy discussion, Ellen discovered that one person who fully supported her stand for equality was Lady Elizabeth Macquarie. Ellen knew she had a housekeeper, and he was the governor, but here she had money and wealth, and there seemed to be no class distinction after that. Here, she was known as a wealthy free settler; therefore, she was in all but the top echelon of society. He had yet to learn of Molly's wealth.

~

By the time Bill arrived on New Year's Eve, Ellen had already had three months to get the house in order. She only had that long again until the lease expired, then she had another six-month option if needed. With Bill now here, she, too, wondered what direction their lives would take. If he and Molly were permitted to marry as they wished, he would become head of their household. It irked her a little, but that was the way of things, and she loved him like a son anyway. He would soon discover the strange friendship between the four convict girls and Molly. It seemed Bill had befriended Tom in much the same way. The life ahead of them here in the colony would be interesting.

The Vice Regal couple were officially living at Government House in Parramatta, so they were rarely at church in Sydney. Being New Year, this week was an exception, and they greeted Ellen with a nod and a smile. She bobbed the required curtsy.

With the *General Stewart* arriving, the governor and his lady had come for the weekend festivities. Major Downes had visited the ship with the governor's entourage. Ellen's letters had been enough to tweak their attention. The story of the two young star-crossed lovers arriving as convicts was enough to want to meet them both.

Humphrey Downes had to wait until Bill came for an official interview. He also received other letters from Sir Percival and Sir Robert, explaining the situation, just in case the Ross's and Bill did not hand over their screeds. The major's visit today was not just to deliver Bill but to invite him to meet the governor that afternoon.

The doctor had come along to meet the mysterious Molly Ross that Bill had raved over. At nineteen, she was every bit as beautiful as he said, although gaunt. Like her mother, she was tall, but she had a graceful movement that made her elegant carriage look like she was floating. Her light brown hair was piled high and tied back in a loose *chignon* bun on the top of her head. She had a way of looking at Bill that was enticingly saucy but done with an air of innocence. She had no idea the effect she had on the lad... or did she? She would lower her chin a smidgeon and glance sideways at him. Their eyes would meet, and Bill would drink in her smile, forgetting what he was saying mid-conversation. He watched her for a while, and then Andrew realised she knew and was enjoying every tantalising moment. He laughed to himself; she was a bit of a minx, but he liked what he saw. He realised not many people would ever get the better of Miss Molly Ross. He could see she had learnt a lot on board the *Maria*. However, she seemed none the worse for her journey. He knew that few ships these days were as bad as the *Lady Penrhyn's* journey in 1788, though their voyage had met similar weather.

Many on board that first ship full of female convicts were cruelly treated. Their punishment consisted of thumb screws and iron fetters, and in some cases, they were flogged with a cat of nine tails and their heads shaved.

Things were vastly improved since that trip with Arthur Bowes Smyth in charge. Andrew remembered reading the journal entry, and his words made him join as a Naval Doctor. The diary entry read… *"At about 6 p.m., we had the long wished for the pleasure of seeing the last of them leave the Ship - they were dressed in general very clean…The men convicts got to them very soon after they landed, and it is beyond my abilities to give a just description of the scene of debauchery and riot that ensued during the night."*

That voyage had seen naval medical personnel employed for each convict voyage since the *Lady Penrhyn*, and they had the authority of the navy to overrule the captain if the wellbeing of the convicts was at stake. He owed his current employment to that man. Most of the one hundred women on board the *Lady Penrhyn* had been pack raped as soon as they landed. Some girls were as young as fifteen and, up until then, had probably not been with a man. Andrew was determined to make the journey as humane for the convicts as possible. He knew that the females of the *Lady Penrhyn* had been on board for thirteen months. The six months his convicts had been incarcerated was nothing compared to that.

Thankfully, on this trip, he had only had men. With only a few causing trouble, the rest were free to wander below decks for most of the journey. Andrew knew Doctor Thomas Prosser had been the doctor on the *Maria* this trip. He had already made enquiries and found it to be as peaceful a trip as the *General Stewart* had experienced, although his ship had not met with a violent storm. Andrew knew he would do everything he could to ensure no convicts were treated so inhumanely again. With no convicts to carry home, he would see who remained in the colony and find out when they planned to depart. Major Downes had asked him to accompany them to the afternoon meeting at Hyde Park Barracks. Why? Andrew had no idea, but he wouldn't miss this for quids. The major had left soon after introductions, but Andrew had been enticed to stay for a late luncheon. From what he saw, Miss Molly Ross was everything and more that Bill said. She was a girl who could easily have been the toast of London. Bill's description of her was as a quiet sister-like character. She was far from that. She became the life and soul of the luncheon, keeping them all laughing, and her bubbling joy had been infectious.

At a quarter to two, the group wandered from the house and down the street towards the barracks. Tom had taken up residence in the rooms above the stables and ate his luncheon with his new companions in the kitchen. He would not come to the meeting but rather stay and settle in. He was the oldest of most of the staff, being out-aged only by the butler if that's what one would call him. Josiah Woods was middle-aged with an overgrown girth and had been a footman who, up until he met Bill, was quite pleased with himself and his role. The puffed-up chest decreased somewhat when Tom told him his new boss was a third-generation, trained London butler.

Josiah decided to make the silver spick and span during their absence. He threw himself into doing the job well.

The four walked with the ladies' hands on the gentlemen's arms. The younger couple fell behind somewhat; however, Andrew enjoyed having an elegant lady walking beside him. She was at eye level with him and was a statuesque brunette. Mrs Ellen Ross had taken his breath away. After a stray comment from Bill, discovering that she was nearly the same age as him was a delight. An attractive, lonely widow may be a pleasant way to while away some months in the colony. This particular one seemed to have a lively sense of humour, too.

The four reached Hyde Park Barracks gates just before two o'clock. The sentry was obviously expecting them as he swung the barred grill open for them to enter without even asking. The clang of the gates when they shut behind them made all four jump.

Major Humphrey Downes was standing at his office door, biting his lip and trying hard not to smile at the picture the four made; they were in for a surprise. They looked as though they could have been out for a stroll in London rather than entering a convict compound halfway across the world. Bill had bathed and donned his best London attire.

The day was scorching hot; even under their parasols and hats, the ladies had beads of perspiration trickling down their foreheads. The men in their tailored woollen coats felt like they were melting.

The person who had requested their presence was waiting inside the darkened room. The young major greeted them and ushered them into the cool office.

The building they were now in was constructed of thick sandstone. The walls were nearly two feet thick, and the room inside was quite a pleasant temperature. Sitting on a drink tray on his desk was a pitcher of pink fluid and five glasses. Humphrey poured a cool drink for them all and then handed them around. The apple-flavoured concoction was delicious.

"Oh, I must say, major, this is a bit of all right," Bill said as he drained the contents of his glass.

Major Downes smiled. "It's a local fruit, lad. Lilli Pilli juice with a hint of honey and lemon. Too right, it's good! Sadly, it's seasonal."

Andrew saw who was standing quietly in the corner. The man was trying not to draw attention to himself. However, Andrew drew in a quick breath. He said, "Your Excellency," and bowed low.

Only then did the others see someone else in the room. Up until now, they had all had their backs to him. All bowed in subservience to the esteemed gentleman.

Governor Lachlan Macquarie had his glass in his hand. "This is an informal meeting, so please take a seat. Doctor, I'm not sure your presence here is warranted, but you may stay if you wish."

Andrew wasn't going to miss this for anything, so he replied, "I'll stay, if I may, sir, as I may be of use."

The governor gave a single nod. His Scottish brogue was a delight to the hearers' ears. "You may, but what I'm going to say will not leave this room, understand? There will be no formal record of this meeting, and what I will discuss is merely an idea, not an order or request." His cocked eyebrow elicited nods from everyone.

He continued. "Mr Miller, I received two letters long before your arrival, followed by a visit from Edward Smith Hall from the Benevolent Society here in Sydney. He, by the way, is a friend of Sir Robert Peel. Let me assure you that I already know quite a bit about you and your background." He flicked his eyes to Ellen, "Madam, even before your arrival, Sir Percival Edison-Browne and Sir Robert Peel had forewarned me of this unusual situation. Both willingly admitted to a miscarriage of justice regarding the supposed crimes of the young folk, and it was only for a technicality that you were both convicted. Sir Percival's first letter to me was sent soon after William's arrest. He revealed all about his son's wayward and abhorrent behaviour. In his next screed, he personally vouched for you both but felt that you would both have a better chance of life here than at home, where neither of you would ever be more than mere servants, let alone land owners. I met him some time ago in London, and he visited me here on one of his many trips abroad. I believe you three were employed as a housekeeper, maid and footman in his house?"

Bill shook his head, saying, "No sir, I was his butler." Bill and Molly glanced at each other, then back to the esteemed gentleman, and then he said, "Sir, we both admitted our guilt of assaults."

Lachlan smiled and said, "Exactly, that was the technicality! Had you not, neither of you would have been convicted. However, that is neither here nor there. The butler, eh? That's even better. I have a proposition for you both, and, madam, this will include you, too, if you're willing. Please take a seat while I explain."

Ellen raised one eyebrow in mock concern. She had met him in church often enough to know his tone. He evidently had some scheme afoot for them all but had not mentioned anything to her earlier. "Sir," she replied with an acquiescent nod of her head.

The governor frowned but responded to her nod with his own. "I require a good accommodation inn in Parramatta, one where the better class of patrons are happy to stay. I have needed this for some time but have been unable to find the appropriate person to oversee my project. Government House is not large enough for many guests, and I will not have my visitors stay at the other drinking houses. I have shut down some of the worst, but I need one where dignitaries are content to dwell for a time. As Mr Miller is a trained London butler, and Miss Ross was a maid in the same house, I have a proposition for you. If the two letters are to be believed, there is some possible connection between the two of you. I do not wish to push you into any situation, but as Miss Ross is still a convict, permission to wed must first be granted before such can occur, should this need arise."

Molly had slipped her hand from Bill's arm and now was holding his hand. Bill felt her fingers squeeze his. He looked down at her and saw the glint of mischief in her glance. "I think that's almost an order, Bill," she chuckled softly.

Her musical laugh was a delight to Ellen's ear. Molly had been almost silent for the weeks leading up to Bill's arrival; today had been a whirlwind of emotions for her.

Ignoring the four adults in the room, Bill turned to Molly, dropped to one knee, and proposed in front of everyone. "My darling Mol, no order is required from anyone. You are my heart, my life-long love. Will you marry me, dear heart, and make me the happiest ex-convict in this new colony?"

Molly was now almost giggling with happiness. Bill had just very publicly proposed. "Yes, of course, Bill." She dearly wished to kiss him, but that would not happen here or now. But later…

Governor Macquarie's deep-throated chuckle broke the awkward silence. "Well, I didn't expect such a public declaration, but it will do; pity you are not in Scotland, as that would constitute a marriage. I shall get John Campbell, the Colonial Secretary, to fast-track the permission. He is, by the way, my wife's cousin." He waved his hand in a circular motion. "That's by the by, now, back to what I was saying. Fourteen years ago, a fellow Scotsman died after a long, distinguished naval career. His name was Admiral Adam Duncan from the Battle of Camperdown fame." He saw the blank looks on the ladies' faces, but the major and Bill knew of the man's celebrity. He continued, "In 1797, the English Navy faced the Dutch, and he defeated them soundly. So, I was thinking of naming the new inn 'The Admiral Adam Duncan' or similar. Admiral Nelson was in awe of this man. Does that give you any sense as to his abilities?" He saw the heads nod. They all knew of Admiral Lord Nelson. He continued, "As I said, I do not want this place to be just any inn. I wish to have the best staff employed to run it. Better still, if it is owned by, let us say…" he paused, looking at the newly engaged couple in front of him, "…a qualified London butler and his wife, then I foresee that this proposed establishment will surpass the rooms in the rest of the town if not the colony, other than Government House. What say you?"

Bill knew that God was calling him to do something different other than teaching; however, running a high-class accommodation inn in Parramatta was not an idea he had even contemplated. "Sir, I'm overwhelmed. My education was somewhat narrow, and it did not extend to hotel management, design, or any such idea as this. Don't get me wrong; I know our good Lord had something planned that was not teaching, but this is way out of my field of knowledge."

The governor tipped his head to the side. "So you are not opposed to the idea? Miss Ross, what about you? If you are against my plan, please speak now."

Molly didn't care what she did as long as Bill was with her. She said, "Sir, I did not intentionally hit Bert, but I would have done something to get here to be with Bill. As long as we are together, I don't care. I'll scrub floors, polish pans and cook porridge all day as long as we can be married." She turned to her mother. "Mama, what about you? Will you help us?"

Ellen would have jigged with glee when the governor voiced his idea if she had not already been sitting. It was something along the lines of what she had been thinking with the big house. "Molly, considering the house we have rented, I was already thinking about running some high-class accommodation rooms like a fancy boarding house for long-term occupants. I know the King's Arms in town here is nice, if not lovely, but it's too expensive for longer stays. On our day trip to Parramatta last month, I saw nothing remotely like that in town, so my dearest girl, I'm in! Wild horses won't tear me away from this idea. I love it."

Andrew couldn't keep silent, but his smile vanished at her last words: "Sir and ma'am, you are correct about The King's Arms being too expensive. I am looking for accommodation for a few months myself. If there were something like this, I, for one, would book accommodation until I need to return to England."

The major, who had remained silent until now, said, "Mrs Ross if you wished to start your new business now, I would recommend Doctor Smith as a tenant, as I have known him for a while."

Ellen didn't reply to the major but turned to the doctor and met his steady gaze. He gave her an imperceptible nod. She said, "Governor, it looks like we are starting in a small way now, but do you have any ideas about a building in Parramatta?"

With an invitation for everyone to gather around the desk, the group discussed building a new inn. The governor was now sitting at the major's desk, "Yes, Madam, I have an idea where to build. However, William, I have two options for you. I can build it with a convict building team and install you as manager. The other option is Sir Percival said he had paid you compensation for his son's behaviour. I do not know if you wish to use that money for this project, but if you do, then you would be landowners. I would still use a convict team to build it for you to my specifications."

Standing behind the ladies, Bill said, "Sir, I shall answer that. You are correct that Sir Percival has supplied me with ample funds for such a project. I would be honoured to own the inn. However, I would appreciate it if you could design a plan and arrange a team to build it."

Lachlan relaxed in the chair, nodding. "Good, good. Leave it with me, and I'll send you ideas. Three architects came four years ago: Francis Greenway, Henry Kitchen, and John Watts. The first two came as convicts, the third as a soldier in the 76th regiment. All will do an adequate job for what I have in mind. I think I will get Henry on to this job as he is currently not assigned to government projects. If not, another man in town, Sam Corbett, is doing excellent work. However, he does not actually design the buildings; he only draws what the finished edifice will eventually look like. I shall employ him, too. His son, Danny, is a good builder, but he is situated here in town."

Bill met his gaze. "Sir, as I said, I know nothing about construction; hand me the keys to the finished building, and I shall be happy with whatever you design. We have funds a-plenty between us, and the size of the building will not be a problem. Aunt Ellen is used to running a large London establishment, and Molly has learned much under her tutelage, so a small inn should not be an issue."

Lachlan Macquarie smiled. "I confess I have someone out there I wish you to meet. So, think about coming for a visit sometime after I return to Parramatta. I'll show you all around town and introduce you to some people who you may find useful." Lachlan thought about how to describe his friendship with Perry and Katy White. The Earl of Collingsford refused to use his title. Many years ago, Perry was severely burned, and half his face had melted, yet he braved society and all it entailed to be with Katy. He had arrived on the ship that brought the architects. They had met on the day he arrived and as he had come to Government House in search of his convicted wife. Once reunited, their help had been invaluable in Parramatta, setting up many of the public works he had in the process. It had been his wife, Katy, who had suggested that they needed a better-quality establishment in town. Now that he had found this couple, that project would soon be underway. Lachlan knew what he wanted but wished for the right people to run it. He had hand-picked this family because of their letters of introduction and background.

The group sat tweaking the idea a little, and by the time the four departed from the major's office, the inn concept had been not only born, but the plans were well underway. It would have twenty bedrooms, some of which were for the family. There would be a private family room and a fancy public sitting room that could eventually be a small tap room for customers to quietly and legally drink. The shared dining room would be just off this and suitable for both men and women. The inn was to have a small private stable at the back of the property, but the site he had chosen did not have much room for a carriage house. The public stables would have to accommodate visiting horses and carriages until some other venue could be worked out. Bill knew little about horses, so he was pleased that at least it was not something he would need to learn.

Chapter 15 The Rear Admiral Duncan

$\mathcal{T}$he plans for 'The Rear Admiral Duncan Inn' proceeded with remarkable speed. The word 'Rear' replaced the admiral's name as it sounded better than just the Admiral Duncan Inn, which may have been a greater rank but did not flow. According to what the Governor had told Bill, the man should have been promoted and given a proper rank other than the title of viscount he was awarded. Bill knew all about Admiral Adam Duncan, but he had not told the governor. Since he was little, he and his father had followed all the battles against the French and their allies. The Battle of Cumberland against the Dutch had been a fight of the most excellent tactics by the admiral. Bill knew that Admiral Adam had been awarded the title of viscount after the fabulous victory against the Dutch. He had been elevated to Commander-in-chief two years earlier. The admiral battled not only the Dutch but also a mutiny on the *HMS Venerable*. He had been dealing with that when word came the Dutch fleet had finally put to sea. The strategy he used was unconventional. It was the first time both sides of the ship and all the gun decks had been used in a sea battle. As Duncan had sailed his fleet into the middle of the Dutch, he opened fire from both sides. Having sailed out on a convict ship, sleeping on the gun decks, Bill knew just how confined the space was. The echoing noise of the gun explosions would have been deafening. The darkness would have been alleviated only by the flashes of the guns firing. As the Dutch returned fire, the crew below would not have seen the shots coming. The cacophony of noise would have made the most robust man quake. Bill smiled. No, he would not mind putting their money towards this project.

As they drove around town, Bill looked at the sloping block of land overlooking the Parramatta River. He had first seen the vacant block when they passed it to the official house. Macquarie had another site chosen, but as they were driven through the small town in the unmarked government carriage, Bill had asked to stop at a vacant corner block on the main street. "Sir, may I alight?" Bill stood looking over the grassy embankment that led down to the river. He had not even noticed that the governor now stood beside him.

Lachlan said, "This block is also suitable, William, but it's sloping." The governor was intrigued by the lad's choice of land.

Bill glanced at the man beside him. "Sir, this is perfect. It's in town and not far from Government House. The sloping land will mean that the back verandah can be elevated, and therefore, it should catch the cool river breezes." He stood gazing at the block that would soon be his new home. "A small stable can be built there," he said, pointing to the level area. "The front can be level to the street, and the backyard is big enough for an orchard of sorts plus a cow and chicken coop." He turned to the vice-regal gentleman and said, "Sir, I can visualise what I'd like to see built here. The only difference from your plan is that this is in the middle of town rather than on the outskirts."

"Are you sure you wish to do this, William?" Lachlan Macquarie found it hard to believe that this learnéd young man was prepared to give up his extensive education to run a colonial inn.

"Yes, sir, I will do anything for Molly, and this also means we can take some of the younger girls and train them as maids. I'm sure you can arrange that for us." Bill wondered if he should tell this regal gentleman anything about his faith. He opened his mouth to speak a few times but closed it again.

Lachlan noticed and said, "Spit it out, son. If you are at all uncertain, I could find someone else."

Bill turned to him, surprised at his intuition. "Oh, sir, it's not that at all. May I explain?"

"Of course. You have my full attention, laddie." The governor chuckled. He had learnt that this young man had a deep faith that matched his and his friend Perry's. He also noted that he had not mentioned it.

Bill nodded acknowledgement. "Sir, you know my academic history. I topped almost everything and graduated at the top of every year of study I did. When I finished college, I wondered what door God would open for me. That door was as a butler, sir, something that I had no intention of ever doing. I took my father's position until something else came up. What came up was Bert insulting Molly. Sir, I thumped him for that, and I was sent here. I won't rehash the story because you know everything from the letters. However, on the ship out here, I knew God was calling me from the academic side of my life. Still, I had no idea what His purpose was for me. Then you called us into the major's office. Governor, I am meant to do this. It fits in with what I feel God is calling me to do and preparing us all for, well, this." He waved his hand across the ground in front of them. "Since that first meeting, I am at peace with this decision. I have had a chance to talk to Molly and Aunt Ellen. They both feel that our new role here will be to help train some of the girls who, like Molly, have found circumstances have occurred they had no control over." Bill had been gazing at the view over the sloping block and the Parramatta River. "Sir, I feel this is where we are to build the inn. Right in the middle of town."

Lachlan had barely taken his eyes off the young man. He watched the wave of emotion flash across his face. As Bill spoke his final words, a great tranquillity settled on him. It was as though the stresses of the world had passed by him.

Now that they had chosen the block, Lachlan ordered the carriage to turn and drive further down the street. He pulled up at a lovely two-story home surrounded by a verandah. The building and the man standing outside waiting for him were very welcoming.

The three in the carriage gasped when they saw the man's appearance. His cheek had all but melted. Lachlan had told them about his friend, Perry, but none had realised how horrific and severe the scarring was.

Perry White was expecting them and greeted them with a lop-sided smile.

Both Perry's wife, Katy, and Molly were still convicts. Lachlan had wished these two families to meet for this reason; however, he did not inform either of what that was. He was looking forward to seeing how these two couples got along. If they could work together, then their assistance would be invaluable.

Perry walked to the carriage and handed down the governor, Ellen, Molly and then Bill. The deformed melting of his face would have been horribly painful, but he greeted them all with a crooked smile. Perry and Katy's household had grown substantially since their arrival, as they now had six children. He had arrived with their two daughters, Katy had delivered another son *en route* on a convict ship, and Jem, the eldest boy, had arrived later with his tutor, who had since married their maid and now had their own children. The White's youngest children, twins, were just six months old. Perry bowed and waved them inside. "Welcome to our humble abode."

Lachlan chuckled. Knowing that Perry was an earl and his father, the Duke of Cheatham, lived in one of the largest castles in the British Isles. However, he could not, and would not, share the secret of his real identity. Perry's son Jem had put Lachlan in his place when he described the castle and told the governor that his home was smaller than the gatekeeper's cottage. Regardless, this spacious residence was enough to make Lachlan somewhat jealous. It dwarfed the original section of Government House, and even the two new wings that he had added paled into insignificance to the luxurious rooms of this home. He said, "Now, now, Perry, I know you are proud of your little cottage, but there's no need to rub it in. It's bigger than

Government House was when we arrived."

Perry chortled with laughter. "Not trying to, Lachlan, but I'm just pleased we have a roof over our head and that we are all under one roof rather than three. Also, we now have somewhere to offer your visitors a place to stay. It is far roomier than the cottages in which we first dwelt. After four years here in the colony, we feel settled now." Perry gave directions to his visitors about where to go. "First door on the right, take a seat. We'll be right in." Perry held Lachlan back for a private word.

The three opened the cedar door and entered a spacious, high-ceilinged room furnished in relaxing blue velvets and corduroys. After seating Ellen and Molly, Bill walked to the window that overlooked Church Street. He had not had much chance to see how heavy the passing traffic was and stood watching what came and went. From where he was, he could catch distant glimpses of the river across the verdant field. He wondered how long the block opposite would stay vacant. An assortment of buildings was visible from the window; most were new, and others were in various stages of construction. He had noticed this dwelling as they passed. He also saw the dilapidated courthouse diagonally across the road. Bill presumed this was one of the many projects the governor had earmarked for replacement. He had listed off some twenty buildings already completed or under construction, but from their conversations, he knew that this couple they were about to meet was assisting him with ideas and suggestions.

A lady soon entered, followed by another who looked quite similar. Lachlan and Perry followed in their wake. Perry said, "May I introduce my wife, Catherine, known as Katy, and our cousin, Janey Brien." Janey had brought in the tea tray and then stood to leave. Perry held the door for her, then softly closed it behind her as she left. "Janey is a cousin neither of us knew we had until recently. It's a long story, and I won't go into it, but she is a life convict assigned to me and helps at the gaol, too. Katy has a few years to serve, and her story is an interesting but somewhat convoluted saga. I shall fill you in later."

Lachlan waited until Katy poured the teas, and then he brought up the topic of the new inn. "Katy, when you first arrived, you mentioned the lack of suitable accommodation in town. Young William here came as a convict, but his term expired on landing; Miss Molly is assigned to her mother, but they will fill in the details later if they wish. Suffice it to say that they are both vouched for by Sir Robert Peel himself. Therefore, I have asked them if they would staff the new inn I want to be built here. They refused, saying they would rather own the inn once married. Mrs Ross is part of the consideration as she is an experienced housekeeper, and William has just chosen the site. It will be on the corner of Phillip and Church Streets, two blocks down from here. They will build on the sloping land on the block. I wished you all to meet as you have much in common."

The discussion over tea was interesting. The group discussed the infant town's growth and where Lachlan and Perry saw it heading.

Bill realised that they wanted to fill him in on their dreams of the town's growth, as they would return home to England one day, and he would remain.

Lachlan said, "I'm trying to lay the superstructure of a solid town. We rarely get to build a city from scratch, and I want it done properly. William, I saw you gazing at the dilapidated courthouse. It is on the to-do list; however, I know I will not finish everything before leaving. With Perry and Katy's assistance, we have a list of priorities for which buildings in what areas need doing as a matter of urgency." Lachlan gave Katy a beaming smile. "My Elspeth is also a source of inspiration, so my list grows daily."

Bill wondered why he had been included in the auspicious group. "Sir, why us?"

Lachlan snorted, then chuckled. "Not many convicts arrive with a letter of recommendation from the gentleman who formed London's Police force. William, as Perry here will attest, few here have not arrived to feather their own nest. Consequently, there are few I trust. With your references and astounding qualifications, I shall pick your brains and utilise your education if you permit. I heard from Doctor Andrew Smith that he has already used your language skills *en route* out here?"

Bill nodded, grinning. It was not likely that he'd ever forget meeting Napoleon Bonaparte. "If my education is only used for that meeting alone, sir, it was worth it."

Perry looked at the young man, puzzled at his comment.

Bill grinned. He had not even had a chance to discuss the incredible interview with the ladies. "I met with Bonaparte on the way out."

Those listening gasped. Lachlan raised an eyebrow at his comment. With a nod, he said, "I shall similarly use you if I may, should the need arise."

Bill was amazed. "Your Excellency, I was a butler, albeit with a good education. If you need my skills, I am at your command anytime." Bill gave a bow of his head in acknowledgment of the honour. "Sir, for you to single us out in any manner is our delight. As people of faith, we believed our coming here would be put to God's purpose. All three of us are willing to be tools for His use. Sir Percival has supplied us with funds aplenty, having now banished his younger son and severely crimped the spending of his older son and heir. He furnished us all with more than adequate compensation. Now we must work out how to put this money and us to the best usage possible." Bill swallowed nervously. "Sir, in the short time available to us, we wondered if it were also possible to assist the less fortunate, particularly the younger girls who are at the mercy of the dishonourable men." He noticed Katy's eyes flew to Perry's. "Have I said something, sir, ma'am?"

Katy, who had remained silent until now, answered. "Mr Miller, when

Perry first arrived, we stayed in the guest room at Government House. Soon after that, we rented some cottages down on Phillip Street and were there until this house was completed. These cottages now house the less fortunate women who arrive in the family way or are in an interesting condition." She paused and glanced at Ellen. "But also for widows and abused wives of the free settlers. Lachlan knows all about this, and I'm guessing it's why he has brought you to meet us. Am I right, Lachlan?" Katy's well-aimed question hit the nail on the head.

Lachlan smiled and nodded. "I want to assist as many poor waifs and strays as possible. As you know, I encourage as many as feasible to return to their status before conviction. I have met several others in various situations similar to your stories. I dare say you will meet some of the others soon enough." He glanced around at the five faces focused on him. "I am determined to leave this colony in a much better situation than it was when I arrived, and all of you are some of how I will achieve this. There will be many who will not take the opportunities of this new life and all its potential. However, many will benefit greatly if only we can source those who need our assistance."

Bill, Molly and Ellen all knew that this was to be their new purpose. When they left the White's home, the two families were invited to stay at each other's abodes whenever needed. Perry had a friend in Sydney whom he wished to visit, and the offer of a room in a safe establishment nearby was a delight. He hated staying at the hotel as he received the unwanted stares of everyone.

~

As soon as Bill had chosen the land, Governor Macquarie had the plans drawn up. Within a week of that, he heard that the tradesmen had laid the stone foundations and erected the timber frame of the brick building. As Bill wished, the inn was a level entry at the front and elevated at the rear. The building had a front facade made of stone that wrapped around until the building became raised from the sloping ground. The back of the building was brick until it reached the elevated back rooms. These walls were framed with timber, the design so cleverly done that the blending of the materials was hardly noticeable. By the time they married at the end of January, the building already had a roof frame, and the internal walls were being erected. The three had visited several times to check on the progress, but no changes were required.

Bill had left the inn's design to the governor, who knew what he wanted the town to have. It would sleep eighteen visitors in beds. Other than rooms set aside for family, there were three double beds, and all the rest were twin rooms.

Chapter 16 Changes

 hree weeks after Bill arrived, Molly woke at dawn when their cockerels decided to have a crowing contest outside her window. The duelling birds were a nuisance, but they were necessary to enlarge their chicken coop. Two of the hens were broody, and Molly had slipped another dozen eggs under them to cheat nature slightly.

This morning, however, was her wedding day. She stretched languidly before kicking back the sheet. The summer heat made her appreciate the overnight drop in temperature. The cooler mornings permitted the bulk of the work to be done comfortably before the heat overpowered them. She was sure she would get used to it.

Today, she was going to be married. First, she would have a bath and wash her hair, followed by breakfast with her mother.

Her eyes roamed over the room, and she realised she would no longer be sleeping in this room but would share Bill's suite until the inn was completed. Governor Macquarie had written to him to say it should be ready in a month. It would be up to them to furnish it.

They had already purchased some bedroom furniture, which was in storage until they could move in. Ellen had deposited their money in the bank at Mary Reiby's store.

They had spent the intervening weeks scouring the newspapers and buying items needed for their new life.

With money available, they did not skimp on the quality of the furnishings. Every bed had a feather mattress, and all the bed frames in the main rooms were four-post frames or had canopies with netting to keep the flies, spiders, and mosquitoes away.

Molly smiled as she thought of their future together and the new bed Bill had purchased for them. He had insisted on commissioning a new feather mattress with a padded kapok top, as he hated being jabbed by the quill tips from the feathers.

She blushed when she thought of what they would be doing tonight. Bill had always treated her as a lady, and he had never attempted to overstep the bounds of propriety and preempt their vows.

Living in the cramped quarters of the convict deck, little was left to the imagination regarding the soldiers coming for their night calls on the willing girls. She tried not to listen, but the cries or sighs left little to her imagination. The cries were from girls who had been assaulted, but the streetwalkers emitted sighs of delight and long cackles of laughter, flaunting their actions to the innocent girls nearby. She was no longer the innocent girl as she knew what men did when they forced themselves on a woman. She had thankfully escaped that indignity, but others hadn't. The first descriptions from the young girls had inadvertently opened Molly's eyes and ears to what occurred to a man's nether regions when stimulated and where his then enlarged appendage went. She crossed her legs at the thought of that occurring to her.

When her mother came in last night to tell her the ways of a man and a woman, she realised that such an act could be beautiful if done with love, hence the sighs from the bawdy girls. Ellen also said that the first time hurt, which explained why the young girls had cried. Her mother had also explained that this was how babies were made, and she had used the term 'joys of marriage.'

Thankfully, they had sat in the dark to discuss this, as Molly had flushed scarlet when she thought of discussing such an intimate thing with her mother. She had felt a change in Bill's nether regions when they had kissed, and now she understood why that had occurred. She grinned and looked forward to tonight.

Just over three months ago, she was on a convict ship locked below decks and teaching the others to read. Today, she was to marry the love of her life. She threw back the sheet and rose to get on with the day.

~

Bill stayed at the King's Arms hotel the night before the wedding, and they would have their honeymoon there. He woke with thoughts of their future. He reached out and ran his hand over the pillow next to him. Tonight, Molly would be lying there.

The governor's plan was exciting. Bill had been unhappy as a butler, but it was a good-paying job that kept him close to Molly. Owning land and running their inn was way beyond their wildest dreams in London. Much of their money would be set aside for their future, but they wanted everything to be of the very best quality.

Even back in England, owning an inn would never have happened. In this town, anyone who worked hard could succeed and make a place for themselves. He knew his education could be used by tutoring their children when they arrived. Only the good Lord knew what roles they would one day hold in the colony!

With money at his disposal and virtually nothing else to do, Bill decided that, as Molly was not permitted to leave the colony, two weeks in the classy King's Arms Inn was as good a place as any for a honeymoon.

He would take lots of notes of what they liked while staying there, and then they would try to replicate it for their inn. Here, they could get room service, and their room had an adjoining bathing room. Unfortunately, that was unlikely to be replicated. However, the idea of a bathing room was possible. It could drain directly into the garden.

From the fancy hotel, they could walk to the various parks and gardens in town and occasionally visit Ellen. They also spent a lot of time shopping for their future. There were bolts of fabric for curtains, more for bedding, table linen, antimacassars for the chairs and doilies for the side tables; some heavy linen was chosen for those smaller items. They also purchased two large bolts of netting to keep the mosquitos, spiders and geckos at bay.

Molly and Ellen would have much sewing to do before they could open.

They would be able to scour the shops for clothing and buy what they needed. Being fair-skinned, Molly needed a wide-brim straw hat, and Bill wanted some work clothing as he had very little in the way of that amongst his possessions. He had been delighted that all his clothes, including his trophies and awards, had been brought with Ellen. She had even packed his father's and grandfather's things that he had wanted to keep, and she had ensured that his grandfather's fob watch had been carefully packed in a waterproof leather pouch. The livery they had worn was not required, but as Sir Percival owned that anyway, he didn't want it. He would have given it away. That part of his life was over forever. He was now his own master.

The week Bill arrived, he discovered a jeweller in town. The first item he purchased was the gold cross on a solid link chain that Molly had always wanted, and he planned to give it to her as a wedding gift. He had also bought a plain gold wedding band and an engagement ring with a Ceylonese sapphire, which she already wore.

It was now the end of January, and they would not move into the new inn at Parramatta for a month or so. Therefore, their marriage would be held at St. Phillip's church in Sydney.

Andrew Smith, Doctor Thomas Prosser, and one of their friends, Robert Espie, would attend, as would two of the military. Major Downes and his friend Major Tim Hinds asked if they could be present.

This church was the second building, as the original one had burnt down long ago. The new church had been officially opened nine years earlier.

With a chuckle at his laziness, Bill hauled himself upright in the comfortable bed, knowing that he would share it with Molly tonight. He turned and looked at the pillow where she would sleep tonight and smiled.

He rose to prepare for his wedding.

~

A teary Ellen walked Molly down the aisle and gave her away.

Molly had almost dragged her mother towards Bill, who stood waiting with a big smile. She giggled most of the way as she was keen to be married to her beloved. Today, she would realise her dreams, and Bill would become hers forever. She would be no shrinking violet for him.

Andrew Smith stood beside Bill as his best man, but his eyes had been on the bride's mother. His feelings for her had deepened over the past month, but she only wished for friendship. However, he had finally admitted his feelings for her were not just as a friend. He had been shattered when she kept him at arm's length. For the first time in his life, his heart hurt.

Both Ellen and Andrew signed as witnesses in the register. Banns had not needed to be called, as they had special permission from the governor. However, Ellen insisted that Molly wear a proper gown to be married. She had purchased a bolt of ivory satin in London, planning to make a dress for Molly for this auspicious event. With everything that had occurred, her best intentions of having the gown ready had been forgotten in the untimely early arrival of Molly. When Molly mentioned a dress, Ellen remembered the fabric she had purchased in London. In the intervening weeks, they hastily made the beautiful gown Molly now wore. She looked lovely.

Molly, now nearly twenty, craved to have Bill's child and hoped to start a family as soon as they could. Most other girls her age had at least one baby.

~

The young ones had moved into their new but unfinished inn. Ellen remained at her house in Sydney to give the young couple some breathing space and have some alone time before the inn officially opened at the end of the month. However, she found that being alone was not all she desired. Ellen had just received a letter from Molly. Sadly, in the weeks since their marriage, no child had started.

Ellen needed to write back, encouraging them and explaining the lack of food causing her monthly flow to stop. But she was sad. Sad and lonely in the big, almost empty house. Andrew's regular excursions were the only relief from the monotony of her daily life. She sighed and quietly said to herself, "Ahh, Andrew!" A smile flickered over her lips. She had not thought she would ever feel the way she did now. Not since Sam died had her heart fluttered over anyone. She jumped when she heard a man's voice.

Andrew was one of some eight boarders at Ellen's luxury boarding rooms, and she knew he would soon need to leave, although he had said nothing about his departure. She had set aside some private rooms for herself, but the other main living rooms, the parlour, the sitting room, and the music room were for the guests. The office and withdrawing room-cum small parlour was at the rear of the ground floor, and she kept these for herself and her family.

~

Although the Rear Admiral Duncan Inn was finished, it was not fully furnished or open for business. As Bill requested, he was handed the keys when the building was completed; they undertook the fit-out together. The construction costs were £112 for the materials. This was a small amount for such a vast inn, but the labour had been free. The building had twenty rooms, most of which were bedrooms. However, they had spent nearly £1,000 purchasing top-quality furniture and decorating the rooms. All the feather mattresses had to be individually ordered, and these would take time to deliver. All needed mats, nets, and other assorted items. They also had to purchase plants for their orchard and construct a barn for their cow. They decided not to build a proper stable, but Tom had a purpose-built room in the small barn.

Bill and Molly had used the time to settle into married life and have an extended honeymoon. They had initially moved into one of the larger rooms at the inn but decided to move their master bedroom to a smaller room with a larger fireplace and a full-width built-in wardrobe and shelving covering an entire wall. It overlooked the river, and this room would become their sanctuary. There was a smaller room on either side of their bedroom, and they hoped that one day these would be their children's rooms, but that was for the future. At the back of the inn were the two largest double rooms. Both had separate entries from the wide, circling verandah and back access to steps.

~

In the weeks since the wedding, Andrew and Ellen often wandered around Hyde Park together and sat in the parlour alone in the evenings. A lot of laughter often accompanied their companionship. Once again, Andrew had broached the subject of developing the relationship, but Ellen still refused. Knowing he would leave, she still only consented to friendship. She also drew the line at anything physical. He was itching to hold her, but she held him at arm's length.

~

Over the weeks, they were often seen together and partnered for various functions. She had no intention of remarrying and planned to spend her golden years with Bill and Molly, helping the colony's less fortunate girls.

Ellen was approaching forty and in the prime of her life. She was a statuesque brunette with no grey hair, but she was now alone and feeling it dreadfully.

More weeks passed.

News from Molly that a second month had passed without her conceiving worried her. Ellen was sad for her daughter. Molly had confided that her monthly flow had returned but was not regular. She knew that having been on such scant rations for an extended time, Molly's now waif-like, stick-thin body would take time to right itself. Being sad and somewhat depressed, Ellen had taken refuge in her private withdrawing room.

Andrew was the only guest permitted entrance to her sanctuary. Here, they could talk freely and drop the facade of the polite world. Being a widow had certain benefits. Today, he entered and found her somewhat distraught. He had caught her at a teary moment after she had received Molly's letter. He walked in as she stood gazing into the fireplace; tears were streaming down her face. His compassion was stirred, disregarding her wish for no physical contact; he gently drew her into his arms for a hug.

Ellen had not felt such personal comfort since Sam's death years earlier, and she desperately needed it now. She wanted Andrew close and knew he cared for her. Now, she was weeping on his shoulder. Overwhelmed by the emotions, she forgot her resolve not to become involved. Rather than pull away from his embrace, with her hands placed on his chest, she lifted her lips to his for a long-desired kiss.

Andrew had wished to do this since first meeting her. To now have her responding to his caress was a sheer delight. He had only intended to hold her and bring her comfort. The possibility of also kissing her delightful rose-scented hair was also something he wished to do. However, the invitation to kiss her reddened lips was one not to be rebuffed. His first gentle kiss deepened into a passionate and hungry one from both. He enfolded her in his arms, crushing her well-endowed figure into his muscular body.

Ellen was shocked when his tongue touched her lips and pushed them open; Sam had never kissed her this way. She opened her lips to his probing, and a bolt of lustful emotions shot through her. She was shocked when her desire for this man made her step closer to him and press her body along the entire length of his. She was stunned when, through their clothing, she felt the stirring of his physical response to her closeness. She was also shocked at herself that she did not want him to stop. His hands moved up and down her back, pulling her closer to him. Their bodies were now almost welded together.

Some time ago, and she had no idea when, her arms had snaked around his neck, and her fingers threaded themselves into his glorious locks while she enjoyed every moment of the heady encounter.

Andrew knew he needed to pull back now or would not answer for the consequences. He lifted his head and released her slowly. He had thought her beautiful before, but having been thoroughly kissed, her lips were reddened and her face glowing with happiness. She pulled back in his arms as he gazed lovingly at her. "Ellen, marry me and come back with me. I find that I have delayed my departure longer than necessary so I can be by your side; however, soon, I must leave. My naval duties call. I love you so much that it hurts. It would break my heart to leave you here."

Ellen didn't pull away but rested her head on his chest. The past weeks of loneliness in a strange country made her think hard about her future. Bill and Molly were now settled; children would eventually come; she was sure about that. She was financially secure, as were the children. She knew she had to release her hold on them at some time. She pulled back a little and watched the micro frown cross his brow. His face was dear to her. He was waiting for an answer. Gazing up at him, she asked, "Can we return occasionally? They are all I have in the world."

Andrew was delighted. "If that is your only condition for accepting my offer, then yes, absolutely. We can even live here once I have completed my naval commission. If we pay for your passage, you can even travel with me on my journeys. However, I must return home to do that. In the meantime, I am at your command."

Ellen's face was glowing with delight. "Then yes, I'll marry you, dear Andrew, but can we get a special licence? I don't want you to move out, but I can't have you in the house close to me without…" She couldn't finish but blushed delightfully. Her head once again fell to his shoulder.

Andrew chuckled. "Willingly, I shall stay at the King's Arms Hotel tonight and until we wed. I came to tell you that I will leave in a few weeks. I am booked on the *Shipley*, and it's due to depart before the end of March. Robert Espie and some of the other medics are returning on her."

Ellen was as shy as a schoolgirl. She blushed again and then looked up at her new fiancé. "Do you really need to go immediately for the licence?" Her arms once again snaked around his neck.

"No!" His reply was to lower his head to her willing lips invitingly offered him. If she thought his kisses before were delightful, unleashing his pent-up passion was overwhelming. She discovered that he had been holding his emotions well in check. He now released all his love into the embrace.

She responded in kind.

He pushed her away only minutes later and pleaded for mercy with a laugh. "My darling Ellen, we are leaving to get special permission to marry immediately. Today, if the governor is in town, tomorrow at the latest. One more kiss like that, and I will carry you upstairs regardless of convention. Grab your hat and coat, and we shall leave now." He needed to bend over to relieve the pressure on his nether regions. At his words, he felt Ellen's hand gently caress his cheek.

She chuckled and said, "Yes, I will go." She paused at the door and turned back to look at him. "Andrew, I didn't say it before, but I love you too." She didn't wait for his reply but shut the door quietly behind her.

Andrew grinned but didn't reply. He adored her, too.

Hours later, the Colonial Secretary applied to the governor for emergency permission for them to marry due to Andrew's imminent departure. The message was sent immediately to Parramatta, where the governor resided.

After Andrew and Ellen returned from the Colonial Secretary's office, Ellen mentioned that she had offered to buy the Hyde Park house. Andrew was thrilled as it was not far from the new hospital. He had already been asked to work there should he wish. On his return, he would take up the offer; he had mentioned his intentions to D'arcy Wentworth.

The following day, accompanying the permission letter from the governor arrived. However, so did Bill and Molly, who had decided to come for a quick visit. They were shocked but delighted at the unfolding romance. At four that afternoon, Bill gave his mother-in-law away to his friend in a quiet wedding ceremony in the same church that had seen them married weeks earlier.

Bill smiled at his beloved Molly behind the backs of the couple as they said their vows. They were delighted to be able to be at Ellen's wedding. Both would be sad to see them leave but knew their lives would now be here in the colony. Andrew said they would return and settle in the Hyde Park house. He was thrilled when Andrew told him he would bring Ellen back after returning to London and resigning. He could work here as a doctor at the new Rum Hospital.

~

With no furniture shops in the Parramatta area, Bill and Molly scoured the newspapers weekly and slowly sourced enough beds to furnish most of the rooms. They could find the frames, but the feather mattresses had to be made for them, as did the kapok toppers. They had come to Sydney to arrange for delivery of the final items needed for the grand opening at the end of the month. They had found and purchased the final single beds required. The new inn was large enough to have a formal sitting room and a smaller family one across from their room.

With Ellen leaving, arrangements were needed for a caretaker of her new house. Some other residents at the Hyde Park house were senior military men who wished for a little more comfort when off duty. One older soldier, Robin Henge, wanted to resign his commission, and Andrew offered him the opportunity to run the boarding house in their absence.

With the caretaker now sorted, Andrew and Ellen were happy to hide in their room and enjoy their honeymoon. They had only two or three weeks until the *Shipley* was due to depart, then many months on board with little to do but get to know each other and relish their intimacy.

In the short time before they left, they spent a few nights at the new inn in Parramatta before it opened. They stayed in one of the large back rooms and delighted in the luxury of the furnishings. Bill had spared no expense furnishing these two guest rooms. They also had kapok-covered feather mattresses and this made the beds extremely comfortable.

Ellen ran her trained eyes over each room and noted what each venue required. A lamp was needed here or a shelf there; one room needed a mat as the floorboards had gaps, and the wind whistled through. They suggested a series of hooks behind each of the doors. Ellen suggested adding a basin and water ewer in all the rooms, plus a washstand and chamber pot in a specially lined bedside cupboard to stop the smell. She also suggested that the main rooms needed dressing screens as the glass doors gave little privacy during the day. All of these things were sourced before the opening.

Andrew suggested a valet stand in each room, something to hold a coat, hat, fob watch, etc. He also suggested a mirror, and, for a final touch, they added a Bible to each guest room.

The formal visitors' sitting room had Bill's valuable ancient texts on a shelf and a few other tomes and novels they had sourced. Bill thought the bookshelf looked sadly empty but doubted he would get much chance to read once business picked up. Some of the tomes he knew by heart.

Once Ellen had approved everything else at the inn, they were ready for the grand opening.

The *Shipley's* sailing date had been pushed back to early April. They were awaiting a new sailing date so Ellen and Andrew could come and stay the two nights before the official opening.

The inn opened with the fanfare of a wonderful write-up in the local newspaper. They had an open house at the end of March. Molly had been cooking up a storm, and the morning of the function, she had made over one hundred tiny bite-size feather-light scones. She had also sourced some delightful local berries, known as lilli pillies, and made a delicious cordial, which she bottled for later use. Major Downes had told them about these fruits when they arrived.

Due to her interest in cooking, Molly quickly discovered that the various honey varieties made a difference in the flavour; some were bitter, and some were sweet. She added some light honey and served this with a slice or two of lemon. As it was a hot day, the visitors quickly consumed the sweet pink beverage.

Governor and Mrs Macquarie were some of the first arrivals. The governor had intentionally stayed in the background since arranging the construction.

As Bill and Molly showed them through the building, Lachlan said, "This is perfect. I will be proud to have my guests stay here. Especially in these two back rooms. You have achieved a much better quality of accommodation than I expected."

Each room was tastefully furnished and had all the conveniences required for comfort. There was not only a Bible, a lamp, books, bedside tables, mats, and a valet stand but also all the other items suggested by Andrew and Ellen. Personal touches like a brush, hair pins, a comb, and various other items required for personal grooming sat on each bedside table.

The governor congratulated the young couple, and then, after nearly an hour at the venue, they took their leave after completing a tour of each room. After the vice-regal couple had gone, the inn slowly emptied of all the visitors. Bill and Molly were left with the clean-up. Ellen and Andrew got stuck into the dishes as the young ones did the major work.

The opening was a great success, and the local newspaper published a second article about the function the following day.

The inn now just needed a clientele.

Tom had taken up residence in the new barn loft and had taken responsibility for the new cow. Bill had bought an old dairy cow from Doctor John Harris, who owned the Ultimo dairy. She was nearing the end of her milking life and was no longer commercially viable. However, Tom was in love. He had named her Daisy, and Molly could hear him singing to her morning and evening as he milked.

Andrew and Ellen returned to Sydney as the ship was readying to leave. They needed to move their luggage on board and settle into their cabins.

Andrew was one of eight naval surgeons returning on this ship. Robert Espie, William Hamilton, Thomas Roylance, Henry Ryan, Morgan Price, John Johnson, and John Whitmarch joined them. Andrew was aware that none of his peers knew he had married, and now he realised they had to face the music.

Ellen was greeted and warmly welcomed by the cluster of doctors. They had stowed the bulk of the luggage in the hold but had yet to unpack their cabin luggage.

They were about to start when the captain knocked on their door. "Doctor Smith, we will need to delay departure for another couple of days, and I thought you may wish to delay your unpacking."

Andrew turned to look at his wife. He saw her nod.

When they found the new sailing date was three days away, they had a lovely comfortable feather bed at the house, and they decided to move back there until departure. They were exhausted after the inn opening, packing their home, and various changes in arrangements. The big feather bed awaited them.

Ellen awoke to the kookaburras' chorus at dawn. She lay looking at the handsome face on the pillow next to her. Her long dark tresses hung in ruffled ringlets around her face.

Thinking back to Sam and her short but happy marriage to him, she smiled and praised God that he had brought another wonderful man into her life. The memories of those heady early days of romance flooded over her; the last weeks since their marriage had been a delight.

However… Ellen's reverie froze.

Weeks!

They had been married for the better part of a month, and she had not had her monthly cycle since the week before their marriage. Swinging her legs out from under the blankets to avoid disturbing Andrew, her gentle movement woke him.

He saw his naked wife sitting on the side of their bed. "Ellen, is something wrong?" His hand slid around her waist to pull her back to him for what had become a regular and lovely morning ritual. She did not need corsets of any sort, not that she would have worn them in bed. This morning, her flesh was soft and supple under his hands. They had not donned their night attire after their passion of last night.

Ellen turned to him, and he saw she was very pale and somewhat perplexed.

Now concerned, he asked again, "Sweetheart, what's wrong?" He pulled the sheet up and covered himself. His desire for her was quite evident.

Knowing he was a doctor, she knew what she had to say would need no explanation. If only she knew how to say it. Her mouth opened and then closed again.

This happened twice before she blurted out, "My flow was due last week, and it didn't come."

Andrew took a moment to comprehend her words, and then he realised, "You're with child?" He pulled her back into the bed and cradled her in his arms.

Ellen nodded, then took his hand and placed it on her stomach. "Possibly, as I'm never late, so I could be and probably am. I always have been regular, and the only time I was late was when Molly was on the way." She snuggled into him. "I'm not saying I am with child, but I'm only thirty-nine, and I have not reached the age that my flow should stop." She wasn't sure if she was happy or not. "It never occurred to me we would have a baby."

Neither of them had thought this was a possibility.

Andrew was stunned. "I'm delighted, but I admit I'd never thought about us having children. I'm just over forty, and I never expected to be a father." He drew her tightly to him, and they lay cocooned, thinking about what possibilities lay before them.

After some minutes, Andrew chuckled and said, "We're going to have a baby, sweetheart. We might soon be parents!" With his thumb, he caressed her cheek.

She lay contentedly in his arms for some time; then Ellen moved so she could look at him as she spoke. "So, you don't mind?"

Andrew gave a hoot of joy. "Mind! Why would I mind?" He set about showing her how happy he was about the news. "Have you worked out yet that I'm delighted? However, we will need to do some shopping."

Ellen nodded with a smile. She did not look forward to telling Molly.

They were very late out of bed and emerged from their room, still somewhat in a daze.

They now had only three days to prepare for the possible birth of a child on the vessel home. With eight doctors on board to attend to her, Ellen was not fearful that she would need extra assistance on the ship, but she was not looking forward to telling Molly and Bill, as they barely had time to adjust to the news themselves.

Molly was hurting enough as it was because she had not conceived a child herself.

Ellen knew the young ones were returning tomorrow for a few days before the farewell. She knew she had to let them know of her suspected condition.

Chapter 17 Seeing Ghosts

*M*olly and Bill planned to spend the day wandering around town, placing advertising around the port in Sydney. Owning a fancy inn was all very well, but no one had booked to stay. Having the vessel's departure pushed back had given Bill time to print some posters before returning to farewell Ellen and Andrew. Hopefully, the *Shipley* would not need to delay leaving again. Mr Stewart at the King's Arms had taken a few brochures and willingly agreed to recommend their inn. He knew it was endorsed by the Governor, as was his establishment. Bill also took some of Mr Stewart's brochures.

Their arrival in Sydney was interesting. Andrew met them at the door, greeted them, and then asked them to follow him. He led them into the private sitting room at the back of the house, where Ellen awaited them.

As always, Molly gave her mother a big hug. Ellen's look was one of utter confusion. "Mama, what's wrong? Are you no longer leaving?" She glanced at her stepfather for clarification.

Instead, he came and put his arm around Ellen's waist. "No, Molly, it's not that. It's that we have made an interesting discovery. Astoundingly surprising, too, and well, we're not quite sure how to tell you."

Words sprung to Bill's tongue, but he dared not voice them although his eyes flew open.

Ellen could see by his expression that he had guessed as his eyes dropped to her waist.

Molly had picked up on the one word she wished to hear concerning herself: "You're having a baby? Is that the interesting condition you mean? Really?" She was ready to weep but excited when she heard the news.

Ellen blushed, nodding very slowly. She was flustered and embarrassed but replied, "I'm only a little bit interesting, like a week or so late, but as we leave tomorrow, I thought you needed to know the possibility." She turned to Andrew and nervously asked, "Can I be a little bit interesting? I suppose not; I either am or not, but time will tell." She was babbling with nerves as she knew that Molly had now realised what activity was required for this to occur.

Molly reached out for her mother, and while hugging her, she saw Bill congratulating Andrew. Her own emotions were in turmoil; excitement was intermingled with raging jealousy.

Ellen understood. She hugged her daughter and whispered, "I'm so sorry, my sweet girl."

Molly had just had another month pass with no child started. They had come to sit and talk it over with Andrew, but this news had overwhelmed her. At her mother's empathetic words, the tears finally came.

Bill was immediately at her side, knowing what had caused her sadness. He knew now was the time to have the conversation, so he pulled Molly to the settee and pointed to the other sofa for Ellen and Andrew.

One of the girls brought in a tea tray and then vanished. With the door closed, the ins and outs of having a baby were the topic of conversation.

Andrew, with his medical training, pointed out that she had been on almost starvation rations on the voyage out. She had lost so much weight that conceiving a child while so thin was problematic. He had had little to do with birthing, but it had certainly been covered in his lectures at college. He had heard then of the women who had no food, of stopping their monthly flow. Thankfully, the convict voyages he had done were all males. But, some of the other doctors were well-versed in the female reproductive cycle and possible problems. He said that she would unlikely conceive until Molly put on a little bit of weight and her monthly cycle was back into its normal rhythm. He said, "Molly, it could take a couple of years, but you are both young. Concentrate on the inn and on enjoying the joys of marriage. Not many couples get time to adjust to marriage before children arrive. Trust me, the knowledge of this situation is overwhelming. Ask your mother."

Molly looked at her mother. Ellen nodded in agreement. She said, "Use that time to settle into marriage, sweetheart. We'll be back in a couple of years, and I bet you will be cradling a little one by then."

Molly smiled, then turned to Bill for comfort but held back her tears. Her mind started concocting a delectable menu for home, and she was determined to regain her curves. She was aware that her flow had indeed stopped on board, and even now, when it came, it was irregular and heavy. Now she knew that once she had a normal flow, she would probably conceive a baby; she realised the wisdom of Andrew's words. She looked at

Bill and said, "You told me I wasn't eating enough." Bill kissed her forehead in response.

~

After a frantic shopping expedition and preparing for the arrival of an unexpected child, Molly and Bill helped reload the small amount of luggage that Andrew and Ellen had brought from the ship.

The *Shipley* sailed on the afternoon tide the following day. Once on board, they looked around the cabins and mess room. The captain told them sailing was imminent, and the gangplank was about to be raised.

Molly was teary but held them back. When she saw her mother again, she would likely have a sibling. Hopefully, they would have a child or two by then. Two years! Changes had occurred so fast that it was hard to believe that Bill had only been in the colony for four months and that seven months had passed since her arrival. They now owned their new inn and oversaw the house in Sydney for her mother. With a final hug, they parted.

The gangplank was raised, and the ropes pulled on board.

Molly clung to Bill's arm while watching her mother sail away. The voyage would mean an onboard birth as they sailed via China to source cargo.

The young couple waited until the ship was no longer visible before leaving the dockland. After putting up some posters, they returned to Parramatta to start their new lives without a parent at hand.

As the ship neared Sydney Heads, Andrew told the captain of their discovery. Captain Moncrief was slightly horrified at the news that Ellen was possibly expecting. He then realised she couldn't be in better hands with eight naval surgeons on board as passengers.

~

The posters Bill had erected worked, and the business picked up to a brisk turnover of clientele. Mr Stewart often sent them clients, too.

Molly's cooking was becoming well known, and they discovered Tom Yates was part of the reason for that. Although he refused to come inside and eat with them, Molly would take out a plate for him, and he thought he was in seventh heaven.

Unbeknownst to Bill, Tom had been one of their best advertisements. Tom spoke to everyone he could and told them of the beautiful new inn where one could sleep undisturbed. It was a place where the best food possible was found, including scones so light they almost floated off the plate, mattresses so soft it was like sleeping on a cloud, and nets on the beds to keep the beasties away.

~

Months passed, as did winter.

Tom's quarters in the stables were warm and toasty, but he still stank as he refused to wash himself or his clothing in case they fell apart.

Daisy was only producing a little milk, but Tom still managed to strip enough from her to supply their needs.

After six months, Bill and Molly finally received a letter from Ellen via a ship leaving China for Sydney. She was undoubtedly with child and was due around Christmas. She wrote that her growing condition became more awkward on a moving sailing ship as she was unbalanced. Now over the shock, her mother's letter made Molly chuckle.

Ellen said she had forgotten how cumbersome being off-centre was. The eight doctors on board were all clucking like mother hens, and sometimes, she would refuse to leave her cabin to get some peace. They had met a ship heading to Sydney, and Ellen enclosed a box of black Oolong tea and a bolt of beautiful damask silk that Molly could use as she wished. There were also ten yards of the most exquisite sheer white silk for her to make some luxurious drawers and a camisole or two.

The intervening months since Ellen and Andrew departed were busy ones for Bill and Molly. Perry and Katy White had been excellent for moral support and spreading the word about their upper-class accommodation. The governor used their inn as overflow for official functions.

Katy had stepped in where Ellen had left off. She had delivered twins not long before they met, and now a year old, the two tiny tots liked to wander up to the inn. It was as far as they could walk, and they were often accompanied by some of their siblings, Mia, Jem, Lou, or Davy, who ranged from five to ten. The short distance was not even out of eyesight from their home.

Molly always had some of her delicious pink cordial on hand, and if she was not busy, she would stop whatever she was doing and whip up a batch of gem scones for them. It was this treat that they came for; however, their presence, as delightful as it was, made Molly feel sad. She thought back to Andrew's words about settling into marriage without children. She still thought it strange she now had a stepfather. She had been stunned when her mother told her she might be expecting. Having been married for a few months, the thought of her mother doing what was required to produce a baby made her recoil in horror. Surely, she was too old for that activity? She was right about one thing: they had discovered that it was a very enjoyable activity. Bill's actions now explained the sighs of delight from the girls on board. The idea of her mother's activities, a distended stomach, and how she would cope if she were in that condition made her remember that God was in control and He knew best, but it was so hard to trust Him.

~

The Rear Admiral Duncan Inn was fully booked for Christmas week. In the stinking heat of the summer weather, Molly felt almost relieved that she did not need to cope with morning sickness. At least her flow had become regular once more.

Eight weeks earlier, she had not had her flow for two months and had wondered if she had finally conceived, but the week before the Christmas rush started, it returned. Emotions washed over her anew, and she had cried herself to sleep in Bill's arms more than once.

All the beds at the inn were fully booked back to back. That meant so many sheets to wash and so much food to cook that Molly was frantically busy. Thankfully, there was no tap room at the inn, and Bill was able to help with the cleaning and washing. When building the inn, they had planned that Ellen would be there to help them run the inn, but with her now gone, they wondered if they should get one of the girls from Sydney to come and help. Realising they had no spare beds for a maid as they had never finished the staff area under the back verandah, they managed their first rush independently. They would enclose the area downstairs and add some staff rooms. They would eventually need some help but put that on the to-do list.

~

New Year's Day 1820 came and went, and with it, a new convict ship arrived. This particular ship brought a friend of Perry's and someone Bill knew he had met in London. However, this man was a major in the 48th Regiment, but Bill was sure it was the same man, so he must have enlisted. As the almost white blonde-haired man showed no recognition, he wondered if he was mistaken; then Bill realised servants were always invisible. Lord David Lockley had been a friend of Errol's from his repeat year at university and a frequent visitor to the house. Shortly before Bill's arrest, David's brother, Edward, came to the London residence with him. Bill knew David to be a marquess, so why was his brother here? Bill's glances at the man were met with blank looks. Mayhap this man was not him, but as alike to be his brother. He realised the second son of the family often joined the military and figured this must undoubtedly be a younger brother. But this man certainly had the same first name.

Bill's question about Ned Grace's identity would remain unsolved for many a year.

One afternoon, about a week later, Bill was helping Molly fold the sheets after the Christmas rush, and they heard a knock at the back door. Presuming it was Tom coming for some food, Bill called, "Door's open; come in."

The appearance of another fair-haired man about the same age made him drop the sheet. This was not Perry's friend, Ned; however, he could have been another brother. Bill knew four boys were in the duke's family, and the other two were named Paul and Douglas.

The unexpected visitor said, "Hello, sir. I'm Charles Lockley, and Mr White was wondering if you and Mrs Miller would like to come for dinner tonight."

Bill's jaw dropped open. Here was another Lockley, and they looked so similar to David they could all well be brothers. How many of them were there? Was there a brother who was not acknowledged in Debretts? Bill was so shocked that he said, "Pardon?"

Charles repeated his request.

Bill saw Molly nodding. She whispered, "No one staying in tonight, Bill, and it will save me cooking."

Bill regained his voice. "Thank you, what did you say your name was?" He needed to check he had not misheard.

"Charles Lockley, sir," came the well-modulated reply that sounded much like David's. "I have been assigned to Mr White instead of Abel Jones, along with a convicted lady, Sarah McCarthy, known as Sal. She's to help with the laundry and do Major Grace's washing and cleaning."

Knowing that the White household was growing as their tutor's wife had not long given birth, Molly looked at the single-cane basket load of laundry at that house and smiled.

Bill was still puzzled that two clones of the man he had known in London had turned up on the one ship, and to top it off, this one's name was Lockley as well. Swallowing, Bill replied, "Yes, thank you, we would love to come." He wondered if Major Ned would be there so he could compare them.

The man said, "Mr White said six o'clock if that's not too early. It's to be a family dinner." Charles gave a formal bow and left the way he had come in.

When the door closed behind him, Molly said, "You look like you've seen a ghost. What's wrong, Bill?"

He sank onto the bed. The laundry was forgotten as Bill filled Molly in about the man he had seen in London. He had never been officially introduced as he was only the butler, but it was one of the nights he had needed to go to White's Club in St James to collect a very drunk Errol. The fact that this man was himself a member of White's Club, if it were indeed Lord Edward, made him think back to that night. Errol's friend, Lord David Lockley, suggested he apply to Brooks Club. However, Brooks politely declined Errol's application, so Bill was aware of his employer's depression and was on hand to support his friend. How Errol managed to get into White's in London was beyond Bill's understanding; he presumed he had purchased a membership. Then again, maybe Lord David had paid?

That fateful night, only a week before the altercation that saw him convicted, Bill had seen the esteemed arbiter of fashion, the great Beau Brummell. He may not have even noticed the second blonde gentleman if he had not kindly assisted in removing Errol from the hallowed halls and all but carrying him home.

Bill had learnt one thing about this new colony. Many were here using names that were not necessarily their own. If either of these two men were incognito, then it was no business of his. He would accept them at face value.

If Major Ned Grace and Charles Lockley were indeed related, time would tell. Either way, they were a link to home, so he would try to befriend them both.

After discussing this topic, Molly said, "I presume the major is here under an assumed name; we shall keep his secret, Bill. He is obviously hiding for a reason. Maybe he and snooty Lord David had a falling out."

Bill agreed but said nothing.

~

Charles and Sal married only a few weeks after the dinner invitation. Bill and Molly were surprised at the speed of their nuptials, but Perry explained that Sal had been accosted, and Charles wished to protect her the only way he could.

Eight weeks after the Lockley's marriage, Bill informed Molly that Sal was expecting a child and that she was due at the end of spring. Bill had taken her in his arms to break the news, and as expected, Molly melted onto his shoulder in tears, overwhelmed that even after more than a year, she had not conceived; however, she was still woefully thin. Bill surreptitiously measured her waist with his hands to see if she was gaining weight. He had loved her curves from her youth. After only a few tears, Molly pulled from his arms and, with a shake of her head, said, "I must go and tell Sal how pleased I am for her."

Bill smiled and released her. He quickly kissed her. "Sweet Molly, not only do I love you, but I am so proud of you. If we never have children, at least I have you." The glowing joy on her face surprised him.

Her hand reached up and cupped his cheek. The loving look she gave him comforted him. "Bill, I'm finally putting on weight, but I have handed that situation to God. I know His timing is always right; however, I freely admit it's hard seeing others so happy, first Mother, and now Sal." She reached up and gave him a quick peck on his lips before continuing. "I find it hard to believe Mother fell with a child so quickly. She will have delivered it by now, so I have another sibling somewhere. I've not heard anything from them since China. Katy's servants, Lucy and Buck, had Judith last year and now Sal and Charles. My heart hurts, and my arms are empty, and I miss Mama so much."

Bill knew what she meant. Each month that passed, he would see Molly's tears were triggered when her monthly bleed returned once more. Each time, once the tears dried, she would shake her head and get on with life. Bill's adoration of her grew. Molly blew her nose and set off to see her friends and congratulate them. Now working as a houseman and gardener for the Whites, Charles had grown closer to Bill. Molly and Sal had become kindred spirits. Charles had initially been standoffish until he found that Bill had also arrived as a convict. Bill explained that Molly was still officially serving her time, and her sentence would expire that coming Christmas.

When Sal discovered their history, she too accepted the hand of friendship.

It was a friendship that would last a lifetime.

~

By the end of winter, Sal found walking any distance awkward. Gone was her sylph-like figure, and she had a decidedly large bump at the front that looked like a melon under her gown. When Sal visited her friend on one of her constitutional walks, she noticed a wave of melancholy pass across her friend's face. She enquired, "Mol, is something the matter?"

Molly met her friend's question with sadness; her eyes dropped to Sal's stomach, then returned to her face. "Not wrong precisely, but maybe wrong with me. I seem unable to conceive a child, and I willingly admit I am more than jealous of those who fall so easily. Even my mother fell mere days after her second marriage." Molly was unable to keep the tears from her eyes.

Sal's girth was certainly cumbersome, but her compassion was stirred, and she drew her friend into a loving hug; the babe within kicked as she did so. Sal said with great love, "Dear Molly, you are woefully thin. I'm guessing that the food on the ship was inadequate?"

Molly nodded. "We left London with plenty of food on board, but much of it was spoiled by the rough seas we struck. I was quite curvaceous when I was arrested. The doctor was wonderful and gave me as much as he possibly could, but I lost a lot of weight; I was not sick with a disease. The rations we were on kept us alive, but only just. The meat was slimy and made my illness worse. One blessing was that most of us did not have our flow when on the vessel."

Sal thumbed away her tears. As she hugged her, she could feel her bones through her gown. "Then we'll have to work on getting your weight back, my dear. We'll start by adding some good black porter to your diet."

Molly shuddered. "But Sal, I don't like beer, let alone the black stuff. If I must drink cold fluids, it's cider or my pink cordial."

Sal chuckled. She didn't like beer either. She said, "Well, I suppose it depends on how much you want a child. Your body is malnourished, Molly, and you must build it up before it can cope with carrying a baby. If you conceived now, you could well lose it."

The look of horror on Molly's face told Sal of her concern.

Sal continued, knowing she had to make her point. "Molly, if you have put on weight since your arrival, I would have hated seeing you when you landed. You are nothing but skin and bones now." She took her friend's bony hands and caressed the back of them, waiting for Molly to digest the comment. Sal saw her nod slowly.

Molly knew her friend was correct. But Bill liked her new slim figure. His hands easily spanned her waist now, as he often did this when he came up behind her before hugging her. His hands wandered pleasurably over her body before he turned her around for a loving embrace. Often, they would end up back in their bedroom. However, he had fallen for her when she was curvy. Even with the many chances of conception, nothing happened.

Molly frowned. "Fine, then feed me the ghastly stuff and fatten me up like a pig to the slaughter." She shuddered. "I really don't like any of those drinks, beer, ale, lager, or that horrible thick black porter. If I must drink something, I'd rather have a nip of brandy."

Sal chuckled at her reluctance. She explained, "Porter and all the black beers have all sorts of goodness in them and will help build up your body. If you can find a thick black stout, that's even better. I used to make my mama drink it for her health. Also, add a huge dollop of cream to your porridge and drink lots of milk."

Molly's face screwed up. "If that's the price I must pay, my diet is in your hands, Sal."

The two women sat, and Molly wrote what they usually ate for a meal. It was healthy but weighed heavily on the vegetables they grew in the backyard. There was little fat on the native meats, which were only available once a week if that.

Molly also admitted that although they had a cow, she didn't give much milk. Then added, "There's a new girl, Jennifer Kellow Williams, up at the dairy, and she said I can have what I want, but I hate to ask her. I keep Daisy's milk for cooking, or I serve it to Bill or give it to the guests. Our meat is usually possum or lean kangaroo tail, made into a stew." Molly knew that Bill and Tom shared most of this, as the rich roo meat had once made her a bit sick. She didn't snack between meals, and, as she'd been taught, she never finished everything on her plate.

Sal bit her lips, eventually saying, "In this place, Molly, manners have little to do with rations. Here we have food, and the manners we used in London are not for here. From today forward, you will make scones or biscuits regularly and eat them with your morning and afternoon teas. Add jam and cream, and enjoy what you cook for others. I now insist you finish all your meals and eat the fatty bits. Serve decent portions for yourself, and do not go without the food you need. You must also drink milk, cream, and cheese and eat your vegetables, including potatoes. Take Jennifer up on her offer of milk and cream; if you don't, I will talk to her on Sunday. Add rice or potatoes to every main meal, and you must eat all of those, too, not just feed the men. Every mouthful you eat, think, this is for a baby."

A tear ran down Molly's cheek, but Sal saw her listening intently. Sal's eyes met Molly's, and she said, "Get Jennifer to bring you some clotted cream and cheeses from the Government Dairy. Their cheeses are delicious and, in your case, not a luxury. You told me she offered to let you become a taster for her new varieties; take her up on her offer. Her cheese is made with the fat from the milk, which will help with the weight gain."

Molly was still teary, but she held her friend's gaze.

Sal's raised eyebrows silently questioned her determination to put on weight. Molly nodded and sniffed in a very unladylike way. She knew Sal was right. Her mother and Andrew had imparted much the same wisdom. Sal took her hand. "Mol, I want to see you letting out your gowns each month from now on, and you must also tell Bill. He may like you slim, but slim to the point of illness is unhealthy. Do you understand me?"

~

By the time little Charles John Lockley arrived in November 1820, Molly had let her gowns out twice. She still had a long way to go, but it was a good start. Bill was delighted to see her curves returning. He had admitted that he had spanned her waist to see if she was gaining weight, not wanting to embarrass her by asking. "I liked your rounded, curvy bits, love."

Charles and Sal were deliriously happy with the birth of their first child, Charlie. When the baby grinned to release a burp, he had two big dimples in his cheeks. He was the most adorable cherubic baby with big blue eyes and an infectious giggle.

Molly saw the dimples and looked at his parents. She had noticed Major Ned had similar indentations but not Charles. She had also realised the similarity between the two men.

Sal realised her query. "Charles has dimples but hates showing them, so he rarely grins broadly."

With that, Charles gave one of his very rare big grins; his face was flushed scarlet. Two deep holes popped in his cheeks. He said, "My sister has them too. Apparently, Father also had them as well, but he died when I was five, and I can hardly remember him." With a quick kiss on Sal's brow, Charles returned to work after leaving the two women to gush over his son.

~

The Rear Admiral Duncan Inn was fully booked again over Christmas week. Molly had again let out her gowns, but her flow was now regular. Bill's fingers could still circle her waist, but at long last, his fingertips no longer overlapped; they only just met. Molly was delighted that Bill's appetite for her had increased with the return of some of her curves. Her healthy glow grew, too. She had no idea that this had even been her deep-seated fear that Bill would not like her a little plumper. However, that was certainly not the case. His hands often explored her curvaceous figure whenever they were alone. Molly's shocked giggle delighted him. He repeatedly added that if they had no children, he still had her.

After a hectic week of non-stop patrons, a lull occurred. They had no bookings over the new year and for a few weeks through early January. They took the time to do some minor repairs and relax. Bill hoped they would have some walk-in customers to fill their empty beds. During this quiet period, he asked Governor Macquarie if he would mind them converting the formal sitting room into a small, almost private tap room for his patrons. The

Governor was delighted as there was no such place as an upper-class English Pub in the town. He fully intended to patronise it himself.

In a very short time, part of the wide front verandah had been remodelled and converted to access the classy sitting room, which they rarely used, into a closed-off bar, small taproom, and men's lounge. A high bar was constructed of beautiful polished red gum timber. There were six barstools, and the shelf behind had a variety of fancy bottles. They ranged from top French cognac to locally brewed rum and almost everything in between.

Lachlan was pleased to see that there were two varieties of Scotch. Bill had sourced Glenlivet and Heatherbrae whisky. Heatherbrae was his favourite, but he rarely found any. Henry Gates's bond store in Sydney had a wide range of spirits that he now purchased.

Mid-morning on the tenth day of the new year, a carriage pulled up at the front of the inn. Bill was cleaning the front room when he became aware of a vehicle approaching then it pulled up outside. He stood to greet the new arrivals.

Molly heard Bill's animated and excited chatter and stuck her head out of the kitchen to see who it was. The sight of two very familiar faces made her fly out the door and into her mother's arms. The two women were in tears. Molly had not even noticed the little girl in her stepfather's arms. The men ushered their wives indoors for a more private welcome.

Bill returned to arrange unloading the mountains of luggage on the hired vehicles.

Molly chattered to her mother and giggled excitedly; however, her conversation was stilled by a single word.

"Mama!" came a cry from behind them. Ellen turned and reached for her youngest daughter. Andrew passed the child over and gave Ellen a quick peck on her lips. "Elle, I'll arrange the luggage with Bill. He says they have room for us, so we can stay as long as we like."

Molly watched the short exchange, still unused to seeing her mother kissing a man, but her only comment was, "I have a sister? Truly? I always wanted a sister." She knew better than to reach out and take the child, but she gave the adorable little girl a gentle caress on her cheek.

The child's brown eyes gazed unblinkingly at Molly. Ellen introduced the half-sisters. "Beccy, I told you about Molly?" The child's head was tucked into her mother's neck. Neither Molly nor Ellen knew if she understood. She turned to look at Molly again and smiled at her, then hid her face against her mother's neck again.

Molly chuckled at her little sister's actions. "She'll come around, Mama, but it's so good to see you. When did you arrive?" Ellen settled herself on the comfortable settee in the small sitting room. "We arrived only yesterday evening on the *Prince Regent*. We thought we would stay in town for a while, but the house in town is full. We decided to risk it and come straight here. The ship brought more convicts, and a miserable bunch they were. We stayed on board last night as Andrew found that our rooms in our house were occupied." With her eyebrows raised questioningly, Ellen said, "Apparently, Robin Henge has moved into our rooms, as he had not expected us to arrive unannounced. I believe married senior soldiers occupy all the rest of the bedrooms, and they are not planning to move out in any hurry." Ellen looked a little miffed at Robin occupying their private quarters.

Molly had wondered about allowing Robin to move into the private area. Still, Bill had given his permission as six senior officers had wished to reside in the nearby quarters. Some were married, and no other married quarters were in the town. The house had a good clientele, and they caused no trouble at all. "Sorry, Mama, but it brings in regular rent, and Robin keeps the place immaculate; however, his room needed to be rented out. We're too busy here to see to itinerant lodgers, and this way, the money is regular. The military oversees the grounds upkeep as part of the contract."

Bill had given permission, not expecting his mother-in-law to arrive back so soon. The family settled into one of the rooms near Bill and Molly's. The double room overlooked the backyard and had a lovely river view. Ellen's favourite room had windows on two sides, which picked up the cool breezes. As it was elevated at the back, they could sleep with the doors open without worrying about snakes entering their room.

The kangaroo stew that evening was stretched with more vegetables. Tom received his bowl full and returned to his room above the milk shed to consume it as usual, and the family sat down to chat and catch up. Bill put up the *no vacancy* sign at the front of the inn and told the family they would take a few days off to enjoy the reunion. The biggest surprise was the news that Ellen was expecting another child. Beccy was only thirteen months old, and Ellen was due to deliver the next child at Eastertide.

The news hit Molly hard. She made an excuse to clear the dinner plates from the table and fled to the kitchen to weep. Her mother would be forty-one by this baby's birth, and Molly was half that age.

After Molly had left the room, Ellen pumped Bill for information. He filled them in before Ellen followed her daughter's path. Molly had not conceived and still found putting on weight difficult. She was slumped on the floor weeping and didn't hear her mother's approach.

A gentle hand on her daughter's cheek made Molly raise her head. Molly wept, "I've tried, Mama, I've tried everything, but I can't have a baby, and I want one so badly that it hurts here." She punched at her chest with a clenched fist.

Ellen managed to get down on the floor beside her daughter and pull her into her arms. Words were not needed; just being hugged was enough.

Chapter 18 New Arrivals and Departures

$\mathcal{W}$ith the arrival of Ellen and Andrew, Molly found that caring for a small child was not as easy as she had first thought.

It had not taken long for Beccy to seek out Molly for a hug or to get something to eat. She would toddle into the kitchen and plop herself on the floor if she was hungry. And say, "Prease ta, Morry, dink." Then, she held out her hands for a drink.

Molly learnt quickly to sneak her adorable sister a biscuit or a tiny bit of cake. Beccy would promptly devour the evidence and ask for more. She also adored Molly's pink cordial.

The sisters bonded as Molly learnt about the joys of parenthood. Changing Becky's soiled napkins was one side of pending parenthood she did not look forward to. Molly knew one large cookie was more than enough for the small girl. She would give Beccy some scalded milk sweetened with clover honey. Thanks to Sal's conversation earlier, Molly had a glass of this sweetened creamy liquid each morning. She added a squashed strawberry when they were in season.

Bill had sourced some bottles of stout for her and brought a pint glass of the brew each evening as she prepared their meal. He was ecstatic when, one time, he put his hands around her waist to find they no longer met. He finally confessed that he was worried that she was so skinny. He swung her around excitedly and explained his joy. Molly's face was filling out and now looked healthy again. Her breasts were also not as saggy. They, too, had begun to perk up, and the glow was starting to fill her cheeks. Gone were the gaunt hollows in her face, along with the sadness in her eyes.

April brought the birth of Molly's brother. Ellen had a hard time with his delivery, and Andrew feared she would not survive the ordeal.

Their friends, Katy White, her nanny, and her maid Lucy, all attended the delivery, with Andrew insisting on being involved. Molly was initially kept from the birthing room until she told her mother she had helped deliver babies on the ship.

After a long hot bath, Andrew soon had Ellen up and walking around the room. She leaned into his shoulder for each contraction.

Molly did as they had done on board with no birthing stool available. Ellen squatted between Molly's legs, and Sal delivered their second child. Sal caught the baby and quickly passed the newborn boy to his father. Andrew checked him over and made him cry so his lungs could fill with air, a pink colouring infused through him. Andrew had insisted on attending in case he needed to intervene. If he had been holding Ellen, that would have been impossible.

Sal waited for the cord to empty before tying it. Andrew snipped his son free from his mother and carried the babe to meet her. The three sat on the bed, cuddling for some time before the afterbirth contractions started. Andrew passed his sleeping son to his elder sister.

Molly gingerly held her new brother as Andrew attended to his wife. He knew the agony that was yet to come. The little boy opened his eyes and gazed at Molly. As the tiny scrap of humanity lay looking up at her, his face screwed up, and a frown appeared on his brow, and she knew that he was going to squawk. She had seen the girls on board the ship put a finger in the child's mouth, so she tried that trick, and the little boy started sucking. All the while, their mother writhed in agony. Molly had walked to the far side of the room. She didn't want to see this bit, as she knew how gory it was. After some time, the afterbirth finally came away, and Molly handed her newest sibling back to his parents.

David Andrew Smith won the heart of the entire growing family. Beccy had taken possession of her brother and often stood guard over him while he slept. Flies were hard to keep out, so she would brush them away from his tiny face.

~

By the time Dave was three months old, the inn had settled into a routine. Ellen and Andrew had settled into their rooms in Parramatta rather than returning to their Sydney home. The two small children were in the room set aside for Bill and Molly's children, which sat unused until now. It held a crib and a cot should visitors require them.

Andrew was volunteering at the Parramatta Hospital. This building was new, and the old timber hospital was no longer used, but the facilities in this new building still needed to be improved. He volunteered his services as they did not need funds. His time was occupied with triaging the new arrivals and taking the pressure off the paid surgeon, who would treat the more serious cases as required. However, Ellen could see his frustration as the hospital did not adequately use his skills.

With Molly on hand to assist her mother with the children, Ellen adored helping in and around the inn.

Andrew loved sitting in the small tap room with Bill at the end of a busy day, talking to a few nicer patrons. He realised he was relaxed and decidedly happy. He had also been invited to join Perry's select group of men for a weekly Bible study around his immense western red cedar table. This gathering was the highlight of his week.

Bill had encouraged Andrew to come after duty at the hospital.

Andrew found that the weight of oppression was lifted from his heart for the first time in many years. Although he loved the healing side of things, the responsibility of someone else's health had never sat easily with him, and to find that so many had been ill on the convict vessels and he had been unable to help them had been hard to release.

On his second visit, Perry asked him to remain after the others had gone. He did and found himself pouring out his worries to the horrifically scarred man. This man knew ostracism, grief, oppression, and sympathy; he offered Andrew empathy and support. Perry listened, gently probed and then offered to pray with him.

Andrew had rarely met a man who relied so entirely on God and said as much.

Perry said, "After this…" He stroked his melted cheek. "I lived as a hermit for a decade. I only had the minister, Justin, who knew where I was. Even my family didn't know, as I lived in a tiny single-room cottage hidden in a back valley of a small estate. I had no one to rely on except God. The only reading material I had was a Bible, so I devoured it. It became my sanity and solace. Then, one day, I found Katy collapsed by the side of a back road. Next to her was a newborn babe. I took them home, and from that day onwards, I began to live again. We married soon after she was well." He sat gazing into the remnants of his cold tea. "Andrew, caring for her gave me purpose. I had no idea she was my cousin until she recognised me. I fought about how attached I had become to her after caring for all her needs while she remained unresponsive. We moved in with Justin's half-sister." He would not admit his folly to his new friend. But hugging a woman who was not his wife nearly destroyed his marriage. Even though the action had been innocent, guilt washed over him. With a crooked grin, he shook off his melancholy and said, "Never put God to the test, as you never know where you will end up. Here in this hellhole, my burns are hardly noticed. I learned to fully live again, but now I know that God can even use my scars, and when I return home, I will ensure that He does."

Over the months, Andrew heard more of their story and Perry's chase across the world after his wife. Knowing someone else had experienced loneliness and survived greatly encouraged Andrew.

Bill's bar had become a genteel place for the free settlers in town to meet for a quiet drink or two. The establishment drew only the upper class of society. Governor Macquarie kept his eye on the facility and occasionally made suggestions that Bill willingly put into place. One was for him to install a few tables indoors for private conversation rather than just the bar and outdoor lounge.

Four small tables were quickly sourced and were occupied most evenings. The small bedroom next door had been turned into a replacement sitting room for the inn. Visitors came frequently, and business was good.

Bill had no trouble with drunkenness or uncouth behaviour, and often, the governor and Perry could be seen enjoying a quiet drink at a small table out of the public eye.

The tap room was only open for a few hours a day after work, and in that time, many came in to enjoy some male fellowship.

Andrew found this time was a delight as he had discovered like-minded friends to while away a few hours. No one ever drank more than one or two ales, and Molly's pink punch was in as much demand as the hard spirits that sat nearly untouched on the top shelf. Bill served a nip or two each night but rarely more than that.

On one such evening in September, Perry dropped a bombshell. Lachlan Macquarie had called Katy and him in for a meeting earlier that day. Everyone knew that Katy's term was up and that she had been given permission to return home with Perry. However, none realised that Governor Lachlan Macquarie had also tendered his resignation.

Lachlan, Elizabeth, and young Lachie Macquarie were leaving the colony. Governor Macquarie had almost single-handedly turned the place from a corrupt penal colony into a lovely place to live. There were still problems, but time should mend those. Lachlan, Perry, and their families planned to leave by the end of the year or soon after.

Shock at the revelation silenced the group for some time.

Bill had seen what had been achieved in the short time he had been in the colony, but the one thing that impressed him most was the Governor's interaction with the local tribes of Aborigines. He knew the grey-haired vice-regal man regularly met with them and supplied food and clothing. As in most groups of humans, there were always troublemakers. Most of those were escaped convicts who had turned to burglary and bush-ranging, but one or two had been angry indigenous locals displaced from their land. Lachlan issued an order to arrest these few individual tribesmen. However, his order had been enacted to the extreme some years before, and Captain Wallis had massacred the entire small tribe.

All were horrified when they heard of the flagrant disregard of instructions and shunned the officer. This captain was friends with John Macarthur and Major Morriset, who had the undesirable nickname of Lasher Morriset. These three men were thorns in the side of those wishing to grow the colony with freed convicts. A fourth man, Commissioner John Thomas Bigge, arrived unannounced soon after Molly and proceeded to undermine and report on the actions of Governor Macquarie. Rather than interview anyone who had worked with the governor, Commissioner Bigge only interviewed those with grievances against him. With this distorted report of mishandling of the colony now completed and filed, Lachlan Macquarie had to return to London to face Lord Bathurst and the accusations made against him in the Bigge report. The small group of friends were distraught. At least Perry and Katy would be returning with them, but the situation left a sour taste in all their mouths.

Bill had come to know the man very well and thoroughly admired him. He would be sad to see him leave. He knew that Major Ned Grace and Perry knew each other from Kent. Their accents had given their upbringing away quite early in their friendship; Charles's was similar. That, along with the visual similarities between Ned and Charles, intrigued Bill. However, the pair remained silent as to any possible relationship between them.

When Perry mentioned to Andrew that he knew Ned from home, he noted the similarity but admitted he knew of no familial relationship between the two men. So Bill presumed that Charles was not one of Major Ned's brothers.

By the time the news of Macquarie's departure was widespread, Molly had realised that there was a possibility that she had finally fallen with child. Sal was well advanced with their second confinement. Molly had been so busy looking after Beccy and Davy that it had not occurred to her that she had missed her flow for the past two months. Her monthlies had regulated mid-last year, and each month brought new tears.

Sal had come to assist with a luncheon Molly was preparing. As the roast meat came from the oven, Molly departed quickly and threw up over the balcony railing. Ellen and Sal followed her exit, and the two stood consoling her as she heaved her heart out. None of the ladies seemed too worried, and soon they were comforting a weeping but giggling Molly. She was undoubtedly with child. She was laughing as she threw up again. Thinking back, Molly worked out when her last flow had been. At a quick estimation, she figured she was due after Easter next year. The Governor and Perry would be gone by then, but Sal and Ellen would be there to assist.

Ellen was delighted. Finally, her prayers had been answered. Molly's joy was evident. "Mama, I'm having a baby!" she squealed with delight. Knowing that her husband needed to hear from her lips, she turned to head indoors only to find him standing in the doorway. She skipped with glee and threw herself into Bill's arms.

Bill had arrived to discover the source of the commotion.

Moments later, Molly was in his arms, saying, "Billy, my darling love, we're finally going to be parents. I've just realised." Her squeal of delight was followed by Bill grabbing her and twirling her around. Luncheon was forgotten for some time as the couple celebrated the excellent news.

After the completion of the delayed meal, Molly plied both women with numerous questions.

Over the following months, Molly soon discovered that running an inn while expecting a child was difficult when she only wished to sleep. She gained a new understanding of her mother's exhaustion during her confinement. The staff room downstairs was complete, and she wondered if they could finally get some help at the inn.

~

October drew near, and Sal was ready to deliver her second child.
Charles and Ned had come at closing time and sat drinking tea after the taproom closed for the night. After the men's Bible study earlier that day, their discussion had turned to faith-based matters. Charles had often been overheard asking deep and searching questions to Ned, but Ned had since found that Bill had a much deeper understanding of faith and how to explain it.

Bill had never let on that he had a degree in Divinity from Oxford in this subject. However, presenting his understanding in simple terms was another matter altogether. His words were too big for a minimally educated man to grasp. Even though he had a deep faith, his knowledge was book learning.

On this particular informal discussion, Perry joined the three men. He said, "I have a minister friend at home who summed up our faith in five lines. It makes it easy to remember. You can make your explanation as deep or simple as you wish from these five points."

Bill was silent, wondering what he meant. He frowned at the well-dressed man beside him.

Ned looked at his friend and asked, "Well, what are they? Don't keep us hanging."

Perry glanced at Charles and Bill and saw both expected him to answer. With a nod, he replied, "Okay, they are 'God, Man, God', then two questions: 'What if you do? What if you don't'?"

Now, all three men at the table with him frowned.

Charles summed up their puzzlement by saying, "Huh?"

Perry motioned that it was time for Bill to shut up the taproom, so Bill pulled down the open sign and closed the front door. The four sat in the quiet room waiting. Bill had overheard Charles's comment, and as he sat grinning, Charles said, "I have no idea what you mean, sir."

Perry smiled and said, "Patience, men! I shall elaborate for you. The first *God* in the story is, God created the world, skies, and everything in it and beyond it, including us."

Ned nodded, but Charles frowned at Bill's grin.

Perry said, "I've heard some people say that they don't even believe in God; they think He is not true, then in the next breath, they blame Him when something goes wrong."

All the listeners agreed as they had all heard people do and say this.

Perry continued, "Anyway, Creator God made mankind, and He made us 'good' and He gave them the Garden of Eden to live in."

The three men all murmured various words of agreement.

Perry continued once more, "Everything that God made was good, and that means perfect, including us. In the garden were two central trees, the Tree of Everlasting Life and the Tree of Knowledge."

Charles gasped. "But what happened because we certainly are not now? Otherwise, we would not be sitting in a convict colony."

Perry grinned his lop-sided smile. "Ahh, well, that's the next bit. The *Man* part." He took a sip of his ale. "When God made everything, including the angels, one named Lucifer thought he was as powerful as God and ended up cast out of Heaven along with a third of all the other angels. These became the demons. Lucifer became who we know as Satan or the devil."

Bill had never heard it explained so clearly. He had realised that that still meant the angels outnumbered demons two to one. He had loved that statistic.

Perry saw that Bill and Ned's gaze didn't waver, and Charles was spellbound. So, Perry continued. "Okay, that was the first sin, and it was amongst the angels, not humans; it was a rebellion against God. But the devil, as Lucifer was now known, wasn't happy with that, so he decided to tempt the perfect humans. Remember, God made humans good. When He did that, God gave them just one rule."

Again, Charles gasped. "Only one? If only we could go back." He gave a sign and then motioned for Perry to continue. Apologising for his interruption, he said, "Sorry!"

Perry chuckled, saying, "The one rule was, 'Do not eat from the Tree of Knowledge'. They could eat any of the perfect fruit or vegetables from any other trees that grew around them. Note I said *any* tree, including from the Tree of Life, where they, and therefore us, could have lived forever. Lucifer took the form of a snake and offered Eve a taste of the enticing forbidden fruit, and by doing so, he lied to her. She took the fruit and ate it, then offered some to Adam. He also ate, knowing it was the fruit from the forbidden tree. So, sin entered into the world." Perry let that sink in for a bit and answered a few questions.

Bill remained silent. Theologically, the explanation had been perfect so far. A beatific smile had settled onto his lips.

Perry noticed but said nothing.

Charles lay back and folded his arms. "Fine, then what happened?"

Ned looked at his clone and raised an eyebrow. He knew Perry was, in reality, an earl, and Charles did not talk to him respectfully. However, he remained quiet. Perry gave his friend a subtle shake of his head and a frown. Ned ignored him and gave Charles a filthy look, which, unfortunately, he did not see.

Seeing Charles was waiting for an answer, Perry continued his account. "Then we get back to *God* again. God loves us unconditionally, unequivocally and eternally. He promised us a pathway back to Him. He supplied that by sending His son to take our sins and die. Jesus was, and is, perfect as we had once been. When He died on the cross, He took our sins and disobedience onto Himself. However, by doing that, Jesus unlocked the doorway back to Heaven. In that battle over life and death, Lucifer lost. Jesus came back to life and still lives to this day. The devil was defeated that day but doesn't realise that he has already lost the final battle between good and evil. The pathway back to God is permanently open again for anyone who seeks Him. Satan can't close it ever again." Perry chuckled. "Justin, my friend, said that Satan didn't even realise he was in a battle that had begun at Creation and would last for Eternity, or if he did, not what he was fighting for. Either way, Jesus won."

Bill had never heard his entire three-year degree at university summed up so simply. He shook his head in amazement. Listening intently, he queried, "So what of the two questions?"

Perry smiled at the reserved probe. He, too, had pondered over this when his friend Justin Williams had first mentioned it to him. The childlike questions had been so blatantly obvious he had missed their importance. With a nod to Bill, Perry said, "In reality, I suppose there is only one question, not two. Think of it as a two-part one. They are to either accept and believe or reject. Hence, 'What if you do?' and 'What if you don't?' Our faith is that simple. We either choose to believe, or we reject and follow our own pathway to sin and follow the devil, Satan, or Lucifer as he was originally known, and all his temptations. Denial that sin exists is one of the biggest problems. You can't repent of something if you don't believe you have done wrong."

Ned had been sitting with a smile on his face. "I've heard this before, Perry, perhaps not quite so simply put, but in essence, the same. Each time, my faith gets a reboot. We get tied down with big words when only a childlike acceptance is enough. This Bible study has opened a new understanding for me, and I've gone to church all my life. I know God loves us, forgives us, and wants us back into His fold. My mother explained it with the story of the lost sheep. We are that lost lamb. When she told me that as a child, I have never forgotten it."

Charles sat in awe at what he had just heard. Ned had tried to explain it, but Perry's concise explanation was easy to follow. "I can do that! If that's it, following what's right is not too hard. I got sent out for something I didn't do anyway, so it's not like I'm a crook." Three pairs of eyes were upon him. He explained, "I got charged with sheep stealing and transported, but I was at work. I could prove it too, but I still had the sheep in my yard." Charles shrugged. It was no use crying over spilt milk. It had happened, and his only regret was that his mother and sister were now alone. Life here was good, and now he had Sal. His family had needed the small amount of pay his job brought in, and now they had little to no income but the mystery money that arrived monthly.

The conversation turned back to life in the colony and then what Perry would do on his return home. That question from Bill brought up the topic of Elizabeth Fry. Her amazing work of assisting the convict women on board the ships and the difference it made for them made Ned think about his possible role in the colony. All three women, Katy, Molly, and Sal, had all been assisted by her in London. From this conversation, they discovered that Katy had been the first convict she had visited, which had developed into Mrs Fry's growing charity work.

Ned sat listening hard. Bill and Charles were, or had been, convicts and could do little to assist, but as a military man and a major at that, he was in a position to do something about some of the younger girls, so he did. With the opening of the Female Factory in February of that year, the situation had eased slightly. However, so much more was required. Molly, Sal, Katy, and her cousin Janey were examples of different types of female convicts, and he saw a way to assist them. He would seek out safe houses throughout the area and place the chosen few in places of safety and sanctuary. His friends Humphrey Downes and Tim Hinds were doing the same in Sydney.

Perry saw a frown settle on his brow. "Ned, what's up? You look to have the weight of the world on your shoulders."

Realising Perry was correct, Ned straightened up. "I've just had a thought, that's all. Elizabeth Fry's work is brilliant. Both Sal and Molly benefitted, as have thousands of other women, but it was because of Katy that Elizabeth Fry started her project."

Perry gave him a single raised eyebrow glance, then nodded.

Ned gave a dimpled grin. "Okay, it was also after a few conversations with you and introducing her to your minister friend Justin, whom she already knew, by the way." He chuckled. "But that's by the by! Once the girls, like your three wives, are here in the colony, there is little hope of keeping them safe. I know some who abuse their assigned women before they even get them home. One man, Cyrus Black, out on the Hawkesbury is so vile that I shudder to think how the poor girl assigned to him is coping. Caroline Shelley was allocated to him only a few weeks ago."

Bill knew the filthy man and exclaimed, "Cor, poor girl!"

Ned shuddered, and then he explained. "Cyrus lives in a bark hovel at

Castlereagh near the edge of the Nepean River, not far from Ben Parker's leatherwork factory. Anyway, Cyrus's furnishings are sparse, to say the least." Ned felt bile hit his mouth when he thought of the foul man. He said, "Even as a major, I have no authority to protect the girls. I had reason to visit the Blacks soon after she was assigned to him, and Caroline was covered in the most appalling bruises, so I'm guessing he uses her as a punching bag as well as a bed warmer. Reverend Marsden married them in one of his quickie weddings at the factory, so legally, the girl is the man's possession, and therefore, he can do what he wishes with her. My hands are tied." He groaned as though in pain. "Consequently, I cannot help her, and quite honestly, I feel she will end up dead. I try to stop men like him from getting carnally innocent girls. So, after this conversation, I plan to set up a group of safe places where I can send the younger ones. I have a few already."

Ned had been devastated when he saw the colour of Caroline's face. He had been asked to call on the farm to confirm that the convict girl was still there as he had heard that she had never been seen outdoors. Now he knew why. When he arrived, the noises emanating from inside the hovel made him wait a few minutes. The bed, such as it was, was currently in use, and he did not wish to interrupt the couple's activities. He had walked across the two-wheel track and looked at the ford near the next-door farm. By the time he returned some twenty minutes later, they had both risen from the bed, and he saw Cyrus heading out to the yard. He knocked, and with one glance at the girl, her nose bleeding, her robes in great disarray, and her bodice torn to the waist, he now wished he had disturbed them when he first arrived. She was in tears. Cyrus had obviously seen him drawing near to the shack and arrived back panting. Cyrus's breath was what first assailed Ned's nostrils. The stench of the man's breath and his blackened teeth made Ned wish to step back a few paces. However, he stood at the door as he was not invited inside. The filthy creature spat a stream of black chewing tobacco onto the hut floor and motioned for Caroline to clean it up. She did so without hesitation. Ned realised she had learnt to do as ordered or pay the consequences. His heart sank.

Six months later, he had already found one or two needy girls and sent them to Perry. Sal had been the first rescue on his first day in the colony; other girls had followed. The government dairy had taken more than a few, and Elizabeth Macquarie had persuaded Elizabeth Macarthur to take two girls for their private dairy. Jennifer and Billy Williams had their new dairy open, and they had also asked for a group of young milkmaids. He had been assigned to oversee Jennifer when he first arrived and had come to know the William's family well. Bill and Molly Miller had added a few pallet beds downstairs in the unlined storeroom for emergency placements, but it wasn't enough. Hundreds, if not thousands, more places were needed. He felt overwhelmed. It was never going to be enough. With Perry leaving, the three cottages he rented in Phillip Street would no longer be available to hide the most vulnerable. He wished there was some way that the cottages or some other form of accommodation could be accessed. He gave a resigned sigh.

Charles had been biding his time in replying to Ned's comments. Charles had recently discovered that Perry was an earl and Ned was the major in charge of the convicts. The eclectic group were friends, yet not friends. They were brothers in Christ, and that broke down the social barriers. It was more that they had all been thrown together by an unknown hand. Charles had little idea why he was considered good enough to socialise with men of this calibre. However, here he was, sitting at a table as an equal. As there had been no mention of the date Perry was actually to leave, Charles knew that this could well be one of the last times they were all together.

The conversation at the table had fallen into a lull.

Charles finally said, "Sirs, I was summoned by the governor this week, and with Mr White leaving, I knew I would be reassigned. Major Ned, I had thought you would suggest that we go somewhere else, but not so. The governor has a different idea. After receiving my 'Ticket of Leave' early as a reward for assisting in suppressing that mutiny, the governor found out that I was literate and requested that I manage the Government Stores for the town. You may not know that I've been doing that from Mr White's house for a few weeks." The listeners all nodded in acknowledgment. Charles continued, "Well…" He paused and swallowed. "…Governor Macquarie also asked if Sal and I would like to run a new sailors' inn. Not a fancy one like yours, Bill, but one that is cheap accommodation with a small taproom for the sailors and travellers who wish for a quiet hammock in the loft. In our case, it will be in a new barn loft for the night. It is what he is building down at the end of George Street near the King's Wharf jetty. *The Jolly Sailor Inn* will have a huge public stable complex with a barn with a big quadrangle forecourt that backs onto that grassy slope that leads down to the wharf. I think he will be reusing some of the old barracks infrastructure as the store. Apparently, one of the soldiers is helping finance the project, but I was not told which one." He glanced at Ned, wondering if it was indeed him

They pumped Charles for more information about the new facility.

Bill was thrilled, but Charles's new work meant they would see little of each other. Their inns would only be a few streets away, so Sundays would be their only rest time for socialising.

Ned lay back smiling. He hoped Charles would never find out that he was the instigator of the idea and also that he was indeed one of the secret financiers and had recommended Charles to the governor via Perry. He had brought a large wad of money with him; this way, he could almost have a home base where he could relax. His money currently sat in the new bank, and as it was getting very little interest, he thought he might as well use some of it. However, he was not the only sponsor. Another mystery man was, too.

~

Bill had an inn full of guests, and with Molly recovering from her morning sickness, he realised he would have his hands full coping with everything.

Perry was throwing Ned a birthday party.

Ned's birthday was Tuesday, October 16th, 1821. It was a belated twenty-first party, as last year; his coming-of-age slid by unnoticed and, therefore, uncelebrated. Being a major at only twenty-two was all well and good, but being halfway around the world from your family was hard. Perry thought a private informal luncheon would be perfect. The Miller household was all invited but politely declined due to other commitments. Andrew was at work, and Ellen was cooking the evening meal for the full inn while Molly babysat. The luncheon was eaten and packed away before anyone realised Katy, Charles, and Sal had vanished.

By early afternoon, eleven-month-old Charlie realised he had not seen his parents for some time; however, the whereabouts of the missing couple were soon explained with the cry of a new voice.

Sal had delivered a second son with the assistance of her mistress, Katy. The first person to be asked to cradle the newborn child was Ned.

Charles placed the baby boy in his friend's arms. "Major Ned, we thought you would like to meet your name's sake, Edward John Lockley, to be known as Eddie."

Ned had plenty of experience holding Charlie; therefore, he carefully took the baby from his friend's arms. The tiny babe, who had just been fed, emitted an almighty burp. "Well, my lad, that's not very gentlemanly of you, is it? I'm sure you will grow into your exalted name." He chuckled as the babe gave a windy smile, and Ned realised they both had dimples in the same places. He gasped but chuckled. Charles knew he had them. The two men were so similar in appearance; he wished he could find out if there was some connection between them, but he hardly dared to enquire further. He knew that to do so would mean that Major Edward Grace, or Ned, would need to reveal his true identity as Lord Edward John Charles Lockley, older namesake to the child he now held. Ned knew that Perry was the only one in the room who knew the name's significance. Their eyes met in silent acknowledgment of the moniker.

In England, Ned's father was the Duke of Gracemere, while his older brother David was the Marquess. Ned and his two younger brothers were all spares, so Ned joined up and tried to live a normal life half a world away. Only Perry knew that his family had no idea of his 'new' enlisted name. He was incognito for the first time in his life. The first months away from home were difficult. He no longer had access to servants to fulfil his every wish. Here he had Sal, who washed his clothing and cleaned his room but nothing else. Because Perry knew his circumstances, she had been permitted to work at both jobs. With Charles's news that he would now run the new inn, Sal had promised that she would continue attending to Ned's clothing and room. Perry's maid, Lucy, was filling in while Sal was on leave.

Perry had also arranged to sell most of the furniture with the house. However, the buyer did not want the large dining table and chairs. He said, "Charles, as I'll be leaving and your new inn will need a table, I would love to offer you my extension table so Ned could still eat and hopefully pray around it. Would you accept this to celebrate the birth of your second child? I want to think that one day, little Eddie will be able to own it himself."

Charles glanced at Sal, and she nodded. He said, "I would be honoured, sir."

~

Bill and Molly were preparing for the birth of their first child while Charles and Sal were settling into their new inn.

A few days earlier, Molly had walked the front garden at Government House collecting pine resin for her next project. She had been able to buy some beeswax as she needed to make more wax wraps, but she required resin. With summer near, these wraps were brilliant at keeping the flies off the food. She washed the calico squares and was ready to make them when she realised she had run out of pine resin. A giant pine tree inside the Government House gate had a significant trickle of resin dribbling down its trunk. There were some bunya pine trees near the building site for the Female Factory, but she dared not go there alone. She wasn't sure either species of pine would even work. At least there were guards on sentry duty at the gates of Government House, so it was safer, and it was not far from the inn. Molly took a basket and knife and headed up to the tree to spend a pleasant half-hour collecting the resin.

The two-story plan of Charles and Sal's new home was designed to stretch. Like Bill's inn, it was built on a slope. The main entrance was on ground level and contained the living quarters for the family. There was also a loft, but it would remain unused for the moment. The lowest floor was a storeroom, which was a single room; however, it had three sets of solid bunks hidden behind a shelving wall, similar to the convict ships. Ned and Charles planned to use this room for emergency women's accommodation. The men had done the fit-out themselves rather than have a convict crew know of its whereabouts.

The young family did not need to use the loft, but a narrow staircase was hidden in a false cupboard should they require the extra space. It would be both cold and hot up there as a timber extension. However, they could add walls and expand upstairs if required. In the meantime, it was used as storage. The building had three bedrooms: a kitchen, an enormous dining room, and a family room. There was nothing fancy in the design, but as Perry and Katy had offered Charles their incredible extending dining room table from their house, the plan of the inn was adjusted accordingly, including a double door into this room.

When it came time to move, it took ten soldiers to carry the exquisite piece of furniture to its new home. More carried the large matching sideboard that joined it. Other soldiers followed with the ten chairs and two small bench seats. The line of red-coated soldiers carrying furniture looked like a trail of ants walking down Phillip Street to the Charles Street inn. The table fitted perfectly.

The rooms were furnished with three double beds. In two rooms, the hanging space was a rod hidden by a curtain. Charles and Sal's room had a large wardrobe built into the wall.

Ned knew Perry's staff had eaten around this large table with the family. He had regularly had a meal there himself. It was a place where Perry had broken down barriers. Charles had promised Ned would continue to be welcomed for a regular Sunday evening meal. Ned loved this time of family fun and fellowship. He adored the little boys, and they were his godsons.

The men had sat at this dining room table and had Bible studies around this expansive surface. All had freely discussed faith; even the children were encouraged to ask questions. In England, none of that could have occurred. He was fully aware of the status of the eclectic group. Ned had regularly visited Perry's homes when at school. Perry had been his mentor, and he was six years older. His father had a castle to rival his family seat. Castle Gracemere and Cheatham Castle were two of the largest in the country. As both were sons of dukes, they had been buddied at school. When Perry finished schooling, he challenged Ned to mentor other boys. He did, and now he would continue to do something similar.

He thought of Charles, a convict who was growing in his faith; of Buck, Perry's son's tutor; and of Bill, an ex-convict innkeeper. Then there were Billy and Bryn Williams, Cornish dairymen who ran the dairy with Jennifer. They joined the group when they could. The eclectic group occasionally included the Vice Regal Gentleman himself. Lachlan Macquarie often sought out some of them for friendship and fellowship.

Ned would miss Perry and Lachlan when they left, but he would no longer be alone. Charles and Sal absorbed him into their growing family. Being Godfather to their two sons made him feel as though he belonged.

Perry promised to visit his parents on his return and, without giving too much away, to tell them he was both happy and content.

Charles was determined to continue this tradition. Bill and Molly joined them when possible while Ellen and Andrew held the fort at their own inn. Another couple came when they could. George and Charlotte Ellis had a tannery on the outskirts of town and often tried to join them. They were all friends from Church.

Charlotte's family, the Rosedales, had arrived years earlier at the invitation of Governor Hunter and had been instrumental in teaching many how to farm the virgin arid and parched land. Charles and George had become firm friends.

Ned found that being the soldier in charge of Charles presented its own difficulties. Over the past year, they had used first names in private, but they were careful to keep things official in public. Neither had mentioned the elephant in the room. Ned was waiting for Charles to say something, but the questions never came. Maybe Charles had never looked in a mirror. Charles accepted him as a friend and never asked more than he was prepared to give. He wondered if he was even aware of the similarity as he may not have a mirror. He decided not to prod the bees' nest.

~

The farewell to the Macquarie's and Whites occurred in early February 1822. The replacement governor, Thomas Brisbane, had arrived some months before. Guy Manning served as his private security guard and soon joined the prayer group, and his young wife Martha came when she could. Lachlan escorted the new Governor around the town and introduced him to everyone required, including the Aboriginal tribal leaders. Compared to the squalid hovel Lachlan had inherited some twelve years previously, the main town of Sydney was almost unrecognisable. Many gleaming golden Georgian edifices now lined various streets. There was law and order and an operational hospital known as the Rum Hospital, as it had been constructed from rum tariffs, with extensions for that edifice already needed. The mint and numerous other public buildings had been completed, and more were planned or under construction.

Ned knew that the new barracks and Female Factory in Parramatta were two crucial buildings Lachlan had constructed. The remains of the old redoubt below the current official residence, the previous barracks, and soldier accommodation were still there. They were now in a significant state of decay. Parramatta also had a new hospital and other public buildings. Ned knew that his friend Perry had been silently instrumental in working behind the scenes to read the sentiment in the community and let Lachlan know where to act next. Another family had joined the departing ship, and that was Phil Bentley's family. Phil was another of Perry's friends and he was also returning home with his family.

The family groups sailed out on the *Surrey*, and Ned stood watching his friends leave. Another soldier stood next to him. Major Tom Turner was also from Kent in England, and the two men had been charged to watch over two other emancipated convicts from their area at home. With Perry's departure, Ned felt somewhat bereft, so Tom Turner's presence beside him was comforting. The older major saw Ned's face and said, "Come on, Ned, let's go see Sam and Annie. I presume you will head back to Parramatta tonight?"

Ned nodded assent to both comments. The conversation they had recently with Perry as he said his farewells weighed heavily on him.

Perry had long ago admitted to Ned that was aware of his friend Sam's history and why Ned had befriended him. He knew Ned was watching out for him for his father and sending news and reports home. However, the letter Perry held revealed the family secret. Ned had said it was for his father, but it was addressed to a duke. After reading the name on the letter, Perry realised that Sam's biological father was really James, Duke of Malvern, not Philip, Earl of Meldon. Perry gasped. He realised Sam was a younger version of the duke. He wondered if Ned knew the story. Perry understood and promised to support his friend when the time came.

Tom had just shared more details with Perry while waiting for Lachlan's arrival. The fact that the duke and earl were neighbours made Tom's revelation surprising, but it all made sense. Tom had told Ned that Perry also carried a letter for Annie's mother, as Lady Broome-Hall was Perry's cousin. He then mentioned a word that initially confused him. "Ned, think of a cuckoo. It lays its eggs in another bird's next." He then crossed his hands over each other, motioning a swap. Major

Tom admitted that neither of their friends realised their own background. He had been employed by Annie's mother to watch over her just as Ned had been asked to watch over Sam. "Mr Perry, I am only telling you as I have heard Lord Nigel, Sam's elder brother, is dead. Lord Philip sent some attorneys and told him that he was the heir. Sam will need you near when he returns home. For I know who you are, too, my friend. You will need to return home one day."

Ned nodded. The immoral situation of some of the nobility and the corruption it condoned, which was so popular in many of the upper echelons of that society, disgusted Ned. He wondered how many of the heirs of the big houses in England were the real biological sons of their so-called fathers. Thankfully, he knew that the Duke of Gracemere fathered him and his brothers as they all were clones of his father. Unfortunately, so was Charles, and Ned knew no other Lockley cousins. He had an unvoiced question of wondering if Charles Lockley was a by-blow of his father and had been hidden away here. His friend mentioned that his father had died when he was five. It made him wonder if his father was really still alive and if he was the connection between them. Was this why Charles had been falsely accused and banished far beyond the sight of his family? Surely, his father had not strayed from his beloved mother's bed, but who else could have fathered his friend? Was Charles his half-brother? Would he ever be able to find out? Probably not, so in the meantime, while he was here, Charles was his friend, and that's how it would stay. Tom and Perry were the only ones who asked, and Ned answered them honestly; he had no idea if Charles was related. None at all!

Chapter 19 Tiny Tim

*T*imothy Jerome Miller entered the world two weeks before Easter in 1822. The perfect little boy was worth the wait, heartache, and tears. Timmy's Baptism had a huge turnout of locals. Jennifer and Billy William's son, Bryn Jacob, to be known as Jack, was born the same day, and the two families decided to have the children Baptised together. Everyone knew and loved both young couples.

Unlike other drinking holes, Miller's inn was a classy establishment that only attracted nice clientele to the town. Even women were welcome to sit inside at the tables and have a cool cider, ginger beer, or lilli pilli cordial.

On the auspicious day, when Reverend Marsden took Tim in his arms to do the Baptism, the little boy reached up and grabbed his preaching bands. As these were starched, they crunched in the baby's hand and now had creases. This did not impress the rotund, dour gentleman.

Charles and Ned stood as Godfathers, with Sal as Godmother to the young lad. Bill had asked Andrew, but he refused because he said he was too old. He felt a Godfather needed to be someone younger who would still be around as the child grew. He was step-grandfather, and that was enough.

The Williams family had to return to the dairy straight after the service. However, the rest of the extended group of friends retired to the courtyard at the Jolly Sailor Inn to welcome the babies into the family of God.

Timmy was the most beautiful babe from the moment of his birth. As he grew, he was a sponge for any knowledge. He was also a forward baby, achieving his milestones early. He was sitting unaided at four months, walking at ten months old, and by the time he turned one, he would ask for things in entire grammatically correct sentences. His father spoke to him in French, as his father had done, and he could speak the language as easily as English. His uncle Davy was only nine months older, and Timmy outstripped him in nearly everything. The two little lads and Beccy were taken into the hearts of the four doting adults.

Life at the inn was good. Molly, in particular, blossomed to the point of almost glowing. She had Bill's son in her arms, and her life was complete and her heart content. If she only had one child, then she would be happy.

Bill knew that he could teach Tim at home, and by doing so, surely, his education would be put to good use in this lad's future. He wondered what future Timmy would have in this new classless world.

Charles and Bill found a deep friendship anchored in faith. Molly, Sal, and Ellen learned a lot from each other. Ellen mothered the various younger women. They often met at Charles's big dining room table with Andrew and the seven friends; as they always included Ned, they had some wonderful evenings. The women retreated either to the kitchen or the wide verandah at the back.

Andrew had purchased a Broadwood box-shaped piano and installed it in the public sitting room in Bill's Inn. Sing-along evenings on wet nights when the inns were empty were enjoyed by all.

By the time Timmy was eighteen months old, Molly was expecting again. She had only realised her condition as her breasts were again getting tender. Timmy was still having a night feed so she could rock him off to sleep, so she had not expected to fall with child again so quickly. She had indeed put on some extra weight while expecting Timmy. However, this added to her loveliness. She was nearly the blushing beauty she had been as a girl. She had not realised how much the convict voyage had taken out of her. She was also beginning to recover mentally. Helping others in a similar situation had been a healing balm.

Bill was more in love with her now than even when they married. His feelings had grown and developed. Bringing a child into his family had been an overwhelming responsibility he had not expected. Having lost his own parents, Ellen was as close to a mother as he could remember. Andrew was a doctor but was a new father himself. However, Andrew had the most experience as a father compared to Charles and himself, plus he also had the background and education as a doctor.

Life at the Rear Admiral Duncan and the Jolly Sailor Inns became busier daily. On Sundays, both venues were closed to new patrons, and all guests were awake in time for the 7 a.m. service at St John's Parramatta. The Ellis, Rosedale and Williams families joined them occasionally, but the Ellis' often headed to one of the extended Rosedale farms.

~

Grace Letitia Miller was born mid-morning on a Sunday in January 1823. Andrew, Ellen, and Sal helped with Molly's confinement.

Charles and Bill were on babysitting duty and had six little ones to oversee. Andrew and Ellen's little ones were growing fast. Charles and Sal had a third child, a beautiful one-year-old cherub named Elizabeth, after Charles's mother and sister, but they had shortened her name to Liza. Her adorable shock of blonde curls and big blue eyes looked out on the world, where she greeted everyone and everything with an angelic smile. Where her older brothers, Charlie and Eddie, were mini-clones of their father, Liza was like Sal.

They had all missed church that morning as Molly had gone into labour at dawn. However, Gracie's arrival on a Sunday morning was otherwise very convenient. Sal even had time to feed her patrons and children before assisting with the birth.

The young fathers had their hands full with six little ones to look after. Sal was already expecting again and was due to deliver later that year. Their children were barely a year apart.

~

By the time Sal delivered her fourth baby, Susanna, called Anna, Ellen could see that Andrew was becoming even more frustrated with the hospital in town. For such a well-trained surgeon, he was only used for operations if a significant emergency occurred.

Molly had already discussed with her mother how long they would stay in the colony. She could tell from her mother's demeanour that it had been a topic of conversation already discussed in the privacy of their bedroom. She knew they would leave. She was surprised that, although sad, she was not as shattered as expected. Her life was now with Bill and her new little family. Her mother's life was now with Andrew, Beccy, and Dave. Thankfully, being literate, they could write.

She was right. Andrew and Ellen Smith and the two small children departed in November 1824. The *Prince Regent* carried the family away with Captain Lamb at the helm.

Molly held her emotions in check until the ship had rounded the point and was out of sight; then, the tears flowed.

Bill had wondered about the wisdom of seeing them off in Sydney, but he knew how close they were and that every moment was valuable. Farewelling Ellen was like saying goodbye to his own mother. At least Andrew would care for her as best he could. Captain Lamb carried a letter for them, which he would give them once at sea. It brought the news that Molly was expecting again. They had decided not to tell them before they sailed as they knew Ellen would wish to stay. Now, the die was cast, and they were gone.

Bill's stomach roiled as he realised they might not see him again. They were about to turn and leave when a soldier appeared beside him. "Hello, William. It's a sad day for us all today! I had friends leave on that ship."

Bill nodded.

Molly was still in his arms, weeping. She sniffed and dried her eyes.

Major Humphrey Downes had recognised the young couple and came to ask how the inn was going. Few knew of the previous governor's involvement, and that's how the Millers wished to keep it. He said, "I just came to see if all is well in Parramatta. As you know, I rarely get out there, but when I do, it's normally for a flying visit."

Molly had recovered somewhat and now stood with Gracie in her arms. Timmy was with Sal for the night. There were no guests, and Tom was keeping watch on the inn. He had decided he was not well enough dressed to eat there now, so he had moved to Sal's kitchen for his daily hot meal.

The Parramatta ferry wasn't running today as the tides were too low, so they had about an hour to kill before catching the transport coach back home.

Major Downes kept chatting and said, "Any chance you can return to my office? Molly, you can feed and change the baby there too."

Bill glanced at Molly and saw her nod.

The pretty baby emitted an unpleasant odour, so they all realised Gracie needed a change. There was no privacy near the dockland to feed the child, so a refuge in the cool office would be wonderful.

Bill had their baby bag over his shoulder but took her elbow as she walked.

Most convicts would be in fear and trepidation if approached by the senior officer in charge of assignments, but not so this couple. The major took the canvas bag from Bill. Now freed of his load, Bill reached for Gracie and took the smelly but giggling child from his wife's arms. The day was heating up and boded to be hot with the possibility of a thunderstorm before the evening came. As they walked, all three glanced at the gathering clouds above. The major and Bill chattered as they walked.

Molly listened with only half her mind on the conversation. Her mother would now be reaching the heads of the harbour, and that thought made her drop her head as the tears flowed again.

Bill knew of her melancholy but could do little to comfort her in public except hook her hand into his arm. It was better to hasten their pace and get her indoors, where he could at least hug her. He had proposed to her in front of this major, so a hug in his office would not be unexpected.

As they walked up the hill, the young major seemed to know everything about the young couple. He asked about Timmy and discussed how advanced his language skills were. He even congratulated the couple on the impending birth of their third child. That news had certainly only been shared with Charles, Sal, and Major Ned.

Bill's head jerked up when he realised who would have told Major Downes. He said, "Major Ned! He would have told you?"

The tall soldier nodded with a grin. "Not much you can keep secret here, so it's better to hear it officially than get a half-truth."

Bill grinned. "I understand, sir. He's become quite close to us, as have Charles and Sal Lockley. Since the Macquaries and Whites left, we have met in the Lockleys' dining room for weekly prayers. The Williams and Ellis's join us when they can, as Lieutenant Guy Manning did when he was with us." He caught the major's eyebrow rising and hoped he'd not said anything untoward.

The major's following comment relieved his anxiety. "You are lucky. Ned is a good chap, and I was pleased to hasten Charles's paperwork and assign him to Perry White on their arrival. I told Ned to fill in his details when they arrived, and he let me know of his placement later. However, a letter had preceded Jack's arrival, and his placement was arranged by the governor personally. Not how things are normally done, but as long as it's legal, that's all I care about. The governor approved them, so that is all that matters." The major smiled at the young man beside him. "Take your cases, for instance."

They had reached the barracks gates, and the three fell silent, not that Molly had said anything. They walked through the opening and towards his office.

The cool office was a delight to Molly. As they entered the office, Molly attended to the child's needs while the men waited outside in the shade. Her first duty was to change the baby. Molly pulled a blanket from the bag to lie her on, and Gracie would be content to sleep on the floor while they talked. She knelt on the stone floor and cleaned Gracie up. As the baby was asleep, she did not need to feed her yet, so she called in the men.

Major Downes said, "Your cases have been discussed a few times with Ned and others in authority. They all know but will remain silent. However, …" He paused, wondering if Molly was listening. "Molly, can you hear me?" the Major asked.

As the baby settled, she could have left her, but she was weeping. Molly was still on her knees on the floor but politely replied, "Yes, sir." Her back was still towards the men, as she didn't want them to see her tears.

The major nodded, "Good because I wanted you here to tell you…" he paused and waited for Molly to turn around. She didn't, so he said, "Molly, please look at me."

Molly stood and turned to face the major; he saw tears on her cheeks.

Thinking something was wrong, Bill went to her side.

Humphrey saw Bill reach for her hand, usher her to a seat, and stand behind her. Humph waited until she was comfortable before continuing. He delivered his news as kindly as possible, but it would be a shock no matter how he worded it. "Bill, Molly, Bert is dead. Before he died, he confessed that it was all his fault, and Bert withdrew the charges before he died in a hospital in Canada. Sir Percival saw to the paperwork in London. I know it's too late, as your time is up. However, your crimes have been expunged; this goes for both of you. He does not want the money returned as he said you deserved none of the accusations. Therefore, you are both here as free settlers rather than emancipists."

Bill was so stunned he stumbled into the chair next to Molly.

Molly bent over and wept in earnest. Her time had finished three years earlier, but the convict label was still one that she had to live with forever. Now, it was gone. Rather than turn to Bill, she moved quickly, scooped up the sleeping child on the ground, and cradled her lovingly. Bill was not surprised by her action. He smiled as he watched her protect their child, then turned to the major. The words Bill spoke surprised both Molly and the soldier. "Sir, may I ask a favour?"

The major nodded.

Bill continued, "Our work at the inn is growing. With Major Ned's assistance, we have been able to help many of the younger convict girls who have come through the system. We both wish to keep doing this."

Molly had now come to sit beside him again. She nodded her agreement.

Bill saw her smile at him and her assent. He said, "If word gets out about our new status, it may hinder our efforts to help the needy. So, although we are thrilled and willingly and graciously accept the situation, can you keep it under wraps? Major Ned will, of course, need to know, as will the new governor and those who follow him, but can you ask them not even to tell Charles and Sal? If you are ever asked, please just say, 'They arrived as convicts'."

Molly had reached for his hand again and squeezed it.

The major should have been surprised, but he wasn't. "Sir Percival was right about you two. So was Sir Robert Peel. William Miller, you are one amazing man and Mrs Molly, you are a perfect companion for him." The major smiled and lay back in his chair. "I will do all I can for you both, and, yes, I will keep the news on the down low. As you say, Ned will need to be told, but he can hush it up at your end. I know of your work, and Charles and Sal are doing the same with others. I gather you all work together?"

Bill nodded.

Major Downes continued, "Did you know Charles has leased one of the three cottages that Perry White lived in?"

He saw Bill nod and smile.

Bill had anonymously given Charles the money for a year-long lease of one of the cottages. "I leased another one of Perry's cottages. As Aunt Ellen told you, we were well compensated."

The major gave a half-laugh, "Then, I suppose you know all about hiding the abused free settlers' wives?"

This time, Molly and Bill nodded in unison, but Molly answered. "The need first came to Mother's attention through my step-father, Andrew. Being a doctor, he saw their beaten condition when these poor women arrived at the hospital. We needed somewhere they could heal. Often, their husbands would abandon them, sometimes even offering to sell their wives at the markets. Phil's wife, Fanny, was one of those women; the community donated the funds to buy her freedom. Sir, I was horrified, as was Mama. So, we spoke to Katy White before she left, and she suggested we rent their old cottages. There, the women could heal in peace and out of the public eye's scrutiny. We have taken a long lease on the top cottage as it's the largest one and closest to us. Charles and Sal have the lowest one as it is closest to them."

Major Downes's arms unfolded. "I should have guessed it was Doctor Smith. He's aptly suited to your mother. Together, they make a formidable team. I find it hard to believe that she was ever just a servant." He heard Molly give a micro intake of breath. He said, "She was a servant, wasn't she?"

Molly looked at Bill, who gave her an imperceptible nod. She explained her hesitation. "Yes and no, sir; you see, Bill's Papa hired her, knowing her story. Yes, she worked as a housekeeper, but only Bill and I knew her true status. Mother is the oldest legitimate child of the previous Earl of Weedham from his first marriage. She and her sister left on the same day, and each married. The year before we were arrested, Aunt Narelle died by her husband's hand. Hence, we are willing to help those in a similar situation. My grandfather fathered numerous children by various maids, and shortly before he remarried for a second time, Mama left her home to be with Papa. The earl had another daughter, Mary, from his second marriage, with whom Perry and Katy White lived for five years. We never told them that Mary is my aunt, sir, and I ask that you do not either should you ever contact them. After Mary's mother died, Grandfather married for a third time and finally had a son, David. I have never met him. My grandfather was a horrible womaniser; therefore, Mother refused to turn to him for assistance when Papa died. Bill's father was the only one who knew her full story as he was friends with Papa. Grandfather paid for all my half-uncles to train as ministers but abandoned the illegitimate daughters and all their mothers completely. One of my mother's younger half-brothers has been training in Rome as his mother was a catholic; the others were sent to English colleges. Perry mentioned his friend, Reverend Justin Williams, and I know him to be one of the older boys."

The major could not have been more surprised if Molly had hit him. He fired two questions at them. "You didn't tell them you were related to them both? Or that you're an earl's granddaughter?"

Both young people shook their heads. The look of astonishment on his face made Bill chuckle. Bill liked this young man, and it would be interesting to see if his attitude to them had changed.

Molly smiled at Bill's chuckle. She said, "So, yes and no, sir, I may have been born in an entitled family, but now I'm content to be Bill's wife and our children's mother and to assist in running the best inn in Parramatta. Major Downes, life at the Rear Admiral Duncan Inn is good. Even in England, I would not have been so happy. Had my grandfather known of my existence, he would have married me off to some lecherous peer for the sake of status on the London marriage mart. I would have been presented at court as a trophy wife and had a miserable life tied to some man I did not even like. He tried to do the same to Mama and Aunt Narelle, but Mama met the valet of one of the nobility and fell madly in love with him. They had a run-away marriage of sorts. Papa's grandfather was a bishop and arranged a Special Licence for them for free. They lived with him until they found a new position; that was how they met Bill's Papa. Aunt Narelle married at the same time as my parents, but they went to Gretna Green. Her husband thought she would bring money, and although she had her jewels, they sold them. He spent that money quickly, and then he started in on the drink. My mother's half-sister, Aunt Mary, does not even know I exist; if she does, she has no idea where I am. I intend to keep it that way. As I said, I have never met Uncle David, who's now the earl, but Mama has, and she likes him, and that's why my brother was named so. He is nothing like his father and is helping clean up the mess." Molly blushed slightly at her revelation. "Grandfather is dead, so Mama went and introduced herself to her younger brother when they were there. He knows we are here and what we are doing."

Major Downes's gaze flicked from one face to the other. She was the granddaughter and niece of the Earl of Weedham. He had found out that Perry White was the Earl of Collingsford only shortly before they departed. Being a younger peer's son, he knew all about keeping a title quiet. His friend Tim Hinds was another such soldier. Ned and Perry had been conversing, unaware they could be overheard in the major's office. He had suspicions about Ned but could not determine which family he belonged to. He knew of no family named Grace in the Peerage. He had checked an older edition of Debrett's Peerage at the library but found no such entry. He presumed he was under a pseudonym.

Ned and Perry had been talking to Tom Turner, who later confirmed the status of the now-departed person. Perry had taken Katy home to England two years ago.

There were rumours of another titled gentleman, and Humphrey guessed it could well be their mutual friend Sam Corbett, the builder. The cabbie had once let something slip about a pair of visiting lawyers from London and being dismissed by him quite rudely.

After some moments of stunned silence, Major Downes swallowed and said, "Fine, I will keep your status quiet and your histories. I'm a third son myself, and that's no secret, but don't spread it around. So, please know you can come to Ned, Tim Hinds, and me should you need anything. And I mean anything at all. You two have done more for the government than can or will ever be acknowledged. Bill, Doctor Smith told me about your meeting with Bonaparte and many other things I will not go into now. Just know everything you have done and will do is appreciated by the authorities and me."

Bill and Molly thanked him.

Bill realised that Gracie was awake and needed a feed. He stood and suggested they wait outside while Molly fed the babe.

As they departed, Bill said, "Sir, as Molly already said, here we have a life we love. I have no secret past as I was a London butler and also the son and grandson of one. I fell in love with the housekeeper's daughter and love her as just that. I had achieved the top of my career by the age of twenty-one, and I can't say I liked it. I would never have been permitted to step outside my class or marry Molly in England if it were known she was a peer's daughter. Here, in Parramatta, we have security and can help people."

Bill gazed at Molly adoringly. "Running an inn may not have been my idea of how I would spend my life, but God had other plans, and He's never wrong. Our Timmy is showing signs of being a bright lad, and I shall continue to tutor him as he grows. Who knows where he could end up? He may even become a lawmaker in this colony and hold a place of trust and authority. In which case, the expungement of our convictions will become known, as will Molly's illustrious background. We only want our children to have the freedom and choice of a life without class expectations. I'm sure you know what I mean?"

The major looked around to see if anyone was at hand. No one was. "I know what you mean, Bill. I am escaping it too, as I'm guessing you have realised?"

Bill nodded and cocked his head, hoping Humphrey would elaborate.

The major continued quietly, "As a third son, I'm not even a spare! I'm the spares' spare, and my eldest brother has a son, so I'm bumped well down the line." He chuckled. "At least my father taught me to follow orders." His eyes twinkled with fun. "Now I get to give them."

Bill said, "I figured so, Major Tim, too, as you are cut from the same cloth." He knew Ned's status, so he left him out of the comments.

Humphrey nodded with a grin but said no more on that topic.

Molly said the baby had been changed again, but she had yet to feed her. She would need nearly half an hour for that.

Telling his guard he was to refrain from permitting anyone entry to his office, Humphrey walked Bill down to the bakery within the compound. He smiled and said, "Let's see if they have any leftover bread. It normally gets fed to the animals, but it's delicious. Take some home. Lockley could probably do with some, too."

By the time Molly exited the cool office, it was time for the couple to leave.

Humphrey Downes said, "Bill, you were sent here for defending her honour. For that alone, I honour you." He gave him a bow of great respect.

"So, I have a surprise for you."

Humphrey pointed to the government carriage in the quadrangle. He said, "Your transport awaits." Unbeknownst to them, Major Downes had arranged for an unmarked government carriage to be brought around to convey them back to Parramatta.

They would travel in some style rather than be squashed in the public conveyance.

Bill thanked him, hoisted the canvas baby bag and a box of bread into the vehicle and assisted Molly inside.

The rocking of the carriage soon had the little girl asleep again.

Bill turned to Molly and smiled. "I'd do it all again, you know. Any man who hurts you needs to answer to me," he said.

"I know, and thank you." Molly rested her head against him, and he slid his arm around her shoulder and drew her close. "I really didn't mean to thwack Bert, but it meant that we could be together here."

They lay back to enjoy the trip.

~

Hours later, the government carriage dropped them at the front door of the Rear Admiral Duncan Inn.

As Bill assisted Molly in alighting, he turned to unload the bread. With a wave, he thanked the driver, who drove off.

Bill said to his beloved Molly, "We're home, darling one. One day, I will buy a fancy sign with the name in beautiful calligraphy to hang on the wall."

Molly didn't care who saw; she turned to Bill and said, "The major was right; you stood in defence of my honour, and because of that, we are here and free. Look at this magnificent place God has placed us in. Together, we will work for His honour and assist in defending those less fortunate women who have no voice and no champion. Those poor wretches don't have a man like you to stand up for them."

Sal Lockley had seen the carriage pull up at the inn and set off up the hill with Timmy and her children.

Molly stood and waved at the slowly approaching group.

The creak of a door opening behind her made her turn.

Peeping around the edge of the door was a bruised and beaten young girl. She inched open the inn's front door and softly welcomed the returning couple.

Ned had told them yesterday that a young abused girl would arrive from the Female Factory today. Molly had forgotten she was coming. She was to be trained as a maid and placed somewhere safe. Thankfully, old Tom had let her inside.

With a smile at each other, Bill and Molly swung into action in their new life. They shook off the remnants of their past. The that firmly behind them, they set to work.

While careful not to crush the baby, Bill quickly kissed his beautiful wife's lips. "Tally-ho, love, it looks like we have work to do!" He ushered his beloved wife into the inn. He followed with the smelly nappy bag and the box of bread. Sal could take some home for their use. He would deliver some to the cottages, and they would keep a loaf or two for the inn.

They set about preparing for their life ahead.

Tonight, they had one young girl to settle into her new abode. Their work had begun in earnest.

Bill and Molly's story continues in 'The Lockleys of Parramatta' series.

Honest **Reviews** *or star ratings of my books help bring them to the attention of other readers who are more likely to read something from a new-to-them author if it has more reviews. You can easily leave a quick rating or a short review on* **Amazon or Goodreads**.

Characters

Herbert Timothy **Miller**
m **Grace** Blackman
  #1 **Jerome** William Miller
  m **Letitia** Jones d 1800
    #1 William (**Bill**) Timothy **Miller** b mid-1797
    m late Jan 1819 Mary **Molly** Ross b 1800 in Parramatta, dau of Ellen and Sam Ross
    4 Children   (*term expires Christmas 1821*)
        #1 **Timothy Jerome**   b March 1822   m 1843 Susanna (**Anna**) Lockley
            #2 **Grace Letitia**   b 1824   m 1841 **Charlie Lockley**
            #3 **Samuel William**   b 1828 (Sammy) m 1851 Isabella '**Belle**' Ellis
            #4 **Ellen Mary**   b 1830   m 8/1856 **Luke Lockley**
Sam Ross b 1776   d 1802 (*war wounds*)
m 1799 **Ellen** White b 1781 (*daug. Earl of Weedham's 1st marriage, Narelle b 1782 - full sister. ½ sister to Mary, half brother David and numerous illegitimate half brothers, Justin and Hugh are two*)
    1 Mary Ellen Ross (**Molly**) b 1800 (*see above*)
m2 March 1819 **Andrew** David Smith - Doctor from *General Stewart,* convict ship
    #1 Rebecca (Beccy) b Dec 1819
    #2 David   b April 1821

Sir **Percival Edison-Browne**, Baronet,
m 1794 Erminetrude (Tuppence) Tippy b 1800
    #1 **Errol** Edison-Browne b 1795
    #2 Cuthbert (**Bert**) Edison-Browne b late 1796 d 1820 in Canada
Algernon Makepeace - tutor for the Edison-Browne family
Basil Gomes - Librarian and historian for Sir Percival
James new butler
Toby, Phillip and Cedric footmen in London
Sophie and Rebecca (Becca) - Molly's friends and Ellen's new maids
Esther and Ruth - two Jewish sisters, all maids in training
        Cedrick (Ceddie) Dickerson - hackney cab driver
Josiah Woods - Ellen's butler in Sydney
Major Humphrey **Downes** - Assignment officer
Robin Henge - caretaker for Ellen's Sydney house

    Earl Philip Harrington d Feb 1808 - shooting accident - 5th Earl
    M 1805 Catherine (**Katy**) Jane White b 1783 (convicted as Kate Harrison)
        #1 boy stillborn b 1806
        #2 Mary (**Mia**) Phillipa b 4 April 1808 at Harrington Hall, (The Lady Mary)
    m2 May 1808 Peregrin (**Perry**) White b 1772 - Katy's 3rd cousin (12th Earl of Collingsford from age 26) *Fire Katy 14, Perry 24 in 1798*
        #1 Jeramy (**Jem**) Peregrin b Feb 1809 - 1st Marquess of Oxhill from 1843,
        #2 Louisa Jane (**Lou**) b 1811 m **Paul** Lockley - Ned's 2nd youngest brother.
        #3 David (**Davy**) Jacob James b 25 Dec 1813
        #4 Colin (**Col**) Edward 24 June 1818 twin
        #5 Joanna (**Jo**) Catherine 24 June 1818 twin (Twinny)

    Ned Grace - 2nd son of Duke of Gracemere
     3 Brothers, Marquess David, Paul and Douglas
    Charles Lockley
    m Feb 1820 **Sal** McCarthy
        Charlie b Nov 1820
        Eddie b 16 Oct 1821
        Liza b Jan 1823
        Anna b mid 1824

Elizabeth Fry
Lachlan & Elizabeth Macquarie
General Stewart crew
Captain **Robert Grainger** - Captain of the *General Stewart*
Other incidental names are mentioned:- John Macarthur, Samuel
Marsden, Major Morriset, Captain Wallace, and **Commissioner John Bigge.** All
are historically accurate
Admiral Adam Duncan
Surgeon Superintendent **Andrew Smith**

*(NB As far as I can find, **Andrew Smith** only did the one Convict ship trip. He returned
on the Shipley on 3 April 1819 along with seven other naval doctors. In my story, I have him
marry Ellen Ross and later return to the colony with her, and they have children.) In reality, I have
been unable to find out what happened to him once the Shipley returned to England.*

*Another Doctor, Andrew Smith, made a journey on the John Renwick in 1838. But
apparently, it is a different doctor.*
h t t p s : / / f r e e s e t t l e r o r f e l o n . c o m /
surgeon_superintendents.htm#:~:text=Convict%20ship%20surgeons%20played%20a,crew%20aboard%20t
hese%20prison%20ships

Admiral Adam Duncan *(extract from article below)*

Adam Duncan was born in Dundee on July 1, 1731, to a family that had long
been active in the city's affairs.

Duncan became a Rear Admiral in 1787 and a vice Admiral in 1793. In 1795
he was given command of a newly organized North Sea fleet. The armies of
Revolutionary France had just overrun the Netherlands, and the small but efficient
Dutch navy was now a British enemy.

In April 1797, the sailors of the Channel Fleet refused to sail in protest
against poor food, brutal discipline, and salaries that had not changed in more than a
century. The mutinies spread from Spithead to the Nore in May. Admiral Duncan,
who at 6'4" literally stood head and shoulders above the crowd, maintained discipline
aboard his flagship Venerable by force of personality. Duncan's fleet was taking on
supplies at Yarmouth when word came that the Dutch were at sea. The two fleets
met on the afternoon of October 11, 1797 off the village of Camperdown. Realising
that if he took time to form a line of battle, the Dutch fleet would escape, Duncan
attacked in two columns, anticipating the tactics that Nelson would use later at
Trafalgar.

Both fleets had sixteen ships of the line, and the British prevailed only after
three and a half hours of desperate fighting. Nine Dutch ships of the line and two
frigates were captured. Two of the prizes sank afterwards, and the rest were fit only
for firewood. The British fleet lost 1,140 men. The defeated Admiral de Winter, who
matched Duncan's size and stature, was amazed that they had both escaped injury.

Admiral Duncan returned to a hero's welcome. He was inducted into the
House of Lords as Baron Duncan of Lundie and Viscount Duncan of
Camperdown.

*https://www.robertson.org/FC_Admiral_Lord_Adam_Duncan.html If you loved this
book, these are similar.*

Powers and Duties of the Surgeon Superintendent: 1837

* The superintendent surgeon joins the ship before the convicts are put on board and have the whole superintendence of them.

* During the whole voyage, the convicts are under his superintendence; he may inflict punishment by a limited number of lashes.

* He is bound to preserve discipline and is responsible to the Admiralty.

* The convicts might complain of his conduct on their arrival at Sydney to the visiting officer from the Colonial Secretary's office.

* The surgeon superintendent keeps a journal, which is inspected by the governor and by the Admiralty.

* He carries out a copy of the record of the crimes committed by each convict.

* If there is no chaplain on board, the surgeon superintendent reads prayers and, sometimes, a sermon on Sunday when the weather permits.

* The superintendent surgeon does not leave until all the stores have been removed from the ship.

Bibliography

Elizabeth Fry information
https://www.gutenberg.org/files/16606/16606-h/16606-h.htm

Hyde Park House Sept 1818
https://trove.nla.gov.au/newspaper/article/2178215/493928

Newspaper advert for cottage - was actually Nov 1818
https://trove.nla.gov.au/newspaper/article/2178362?searchTerm=rent%2C%20parramatta

Convict ship information
https://www.gutenberg.org/files/16606/16606-h/16606-h.htm

'Maria'- Surgeons Log
https://www.femaleconvicts.org.au/docs2/ships/SurgeonsJournal_Maria1818.pdf

General Stewart ship 1818/Andrew Smith - surgeon
http://www.freesettlerorfelon.com/andrew_smith_surgeon.html
NB There is no surgeon's journal for 'General Stewart.' Captain's Log lists deaths but no details, so I have used a writer's licence.
NB This Doctor Andrew Smith is probably NOT the same one who served with Florence Nightingale in Scutari. That one had served 17 years in Africa while this one was doing the Sydney run. I can find no more information about this Andrew Smith after returning on the Shipley in 1819. Another Andrew Smith did another convict journey on the John Renwick in 1838. I do not know if it is the same one.
https://freesettlerorfelon.com/surgeon_superintendents.htm#:~:text=Convict%20ship%20surgeons%20played%20a,crew%20aboard%20these%20prison%20ships

Further reading - Female Convicts - "Whores and female convicts."
https://theconversation.com/whores-damned-whores-and-female-convicts-why-our-history-does-early-australian-colonial-women-a-grave-injustice-4894

Lady Penrhyn 1788 convict ship.
https://dictionaryofsydney.org/entry/lady_penrhyn

Admiral Adam Duncan
https://www.robertson.org/FC_Admiral_Lord_Adam_Duncan.html

A First Fleet Convict Story 1788

A First Fleet story with the descriptions taken directly from the Journal of Doctor Author Bowes Smith who was the doctor on board the Lady Penrhyn.

Gentle Annie Soames

Her dreams lead to unexpected outcomes. An Australian First Fleet story.

Annie Soames is a girl beloved by the community but not afraid to voice her desires. That leads to trouble, illicit love, and a world turned upside down.

Oliver Quilpie, the recently married Marquess, discovers his arranged union is not to his taste; he is drawn to his wife's companion. Unfortunately, he is unable to keep his hands off her. For revenge, Annie mimics his every move while riding but is dressed as a highwayman. However, she had now fallen in love with him. This action finally leads to her arrest and transportation to a faraway land.

After some years, Oliver's wife dies, and his thoughts turn to Annie. He seeks to find her, but she has vanished. He is horrified to discover she was transported to New South Wales as a convict on the *Lady Penrhyn.* He follows with a shipload of supplies on the *Kitty.* Will Annie want to see him?

ISBN 9780645441574   ISBN ebook 9781923097063

July 2024

The Hunter to Macquarie Collection 1795-1822

When Upon Life's Billows

Sydney 1795-1821 - Governor John Hunter

Captain John Hunter was born to a life at sea. The wind blows where no man knows, and John is caught up in the tempest. Although wrecking his ship, the *HMS Sirius,* in 1790, he became the second Governor of the rough and filthy penal settlement of New South Wales. He always seems to be in the wrong place at the wrong time, trusting the wrong people.

Helena Rosedale is not a typical female convict. She fights tooth and nail to stop the men from abusing her. She gains the name of Helena the Hellcat.

Crispin Milroy is alone in the world and one of the new Governor's security detail. Can he win the fair lady's heart? Life in 1795 in Sydney Cove is raw at best. Food is scarce, and disease often ravages the settlement. Life throws everything except death at these three, yet somehow, they survive. Why does John trust this young couple when others betray him?

What trials must Helena and Crispin endure to make their new lives in this raw town bearable? How can John ease their path?

ISBN: 9780645783339   ebook ISBN: 9780645783346

Coming 2025

Saddler's Song

London 1790s to Parramatta 1840s

George Ellis is a tanner's son living on the outskirts of London. When disease takes his family. Alone and hurting, he seeks to find a new life for himself. Hearing from a friend about the possibility of setting up a business in New South Wales, he sells up and leaves all he knows. His beloved violin is his most valuable item, and his talent for making beautiful music is hidden from all but a few.

Ben Parker is a saddler, like George; he is also alone in the world. Ben also sells up to move to the new colony. The two young men meet and combine their skills to start afresh in a new world. During the journey out, George's skill as a violinist is revealed. On arrival, they find accommodation with a family with many lovely daughters. Two of these girls steal their hearts, but how will the business survive in an animal-starved land where access to leather is limited? What is the saddler's song?

ISBN : 9780645783353   eISBN: 9780645783360

Coming 2025

Tuppence to Pass

London 1800s to Parramatta 1820s - Governor Lachlan Macquarie

Josh Callan is a London lad who makes the best of the life that has been dealt to him. Stealing from the man who killed his father gives the family a change of direction. Josh is arrested, but the judge belittles him, saying he's not worth tuppence. He is transported to the penal colony of Sydney as a convict just as **Governor Macquarie's** term starts. He proves his worth and falls on his feet, becoming the Governor's groom and confidante.

Life in the Colonial town opens opportunities they could never have dreamed about in England, but can Josh find his niche?

Where will this strange friendship take Josh and his family?

ISBN : 9781923097070   eISBN: 9781923097087

Coming 2025

His Majesty's Pageboy
London to Emu Plains, Australia, in the 1800s

Jack Turner was born into a life of pomp and privilege that was not rightfully his. He was brought to the royal court for his own protection. By the age of ten, he was King George the Third's pageboy and known as Lord John. For years, Jack roils against the immorality of society and the shallowness of people; then, he meets an unspoiled young girl amongst the mire of humanity whose purity stands out. He is unable to pursue her before his life hits a wall.

Martha Alexander is the daughter of a wealthy shipping merchant. She has been presented to London's second tier of society, where she meets the young man of her dreams. She is expected to marry well, and Lord John sets her heart fluttering. However, her father's drinking shatters her future. He was made to sign all his possessions away while drunk, unknowingly including his daughter. Refusing a forced marriage changes her life. How do these two end up as convicts in Australia?

Paperback ISBN 9781923097308   eISBN 978192309792
Coming 2026

Far From the Whispering Sheoaks
Set in Australia in the 1820s

Fanny Little was in the wrong place doing something she thought was legal. Her actions see her arrested, tried and banished. She is assigned from the female prison to ex-soldier Gordon McKenzie and soon finds herself in a despicable and humiliating situation of being sold in the public marketplace.

Phil Bentley is a man running from his jealous uncle, and he finds solace in a secluded farm half a world away. With the community on their side, can Phil save Fanny from Gordon's vile abuse? Why is their relationship destined to court controversy? And who is Jas? Why does Gordon wish to harm the child? Will they ever escape the shadows that are chasing them?

Paperback ISBN 9781923097315   eISBN9781923097322
Coming 2026

Unlikely Convict Ladies Trilogy 1792-1840s
Dancing to her Own Tune
Co-authored by Sheila Hunter and Sara Powter
Sydney 1790s to England 1830s

Annie White is released after serving seven years as a convict in Sydney. She gets a visitor who, with his help, she can start a baking business. She is then asked to assist another sick man, **Sam** Corbett. Annie nurses him back to health, and a relationship develops. They settle into a life together, barely making ends meet; she realises she's expecting a child. Sam has his past laid bare and must adjust to the revelations. They both must face their accusers and find that the answers to their questions are not what they thought. Their life experiences seem to cling to them, and unable to shake them off, they end up back in England. They must face their ghosts and discover they are not who they think they are. How can they turn their anger and spite into love and forgiveness? The Dance of Life goes on.

ISBN 9780645110715   ISBN9780645110722
Long-listed in the Historical Fiction Company Competition 2022
https://amazon.com/dp/064511071X   https://amazon.com/dp/B09JC378YV

Amelia's Tears
Parramatta 1828 – England 1840s

Amelia Westaweller awaits her assignment in the Parramatta Female Prison. Forced to leave the relative safety of gaol, she is assigned and now faces her worst nightmare. A foul man claims her and makes her life a living hell. Then, her world goes black. A glimmer of hope arises when she hears from her brother, Jim, who has enlisted a friend to help her. She writes to Jim, pouring out her heart and telling him of the horrors of her new life. He encourages her to stay firm in her faith. All she can do is pray. When Major **Ned** Grace, her brother's friend, enters her life in Parramatta, he starts to ease her path. Things have changed, as now she has a child in tow. How can Amelia forge a new life for herself? What man could want her with her background and a child at her side? Who is the gentleman who turns her tears of sadness into tears of great joy?

ISBN: 9780645110739   eISBN: 978-0-6451107-4-6 Hard Cover ISBN 979-842061-7953
https://amazon.com/dp/0645110736   https://amazon.com/dp/B09SS855BR

A Lady in Irons
England 1800s - Parramatta 1808+
Katy Harrington is mourning the death of her husband after he died in a shooting accident. Barely coping, she awaits the birth of their child. If it's a girl, she must hand the family home to her husband's brother. The day after giving birth to a daughter, she and her daughter are left on the side of a road. She collapses and is found by someone she thought had died in a fire ten years before. **Perry White**, badly scarred himself, nurses her back to health. They marry and move in with her widowed friend, Mary.

After some years, she discovers her husband and friend in each other's arms. Now living in a love triangle, she flees. Grasping the only straw available, she intentionally gets arrested and is sent to a colony far away. By doing this, her marriage can be annulled.

What happens in the Colony is different from what she expects. Governor Macquarie comes to her rescue, but what of Perry and her children?

ISBN: 9780645110784   eISBN:9780645441505

https://amazon.com/dp/0645110787   https://amazon.com/dp/B0BCWSXB9Z

The Convict Birthstain Collection 1830-1840s

NO MORE, MY *Love*
Hunter Valley, NSW 1820s
Jess Elkin is distraught when tragedy ravages her family. She becomes the victim of a carriage accident and is nursed back to health by the driver, **Marcus Ryan**. Marcus was not expecting to fall in love. Yet, when Jess's fortunes suddenly turn for the worse, Marcus must decide how far he will go to pursue her. As time passes in Newcastle, Australia, Marcus must take a business trip and is taken by pirates. Jess is left wondering if her will keep his promise to return to her… Will she ever see him alive again?

ISBN: 9780645441536   eISBN 9780645441581

Long-listed in the Historical Fiction Company Competition 2023

https://amazon.com/dp/0645441538   https://amazon.com/dp/B0BSBH143Q

The Vine Weaver
Hawkesbury River area 1820s+
New Beginnings and Old Threats
In the 1820s, Australia, **Joel and Hetty Walker** live on a secluded farm on the Hawkesbury River, which becomes a healing haven for the protection of young convict women. A series of events brings **Fran Rea** to Hetty's attention, and she is taken to the farm. Fran and Hetty develop a cottage industry under the compassionate eye of farmhand **Hector Macdougal;** Hector's loving words change lives. It is to him that Fran turns when threatened.

The vines now must draw them close to survive the future revelations, and of those, there are many.

ISBN: 9780645441512   eISBN: 9780645441529

Long-listed in the Historical Fiction Company Competition 2023

https://amazon.com/dp/0645441511   https://amazon.com/dp/B0C6Z552Y2

The story continues in Scotch at The Rocks…

Scotch at The Rocks
Glasgow, Scotland, early 1800s to The Rocks, Sydney 1830s
Orphaned children Brodie Stewart and Heather Anderson live on Glasgow's streets. Although hungry, somehow they survive and keep out of trouble. Heather finds a job and looks to be settled; things go pear-shaped for them both. Eventually, they marry by declaration, yet even that gets messed up, and they are both arrested soon after they make their vow. In 1838, they were transported to Sydney as convicts. Heather arrives within weeks of Brodie, and they are assigned close to each other. They are now living on the docklands in Sydney, called The Rocks. They now have to forge a new life halfway across the world from their homeland.

Adventures abound, and Brodie gets press-ganged. While he's away, Heather's life changes and soon, she's officially selling Scotch Whisky at a shop in The Rocks.

You can take a Scot out of Scotland, but where did the Scotch come from?

ISBN 9780645441550 ebook 9781923097001 Large Print 9781923097254

November 2023

Waiting at the Sliprails
The Bathurst Road 1830s
A Convict's Tale

Bea Dawes's term of conviction nears an end, and she has few options other than marriage to a stranger or going on the street.

Jack Barnes, the hired drover, wants a wife. Bea accepts his offer; then, she discovers that he could be gone for months, leaving her alone with **Billy and Netty**, part of the tribe of an Aboriginal tribe who live on his secluded farm. Bea learns to love her husband and also this wonderful aboriginal couple.

Drought ravages the farm, and Jack must hit the long paddock with the flock. In his absence, a visitor arrives, threatening to destroy everything she has worked so hard for. Can Bea touch her heart? Can she cope? Will the drought ever end? And when will Jack return?

ISBN: 9780645441543   eISBN: 9781923097032

August 2023

Convict Shadows of the Past
Two Jennifers, two hundred years apart

When aged eight, **Jenny** Kellow learns of her convict family history and discovers that she was named after a convict from nearly two hundred years ago. Her grandfather's stories inspire her to dig deeper into her ancestors' convict past. From her grandfather, she hears stories of bushrangers, convicts, and life in the infant colony of Parramatta. She sets about retracing the footsteps of her convict great-great-great-grandmother to honour her. Jenny's search starts with microfiche back in the 60s, and she learns about the small tin mining town in Cornwall and the production of a cheese that sets London afire. She discovers her ancestor, **Jennifer Kellow,** has brought these cheese-making skills to Parramatta, where she taught others her craft. Echoes of the past can still be heard if you know where to listen.

Who was the first Jennifer, and what does she have to do with cheese? Why is she so elusive? Did Jenny's ancestor, Jennifer, ever see those two small crosses carved into the bricks of the Female Factory? Would Jenny ever find out her ancestor's story?

ISBN: 9780645783315   ISBN ebook 9780645783322

A NaNoWriMo 2022 book winner

January 2024

In Defence of Her Honour
London 1800s to Parramatta 1819

Bill Miller had been raised and educated with the sons of the family. The youngest, Bert, had been his best friend. However, jealousy intervenes when Bill's excellent schoolwork curtails their friendship. He wins a scholarship and enters Oxford University. When Bill's father, the old butler, dies unexpectedly, Bert insists that Bill take over the position, but it's more to oppress him. Bert's jealousy grows and festers. Now looking for a way to rid themselves of their new butler, a ruckus ensues, and Bill is arrested for assaulting Bert. The housekeeper and her daughter, **Molly Ross,** vouch for him, but it's too late; Bill has been arrested and sentenced to be transported. With Bill gone, Molly now needs to defend herself from Bert. After hitting him with a pan, she is arrested and sent to Sydney. Bill and Molly arrive with letters of introduction and compensation from Bert's father. Soon, they will be running the best inn in Parramatta with an endorsement from the governor.

ISBN 9780645441567   ISBN ebook 9781923097049

April 2024

I Can't Stop Tomorrow
Irish Famine 1840s to Avoca Beach, Australia

Escaping bigotry and prejudice in Ireland, the **O'Shane** family lives on a secluded farm on the west coast of Ireland. The potato blight soon decimates their farm. It's always darkest before dawn, and the two remaining girls cling to the hope of a new life. With the kindness of strangers, the eldest girls, **Clare** and **Kerry O'Shane**, head to their cousin, Sal Lockley, in Parramatta, Australia. A new, wonderful life awaits them both. **Shéamus Connor** is the annoying teenage boy who reluctantly draws Clare's affection. However, living in a convict town means ruffians abound.

John Moore is an angry and troubled Irishman, content to live alone on another secluded farm until he discovers Clare and two other lads need rescuing.

Can John protect her from the pain inflicted by an evil world?

Can Shéamus find his lost love who had fled?

ISBN: 9780645441598   ISBN ebook 9781923097056

October 2024

Madeline's Boy
England 1830s to New South Wales 1840

All is not straightforward when money and a title are involved.

Madeline Brougham is asked to care for her best friend's orphaned son when his life is in danger. **Christopher Downes** is the pawn between a greedy, unscrupulous uncle and his inheritance. Maddie must do everything she can to keep him safe, including moving halfway around the globe to take Chip to his guardian, Major Humphrey Downes, in the Australian Corps in Sydney. Humphrey's best friend, another soldier, **Major Tim Hinds**, meets Maddie, and with the support of these two men, a chase around the colony ensues. Will Maddie and Tim be able to find happiness together?

Can the three adults keep Chip safe until he's old enough to claim his inheritance?

ISBN: 9780645783308   ISBN ebook 9781923097094

Dec 2024

Jam or Marmalade for Tea
England 1820s to New South Wales 1825 (Brisbane Era)

Martha Hamilton is the eldest of four orphans struggling to survive on their own. Caught stealing, she is tried, convicted, and transported to New South Wales. With her family gone, she becomes despondent. Life holds no meaning for her, and The ocean waves look inviting.

Captain Guy Manning is a frustrated and injured redcoat soldier returning to Sydney to take up a new assignment. He notices Martha trying to jump overboard and rescues her. How do two cats bring them together?

A convict ship is no place for romance, and she's far too young anyway, isn't she?

Can Guy save her and forge a life together for them? What connections does he have to try and save her siblings? Why is marmalade important for their future?

Paperback ISBN 9781923097933   eISBN9781923097285

A NaNoWriMo 2023 book winner

October 2025

A 100-year, six-part Australian Colonial series

<u>The Lockleys of Parramatta 1800-1900</u>

Hands upon the Anvil

A blacksmith's life and love are more than work

<u>Parramatta 1830s</u>

Eddie Lockley's parents were transported for their crimes. Can a steadfast lad rise above his origins and guide others to succeed in a land of opportunity? Ten-year-old Eddie longs to help his mum and dad. Living in a convict town with his family, the keen youngster has been working with the local blacksmith since his sixth birthday. But when a lieutenant doesn't stop abusing his older brother, the young boy yearns for the day when he can stand up and end the torment. Though he's thrilled when his mentor offers to send him off to learn his letters, Eddie fears he won't be around to watch his sibling's back. But as he takes on the biggest adventure of his life, the brave believer soon discovers God is looking out for everyone he loves. Does this young man in the making have what it takes to change everything for the better?

<u>ISBN</u> 9780994578235 Ebook <u>ISBN</u> 978-0-9945782-5-9 Hardcover 9798496177368

Released 2021

https://amazon.com/dp/0994578237 https://amazon.com/dp/B08TB51L19

Out Where The Brolgas Dance

Gold is found, and so is love

<u>Parramatta 1840s</u>

How can a question change so many people?

It's the 1840s, and discoveries across the Blue Mountains continue. Major Mitchell's new road is complete, and towns are planned and being built. Abundant land is available for those who want it.

William "Wills" Lockley, 18, has laid a solid foundation for a respectable career as a blacksmith, but the Lockley lust for adventure flows deeply within his veins. He dreads the monotony of work at the blacksmith's forge and yearns for adventure in a new frontier. Wills meets six Englishmen (*Coping with what is now known as PTSD*) who have the means to make his dreams come true. What they discover changes the Colony and their lives forever. Gold fever ensues. In the West, Wills has to deal with an uncertain romance. Does she even want him?

<u>ISBN</u> 9780994578242 Ebook <u>ISBN</u> 978-0-9945782-6-6 Hardcover <u>ISBN</u> 9798755445504
LP ISBN 9781923097155

Released 2021

https://amazon.com/dp/0994578245 https://amazon.com/dp/B08T6NS3XX

Diamonds in the Dirt

Diamonds, love and money… but there is much more to life.

<u>Parramatta 1850s</u>

Luke Lockley, the youngest Lockley son, has completed University, and his life has no direction. No job, no money, and no love. Desperately alone, he prays for guidance. How can Luke trust that God has a plan for him if he can't even find a job? He does the only thing he can … he prays. Within a week, life has changed … oh, how it has changed as his brother Wills turns up with a suggestion. Would Luke be interested in joining the expedition with John Evans? **Reverend William Clarke** needs assistance on a Government Mineral Survey. The challenge, adventure and finds are life-changing for many. However, it gives Luke meaning, purpose and direction. The condition of his heart problems also takes a turn. Can he walk away?

<u>ISBN</u>:9780994578273 Ebook <u>ISBN</u>: 978-0-9945782-8-0 Hard cover <u>ISBN</u> 979-8788011141

Released 2022

https://amazon.com/dp/099457827X https://amazon.com/dp/B09NH1MLXZ

The Earl's Shadow

Who or what is the 'shadow'? How does it affect so many?
Parramatta 1860s

Charles Lockley is the Earl of Coxheath. He spent his youth as a convict in Parramatta and had no idea he was an Earl. He had minimal education and few social skills. His eldest son, **Charlie,** is no different.

Now faced with his own mortality, Charles has to work out how to live the remainder of his life after a near-death experience. He is called to step way out of his comfort zone in London. His action will change the world for many. The echoes from the past still haunt Charlie. London is calling the family, and they can't postpone the trip. How does the Cobb and Co. coach driver **Jim Leslie** fit in? And precisely what is *'The Earl's Shadow'* that he speaks about? What happens if the 'Shadow' is gone?

ISBN: 9780645110708 Ebook ISBN 978-0-9945782-9-7
Released June 2022
https://amazon.com/dp/0645110701   https://amazon.com/dp/B0B158SKSK

Once a Jolly Swagman

An old black Billy Can contain the secrets of an incredible life
An Australian Historical Novel
Set in 1870s Parramatta and Kent, UK

Rick Lockley, battling his family's expectations, runs away to find himself. **Jack**, a jolly swagman, takes him under his care. Even after years together, Rick knows little about the old man.

On his death, Jack leaves Rick his precious billy can; the contents reveal Jack's identity. Stunned, Rick must travel to England to finalise Jack's wishes. There, he uncovers Jack's life of love, betrayal and a link to his own family. Rick also discovers there is much more to learn about this enigmatic man.

ISBN 9780645110753   Ebook ISBN 978-0-6451107-6-0
Released Sept 2022
https://amazon.com/dp/0645110752   https://amazon.com/dp/B0B5JN1WCV

Jonty's Journey

Gems, Love, Artists and a Golden Lion
Australia and South Africa 1880-1902

Sydney Jeweller Jonty Evans' passion for gems takes him to Africa at a volatile time. He finds the diamonds he wants and is given a lion cub. Jonty is all but kidnapped. His experiences in the Transvaal plunge him into questioning everything he knows of life. Soon, nightmares haunt him. (Now known as PTSD.)

On return home, he nearly messes up his love life with **Lottie** before it even starts, and he struggles to settle. Lottie's father, **Luke** Lockley from Parramatta, takes him in hand and points him to someone who can help.

Jonty is then recalled to Africa as a liaison and reconnects with his lion, Chimbu, when he saves the life of his security detail. His life journey introduces him to the most amazing Heidelberg artists, politicians, poets, rebels, and the scapegoat soldier Harry Breaker Morant. Can Jonty bury the past and regain the peace he's lost?

ISBN 9780645110777 HC ISBN 9781923097124   Ebook ISBN: 978-0-6451107-9-1
Released Feb 2023
https://amazon.com/dp/0645110779   https://amazon.com/dp/B0BLJ7ND1Q

Australian Colonial Trilogy 1840s
By Sheila Hunter
Co-Winner of 1999 NSW Senior Citizen of the Year, In the Year of the Senior Citizen

Mattie
Coming of Age in Convict Australia

Twelve-year-old London street urchin **Mattie Paul** is convicted of petty theft and sentenced to seven years of transportation to the penal colony of Port Jackson, NSW. Peg, another female convict, takes Mattie under her wing and gives her a chance to make something of her life by teaching her to read. Mattie seizes every opportunity that comes her way. Though life is not particularly kind to her, she battles through earning her freedom, marrying and becoming a mother in her homeland. On this journey, she encounters bushrangers, is widowed, and becomes an entrepreneur in the Bathurst goldfields. She mixes with escaped convicts, but her spirit is indomitable, and she becomes a pillar and much-loved treasure of her adopted community. Mattie may be a fictional character, but her experiences are only too real and invest us in immersing ourselves in the lives of those remarkable women who helped to make Australia what it is today. *(Mattie's story continues in The Lockleys of Parramatta - bk 2+)*

ISBN 9781503252370 & ebook AISN BOOTTEDBTO

(The story continues in The Earl's Shadow & Once a Jolly Swagman)
Released 2015
https://amazon.com/dp/150325237X   https://amazon.com/dp/B00TTEDBT0

Ricky
A boy in Colonial Australia

Ricky English and his mother immigrated from England to join his father in the new Colony of Sydney. Upon arrival, there was no sign of his father. Ricky's mum uses the tiny amount of money they brought to get lodgings in a run-down building. Things go from bad to worse when his mother dies; he is thrown out of the rooms, and the caretakers confiscate all their possessions.

Ricky lives on the streets of Sydney Town as a street waif. Ricky finds safe places to sleep and befriends freed convicts who can help him survive. One day, he encounters a lost child and helps reunite her with her family. These people try to help him, but he insists on doing things his way because of his stubbornness. However, he has found a mentor and confidante. The story follows him through his life. He survives and turns his life around, helping others along the way. **(The Story continues in Jonty's Journey)**

Paperback ISBN 9780994578211   Kindle ASIN: B00MLYN6IG
Released 2014
https://amazon.com/dp/1500770574   https://amazon.com/dp/B00MLYN6IG

The Heather to The Hawkesbury
Four Scottish families brave a new life in a strange land.

Mary Macdonald and husband **Murd** and family; her brother **Fergus** MacKenzie; sister-in-law **Caro** MacLeod; cousin **Alex** Fraser and all their families who have had to emigrate from the Isle of Skye during the "Clearances."

The story follows the four families from Scotland on the ship out to the NSW colony in the 1850s. Mary does not cope with the changes and losses that occur in the first months in the colony. The other women in the family rely on her, and she nearly crumbles. The families struggle together through accidents, losses, trials, floods, and hard work and forge a strong bond with their new country. Trials, tribulations and triumphs see the four families make a firm mark in their new homeland. The immigrants from Scotland helped make Australia what it is today.

ISBN 978994578228   ebook AISN B01A21JYWQ   Large Print ISBN1533473641
Available on Amazon/Kindle & Large Print
Released 2016
https://amazon.com/dp/1503251438   https://amazon.com/dp/B01A21JYWQ

Sara's Author Bio

Sheila Hunter and Sara Powter were a passionate mother-and-daughter team of amateur genealogists. While working together on their family tree, Sheila and Sara made many captivating discoveries. The greatest of these was finding four convicts, and these four had very different perspectives. They were sent to Australia from 1792 to 1814 during the height of Convict transportation. Before her *passing* in 2002, Sheila adapted some of these histories into enchanting stories, her Australian Colonial Trilogy. Sara later had these published. A fourth she left unfinished, and this inspired her to complete it. However, before she did, **The Lockleys of Parramatta** were created. The first two in the series were completed before she completed '**Dancing to Her Own Tune**' for her mother. (*Sheila wrote the first 30k words*)

Vividly living through the Colonial Era, these books delve further into the theme of overcoming adversity in Colonial Australia and how it developed, the demise of the Convict system and the discovery of mineral wealth.

Sara intricately weaves accurate archival data and a charming narrative to create a series of tales of faith, love, loss, and redemption.

And so, two hundred years after her family arrived in Australia, Sara continues the Australian Colonial stories started in **Lockleys of Parramatta,** followed by the **Unlikely Convict Ladies** Trilogy. **The Hunter to Macquarie Collection** and **The Convict Birthstain Collection** are all stand-alone novels. More Historical Fiction books are to follow… as they are already in the editors' queue.

See Sara's web page to keep up to date with more stories.

With an online store available for a signed copy of Sara's books.

www.sarapowter.com.au   (*Australian Postage only*)

Amazon Aus QR

Feel free to email me at
saragpowter@gmail.com
(*Australian Postage only*)

Feel free to email me at
saragpowter@gmail.com

BOOK BUB https://partners.bookbub.com/authors/6273615/edit

FACEBOOK https://www.facebook.com/profile.php?id=100063887262514

FREE Newsletter signup
https://preview.mailerlite.io/preview/41388/
sites/77987646202184961/wCAAcK